D0383688

Praise for Novels by Brandilyn Collins

Over the Edge

"*Over the Edge* is an excellent mystery. I got involved in the story, and instead of my usual thirty-minute read before bed, I finished the book in four evenings. *Over the Edge* actively portrays the patient with the myriad symptoms seen in acute or chronic Lyme. This is especially true for those patients not fortunate enough to know about testing or find a Lyme literate physician."

—Dr. Nick S. Harris, President/CEO of IGeneX, Inc.

"Brandilyn Collins has written a 'who dunnit' mystery that is fun to read. More importantly she has exposed some of the clinical picture and revealed the evidence in the medical literature that at least some patients suffering with chronic Lyme have persistent active infection that responds to antibiotic therapy. Collins also reveals lateralization of 'sides' in those who treat Lyme: both sides read the same medical literature, but one group of scientists chooses to look at articles stating there is active infection that requires antibiotic to eradicate, and another group points to literature that reveals the spirochete of Lyme might cause an autoimmune process in some patients, causing persistent disease."

—Dr. Christine Green

"Meticulously researched and captivating, *Over the Edge* shows the plight of those who suffer from Lyme, and the intensely emotional "Lyme wars" between patients and the medical community. If you know someone who suffers from Lyme, you need to read this compelling novel."

—Lydia Niederwerfer, founder of Lyme-Aware,
http://lyme-aware.org

"This book stayed with me long after I put it down. Not only was it a page-turner, but the storyline about Lyme disease was fascinating and eye-opening. *Over the Edge* will raise awareness about this horrible disease and validate those who suffer with it."

—Terri Blackstock, author of *Predator* and *Intervention*

"*Over the Edge* will draw you in early and keep you glued until the end with an unexpected twist. Humans can only be pushed so far, then they react. This is an excellent fictional portrayal of that frustration felt by so many right now in North America as medical professionals and researchers become pitchmen for corporations who do not have your good health at heart."

—Jim Wilson, President, Canadian Lyme Disease Foundation,
www.canlyme.com

Deceit

" . . . good storytelling and notable mystery . . . an enticing read [that poses] tough questions about truth and lies, power and control, faith and forgiveness."

—*Publishers Weekly*

"Solidly constructed . . . a strong and immediately likable protagonist. One of the Top Ten Inspirational Novels of 2010."

—*Booklist*

"Filled with excitement and intrigue, Collins' latest will keep the reader quickly turning pages . . . This tightly plotted mystery, filled with quirky characters, will appeal to suspense lovers everywhere."

—*RT Book Reviews*

". . . pulse-accelerating, winding, twisting storyline [that will] keep your attention riveted to the action until the very end."

—*Christian Retailing*

Exposure

". . . a hefty dose of action and suspense with a superb conclusion."

—*RT Bookreviews*

"Brandilyn Collins, the queen of Seatbelt Suspense®, certainly lives up to her well-deserved reputation. *Exposure* has more twists and turns than a Coney Island roller coaster . . . Intertwining storylines collide in this action-packed drama of suspense and intrigue. Highly recommended."

—*CBA Retailers + Resources*

"Captivating . . . the alternating plot lines and compelling characters in *Exposure* will capture the reader's attention, but the twist of events at the end is most rewarding."

—*Christian Retailing*

"Mesmerizing mystery . . . a fast-paced, twisting tale of desperate choices."

—*TitleTrakk.com*

"[Collins is] a master of her craft . . . intensity, tension, high-caliber suspense, and engaging mystery."

—*The Christian Manifesto*

Dark Pursuit

"Lean style and absorbing plot . . . Brandilyn Collins is a master of suspense."

—*CBA Retailers + Resources*

"Intense . . . engaging . . . whiplash-inducing plot twists . . . the concepts of forgiveness, restoration, selflessness, and sacrifice made this book not only enjoyable, but a worthwhile read."

—*Thrill Writer*

"Moves from fast to fierce."

—*TitleTrakk.com*

"Thrilling . . . characters practically leap off the page with their quirks and inclinations."

—*Tennessee Christian Reader*

Amber Morn

". . . a harrowing hostage drama . . . essential reading."

—*Library Journal*

"The queen of seatbelt suspense delivers as promised. Her short sentences and strong word choices create a 'here and now' reading experience like no other."

—*TitleTrakk.com*

"Heart-pounding . . . the satisfying and meaningful ending comes as a relief after the breakneck pace of the story."

—*RT Bookreviews*

"High octane suspense . . . a powerful ensemble performance."

—*BookshelfReview.com*

Crimson Eve

"One of the Best Books of 2007 . . . Top Christian suspense of the year."

—*Library Journal, starred review*

"The excitement starts on page one and doesn't stop until the shocking end . . . [*Crimson Eve*] is fast-paced and thrilling."

—*Romantic Times*

"The action starts with a bang . . . and the pace doesn't let up until this fabulous racehorse of a story crosses the finish line.

—*Christian Retailing*

"An unparalleled cat and mouse game wrought with mystery and surprise."

—*TitleTrakk.com*

Coral Moon

"A chilling mystery. Not one to be read alone at night."

—*RT BOOKclub*

"Thrilling . . . one of those rare books you hurry through, almost breathlessly, to find out what happens."

—*Spokane Living*

". . . a fascinating tale laced with supernatural chills and gut-wrenching suspense.

—*Christian Library Journal*

Violet Dawn

". . . fast-paced . . . interesting details of police procedure and crime scene investigation . . . beautifully developed [characters] . . ."

—*Publishers Weekly*

"A sympathetic heroine...effective flashbacks . . . Collins knows how to weave faith into a rich tale."

—*Library Journal*

"Collins expertly melds flashbacks with present-day events to provide a smooth yet deliciously intense flow . . . quirky townsfolk will help drive the next books in the series."

—*RT BOOKclub*

"Skillfully written . . . Imaginative style and exquisite suspense."

—*1340mag.com*

Web of Lies

"A master storyteller . . . Collins deftly finesses the accelerator on this knuckle-chomping ride."

—*RT BOOKclub*

"fast-paced . . . mentally challenging and genuinely entertaining."

—*Christian Book Previews*

Dead of Night

"Collins' polished plotting sparkles . . . unique word twists on the psychotic serial killer mentality. Lock your doors, pull your shades— and read this book at noon."

—*RT BOOKclub*, Top Pick

". . . this one is up there in the stratosphere . . . Collins has it in her to give an author like Patricia Cornwell a run for her money."

—*Faithfulreader.com*

". . . spine-tingling, hair-raising, edge-of-the-seat suspense."

—*Wordsmith Review*

"A page-turner I couldn't put down, except to check the locks on my doors."

—*Authors Choice Reviews*

Stain of Guilt

"Collins keeps the reader gasping and guessing . . . artistic prose paints vivid pictures . . . High marks for original plotting and superb pacing."

—*RT BOOKClub*

". . . a sinister, tense story with twists and turns that will keep you on the edge of your seat."

—*Wordsmith Shoppe*

Brink of Death

". . . an abundance of real-life faith as well as real-life fear, betrayal and evil. This one kept me gripped from beginning to end."

—*Contemporary Christian Music*

"Collins' deft hand for suspense brings on the shivers."

—*RT BOOKclub*

"Gripping . . . thrills from page one."

—*christianbookpreviews.com*

Dread Champion

"Compelling . . . plenty of intrigue and false trails."

—*Publisher's Weekly*

"Finely-crafted . . . vivid . . . another masterpiece that keeps the reader utterly engrossed."

—*RT BOOKclub*

". . . riveting mystery and courtroom drama."

—*Library Journal*

Eyes of Elisha

"Chilling . . . a confusing, twisting trail that keeps pages turning."

—*Publisher's Weekly*

"A thriller that keeps the reader guessing until the end."

—*Library Journal*

"Unique and intriguing . . . filled with more turns than a winding mountain highway."

—*RT BOOKclub*

"One of the top ten Christian novels of 2001."

—*christianbook.com*

BRANDILYN COLLINS

OVER THE EDGE

BRANDILYN
COLLINS

OVER THE EDGE

PUBLISHING GROUP
Nashville, Tennessee

Other Novels by Brandilyn Collins

Deceit

Exposure

Dark Pursuit

Rayne Tour Series
(cowritten with Amberly Collins)

Always Watching

Last Breath

Final Touch

Kanner Lake Series

Violet Dawn

Coral Moon

Crimson Eve

Coral Moon

Hidden Faces Series

Brink of Death

Stain of Guilt

Dead of Night

Web of Lies

Chelsea Adams Series

Eyes of Elisha

Dread Champion

Bradleyville Series

Cast a Road Before Me

Color the Sidewalk for Me

Capture the Wind for Me

Copyright © 2011 by Brandilyn Collins
All rights reserved.
Printed in the United States of America

978-1-4336-7162-3

Published by B&H Publishing Group
Nashville, Tennessee

Dewey Decimal Classification: F
Subject Heading: MEDICAL NOVELS \ LYME DISEASE—
FICTION \ MYSTERY FICTION

Author represented by the literary agency of Alive
Communications, Inc., 7680 Goddard Street, Suite 200, Colorado
Springs, Colorado, 80920, www.alivecommunications.com.

Scripture quotations are taken from the New American Standard
Bible®, Copyright © 1960, 1962, 1963, 1968, 1971, 1972, 1973,
1975, 1977, 1995 by The Lockman Foundation. Used by permission.
(www.Lockman.org) Also used Holman Christian Standard Bible
(HCSB), Copyright © 1999, 2000, 2002, 2003, 2009 by
Holman Bible Publishers. Used by permission.

1 2 3 4 5 6 7 8 • 15 14 13 12 11

For Lyme sufferers and their families,
And the doctors who treat them.

If I should say, "My foot has slipped,"
Your lovingkindness, O Lord, will hold me up.
(Psalm 94:18 NASB)

Prologue

A VISION DENIED IS A BATTLE LOST.

With a flick of his hand the blackened sky blipped into eerie green. Crouched on the house's back deck, he adjusted his night goggles. The high bushes surrounding the yard illumed, the wizened limbs of a giant oak straggling upward in surreal glow.

He ran his hand over a pocket on his black cargo pants. The vial created a telltale bump against his thigh. His latex-gloved fingers closed around it.

Rising, he crossed the deck in five long strides. He surveyed the lock on the sliding glass door. Not enough light. He raised the goggles, darkness reigning once more. From a left pocket he extracted a tiny flashlight. Aimed its beam at the lock.

A common thief he was not. His mission had required intricate study of skills he'd never dreamed he need possess. The pick of a lock. A stealthy skulk. A means to render unconscious.

He pulled the necessary tools from the same pocket. Holding the flashlight in his mouth, he worked the tools into the lock, manipulating as practiced. The mechanism gave way with a tiny *click*.

He slid the door open.

No alarm sounded. He knew it wouldn't. In this upper crust town, home to Stanford University, alarms were for vacations. Children at home were too apt to set them off.

He replaced the flashlight and tools in his pocket. Slipped inside the house and eased the door shut. Down came his goggles. The large kitchen gleamed into view. His astute nose picked up the lingering scent of pizza, cut with a trace of ammonia. A cleaning agent, perhaps.

The digital clock on the microwave read 2:36 a.m.

From where he stood he could see through open doorways to a den, a hall, and a dining room.

At the threshold to the hall he stopped and reached into the lower right pocket beneath his knee. The three-ounce glass bottle he withdrew had a covered plastic pump spray. The chemical inside was not compatible with metals. He removed the cap and slid it back into his pants.

Holding the bottle with trigger finger on the pump, he advanced into the hall. A left turn, and he stood in the entryway. Straight ahead, a living room. On his left, a staircase. Carpeted.

He lifted a sneakered foot onto the bottom step.

The bedrooms would be upstairs, two occupied. One by nine-year-old Lauren. The second, a master suite, by mother Janessa, called Jannie. She would be alone. Her husband, the highly respected Dr. Brock McNeil, was supposedly imparting his impeccable knowledge at a medical symposium on Lyme disease.

His jaw flexed.

After three steps he reached a landing. He turned left and resumed his inaudible climb.

His heartbeat quickened. Too many emotions funneled into this moment—grief-drenched years, anxiety, the playing out of two lives, and now adrenaline. He willed his pulse into submission. Once he went into action everything would happen quickly. He needed his wits about him.

Within seconds his foot landed on the last stair. To his immediate left stood an open door. He craned his neck to see around the threshold. Empty bedroom. With a quick glance he took in three more open doorways—two bedrooms and one bath, halfway down the hall. The closed door directly in front of him would be a closet. He looked down the length of the hall, saw one open door at the end. That was it. The master bedroom, running the entire depth of the house.

He advanced to the next room on his left. Peered inside. The green-haloed room held a canopied bed and several dressers, a large stuffed lion in one corner. In the bed lay a small form on her back, one arm thrown over the blankets. Lauren. Beside her head was a stuffed animal. He could hear the girl's steady breathing.

His mouth flattened to a thin, hard line. He turned and glared at his targeted bedroom, left fingers curling into his palm.

His legs took him in swift silence to the threshold of Janessa McNeil's door.

With caution he leaned in, glimpsing a large bed to his right. She occupied the closest half, lying on her side facing him. How very thoughtful.

Scarcely drawing oxygen, he stepped into the room.

Her eyes opened.

How——?

His limbs froze. He'd made no sound. Had she sensed his presence, the malevolence in his pores?

Janessa's head lifted from the pillow.

In one fluid motion he strode to the bed, thrust the bottle six inches from her face, and panic-pumped the spray. The chloroform mixture misted over her.

A strangled cry escaped the woman, only to be cut short as her head dropped like a stone.

He stumbled backward, holding his breath, pulse fluttering. When he finally inhaled, a faint sweet smell from the chloroform wafted into his nostrils. Leaning down, he dug the plastic cap from his lower pocket and shoved it onto the spray container. Dropped the thing back into his pants.

For a moment he stood, fingers grasped behind his neck, regaining his equilibrium.

Everything was fine, just fine. No way could she have seen him well enough in the dark.

Remember why you're here.

Visions of the past surfaced, and with them—the anger. The boiling, rancid rage that fueled his days and fired his nights. So what if this sleeping woman was known as quiet and caring? So what if she had a likable, if not beautiful, face? Green eyes that held both caution and hope, smooth skin and an upturned mouth. She looked as if she could be anyone's friend. But at this moment she was nothing to him. Neither was her daughter. Merely a means to a crucial end.

He snatched the vial from his upper pocket.

Raising it before his face, he squinted through the hard plastic. Saw nothing. The infected parasites within were no bigger than the head of a pin. He turned the vial sideways and shook it. Three tiny dark objects slid from the bottom into view.

His lips curled.

This *Ixodes pacificus*, or blacklegged tick, carried spirochetes— spiral-shaped bacteria—that caused Lyme disease in California. And not just a few spirochetes. These ticks were loaded with them, along with numerous coinfections. Thanks to painstaking work the spirochetes had flourished and multiplied in the brains of mice. As the infected baby mice had grown, the sickest were sacrificed, their brains fed to the next generation of ticks.

The spirochetes loved human brain tissue. Janessa McNeil may soon attest to that.

He moved toward the bed. No need to hurry now, nor be anxious. His target would not rouse.

Last summer in their larval stage, the captured ticks had enjoyed their first feeding on an infected mouse. Now as disease-carrying nymphs, they were ready for their second meal. He'd chosen three to hedge his bet that at least one would bite and infect Janessa McNeil.

He leaned over the sleeping woman and opened the vial.

The hungry ticks would bury their mouth parts into Janessa's warm flesh and feed for three to five days. After one to two days they would begin to transmit the spirochetes. Even fully engorged, nymph ticks were so minuscule they could easily go unnoticed on the body. But just to be sure, he held the vial above the woman's temple. Her dark brown hair would provide cover.

Pointing the container downward, he tapped the ticks over the edge.

He slipped the vial back into his right pocket, pulling the flashlight from his left. Then raised his night goggles and turned on the flashlight. He aimed its narrow beam at his victim's temple and leaned in closer, squinting.

Ah. There they were, crawling near her hairline.

With a fingernail he nudged them farther back until they disappeared among the strands of hair.

He straightened and took a moment to revel in his victory. He'd done it. He had really done it. Nothing more to do but hope the disease took hold of Janessa—and soon.

Smiling, he put away his flashlight and lowered the goggles. With a whisper of sound he turned and left the room. Down the stairs he crept, and through the kitchen. He stepped out onto the back deck, closed the sliding door and relocked it with the tools from his pocket.

As he slunk from the backyard, a wild and primal joy surged through him. He smirked at the memory of the green-hued sleeping figure, every fiber of his being anticipating, relishing the fulfillment of his vision.

A battle won.

Justice.

THURSDAY

Chapter 1

THE NIGHTMARES FELT SO REAL.

I'd been sick for three weeks. Aching limbs, sore joints, a weakness in my legs. An odd pain shot around in my chest. The back of my neck hurt, radiating clear up to my skull. A *nuchal* headache, Brock would call it, referring to the back neck muscle. A term I'd never heard until I married a doctor.

Most likely I had some strange lingering flu. A virus had been going around this spring season, although no one seemed to have symptoms like mine.

Then a few days ago the bad dreams started. Horrible scenes of a bug-eyed man standing over my bed. "Does flu ever make you have nightmares?" I asked Brock yesterday as he prepared to leave for work. We stood in the kitchen. He was flipping through papers in his briefcase, searching for something.

He looked up distractedly, his thick brows knitting. The lines between his dark brown eyes deepened. "Never heard that one before."

At 6'2" Brock stood a head taller than I. He'd spent years concerned with the health of others—and the stress showed on his face. At fifty-three to my thirty-six, he looked older than his age but still so handsome. So alive and vibrant and strong. As he expected me to be.

"This isn't what Lyme feels like, is it?" Of all people, my husband would know.

He sifted through more documents, too busy to make eye contact with me. "When would you have been bitten by a deer tick?"

We hadn't been hiking or spending time in the woods. And I was mostly a homebody. "I've been planting flowers." Our house boasted a large, beautiful backyard. Behind us lay open space with plenty of trees. Sometimes the deer jumped the fence and wrought havoc with my plants.

He waved a hand, then snapped his briefcase shut. "Let's give it a few days. If you're not better, we can test for it."

Quintessential Brock. Whatever the situation, including illness—buck up, raise your chin, and this, too, shall pass. That rock hard core strength is what had first attracted me to him. Goodness knows I'd needed some strength of my own in those days.

Now I yearned for gentleness.

We'd met when I was twenty-two, a glued-together version of emotionally broken pieces despite my academic success: a B.A. in marketing, valedictorian of my class. As we dated, Brock wedged bits of his unwavering self-confidence into the gaps I failed to hide. He taught me to believe in myself—because *he* did. Bathed in love, his shaping of me never felt harsh.

But in the last year my husband had slipped from attentive to distracted to aloof. Why? I was no less the wife I'd always been. In fact lately I felt like the old Avis rental car commercial—"we try harder." Brock didn't seem to notice my extra effort.

Our conversation yesterday ended as quickly as it started. With a tight smile aimed in my direction, Brock disappeared out the door to the garage.

I rubbed my neck. Last night I had the nightmare again. This morning I awoke feeling five times worse. No flu had ever hit me like this.

Not a good time to deal with a phone call from my mother. But then, it never was. She'd called a few minutes ago, and now I wished I hadn't answered. I moved the receiver to my other ear.

"You get your housecleaning done today?" Mother's voice held that barbed edge I knew so well—half accusation, half sarcasm. Why did I even bother to talk to her? The woman never changed. "Thursday *is* your day to clean."

I lay on the TV room couch, looking toward the pass-through window into the kitchen. I'd had to move from the other end of the sofa. Facing toward the bright front window hurt my eyes. "Yes, I did." Somehow I'd managed to clean, even though I felt so punky. As soon as I was done I collapsed on the couch and had barely moved since.

"That husband of yours would notice if the house wasn't spotless."

My fingers tightened on the phone—until pain forced them to relax. *That husband* of mine happened to be successful and stable, a one-eighty from my alcoholic and abusive father. My mother could not forgive me for that.

"Why don't you hire a housecleaner, Janessa? You can certainly afford it."

"I'd rather do it myself. Then I know it's done right."

"Well, you always were the perfectionist."

My heart cramped. A perfectionist should be able to fix her own marriage. "I have to go, Mother."

"And do what? You're sick, remember?"

"I have to pick up Lauren soon."

"How's she doing?"

My mother's tone made the question's real meaning all too clear: *I haven't seen my granddaughter in years, so how would I know?*

"Fine."

"Isn't she supposed to be out of school for the year soon?"

"Not until the middle of June."

"Then what's she going to do?"

"Be a kid. Hang out, have friends over."

Like I could never do.

"We were good parents to you, Janessa."

My eyes closed. *How* did my mother do that?

I'd managed to move across the country from my parents years ago, before I met Brock. At this moment the connection to my mother amounted to no more than a tenuous link through invisible phone lines. Or so I told myself. I should hang up. Refuse to answer when she called back.

Truth is, the link between mother and daughter is never so tenuous, even when you want it to be. Even when you know the woman's poison for you. There is no more sacred bond, and when it's broken, defiled, it leaves a cleft in your heart never quite filled.

Although Brock had come closest to filling it as any person could.

Someday soon my mother might hear the dullness in my voice over the phone and guess the expanding new truth about me and Brock. "This paradise of yours will never last," she'd sneered the day of my wedding. How self-satisfied she'd be now to hear of the cracks in our Eden.

"I never said you weren't good parents, Mother."

"You didn't have to."

Enough was enough. I forced myself to sit up. I felt so *tired*. "I need to go."

I clicked off the line.

For a long moment I slumped forward, forearms on my legs, still holding the receiver. Its digital read-out told me the time—2:30. I needed to be at Lauren's private school at 3:00. The drive would take fifteen minutes. I would not be late, not even by sixty seconds. In my own childhood I'd spent far too many hours waiting on my mother—who may or may not show up, depending on my father's level of drunkenness. I had grown up dreaming of my own happy marriage someday, of secure children. Lauren would never be treated as I had been.

I replaced the phone in its holder and pushed to my feet. For a moment I swayed. *Man.* What was this? I arched my shoulders and moved my achy neck from side to side. Maybe two more extra-strength pain relievers would help.

I stepped away from the couch and headed for the kitchen, chiding myself for resting too long. Now I'd be pressed to make dinner on time. The roast needed to slow cook in the oven, and I hadn't cut the potatoes, onions, and carrots. Brock expected his dinner at six thirty. Or whenever after that he happened to come through the door.

My legs felt wobbly as I walked to the stainless steel sink. I gazed down at the defrosted roast. Okay. First a large pan . . .

My eyes fixed on the piece of meat. I stared at the red hunk until I looked through it. My thoughts splayed out . . .

Flattened.

Melted away.

I hung there. Hands on the sink.

I blinked.

What was I . . . ?

The pan.

I crossed the kitchen to a lower cabinet, where I'd have to reach far into the back. Started to bend down.

Don't do it.

I stopped. Made a face at myself. What was that voice in my brain?

My hand reached out again. A knowledge deep inside protested that my legs wouldn't hold me.

Air puffed from my mouth. How silly. My legs were a little weak, that's all. Besides, I had no choice. Dinner required this particular pan, and that was that.

I bent over, opened the cabinet and crouched down.

My legs gave out. Down I went—hard—on my rear end. Pain ricocheted through my shoulders and neck.

Stunned, I sat on the floor, palms flat against the hardwood. After a minute I shook my head. Okay, so I'd fallen. While I was on the floor, I'd at least get the pan. I scooted close to the cabinet, leaned in and withdrew it from the top shelf. I lifted the pan and slid it onto the counter. Closed the cabinet door.

Now to get up.

Twisting to one side, I placed both hands close to each other. Pushed against the floor. My legs wouldn't cooperate. I tried again, managing to work my way onto my knees. My leg muscles felt squishy.

Well now really. This was dumb.

I lifted one knee, positioning a foot beneath my body. Pushed off from the floor—and tumbled over. My head bounced against the cabinet.

"Ungh." I lay on my side, mouth open, my annoyance turning to fear. What was happening? I had to get *up*.

I tried again. And again. Didn't work. Sweat popped out on my body. I couldn't believe this. My arms felt strong enough, though the joints hurt. But my legs just wouldn't . . .

Once more I tried to rise. And failed.

Chapter 2

I SLUMPED ON MY KITCHEN FLOOR, TELLING MYSELF NOT TO panic. Okay, so my legs felt a little weak. I'd manage. In a metaphorical sense, I'd had my legs pulled out from under me time and again as a young girl. I'd never forget one scene when I'd been ten. My mother, huddled in the corner of our dirty living room, cheeks reddened with tears and rage.

"I'm *sick* of him. I can't live like this anymore."

"What're you going to do?" I stood in the doorway, heart rattling. Which was worse, living with a drunk or without him? Mom had no money. At least Dad gave us a house to live in.

My mother raised dull eyes to me. "I want to die."

Breath caught in my throat. "No, you don't."

"Yes, I *do*." She slapped both hands over her face and sobbed.

My fingers bit into my arms. *And what happens to me, Mom? You gonna just leave me alone here with* him?

I swallowed hard. I should go give my mother a hug, cheer her up. But who was ever there to comfort me?

I hung in the doorway, torn and breathless. Finally I turned and fled.

Now in my own home, I felt the roil of determination. I'd grown from that frightened child into a strong adult. I was no longer a victim. And at this moment the clock was ticking. My daughter needed me. I *would* get up.

First I shot a prayer to heaven for help. Then mouth set, I scooted on my rear end across the room. At the sink, I bent my knees and placed both feet flat on the floor. Reached up and wrapped my tender fingers around the lip of the sink. *One, two, go.* With both arms I pulled myself upright.

For a moment I leaned against the counter, hanging onto the granite. Assessing. My legs felt weak, but they would hold me. As long as I didn't crouch down again.

I turned and checked the stove clock. Ten minutes before three.

"Oh, no."

I headed for the door leading into the garage. I had to walk slowly, steadying myself along the way, trailing a hand along the counter, a kitchen chair, the wall. I stepped through the door, then hesitated, hand still on the knob. There was . . . To drive I needed . . . something.

Keys.

I shook my head. I knew that. Something else. Where did I keep my . . . That thing.

Purse.

My mind opened up, and the thoughts ran clear. I kept my purse in the car. And the keys in the ignition.

I walked to my Lexus SUV and slid inside. Hit the remote button to open the garage door. I started the car engine. Reaching inside my purse, I turned on my cell phone. I'd be late getting to school. Lauren might worry and try to call me from the school office.

As I turned my head to back out the car, my neck ached something fierce. Had I ever taken those pain relievers? And my fingers on the steering wheel—the joints *hurt*. The afternoon was so bright. I stopped to put on sunglasses.

I checked the clock. 2:55. I'd be ten minutes late.

How to make this up to Lauren? Maybe bake cookies. If I could manage to stand up. But I hadn't cut those vegetables yet, and the meat needed to be seasoned and put into the oven . . .

An overwhelming sense surged through me. So much to do. I hadn't the strength. Really, I didn't.

I made an irritated sound in my throat. What was *wrong* with me? "For heaven's sake, Jannie, get a grip."

My cell phone rang.

Lauren.

I pulled over to the side of the road. For once I was glad for the California law against holding a cell and driving. My mind couldn't have processed two things at once. I yanked the phone from my purse and hit *talk*. "Hi, sweetie, I'm so sorry, I'm almost there."

A taunting chuckle. "'Sweetie'?" Some man's voice, low and gruff.

I stilled. "Who is this?"

"Feeling a little under the weather these days, Janessa?"

"What?"

"Joints hurting? Maybe your muscles are weak. Has it affected your ability to think? There are over sixty possible symptoms. It hits each person differently."

How did—? "Who *is* this?"

"You'll need to go to a doctor. Oh, right, you're married to one."

That tone—so hate-filled. I drew in my shoulders. "I'm hanging up right n—"

"*Don't.* You want to be stuck feeling like you are?"

"How do you know I'm feeling sick?"

"Because, Janessa. I *made* you that way."

Every vein in my body chilled. My eyes fixed on the clock. Some distant part of my brain registered it turning to 3:00.

This was just some crazy prank call. I clicked off the line.

In seconds the phone rang again. This time I checked the incoming ID. *Private caller.* Couldn't be Lauren.

A second ring. I threw down the cell as if it were a snake. Stared at it.

How did that man know how I felt? *How?*

Of its own accord my hand picked up the phone. My finger hit the *talk* button. I hesitated, then placed the phone to my ear.

"Mrs. McNeil?"

"Who are you?"

"I have no time for your games." The man's tone flattened. "I take it you want to get well."

"What do you mean, you did this to me?"

"I entered your house at night. Your husband was gone to one of his many conferences. I placed three infected ticks on you. Apparently the disease has taken hold. You're now experiencing the symptoms of Lyme."

Lyme.

"Your husband's favorite disease."

"I don't—"

"Let's see how he reacts to his own loved one getting Lyme. Once you finally get a diagnosis, that is. What will he do when a mere three to four weeks of antibiotics doesn't cure you? Imagine Dr. Brock McNeil's wife developing a case of chronic Lyme."

This man was insane. Or some enemy of Brock's. My husband had spent years disproving the existence of chronic Lyme. "There's no such thing."

A pulsing silence. "Tell your body that."

For long seconds we breathed over the line.

This had to be a joke. But the way I was feeling, my foggy mind. And the dreams of that bug-eyed man in my bedroom . . .

No. That would be too bizarre. Too terrifying. There had to be an explanation.

"Did you wear something on your face?" I whispered.

"Night goggles."

I dropped the phone. It bounced off the console onto the floor. I ran a hand through my hair, unable to think, my breath shallow.

"Mrs. McNeil." The words rose up, a voice from hell. "Janessa."

Muscles wooden, I bent over and retrieved the cell. Held it to my ear. The thing burned my fingers. "What do you want from me?"

The man uttered a derisive laugh. "That's for another conversation."

No reply would come.

"Go on now. Pick up your Lauren from school."

I gasped. *"Don't* you—"

"Welcome to the Lyme wars, Janessa."

The line went dead.

Chapter 3

I PULLED THROUGH THE CURVED DRIVEWAY AT LAUREN'S private school, my entire body trembling. The man's voice, his bizarre words, echoed through my head. His claims couldn't be true. I would find a rational explanation. The alternative was unthinkable. To believe a man had broken into my house and *passed Lauren's bedroom* on the way to mine . . .

No. Absolutely not. If I believed that, I'd never be able to sleep in my house again.

I drove slowly, eyes scanning for Lauren. Kids spilled through the grassy area in front of the buildings, cars stopping, doors opening as they clambered inside. I spotted Lauren laughing with her best friend, Katie. They faced each other, Lauren's eyebrows raised and her smile wide. Her hand lay on Katie's shoulder, her heels pumping up and down. That half jump always appeared when Lauren was excited.

Apparently Katie's mom, Maria, wasn't here yet. Maria was one of my closest friends. We'd met when our daughters were in kindergarten. Like Katie, Maria was light-skinned with almost white-blonde hair and blue eyes.

I pulled over to the curb near the girls and put the car in *Park*. Pressing both hands to my temples, I tried to squeeze away the chaotic thoughts in my mind. I still felt so crazy tired, but I had to overcome that. Lauren was a bundle of motion. It took strength just to be around her.

Lauren hugged Katie and bounced over to the car, her glorious thick brown hair catching a breeze. She flung open the rear door and threw her backpack inside. Then jumped into the passenger seat. "Hi!"

I took in her pixie face, the light freckles sprinkled across her nose, and managed a smile. "Hi, sweetie. So sorry I'm late."

"You were? Didn't notice. I was talking to Katie."

Something pricked me inside, but I said nothing.

I pulled away from the curb. "So what happened in school today?"

Lauren put her feet up on the dashboard. I couldn't find the energy to tell her to take them down. "Katie got in a fight with Crystal. You remember who she is? That long blonde-haired girl that's always so mean to everybody? She told Katie her outfit looked 'totally stupid.' That's just what she said, can you believe it? 'Totally stupid.' So I told Crystal if Katie looked stupid *she* looked like a wanna-be clown."

I repressed a chuckle. "Lauren, you shouldn't have said that. Haven't we talked about you keeping out of fights?" We reached the end of the school's driveway. I checked traffic before turning right. Oh, my neck hurt. And my elbows. I just wanted to crawl into bed.

Lauren chattered. Now and then I interjected a comment. But my mind couldn't seem to stay focused. I drove hunched toward the wheel, hyper-aware that I needed to listen and drive at the same time. Such a hard task. And I had to breathe. That was so *tiring*—

"Where are you going?" My daughter's sudden question stabbed my attention.

"Huh?"

"Where are we going?" Lauren pointed left. "Home's that way."

I blinked. I was driving up El Camino . . . Oh. I should have turned left at that last stoplight. Was that correct? For a pulsing moment I couldn't remember.

I tried to laugh. It came out flat. "Guess I just wasn't paying attention." I could feel Lauren's hazel eyes on me, assessing.

How to get back in the right direction? Panic rocked me. I had no idea. I didn't know what I was doing. Heat flicked along my nerves. I took the next right turn onto a smaller road and pulled over to the side.

"Mom, what's wrong with you?" Lauren's voice tinged with fear. Nine-year-old girls were so dependent on their mothers. I leaned back in my seat and took a deep breath.

"Sorry, honey. I'm feeling a little sick. I think it's the flu. Just let me rest for a minute."

I drew in two more long breaths, then plastered a smile on my face. "Okay. Let's turn around." I pulled a U-turn and waited at the stoplight to go left on El Camino. My thoughts had cleared. I knew the way home.

"Sheesh, Mom. You should go home and lie down."

"I thought maybe we'd bake some cookies."

"I don't think so. You're likely to put in a cup of salt instead of sugar."

That was my little comic, but today the words hit too close to home. "I was late coming to school. I wanted to make it up to you."

"Like I said, I didn't care. You don't have to worry so much about me."

I nodded. The complexities of young girls. One minute needy, the next determined to be independent. "Okay."

I managed to get home without another wrong turn. *It's the flu, it's the flu,* chanted through my head. That's all this was. A day or two and I'd be over it. As for the phone call—merely some crackpot.

But how did he know I was sick?

Coincidence. Nothing more.

Lauren bounded into the house, lugging her backpack. She'd head to the refrigerator for something to eat, then settle at the table to do her homework. Those were the rules. No TV and no phone until the homework was done.

I dragged myself into the house, fixated on preparing the roast. Then I'd lie down for awhile. Lauren was already spooning strawberry yogurt into her mouth as she headed toward the kitchen table.

Not until I was taking vegetables out of the refrigerator did the thought hit me: *cell phone*. The man's incoming ID had read *private caller*. Was there any way to trace that number?

I laid the vegetables on the counter and reached for chopping board and knife. From behind me came the sound of Lauren's chair sliding over the hardwood floor. "You have much homework?" I cut into the first potato.

"I always have too much homework."

How Lauren managed to make *A*s and *B*s, I didn't know. The girl's attitude toward school work was laissez-faire at best. She always hurried through assignments, which is why I checked her work every day before releasing her to play.

I cut into the second potato. My hands hurt to hold the knife. And my thoughts swung this way and that. I'd just been thinking something important. What was it?

Tracing the call.

Wait. Why should I need to trace that number? It had been a prank. I'd probably never hear from that man again.

But he'd said my name. He'd mentioned *Lauren's* name. Fresh fear spiraled through me. Not Lauren's name, no. My brain had been fuzzy. Maybe I'd heard wrong. I would never let anyone hurt my daughter.

I'd never seen a tick on my body. Hadn't Brock and I just talked about that yesterday?

The realization flushed me with relief. I dropped the knife with a clatter.

"You okay, Mom?"

I stared at the blue-gray granite. Its swirls reminded me of my own brain waves at the moment. Random. Unpredictable.

"Yes. I just . . . dropped something."

I picked up the knife and resumed cutting. My thoughts wove and dipped as I prepared the vegetables by rote and placed them in a large pan with the meat. The man's hate-filled tone still pulsed within me. I couldn't deny the existence of evil, nor how close it ran with selfishness. I'd grown up with both. But the caller's words were just too off the wall.

As I slid the roast into my oven, the phone rang.

I jumped.

Lauren thrust her chair back from the table. "I'll get it."

"No!" I banged the oven door shut and whirled around.

My daughter looked at me, round-eyed. "Okay, Mom. You don't have to yell." Pouty-faced, she returned to the table.

The man's words drilled my memory: *"That's for another conversation."* I eyed the phone. It rang again.

I crossed the kitchen as fast as my weak legs would take me. I told myself it was just one of Lauren's friends. Maybe one of my own. Or some pesky 800 number salesman. Heart pounding, I bent down to peer at the ID on the receiver.

Private caller.

Chapter 4

ONE HAND GRIPPING THE COUNTER, I STARED AT THE RECEIVER. The phone rang a third time.

Lauren heaved a sigh. "Mom, answer it!"

My hand seemed to float as it reached for the receiver. I faced away from Lauren. For a long second I couldn't find any words to speak.

"Hello?"

"So we meet again." The man's voice ran rough and vibrating.

Turning, I glanced at Lauren. "Just a minute," I whispered into the phone. I made my way out of the kitchen, through the hall and into the front bathroom. Shut the door. I sank onto the closed toilet seat. "Who *are* you? What do you want?"

"How are you feeling?"

"*What* do you want from me?"

"Actually I know how you're feeling. I've seen it up close and personal. Too personal."

"You told me I have Lyme. That you made me have it."

"You do, and I did."

"That's crazy."

"Let me tell you *crazy*, Janessa. Crazy is doctors and researchers denying that a disease exists when patients are suffering right in front of their noses. Crazy is people's lives being reduced to moving from bed to couch, or even dying, because those doctors love their medical reputations and grant money more than they care about others' pain."

I bent over and pressed a hand to my forehead. "I don't know what you're talking about."

"Yes, you do. You know what your husband does. His specialty."

Of course I knew. Brock was a researcher and professor at the prestigious Stanford School of Medicine. He'd spent years studying tick-borne diseases, particularly Lyme.

"You know the committee your husband chairs? The one whose members will be publishing their irrefutable findings"—the words were sneered—"to the entire medical community this coming fall?"

The committee. Brock was its chairperson and most outspoken member. He'd personally appointed most of the other doctors. But what—

"*Janessa!*"

I started. "I-I'm here."

"You know what those findings are going to say?"

I didn't respond.

"What they've always said—lies. That chronic Lyme doesn't exist as an active infection. That a mere four weeks of antibiotics at most kills every spirochete. All those suffering patients out there claiming they've had the disease for years—long after antibiotic treatment— and the doctors who deign to listen to them, are wrong. Either that or just plain crazy in the head."

"What does this have to do with me?"

"You live with the main culprit."

"But . . . the committee's findings are based on scientific studies. They are what they are."

The man laughed deep in his throat. The chilling sound sent a fissure up my spine. "But they're not, you see. Your husband and his cohorts find what they want to find. They enter their research with their minds already made up. They quash dissenting opinions."

"Why would they do that?"

"Tell me something, Mrs. McNeil. What would happen to your husband's scholarly reputation if his life's research was proven *wrong*?"

My mouth opened but no answer came.

"And doesn't he hold patents having to do with Lyme? Maybe he'll come up with a new vaccine some day. That could make him millions of dollars."

"He's—"

"Do you know that selling a Lyme vaccine depends on a narrow definition of the disease?"

"I . . . no." What was he talking about—narrow definition? My head swam.

"And hasn't your dear husband testified on behalf of insurance companies at numerous trials? Trials in which other doctors have been sued for *over-treating* patients who *claim* to have Lyme? I believe he's been paid for his hard work on the stand, correct?"

My breath came in shallow pants. My limbs hurt, my neck ached, and my elbow throbbed from bending to hold the phone. My wavering brain could barely follow this conversation. Why was I even bothering to listen to this?

"Still with me, Janessa?"

I swallowed. "Yes."

"Your husband is the same as the rest of his cronies on that committee. He has a reputation to keep, not to mention the money at stake. Of course their 'findings' support what they've always claimed."

This was too much. This man was accusing the man I loved of being some kind of shyster. Brock's reputation was stellar. He was known across the country for his work in medicine. "You're saying my husband is nothing but a fake?"

"I'm saying he sees what he wants to see. And meanwhile, Janessa, people are *dying*. Brock McNeil has blood on his hands."

"You're insane."

"Really?" Anger trembled in the man's voice. "Perhaps you don't understand how powerful that committee is. Its written report will be touted to all doctors across the country. Physicians everywhere will be told—again—that chronic Lyme exists only in the imagination of self-proclaimed patients and their doctors." The man's tirade grew louder, more virulent. "Those doctors who treat such patients with long-term antibiotics can be brought before their medical boards, have their licenses pulled. All other docs will be afraid to treat Lyme at all, or will only treat it for the mere number of days that the report recommends. And those doctors will continue to be told Lyme probably doesn't even exist in their area. Patients, very sick patients, will come to them and get no help. They'll go undiagnosed for years. Every day they'll feel like you're feeling right now. Only over time they'll get far worse. They'll lose their friends, life as they knew it. And no one will listen to them. And doctors like your husband will tell them it's all in their head!"

I sagged to my left until my shoulder rested against the wall. I so needed to lie down. This man was crazy, yet his diatribe simmered through me. There were people who felt like I did right now—and worse—for *years?* How could they live like that? How could they cope? After a few more days of this . . . whatever it was I expected to be back to normal. I couldn't imagine feeling like this for months. My body already felt like half its strength had wasted away.

"Please." I took a deep breath. My lungs couldn't get enough oxygen. "What do you want?"

"I want you to change your husband's mind."

I blinked.

"I infected you months ago. The spirochetes have had time to multiply and burrow deep into your body tissue. So now I want you to show him how real chronic Lyme is. Shouldn't be too hard once he sees it raging in his beloved wife's body. The problem with doctors like your husband is they're sheltered in their laboratories. They need to get down in the trenches with patients, see what the disease is like up close and personal. You're Exhibit A, Janessa."

He'd done this to *me* because of my husband's research?

"You must convince your husband to relook at his experiments, find his false presumptions." Passion throbbed in the man's words. "I want a very public announcement from Dr. Brock McNeil, stating he is utterly convinced chronic Lyme does exist as an active infection. That the medical community and insurance companies must change their narrow-minded, backward ways of dealing with the disease."

Sure, no problem. I would have laughed had I possessed the energy. No one convinced Brock of anything. Not at work, not at home. Brock McNeil was always right.

"Janessa, do you hear me?"

"I . . . yes."

"You will do this."

"What if I can't?"

"Of course you can. Your husband will want you well. He loves you, doesn't he?"

Did he anymore? I thought of all the late-night meetings in the past few months. Brock's growing coldness.

"How do I get well?" I whispered.

"Once you're finally diagnosed? Which will take some time, since your husband will fight you on that, too. With long-term, high dosage antibiotic treatment. The very treatment doctors like your husband sneer at, and insurance companies love refusing to pay for."

What did he mean—once I was "finally" diagnosed? "How long will it take to get better?"

"Depends on when you start treatment. Months. A year, maybe more. And you'll get a lot worse before you get better."

A year? And *worse?*

"You see, Janessa"—he spoke as if savoring every word—"you have no easy case."

"What?"

"The ticks that bit you carried spirochetes that cause Lyme—*and* three coinfections."

I raised myself upright, my tone hardening. "You're nothing but a liar. None of this is true. I have the flu. I'll get better soon."

"Your kitchen counters are granite, aren't they, Janessa? Sort of a bluish gray. At least that's the best I could make them out in the dark."

I went absolutely still.

"Your daughter, Lauren, sleeps with the door open. Her bedroom is the second on the left at the top of the stairs. Lovely canopied bed. Large stuffed lion in the corner. Very cute."

My fingers gripped the phone. Pain shot through my knuckles, but I hardly noticed. "I'm calling the police."

"You do that. These calls won't be traced to anyone. And I left no sign of a break-in when I picked the lock on your kitchen sliding glass door. Meanwhile, don't forget: you'll still. Be. Sick."

I heard a *click*—and the line fell silent.

Chapter 5

MINUTES SLID BY AS I SAT LIKE A STONE. ALL OF THIS—THE man stalking me, his claims—was too bizarre to be real.

The police. They should know.

I started to press the *talk* button on the phone, then hesitated. What would I tell them? What proof would I have of anything?

Didn't matter. These calls had to be documented.

But my body did not want to comply. I didn't have the energy to meet with a police officer, relate the whole story. My limbs felt like dishrags. And what would I tell Lauren? No way was I going to scare my daughter.

God, what do I do?

I stared at the texture-painted wall before me . . . and my mind numbed out. My vision glazed, my eyes looking *through* the light blue. I hung there, telephone in my hand, knowing I was supposed to do something, that a terrible event had occurred. My thoughts reached out . . . groped. Felt only the spider-webbed corners of my mind.

Dusty awareness puffed through my brain. *Call someone.*

A small gasp escaped me.

I focused on the phone. My forefinger hit the programmed digit to call Brock's direct line at the office. Brock absolutely adored Lauren.

If he thought his daughter was in danger, there would be no end to what he'd do.

His voice machine answered. I wavered, then hung up.

I closed my eyes, trying to *think*. I'd tell Brock when he came home. Lauren could watch TV while we talked privately. Brock would know how to proceed.

A sudden thought burst in my head. Lauren wasn't safe here. That man had broken into our home. He could do it again. For all I knew he was watching our house right now. He obviously knew my schedule. He'd called my cell phone at the right time, then the house line when we returned from school.

We had to get out of here.

I thrust to my feet, then swayed.

Where should we go?

To Katie and Maria's house, that's where. But they lived on the south end of Mountain View. The twenty-minute drive through town may as well be across the country. I wasn't sure I could operate a car. How much worse I'd become just in the last hour.

I sat back down and called Brock's direct line again. Another message. I tried his cell phone, and he picked up. "Hi." His voice rode on pockets of air. "You caught me walking across campus."

My throat closed until I could barely speak his name. "Brock."

"What is it?"

"I . . . I'm real sick. And there's this man. Like a stalker. Called twice. He said he broke into our house. He knew Lauren's bedroom layout and everything—"

"*What?* Where are you?"

"At home. In the bathroom, where Lauren can't hear."

"Are the doors to the house locked?"

They always were. "Yes."

"Did you call the police?"

"No, I couldn't . . . I'm not thinking very well."

"What do you mean?"

"I was so much worse this morning. All these weird symptoms. The man said I have Lyme. He said he put ticks on me some night when you were gone to a conference. And now I'm really bad."

"That's absolutely *insane!*"

"He insists it's true."

"How long ago?"

"He just called—"

"No, how long ago does he claim he put that tick on you?"

"Months ago." I thought of my nightmares about the bug-eyed intruder. "You need to come home, Brock. I don't know what to do. I fell in the kitchen this afternoon and couldn't get up. My legs are all shaky, and my body feels like a truck hit it. Only worse."

"Jannie, you go lie down." Brock's tone was tight and furious. "I'm coming home right now. I'll call the police on the way and ask them to send somebody out. If Jud Maxwell's on duty, he'll come."

Of course, Detective Jud Maxwell. He was married to Brock's administrative assistant, Sarah. I last saw Jud at the Department of Medicine's Christmas party. He was a likeable man, comfortable with who he was. Not in the least intimidated by all the physicians around him. And he so obviously loved his wife. For that reason alone I should have thought of Jud now. Should have called him myself.

"What about Lauren?" I asked. "She'll be scared."

"Tell her it has something to do with my work. We have to protect ourselves, Jannie. This is some nut. Sounds like one of those protestors in the Lyme awareness community stooping to the lowest of low." The derision in Brock's voice could have cut steel. "Now go rest. I'll be there in ten minutes." He hung up.

Somehow I managed to pull to my feet. Phone in hand, I stumbled out of the bathroom, my mind spinning as I went to tell my own child what I'd vowed I never would—a lie.

Chapter 6

THE OFFICER ARRIVED BEFORE BROCK. WHEN THE DOORBELL rang I was lying on the sofa in the den. I sat up and squinted through the window. At the bright light, I winced. An unmarked car sat at the curb. It must be Jud Maxwell. Detectives worked in suits and ties, and didn't drive squad cars.

"Who's that?" Lauren called from the kitchen.

"Keep working. I'll get it." I dragged myself to the door, not looking forward to facing anyone on the police force, even Jud. Surely I'd sound like a lunatic. The story was too crazy.

I opened the door, sunlight pouring in. The brightness daggered my eyes. I gasped and shielded them with one hand. My gaze fell downward to brown shoes and pant legs.

"Mrs. McNeil? Your husband called. I hear you've had some trouble."

I blinked up at his face. Jud was a little on the short side and stocky, with sandy hair and deep brown eyes. "Hi. Yes. Come in." I stepped back, heart grinding as he crossed the threshold. As I moved to close the door, I stumbled.

"You all right?" I felt a hand underneath my forearm.

"Yes. Fine. Just . . . weak."

"Mom? What's going on?"

I turned to see Lauren in the hall, surveying the unknown man with curiosity.

"Don't worry, sweetie. This is just a detective from the police department. He's here to ask questions about something that happened at Daddy's work."

"At work? Then why's he here?"

"Daddy's coming home in a minute to talk to him."

"Is Daddy okay?"

"He's fine."

"What happened?"

"Lauren." My tone edged. "Go finish your homework."

She gave Jud Maxwell a long, unconvinced look before turning back to the kitchen.

I leaned against the wall, looking blankly at the detective. He raised his eyebrows. "Is there somewhere we can go to talk? Looks like you need to sit down."

"Yes."

I led him slowly through the living room and into Brock's wood-paneled office. There I motioned him into one of the overstuffed armchairs. I half fell into the second one before realizing I hadn't shut the door. I eyed it, overcome with weariness. I'd have to get up again.

The muted sound of a door closing drifted from the other end of the house. Relief washed through me. "Brock's home." I listened to him exchange hurried greetings with Lauren and assure her everything was okay.

"Mom's sick," Lauren said.

"I know."

His swift footsteps approached. Jud rose. Brock barreled into the room and closed the door, his eyes on me. His tie, usually so perfect, lay askew, his face flushed. The power he always exuded filled the room, but now it mixed with frightened agitation.

"How are you?" He crossed to me, ignoring Jud, and leaned down to search my face. His gaze was that of both husband and doctor, assessing, evaluating. He placed his hands on either side of my neck, feeling for swollen glands. Rested his fingers against my forehead. I knew he felt no swelling or fever, yet his eyes clouded. The gravity of his gaze filled me with fear. Clearly, he could tell I was much worse than when he last saw me.

Brock hadn't looked at me with such concern in a long time.

Sodden hope for our marriage stirred. I'd been praying for something to change our errant course, something to push us back on a stable path. Maybe this was it. My husband did love me. Maybe I'd just read too much into his recent extra hours at work. He was a busy man.

"I'm . . . okay." I gave him a lopsided smile, even as tears filled my eyes.

Brock patted my shoulder, then turned to the detective. "Jud, thank you for coming so quickly."

"No problem. Glad to help."

The men shook hands. Brock motioned for Jud to resume his seat in the armchair. Brock pulled his rolling work chair around to the front of his desk. He leaned forward, hands clasped between his knees. "Jannie," he said before Jud could speak. "Tell us what's happened."

"Wait a sec." Jud reached into the inside pocket of his jacket and pulled out a small tape recorder. "If you don't mind I need to record this."

"Oh. Sure." Brock glanced over his shoulder at the desk. "Can you set it here?"

"Yeah."

Brock rolled his chair a little to his left. Jud set the tape recorder on the desk and hit a button. He related the date, time, and address.

"Interview with Janessa McNeil and her husband, Dr. Brock McNeil."
He pulled a small pad of paper and pen from his shirt pocket. "Let's
first get your phone numbers, home, work, and cells."

My cell number? I couldn't remember.

Brock rattled off each number. Jud wrote them down as the tape
recorder rolled.

"All right. Thanks. Now." Jud looked at me. "Tell us what
happened."

I licked my lips. Where to start? For a long moment my mind
whited out. I could feel both men watching me, waiting. My cheeks
heated.

"Jannie?" Brock leaned forward and tapped me on the knee.

I stared at his finger . . . and my brain realigned. "You remember
that dream I've had the last few nights? About the bug-eyed man in
our bedroom?"

Brock nodded.

"That really happened. The man said he was wearing night
goggles."

Righteous anger flicked across Brock's face. "Go on."

I told them what I could. How badly I felt, the fall in the kitchen.
The two phone calls. Everything the man said about Lyme—at least
all I could remember. After a while my brain started to fuzz. I sensed
I had lost some pieces, but for the life of me couldn't find them in my
jumbled mind. And somewhere along the way I started to stutter. My
flow of words would suddenly stop, the next one I sought just . . .
gone. After a second or two the word would come, and I'd continue
my story.

By the time I was done, I felt even more exhausted. I rested my
head against the chair's high back, hands limp on the cushioned arms.

Brock pushed to his feet and paced toward the rear window, then
back again. He turned around and leveled a hard look at Jud. "I want
you to find this guy."

Jud tapped the pen against his notebook. "We'll find him."

"And I'll tell you right now—we've got a gun in the house. I've had it for years and never had to use it. But if someone breaks into my home while I'm here—" Brock shook his head. "I won't think twice about shooting."

"I take it your gun is registered."

Brock waved his hand in an impatient *yes.* "Jannie knows how to use it, too. I've made sure of that."

I did? Brock had taught me how to shoot, but that was years ago.

Jud made a note. If he was put off by Brock's harsh attitude, he didn't show it. He looked to me. "Where's your cell phone?"

"In my purse."

"I'll get it." Brock hurried from the room, leaving the door open. I could hear Lauren's anxious voice from the kitchen, asking what was taking so long. My heart panged. Kids' antennae were sensitive. They *knew* when something was wrong. Brock reassured Lauren all was fine.

"I'm done with homework, Dad. Can I watch TV?"

"Yeah." He sounded distracted.

Brock returned, my BlackBerry in hand. He shut the office door and gave the cell to Jud. "Thanks." The detective regarded the phone. "You said no ID came through." He glanced at me.

"It just said private caller."

"Who's your service provider?"

My thoughts blanked. I looked to Brock.

"Verizon." He perched back in his seat.

"And for your landline?"

"AT&T."

Jud laid my cell on the desk and wrote in his notebook.

Brock frowned. "You think you can trace the caller's number without an ID?"

"We can request records of incoming calls from both your landline phone company and your cell provider. Those records will show the number the calls originated from. Question is, will that number lead us to anyone? If the guy used a payphone or paid cash for one of those throwaway cell phones and used a false name to buy it . . ." Jud lifted a hand. "Won't lead us anywhere. That's what a lot of drug dealers are doing these days—using those throwaway phones. On the other hand, if any kind of cell phone was used—even one leading to a fake name—we can trace the call's ping off the nearest cell phone tower. That'll tell us what area the guy called from. The tower pings give us a cone-shaped area that's quite specific."

I closed my eyes. I knew all that cell phone stuff. Had learned it from watching true-crime shows on TV.

"We may also want to put a tap on both phone lines."

At Jud's words, Brock hesitated. "I'm not too keen on having my phone tapped. But I want this guy caught. What he's doing is flat out blackmail. Attempting to change the findings of a major scientific study." Brock shook his head. "It's just . . . it's unbelievable. And who knows what he's done to Jannie."

"He said he infected me with Lyme months ago." I opened my eyes, focusing on my lap.

Brock made a sound in his throat. "He may have lied about when he came. Those nightmares you've been having only started a few days ago, right?"

I nodded.

"I *was* out of town then. If he put ticks on you that recently, you wouldn't be having any symptoms yet, much less this severe. I'm more afraid of other possibilities. I'm taking you to the emergency room tonight. We need to get a full workup started on you right away."

I raised my head. "No."

"Jannie, we have no choice. For all we know he could have injected you with some kind of poison."

Poison?

"Maybe he did tell the truth about when he broke in," Jud said. "It's possible the nightmares started long after the actual event."

Brock nodded. "Maybe. Look, if his story's true, and she's got Lyme—great. A round of antibiotics will take care of it."

"He said I'd need long-term treatment because I've had the disease for awhile."

Brock puffed out air. "Jannie, no matter when you got it—*if* you have Lyme at all—two to four weeks of antibiotics eradicate the spirochetes in the body, it's as simple as that. The man's lying through his teeth. He's one of those nuts in the Lyme community who'll stop at nothing to prove his point. Maybe he's working on some so-called medicine that could be worth millions, if only my committee will declare the disease is serious and widespread." Brock's face contorted. "What's even more amazing is that he thinks he can get away with this. That I would disavow clear scientific findings to please some madman!"

I fixed Brock with a dull stare. I *did not* want to go to the hospital.

Brock and Jud Maxwell continued talking, the detective prodding him for more information about his committee and why its findings were so important. I half listened as Brock explained how the findings were crucial to the correct health care of patients. That they were key in determining treatment procedures, and ultimately insurance companies used them in fixing coverage policies—although insurance was not the committee's focus.

Jud stood and clicked off the tape recorder. "I'd like to check that sliding door in your kitchen—the one the caller said was his entry point. And I'll look around in the backyard."

I looked to Brock. "What'll we tell Lauren?"

"I'll just step out back." Officer Maxwell smiled at me. "I'll be unobtrusive about it."

Brock rose. "I'll take you."

They left the room. I sat like a lump in my chair, listening to the distant mumble of the television. Maybe if Lauren was involved enough in some show she'd pay little attention to the policeman searching her backyard.

Sometime later the men returned, Jud reporting he'd seen nothing. No sign of a break-in or even a scratch on the door lock. No discernible footprints in the grass. I could have told him as much. I'd been through that door and out in the backyard many times in the past few days. If anything were amiss, I'd have spotted it.

The detective prepared to leave. He gave Brock and me each one of his cards. "I'll be in touch with you soon about tapping the phones, Dr. McNeil. And I'll need you to keep me apprised of the hospital test findings."

"Right."

"You're headed to the hospital now?"

No, Brock.

"Yes."

"You need help transporting?"

"We'll be all right." Brock thumbed the corner of the business card. "Look, I want this kept quiet. Last thing we need is for this to be in the media."

Jud held up a hand. "They won't hear it from me. But in investigating this case I will have to talk to your associates at work. Someone may have seen or heard something that will trigger a lead."

Brock frowned. "There's no point in doing that. Nobody at Stanford's going to know a thing. This is the work of some Lyme awareness nut."

I don't *want to go to the hospital.*

"That may well be," Jud said. "But we have to start somewhere. And that *somewhere* is the people around you. In this case those closest to your work."

Brock stared at the detective, clearly not happy. Well, what did he expect? You call the police about a break-in, they have to follow up.

My husband never liked not being in control.

After an awkward moment, Brock gave a curt nod.

He showed Jud Maxwell to the door. I remained in the chair, my mind numb. Vaguely I registered the smell of roast wafting through the house. I looked at my watch. Four forty-five. The meat would be done in another . . . what?

How long did roast take to cook, anyway?

I stared at Brock's desk, trying to remember. Trying to comprehend what was happening.

Could poison act like this? Take away my strength and mind function so quickly?

Brock returned, steely determination in his every move. "All right. I'm taking you to Stanford's emergency room. We need to get tests started as soon as possible."

"But Lauren . . ."

Brock rubbed his forehead. "I'll call your friend—Katie's mom. What's her name?"

I had to think. What *was* my good friend's name? Something with an M. "Maria."

"Maria. We'll take Lauren over there for the night." He leaned down and laid a hand on my knee. "We'll just let her continue to think Jud's visit was about another matter—nothing to do with your illness. All right?"

I nodded.

He straightened and swiveled toward the door.

"Brock, what if it *is* Lyme?"

My husband turned back, a scowl on his face. "Then you're in good shape." His words were curt. "If it's Lyme, antibiotics will soon cure it."

I so wanted to believe that. But the frightening warnings of the man who'd called me still rang in my head.

Chapter 7

THE REST OF THE EVENING BLURRED. BROCK HELPED ME INTO his car, Lauren in tow. Our daughter toted her backpack and a small suitcase. Her cheeks were tearstained. She showed no excitement at staying with her friend on a school night. Instead she'd begged to come with us, stay by my side in the emergency room. I'd argued against Lauren spending the night with Katie. Why couldn't we just pick her up on the way home from the hospital?

"I can help Mom while she's there, Daddy!" Lauren's mouth trembled as she argued one more time.

"Honey, no, you can't." Brock put his hands on Lauren's shoulders and drew her close. "You just stay with Katie and don't worry about anything. I'll take care of your mom."

"You promise?"

"Promise."

I heard the exchange from the front passenger seat, my heart swelling. This was awful. It was one thing to make me sick. But to scare my daughter? To harm Lauren in any way? *That* was unforgivable.

Whatever this man had done to me, I would hunt him down when I was well. I would make him pay.

Brock drove to El Camino and headed south toward Katie's house. I kept my eyes closed, feeling the turns, the stops and starts at intersections. Everything seemed hazy and disconnected. Twice I asked Brock about the roast I'd put in the oven.

"We took it out, Jannie. Remember?"

"Oh." Vaguely I did. "Yes."

At Katie's house, Lauren opened my door to lean in and hug me hard before we drove off. The hug hurt. My muscles were so tender. I tried not to wince.

"Love you, Mom."

"Love you too, honey. I'll see you soon."

Maria crouched down to greet me next, laying a hand on my cheek. "I'll be praying for you."

I gave her a wan smile. Thanks to Maria, who'd talked to me about her faith, I'd become a Christian two years ago. "I can use that."

At the exchange I could feel apathy and disdain roll off Brock. He had no need for God and couldn't understand mine. That is, he *wouldn't* understand. I'd explained it more than once—the cleansing I'd experienced. The new purpose and freedom. God had helped heal the wounds of my past. But Brock wanted no part of it. And he'd talked me out of attending church with Lauren. With his constant work, we had so little time together—and now I wanted to leave him every Sunday morning? Truth was, as much as he'd drawn away from me in the past months, Sunday did seem to be the only day we had together.

Maria stepped back from the car. She and Lauren waved as Brock and I drove away.

On our trip back north to the hospital, silence hovered. Brock finally broke it as we pulled into the emergency room entrance. "We're going to have to tell the doctors about what's happened—the phone calls and our police report. They need to understand why they should be looking for poisons and things they wouldn't normally look for."

"Okay." I licked my lips. "Brock. What do *you* think is wrong with me?"

He hesitated. "I don't know."

We reached the Stanford Hospital emergency room. Brock walked me in as I leaned heavily on his arm. My equilibrium felt off, as if a breeze would tip me over. And the bottoms of my feet had a strange burning sensation. Brock settled me into a chair and went to check me in. The place was nearly empty. I could hear my husband's voice, declaring who he was and demanding that someone see his wife immediately.

I could barely sit up in the waiting chair.

How could this happen so fast? How could I plunge from healthy to hapless in so few days? I stared at the hands twisting in my lap. Maybe Brock was right. That man who'd stalked me had injected me with some kind of poison. Once the doctors found it in my system, they'd know what to do. They'd fix me. In a few days I would be better.

Brock sat down beside me, tapping his knees, his back not touching the chair. Such energy it took to be impatient.

A nurse soon appeared to usher us into a small room. They laid me on a bed and brought me a warmed blanket. A white-coated physician entered, introducing himself as Dr. Sherar. He looked in his sixties, thinning brown hair and a round, friendly face. The kind of doctor you'd instantly trust. He and Brock seemed to know each other. They shook hands. I didn't hold mine out to shake. It would hurt too much.

Once again I explained all my symptoms. They sounded so nonsensical I found myself not wanting to name them all. A bona fide hypochondriac would be proud of my list of complaints.

"This tiredness is so . . ." I had a word, but it wouldn't come. "Different. Weird."

"How so?" Dr. Sherar looked down upon me, a concerned frown etching his forehead.

"It's so fierce. I've been pregnant. Had the flu. All the normal things that make you tired. But this is like . . . you know those lead blankets they put on you for protection when you get an X-ray? How heavy they are? I feel like t-ten of those are on me. But *not* on me. *In* me. Wrapped around my lungs. It's so hard to move. It's like walking in a . . ." The word I wanted ran and hid. I pushed out air, biting my lip. "Swimming pool. With the water up to your neck."

Dr. Sherar and Brock exchanged a glance. "All right. Let's take a look at you."

He lifted my right arm and probed the elbow. Pain shot through me. "Ah!"

"That hurts, huh."

I nodded.

He felt the muscles. I gasped again. My legs were just as bad, as if he were pressing deep bruises. My chest was the worst. "You're pushing too hard!"

"I'm sorry. I'm actually being gentle. The area is very tender."

I didn't want any more. I just wanted to go home. "Please." Tears blurred my eyes. "Stop."

Dr. Sherar and Brock left the room. I could hear them talking in low tones in the hall but couldn't make out the words. No matter. I knew Brock was telling Dr. Sherar about the threatening phone calls, discussing with him the various poisons that may have been injected into me.

Long minutes ticked by. I drifted into a fitful sleep.

A nurse awoke me to take blood. She drew vials of it. "Hey, gonna leave me some?" I gave her what I knew was a pasty smile. She patted my shoulder.

"Almost done."

I also gave them a urine sample.

Dr. Sherar and Brock returned. "Mrs. McNeil," Dr. Sherar nodded at me, "we'd like you to stay the night. There are tests we need to run on you tomorrow."

My mouth opened. I looked from him to my husband, betrayal sluicing through my veins. I thought of Lauren with her suitcase, preparing to stay the night with Katie. Brock had known this would happen.

"Why can't I just come back tomorrow?"

"Jannie." Brock's voice was firm. "You need to stay."

Dr. Sherar picked up my chart. "Who's your regular physician?"

"Dr. Oppenheimer. But he's an OB/GYN."

"You don't have a family physician, a general practitioner?"

"No. I . . . I've always been so healthy." I looked from the doctor to Brock. "I really don't want to stay."

Dr. Sherar patted my arm. "Few people do. But we think it's important in your case to check you out thoroughly. We'll make sure you see some specialists here."

I protested a third time, but my words fell on deaf ears. Before I knew it, Brock had secured me a private room. He saw that I was provided with necessities like a toothbrush and toothpaste.

Ensconced in a cranked-up bed with three pillows for support, I called Maria's house to talk to Lauren. I'd insisted to Brock on breaking the news myself. If he thought me completely helpless he had another thing coming. I still hadn't forgiven him for tricking me into admission.

"I'll be home tomorrow, sweetie." I kept my voice as steady as possible. My elbow could not get comfortable. I had to bend it too much to hold the phone. "Then I'll be with you again."

"I don't want you staying in the hospital." The last word stretched out, turned off-key. Lauren sniffled over the line.

"It's okay, honey, don't you worry. I'll get better soon. You'll see."
As I hung up I shot Brock a dark look.

He hung around, pacing, until a nurse brought me dinner.
Chicken and mashed potatoes and peas. A roll and butter. I surveyed
the meal, not in the least bit hungry.

Brock planted a kiss on my head. "Now that you're settled,
I should go."

"Already?"

He made a *tsk*ing sound. "I have to get back to the office and wrap
up some things. I hadn't expected to leave so soon. On the way I'm
going to call Jud, tell him you'll be staying here tonight."

I gazed at him, a dozen questions and suspicions filtering through
my head. None would form into words. Some I pushed to the corner
of my brain marked *No Trespassing.* "Okay."

He gave me a pained smile and turned to go.

I watched the back of him as he walked away from me. "Brock?"

My husband turned.

"I love you."

He nodded. "Love you too, Jannie."

As he disappeared through the door his words drifted through me,
as light and insubstantial as air.

FRIDAY

Chapter 8

AS EXHAUSTED AS I WAS THAT NIGHT I COULD NOT SLEEP. I awoke again and again in a sweat, my body aching as if I'd just endured a triathlon. I thought of Lauren, grateful she wasn't sleeping at our house. She wasn't safe there, none of us were. What were we going to do about that? Could the police post a guard outside our home?

What about Brock tonight, in our bedroom by himself? What if that stalking man came back with a tick for him?

And what Stalking Man had done—it wasn't really blackmail, as Brock claimed. Blackmail was a threat of harm if you didn't do something. But the man had *already* harmed me. So if I didn't convince Brock to change his medical opinion of Lyme—so what?

I stared at the ceiling for a long time, trying to logic through that. Something didn't fit.

The man's a lunatic. Why should anything he does make sense?

When morning finally came I pushed myself from bed and onto shaky legs to visit the bathroom. Every muscle hurt with new desperation, and my body weighed a ton.

Back in bed I called Brock on his cell phone.

"How are you today?"

"Worse."

Silence. "We'll find the cause of this, Jannie."

Let's hope. "Have you heard anything from Jud?"

"I'll be talking with him to see how soon they'll be able to get those phone records. Now you just worry about yourself, okay?" Brock would come by to see me when he could, between classes and lab experiments and all the myriad critical tasks he undertook each day.

As I hung up depression settled over me, coated with fear of the unknown. I wasn't sure of my husband anymore. And I didn't know my own body. I aimed a vacant stare at the wall, dark imaginings filling my head.

God, please help me. I'm drowning here.

From somewhere in the depths of me vague words arose and shimmered. *"God is our refuge and our strength, a very present help in time of trouble."* Where was that from? A psalm? Wherever it came from, I needed that kind of promise right now. I repeated it aloud. Wrapped the words around my heart.

That same hour the tests began.

They drew more blood, why I didn't know. Hadn't they already taken enough? And they took another urine sample. After that I was transported to a room to see a specialist. "What for?" I asked as a buxom nurse helped me into a wheelchair. Her hands were cold and her blonde curls tight.

"They're going to test you for multiple sclerosis, hon."

MS? Is this what Brock suspected?

Rolling down the hall and into the elevator, smelling the antiseptic of mopped floors, I numbed out. People with MS lost the ability to walk. It couldn't be cured. How would I take care of Lauren?

"I don't have MS," I told the nurse. "I have Lyme."

"Well, we're testing for all kinds of things, just to be sure."

The two-part test was horrendous. Surely it came straight out of Nazi Germany. First a nurse attached electrodes to my legs, sending shocks at higher and higher levels until I didn't think I could stand it. I gasped and moaned at each jolt of electricity. If I'd possessed normal energy, if my entire body didn't already ache, I'd have endured it better. I'm no baby when it comes to pain. But I was already worn down. The shocks were followed by long needles stuck deep into my leg muscles while on a computer monitor my nerves twanged a virtual scream.

By the time the procedure was done I was bathed in sweat and trembling.

The doctor studied the test results. "Doesn't look to me like you have MS," he pronounced.

Back in my room I was visited by an infectious disease specialist. Dr. Belkin, a trim man with long-fingered hands, was taking on my case. "We want to be completely thorough, Mrs. McNeil. Your husband insists on it, and we agree." He firmed his lips in a doctorly smile.

Fright banged around inside my chest. Something terrible *was* wrong with me. Enough to make them test for MS. I knew I felt like death on a hot pad, but for them to look at me and *know I was that sick.*

My head moved a fraction of a shake. "I have Lyme."

He regarded me. "How do you know?"

"I . . . just know."

He drew a deep breath. "Well, the lab's running a test for that disease. They're speeding things up for you. We may have those results by the end of the day."

"So I'm not going home today?"

"No, afraid not. We'll finish up testing you by the end of the afternoon. But you're in no shape to go home. We'll want to keep you around until all the results come in."

Brock called around 4:30, asking how I was doing.

"No better. Maybe worse. I don't know. Where's L-Lauren?"

"Maria picked her up with Katie after school. She's going to spend the weekend with them."

"The whole weekend? Why won't you just get her after work?"

"Jannie, she's fine there. I'll want to come see you during the weekend. Plus I have work to do at the office and lab. It's easier if Lauren's taken care of."

"You could bring her. Here, I mean. To see me."

He breathed annoyance over the line—a clear indication the subject was closed. "I've talked with Jud. They are going to place taps on our phone."

"Fine." My voice sounded dull. I was still fixated on spending another night away from home, and the fact that Lauren was staying at Katie's all weekend. Somehow that just didn't sit right. What was Brock not telling me?

Brock cleared his throat. "I'll come see you around 7:00."

I hung up the phone and stared at the closed blinds on the window. They'd been shut against the bright sun all day. Dark suspicions and unease roiled in my chest. The world out there tripped on while I was stuck in this bed.

I would fix this. Somehow. I'd make sure Stalking Man was caught. And like a Siren crooning her song I would woo back the attentions of my husband.

But right now I needed to rest.

My eyes closed, and I drifted off. Sometime later a presence by my bed awakened me. Dr. Belkin. "Hi." His hands were in his white coat pockets. "How you feeling?"

"Hanging in there."

He nodded. "Wanted to tell you we've got results from your blood and urine tests. I won't bore you with the long list of details. But I will say we looked for all kinds of poisons and heavy metals and found nothing unusual in your system. We also did a complete blood workup. We looked at all your systems—endocrine, thyroid, checked your pituitary gland, did liver panels and the rest—and found everything to be in the normal range. Your white blood cell count is a little high but nothing to cause considerable alarm. We did not find signs of viral or bacterial infection. In short, at this point I'm sorry to say we still don't know what's going haywire in your body."

My brain took a moment to process the news. "But . . . Lyme. You promised me you'd test for it."

"We did, Mrs. McNeil. Knowing the claims of this man who's been calling you, we surely wanted to cover that possibility. If you were infected months ago, as he said, antibodies would show up on the test by now. But they didn't. The results were negative."

I stared at him. "Negative?"

He shook his head. "The simple truth is—you don't have Lyme."

Chapter 9

🐜 AT 9 A.M. DETECTIVE JUD MAXWELL STRODE INTO THE STANFORD building that held the business offices for the Department of Medicine. Jud's visit to the McNeil house the previous evening had plagued his sleep, waking him more than once. This case was one of the most bizarre he'd ever encountered. Someone putting infected ticks on a sleeping woman because of her husband's work? How crazy was that? And yet how cunning, when he thought of the planning involved. This was no typical criminal Jud sought.

This was someone with a brilliant, strategic mind.

In the early hours of the morning, Jud had finally given up on sleep and dragged himself to his home computer. There he researched the medical issues surrounding Lyme. He'd had no idea such a war over the disease was raging between doctors and patients. Although his wife, Sarah, was a receptionist in Dr. McNeil's department, she hadn't known that much either.

Now as Jud climbed the steps to the second floor, his mind cycled through the myriad questions he wanted to ask McNeil's lab assistants.

Jud walked through the door that led to the central reception area, and his gaze fell on Sarah behind her wide desk. She looked up and gave him a wan smile. Sarah's brown eyes were usually bright, her mouth upturned. Not today. She'd been stunned to hear Jud's news of the McNeils last night. Sarah thought Jannie McNeil a very sweet woman. And Sarah was very loyal to Brock McNeil. They got along well—but then, Sarah got along with everyone. Truth was, Jud never had liked McNeil very much. Whenever they'd talked at office Christmas parties over the years he'd found the man quite arrogant.

"Hey." Sarah spoke in low tones as Jud stopped before her desk.

"Hi. You all right?"

She tilted her head. "We're all pretty much in shock. 'Course, folks here are just hearing the news as word spreads. At least I've had since last night to process."

Jud didn't make a habit of talking to Sarah about his cases, but last night he hadn't been able to keep quiet about this one. Besides, she was in a position to possibly help.

"Anyway, Alicia and Dane are ready to meet with you," Sarah pushed back from her desk. "They don't seem to think they can be of much help. But they'll do whatever they can."

Jud nodded. "And Dr. McNeil's out till 11?"

"Yeah, he just left for class." She rose. "Who do you want to talk to first?"

"Alicia."

His wife shot him a knowing look. "I'll take you back."

She ushered him down a hall, knocked on the door of a cubicle, and poked in her head. "Jud's here."

"Oh, okay."

Sarah threw Jud a glance and left him to his work. He stepped to the threshold of Alicia Mays's work area.

"Detective Maxwell." Alicia held out her hand. "Let's go across the hall where there's room for you to sit down. You can meet with Dane in there as well."

"Thanks. And I appreciate your seeing me."

She led Jud into an empty office and motioned to a small table. At least this place had a window. They took seats across from each other. Jud set his recorder down and turned it on. Pulled out his notepad and pen.

No doubt about it—Alicia was a looker. Shimmery dark hair and eyes, a lithe figure, and tanned, oval face. Decked out in a red dress-to-kill at last year's Christmas party, she'd been stunning. Now the woman sat back in her chair, trying to look relaxed.

Jud sensed she was anything but.

He spoke the date, time, and place for the recording's sake. "Interview with Alicia Mays." He nodded to her. "First, tell me about your background. Where you graduated from, how long you've worked here."

Alicia clasped her slender fingers on the table. "I graduated from here, Stanford, seven years ago. Then went on to get my masters. Dr. McNeil and Dr. Segal were among my professors. And I was at the top of my class, so when I graduated the job as a lab assistant was offered to me almost immediately. I was thrilled to stay right here and work."

Ah, yes, Dr. Segal. Jud knew one thing from Sarah—despite their surface cordiality, Segal and McNeil were long-time rivals. Apparently one department was too small a place for two raging egos.

"Tell me about what you do here."

Alicia gestured with her head. "I work on research projects in the lab—down the hall. Much of the time I'm there. But for online research and to write notes, whatever, I'm in my little office space."

Alicia's voice had a musical, alluring quality. Even if her answer seemed a bit evasive. She gazed at Jud directly as she spoke, her chin slightly raised.

"What are your hours?"

"During the day. Pretty much nine to five, but we're in and out."

Jud made a note. "By *we* you mean Dane Melford, Dr. McNeil's other lab assistant?"

"Yes."

"Does Dane also assist both doctors McNeil and Segal in the lab?"

She shook her head. "He mostly works with Dr. McNeil. Sometimes he assists other professors in the department when they're shorthanded."

Jud tapped his pen against the paper. "Tell me about your research with Dr. McNeil."

Her eyes flicked away for a moment. "Of course it can get quite technical. But in simple terms, for example, we're studying the transmission of *Borrelia burgdorferi*—the bacteria that cause Lyme—from tick to potential host. It appears that a strain of *Borrelia* deficient in a certain gene product is not able to be transmitted, even though the tick itself is indeed a carrier."

"So without this particular gene, say, if an infected tick bites a human, that person wouldn't get Lyme?"

"Yes."

"And what's the practical application of knowing about that gene?"

"The delineation of a certain gene needed for transmission could lead toward the development of a Lyme vaccine."

A vaccine. "I imagine anyone who develops a vaccine for Lyme could make a lot of money. There must be quite a bit of competition to be the first to accomplish that."

Alicia lifted a shoulder. "Yes, I suppose. Actually a vaccine was developed before, but in 2002 it was pulled off the market. But no doubt many researchers across the country are continuing to try to develop an effective one. There are a lot of complexities involved in succeeding."

"Is Dr. McNeil close?"

She shifted in her chair. "Nowhere near."

What wasn't she telling him? "Might competitors think you're close?"

Alicia gave him a sideways look. "I don't see why they would."

Jud thought about Janessa McNeil's recounting of the threatening phone conversations. The man had made it sound as if he wanted Brock McNeil to reverse his opinion on chronic Lyme. But what if that was just a ruse? What if the guy was a competitor of McNeil's and wanted to upend his research? If millions of dollars were at stake . . .

"What about Dr. Segal's research? Is he also working on Lyme?"

Alicia shook her head. "No. His research is in cancer cells."

"And he's in class this morning?"

"Yes, afraid so."

Jud would have to speak with him another time.

For the next hour Jud questioned Alicia about her thoughts of who could be behind the McNeil's break-in. She claimed to have no idea. Despite her apparent willingness to answer questions, a vague evasiveness continued to coat her responses.

Perhaps Alicia Mays did have something to hide.

But it may have nothing to do with this case.

"Alicia, you obviously work with infected ticks in the lab. Have any gone missing?"

Her eyebrows rose. "From *our* lab? No. Believe me, if your suspect placed ticks on Mrs. McNeil they didn't come from here. There are labs all over the country where *Borrelia* is researched. And maybe they didn't come from a lab at all. It's not as if every infected tick is created through research."

Time was slipping by, and Jud still needed to talk to Dane Melford. He wrapped up the interview and turned off the recorder. Thanked Alicia as he gave her his card. "Please call me if you think of anything. Anything at all."

"I certainly will. I'll go get Dane for you now."

Jud had little time to ponder Alicia's answers before Dane appeared, clad in a lab coat. Jud had chatted with Dane at last year's Christmas party and liked the man. As he remembered, Dane was around forty and a confirmed bachelor. He'd worked with McNeil for a couple years. Dane stood tall and thin, his face a long egg shape, his skin pale.

He took the seat Alicia had vacated, leaning forward to place both arms on the table. "I hope I can give you something. But this"—he spread his hands—"what's happened is beyond me."

"I'll bet. But you never know how some little detail you recall may lead to something."

Dane tilted his head in a *hope so* gesture.

Jud restarted his recorder and stated the details of the interview. "Dane, tell me about your background."

He gave a self-effacing smile. "Nothing as illustrious as Alicia's top-of-the-class performance, I'm afraid." He'd attended San Diego State and graduated in '93. Had lived in California all his life.

"Still not married?"

"Nah. Won't happen."

"Oh, yeah? You may be surprised."

Something flickered across Dane's face. "My parents never got along. I'm talking huge fights, even though they stayed together. And all my uncles and aunts—none of them were happy. I vowed as a kid I'd never get married. Just don't need the stress."

Jud nodded. "I see." But he felt sorry for the man. Sarah—and their two kids—were the most important part of his life.

Jud talked with Dane about his work, how he had eventually moved to northern California and found a job at Stanford. Two years ago he switched to the Department of Medicine and began working with McNeil.

"Dr. McNeil is brilliant. Just so focused. Has long-term vision. I'm glad I get to work with him almost exclusively."

With McNeil's overbearing confidence, Melford was probably a good choice for an assistant. He wasn't the kind of man who would get in the doctor's way. He'd be able to take McNeil's need for control in stride.

"Tell me about your research with Dr. McNeil."

Now this was a subject that brought Dane to animated life. He explained in more detail McNeil's research, how they worked toward the goal of one day creating a vaccine. "I hope to stay with the doctor for years. If anyone can crack this, he will."

Jud asked Dane if he knew of anyone who would want to do Dr. McNeil harm. Perhaps some competitor of McNeil's.

Dane could think of no one. He frowned. "But aren't you looking in the wrong place? As Dr. McNeil described it this morning, the man who did this is part of the Lyme community. Someone who wants to force the doctor's hand regarding his findings on Lyme."

"Do you know much about these Lyme wars, as they're called?"

Dane pushed his lips together. "Not really. I know a little. But mostly we just don't pay attention to their clamor. We've got work to do in our research, and we do it. We can't be swayed by outside opinion." He shook his head. "I'm sure Dr. McNeil is far more aware of what's going on, however. He's the one who's out there in public, speaking in symposiums. And I know he's been verbally attacked. But he doesn't talk about it much. Like I say, he's just really focused."

Jud gazed out the window. "So if you were in my shoes, where would you look for this suspect?"

Dane leaned back and regarded the ceiling. "I'd look at the most vocal advocates in the Lyme community. Who among them may have some criminal background, be capable of such a heinous thing."

"Any thought where someone like that would get hold of an infected tick?"

He thought about it. "He could go into any woods where

Lyme-infected ticks are known to be endemic and catch them in a dragged net, as forest researchers often do."

"He wouldn't know they were infected for sure."

Dane shrugged. "True. But good chance they would be."

The visual picture of dragging a net to catch infected ticks chilled Jud to the bone. It stayed with him as he drove away from Stanford— and pulsed in his mind as he returned to his own office.

Chapter 10

THAT EVENING BROCK CAME TO SEE ME AS PROMISED, STRIDING in with the vim of the outside world. He'd come straight from work, he told me, hadn't stopped for dinner. Brock reached for my hand, brushed my forehead with his fingers. But I sensed little warmth in his actions. *It's the sickness.* Men—even doctors—just didn't know how to handle illness in their own families.

"I don't have Lyme." The words burst from me. News of the test's negative results had throbbed in my veins for the past few hours. I didn't know whether to laugh or cry. Stalking Man was nothing but a liar. A con man, set out to skew my husband's scientific studies. Or so I wanted to believe.

But if I didn't have Lyme, why was I sick?

"I heard." Brock let go of my hand. "I also heard that before those results came in you insisted to every doctor and nurse you saw that you have Lyme."

"I—"

"Doesn't sit very well, Jannie. You intimating to my colleagues that you know more than I do about the very disease I've studied for years."

His words stung. "I'm sorry."

Brock gazed at me—not a warm look. "I talked to Dr. Belkin about all your results."

"So . . . what now?"

"That guy who called you is certifiably nuts. I still want the police to catch him. But now I don't believe he was ever in our house."

Hope lifted its head. "But he knew the layout of our b-bedrooms." I was beginning to stutter again.

"Jannie, we had interior painting done two months ago, remember? Lauren's room and the guest bedroom. We had painters in and out of our house for a number of days. Any one of them could tell you what those rooms looked like."

"You think it was one of those m-men? But what would painters know or even care about your work?"

"I don't know. At any rate I mentioned it to Jud."

My eyes closed in weighted relief. Of course. The painters. Why hadn't I thought of them?

Still . . .

"But he knew our unlisted phone number. And my cell number. He knew Lauren's name."

"Those workers would have been given our numbers when we hired them for the job. As for Lauren, she has numerous items in her room with her name on them."

I stared at the blank TV unit hanging from the wall. Every imagining I'd endured about that man being in our home now replayed itself. I so wanted to believe Brock's words. The man *hadn't* broken into our home. Our house was safe.

"Yes." I nodded, the vastness of my relief making me ache all the more. "Yes."

But the *coincidence* of my illness still pricked.

Brock kept his eyes on me. "The police managed to get our phone records quickly. Turns out it's just as Jud guessed. Your caller used a throwaway cell phone bought under a fake name. They got the phone number he used, but it doesn't lead anywhere."

Stalking Man made this all up—and now he couldn't be traced. *Please, then, just go away and leave me alone.*

I sighed. "Where did he call from? What cell phone tower?"

"You heard Jud explain that? It looked like you weren't even listening."

My eyelids didn't want to stay open. "I heard. Besides I knew about that already. Some true crime show on TV."

Brock stared at me. Something in his eyes . . .

"Where did he c-call from?"

The question hung in the air.

"Brock?"

"Your cell phone call came from the El Camino area in Palo Alto."

I gaped at him. "You mean right near where I was . . . driving to L-Lauren's school?"

He flexed his jaw and nodded.

Stalking Man had been that close? *That close?*

"And the call at home?"

"From our neighborhood."

My breath caught. "You're kidding."

No response.

Panic uncoiled in my limbs. "He's following me! Everywhere! He *was* in our house, Brock. It's not one of those p-painters."

Was he close now? Somewhere in the hospital? Why was he *doing* this?

Brock seemed strangely unaffected. The way he kept looking at me . . .

"I told you they've tapped our phones. If the man calls again, they'll get a recording plus trace where he's calling from. They'll try to get to the area while he's still there."

"Okay." I couldn't think anymore. Couldn't make sense from any of it.

Brock shifted positions. He regarded me with his chin raised and eyes half closed, as if broaching an uncomfortable subject. "Jannie, maybe your illness is psychosomatic. The man said you'd be sick—and you were."

Right. That would explain it—if I hadn't collapsed on the kitchen floor *before* I'd ever heard from the man. But Brock knew that. I looked away.

"Doctors like your husband will tell you it's all in your head." Stalking Man had warned me this would happen.

What was I supposed to do with that? The man had said I was sick, and I was. He'd said Brock would react this way, and he had.

But Stalking Man was crazy. Not to be believed.

I picked at my bedcovers. It's true what they say about the unknown. It's far more frightening to have no answer than to hear one you'd never have wanted. In crisis situations you need a tangible enemy. Someone or something to fight. To bull's-eye with the arrows of your righteous indignation. "The doctor said they want to run more tests tomorrow so . . . maybe they'll find something."

Brock grunted. "Maybe."

Our words lulled. Minutes passed in silence. We seemed to have little to say to each other. Brock mouthed his goodbyes and left. I watched him go, feeling the distance between us crack wider. When he'd rushed home yesterday he seemed so concerned. I couldn't lose his caring, our partnership. No way could I battle this . . . whatever it was alone.

I thought of my childhood, the summer when I was twelve. My father had launched with gusto into one of his week-long drunken binges. Every day he ratcheted up, then loosed by beating me. Then

I fell sick. But I was only faking. I was stuck in that nightmare of a house, too afraid of my father to run away. Instead I threw all my resources into a feigned illness that left me weak and crying with stomach pain in hopes that my dad would feel sorry for me. In hindsight it seemed a silly plan—if the man felt anything for me he wouldn't have beat me in the first place. But surprisingly, it worked. My dad toned down his drinking and took to sitting with me on the couch. When he touched me I felt a gentleness I hadn't known in a long time. For three days I basked in the peace my ailment had wrought. But then my father grew restless. Clearly his concern for me was too much of a burden. Out came the whiskey bottles. His hands again turned harsh. I quickly got better and escaped outside to play with my friends.

Over the next three years, when my dad's behavior warranted it, I pulled the same trick countless times. To this day my mother refers to that era as my *stomach-problem* years. Each time my strange ailment would buy me a day or two of softening in my father. An ephemeral rescue. But oh, the relief.

My phone rang. I jumped, sending shocks of pain through my muscles. I pressed two fingers to my forehead, then reached toward the table on my left for the receiver. Maybe it was Lauren. "Hello?"

"Good evening, Janessa." Stalking Man's voice rode low and snide. My lungs bubbled. "So sorry to hear you're in the hospital."

Chapter 11

FOR A LONG SECOND MY MIND SHUT DOWN. I STARED AT THE closed blinds of my window. How did he know I was here?

I fumbled to find the nurse call button on my right. Pushed it.

"What do you want?" I sounded breathless.

"Just checking to see how your task is coming."

My *task*? I wanted to strangle this man. Anger leaked through me. "Which one would that be? Trying to w-walk? Think with a clear head? Maybe just . . . move without pain."

"*Do* not play with me, Mrs. McNeil. You know very well I mean convincing your husband."

"You're insane. I can't *convince* my husband to refute his scientific f-findings. Besides, I don't even have Lyme."

A pause hovered. "Is that so?"

"Yes, it is so." I shot a glance at the doorway. *Where* was that nurse? "So why don't you just l-leave me alone?"

"Let me guess. Some doctor told you your Lyme test was negative."

"Gee, wasn't that a hard one."

He made a sound in his throat. "Didn't I say you'd entered a war? You're facing the same thing many Lyme patients do. The tests that most doctors and hospitals love to use run anywhere from thirty to fifty percent false negative."

I blinked. "You're telling me the test is *wrong?*"

"Of course it's wrong."

"Maybe your plan just didn't w-work, how about that? Or maybe you were n-never in my house in the first place!"

He chuckled—an evil sound. "Then why are you sick, Mrs. McNeil?"

My mouth closed.

"After they're done testing you for all the things they won't find, go to a doctor who knows how to treat Lyme. There are a few in the Bay Area, although you'll be amazed at the small number. Seven or so in a population of six million. Can you imagine if we had that few oncologists?"

"And what's a Lyme doctor supposed to do?"

"Send you for proper testing, for a start."

"You're *lying.*"

"Am I?"

"I ought to be able to believe a t-test given by a . . . hospital as respected as this one!"

"Agreed. It's shameful. But it's not the hospital's fault. They're merely using the standardized test—the one doctors like your husband hold up as the Holy Grail. Tell me, isn't he worried that your doctors are stumped?"

I thought of Brock's unconvinced tone, the way he'd looked at me.

"Jannie, maybe your illness is psychosomatic."

Why was I even talking to this man, after what he'd put me through?

"If your husband's worried about you, Mrs. McNeil, he'll pursue the answer to your illness, regardless of what it takes. Even if it means seeing past his stubborn mind-set."

The last two words punched me in the gut. Brock *was* stubborn. Was he refusing to see the truth about my sickness because it didn't fit into his neat little box?

I shook my head. "Leave me alone! Do *not* call me again."

"Janessa, you must do what I say."

"He doesn't believe I have Lyme! And besides, what difference would it m-make? I'm already sick. If I change my husband's mind, are you going to wave a magic . . ." The word fled. It made me all the madder. "Wand and make me well?"

A silent, throbbing pause dragged out. My stomach turned over. When the man spoke again his voice fell to thin, sharp silver. "What makes you think I'll stop with you?"

Hang up, I screamed at myself. But my fingers wouldn't let go of the phone.

"You're not the only one who can fall sick, Mrs. McNeil."

"What're you—"

"Kiss your daughter for me."

The line clicked in my ear.

Heat rolled up my body. "No, wait! Listen to me."

Silence.

I lowered the receiver, trembling. Movement on the right caught my eye. I turned my head to see a nurse entering the room. She looked in her late fifties, her hair pepper-and-salt, her demeanor so casual. As if the world hadn't just cracked in two.

"Hello there, you called for me?" She smiled as she approached.

"Why did you take so long? You're too late!"

"Too late for wh—?"

I shook the receiver at her. "I wanted you to hear. I w-wanted somebody to hear his voice, what he was saying." Heat sank teeth into my limbs. I felt sweat pop out on my forehead. I had to get to Lauren, protect her. I had to get *out* of this hospital.

"Who?"

"The man. *Him.* He's c-called three times, threatening. And now he's *threatening my daughter.*"

Her eyes rounded. "What is he saying?"

I hit the off button on the phone, pressed talk. "I have to call my husband." The words were whispered half to myself, my finger stumbling over the numbers as I dialed home. After three rings the message machine clicked on, my own voice answering. With a small cry I ended the call and dialed Brock's cell phone. The nurse stood at my bedside, nonplused.

"Hello." My husband's voice spilled into my ear.

"Brock, he——" All words seized up.

"What?"

"He called again, here in the room. And he said I *do* have Lyme, and you're wr-wrong. And you have to relook at your . . . studies and change your opinion. Or he'll make Lauren sick!"

"Jannie, don't even say such a thing."

"That's what he *said.*" My eyes filled with tears. I couldn't bear to see Lauren in the condition I was in, barely able to walk, to think. The pain was too much for a child. "A nurse is here, she'll tell you." I thrust the phone into the woman's hand, only to remember she'd heard nothing.

She gave me a questioning look, then placed the receiver to her ear. "This is Nurse Evans."

Brock's commanding voice barked from the receiver. I could hear his every word as he asked what she'd heard.

"I didn't hear anything. I walked in and she was just holding the receiver."

"She wasn't talking to anyone?"

"No."

"You sure?"

"Yes. She was just holding it. That's all."

Silence hung in the room. I glowered at the nurse. She shook her head, as if to say *I'm sorry* and handed the phone back to me. "Can I get anything for you?" She studied my face, as if I weren't quite all there.

"We could ask the . . . switchboard. Somebody had to put him through."

"Jannie!" My husband's voice barked through the phone.

She shrugged. "They get so many calls. I'm not sure anyone would remember."

"Jannie!"

I waved the nurse away. *Thanks a lot.* Pressed the phone to my ear. "Brock, I have to come home." I fought to sound steady, but my voice wavered and pitched. "We have to watch Lauren every minute. Somehow he'll get to her. I don't w-want her like this. I don't want this to happen to her!"

"Nothing's going to happen to her."

"But he said—"

"You need to calm down. Take a deep breath."

"I *am* breathing. You need to listen to me."

"Fine. I'm listening. Tell me everything he said."

"He said the Lyme test is no good. It's a f-false negative. And he'll hurt others if you don't start listening to me. And then he let me know he was talking about Lauren. We n-need to tell the police, Brock. They have to know!"

"All right. I'll tell them."

I hesitated. His voice didn't sound right. "You will?"

"Yes."

"Can they watch Lauren closer at school? And Maria should know. She can't let the . . . girls go anywhere this weekend."

"I'll talk to her, too. Now listen to me. I want you to get some rest."

How could I rest? I could barely move, but my mind swooped and plummeted.

"We'll talk more about this tomorrow, Jannie. For tonight Lauren's safe at Katie's."

The receiver felt slick in my fingers. My left elbow throbbed. A new wave of tiredness washed through me, as if my body suddenly realized it had spent what energy it possessed. My head sank deeper into the pillows. "You're not going to call Maria, are you."

My husband breathed over the line, a weary, beleaguered sound. "How do you suppose this man found you in the hospital, Jannie?"

"Don't know. Maybe he f-followed you here and figured it out."

"I teach at the med school. I'm at the hospital on a regular basis."

"Maybe he doesn't know that."

"I thought he knew all about me. How important my opinion is to the medical world."

There was that tone again. Almost accusing. "What are you saying?"

"It's just odd, that's all. He calls on your cell phone, then our home line, and neither call has a traceable ID. You and I agree to have our home phone tapped. The police have your cell. So now you say he calls your private hospital room."

I *say?*

"What are you getting at, Brock?" My nerves prickled. I could not be reading him right.

"Remember that conversation we had some years ago? How when you were young you faked a stomach ache so your father wouldn't treat you so badly?"

My mouth opened, but I said nothing.

"The plan worked. You used it again and again."

Somewhere deep within me a voice whispered that I should have known. Hadn't I thought of this very same thing just after Brock left my room? "Are you saying I'm faking this illness?"

"Are you?"

The question punched me in the stomach. Psychosomatic illness, nothing. My husband didn't want to believe me—period. "And the m-man? His calls?"

"Those calls came from the same areas where you were. Both times."

"Yes. He was so close!"

"Or you made them."

My head dropped back against the pillows. "*I* made them?"

"You could have bought the throwaway cell phone. You said you know all about the tracing methods."

What? I could barely breathe. "And the one here? To my room?"

"No one heard it but you."

No. This was too much. This could not be my husband talking. "Why, Brock? Why would I do all that?"

He released a long sigh. As if we both knew exactly why.

My left arm fell to the bed. The phone bounced on the covers and out of my hand. Half in a daze I picked it up and pressed the button to end the call.

For a long time I lay staring at the wall, my saturated mind trying to understand what was happening. Who my husband had become.

And what I was supposed to do now.

SATURDAY

Chapter 12

I STAYED IN THE HOSPITAL A SECOND FULL DAY, FLOATING IN A sort of purgatory. I wanted to go home and take care of Lauren. Bring her back from Katie's house. In fact I insisted to everyone who would listen that I had to leave—*now*. Dr. Belkin didn't want to discharge me until the tests were finished. He asked Brock to talk some sense into me. How doctors stick together. Brock phoned and said I had to stay another day.

"What for?" I demanded. "Since all this is fake anyway."

What an odd, strained dance we found ourselves in. To music I'd never heard.

"Jannie, Dr. Belkin wants to cover all the bases. Maybe there's something he hasn't found yet."

And you, Brock? If you were my doctor?

The doctors ran more tests on my blood and urine, looking further for this esoteric poison and that. They poked and prodded me, watched me walk (like a wambling sailor) and listened to me talk (stuttering and searching for words). They did a brain scan.

They found nothing.

More fodder for Brock.

Dr. Belkin looked from my chart to my face, then back again. "Perhaps you've developed a case of Chronic Fatigue Syndrome. But it's far too soon for that diagnosis. You certainly have some of the symptoms. Impaired memory and concentration, muscle pain, joint pain, trouble sleeping, and most of all the fatigue. However, we typically wait to see if symptoms other than fatigue are present for more than six months. Until that time we'll keep an eye on you and see if you don't get better on your own."

Brock called again later in the day. I wondered why he bothered. Neither of us mentioned the *faking it* conversation. But it hung between us, overripe. The spoiling fruit of his suspicion. We would talk of it again—I knew that from the authoritarian tone in his voice. He was waiting for the right time. Maybe when I came home.

Made me want to stay in the hospital.

In the afternoon Brock brought Lauren to visit. She came at me as I sat up in bed, her arms wide for a hug. I cringed. "Oh, sweetie, I'm s-sorry. My body hurts so much it's hard to be hugged. Just pat me on the . . . cheek, okay?"

Teary-eyed, she laid her fingers against my face. "You're talking funny."

"I know."

"I miss you."

"I miss you too. I'm coming home tomorrow."

"Are you any better?"

How I wished I could say yes. I managed a smile. "A little."

We talked about school. Perched on the edge of my bed, Lauren chattered about her friends, her too-much homework for the weekend. Her lively conversation tasted bittersweet. How her nine-year-old world had gone on without me.

Brock sat on a chair in the corner, listening and withdrawn. He did not smile at me, barely looked me in the eye.

And he watched Lauren with a protective gaze that made me shiver.

Chapter 13

JUD MAXWELL SLUNG DOWN THE PHONE IN HIS CRAMPED OFFICE and hunched over his computer. Six o'clock on a Saturday night—and no going home anytime soon. Three more house burglaries in the last two days in Palo Alto—two last night and one today in broad daylight. That made seven altogether in the last two weeks. Chief of Police Jeff Kraminsky was not happy. With the media and angered public breathing down his neck, he wanted the crimes solved *now*.

A little hard without one suspect fingerprint yet. The perp had taken precautions.

Despite Jud's extra stress the McNeil case bubbled in the back of his mind. He wasn't happy about being pulled away from it to focus on the burglaries. But fact was, he had nothing to go on. As promised, Brock McNeil was updating him on Mrs. McNeil's condition and test results. So far the tests had all returned normal. And no more threatening phone calls had come in. The tracings on the two she'd received had been disturbing. The suspect was right in the area. But then he'd fallen quiet.

Jud peered at his monitor, trying to refocus. Before his phone rang he'd been in the middle of typing up his report of the latest burglary.

His fingers found the computer keys to continue—and his phone went off again.

Muttering under his breath, Jud yanked up the receiver. "Maxwell."

"Jud, you have a visitor here who wants to see you." It was Glenda's smoke-husky voice, out at the front desk.

Jud groaned. "Who is it?"

"Dr. Brock McNeil."

Jud blinked. McNeil to see him *here*? Maybe he had news about the final test results. "I'll be right out." He dropped the receiver into its cradle and shoved back his chair.

A moment later Jud strode into the waiting area, his gaze lighting on Dr. McNeil, clad in khakis and a polo shirt. The man was pacing, agitation rolling off him. He glanced up and saw Jud, and relief flickered across his face.

"Dr. McNeil." Jud stuck out his hand.

The man shook it briefly. "Thank you for seeing me."

Thank you? Didn't sound like the same brash, take-charge man from Thursday night. "No problem. Come on back to my office."

Jud led the way down the hall and into his quarters, extending an arm to invite McNeil to step in first. The doctor entered and looked around, face pinched with distraction.

"Sorry it's so cluttered in here." Jud grabbed a stack of files from the extra wooden chair and dropped them on his desk. "Have a seat."

McNeil sat down. Jud claimed his battered chair behind the desk, moving aside his notes from the burglaries. "Have you been trying to get hold of me today? Sorry I've been busy with another case."

"No, I just thought I'd try to catch you." The doctor straightened his back. The hesitation melted from his demeanor, replaced with a steely determination. "I need to talk to you about Jannie."

Jud leaned back and his chair squeaked. "You have new information?"

McNeil pulled in a deep breath. "You know about the test results from yesterday. All normal. And today—same thing. They can't find one thing wrong with her."

Jud mulled that over. "No poisons. No infections. No . . . anything."

"Correct."

Interesting. "So what do you think?"

McNeil ran a knuckle under his chin as he contemplated Jud's scratched-up desk. "I think . . ." He shifted in his seat. Tilted his head back with a sigh. "This isn't going to be easy to say."

"Okay." Jud nodded, then waited. He'd learned years ago not to fill the silence. Let the witness or suspect fill it instead. Never know what interesting information you'll get.

The doctor looked down at his hands. His jaw moved to one side, his forehead puckering. "I'm afraid she's faking."

Jud fought to keep the surprise from his face. "Faking her illness?"

"All of it. Her illness. And the man's phone calls."

Wow. Jud leaned forward, clasping his hands on the desk. What question to ask first? "Is she the kind of woman who would do that?" Jud never would have guessed such a thing.

McNeil cleared his throat again. "Not usually. I mean, never before in our marriage has she pulled anything like this. She's always been trustworthy. But now . . . And then there's her past. Plus the facts at hand that I just can't ignore."

The doctor looked pained, as if the very conversation was hurtful to him.

"I see." Jud slid a pad of paper toward himself and found a pen. Clearly there were numerous issues to sort through here. "If you don't mind I'd like to take notes."

McNeil pressed his lips, then nodded.

"So . . . let's start with the 'facts at hand.'" Jud wrote a number 1 on his page and circled it. "Tell me the first."

"The negative test results."

Jud wrote down the answer. "But surely this has happened before with patients. Something so esoteric or rare is wrong with a person that it takes a long time to find the cause."

"Yes, but you're forgetting one thing. According to Jannie's unwavering story, she's supposed to have Lyme. She doesn't. Yet she still insists on it. Of course we worked her up for everything else just to be sure. But I've spoken to the physicians and nurses attending her at the hospital. They all say she keeps insisting she has Lyme—the very disease on which I've built my reputation." Bitterness edged into McNeil's tone. "To make her story work, she *has* to have the disease."

"But if she's faking, she'd know the tests would show negative."

"True. And she's got the perfect comeback—the same thing all those *chronic* Lyme patients out there claim. The tests are wrong." He shrugged. "As for all the other workups she had to endure, I'm sure she never expected me to send her to the hospital in the first place."

Jud frowned, his gaze wandering to his monitor. The screen saver had kicked in, rolling an aimless ball. "She looks so sick."

"Yes. Well. She's had practice."

Jud raised his eyebrows. "Practice?"

McNeil nodded. "It happened in her childhood. Jannie's the daughter of an alcoholic. A horrible man who abused her both physically and emotionally. Then one day she figured out how to pull some real, caring attention from him . . ."

Jud took notes as he listened to the disturbing stories from Jannie McNeil's childhood. The stomach aches she faked. Her repeat performances because of their effectiveness.

McNeil shook his head. "Took her years to open up to me about this. When she finally did, I felt terrible for her. That a child should need to do that just to see some tenderness from her father. And part of me was confused, because the Jannie I knew wore her emotions on her sleeve. How did she ever fake something well enough to fool her callous father? And her mother? I'll never forget Jannie's answer. She said, 'I was great at it because I had to be. I needed to survive.'"

The last word hung in the air. Jud dwelt on it for a moment, then struggled to place the Janessa McNeil he knew into this new context of deceit. Faking an illness as a child was one thing—and in her situation understandable. But launching this kind of scheme as an adult, as a caring mother with a daughter to take care of . . . What in the world would push a stable woman to do such a thing?

A cold light dawned in Jud's head.

He tapped his pen against the paper. "So number one—we've got the test results. Nothing to indicate she's sick in any way." He wrote 2 on his paper and circled it. "Second, we've got . . . ?"

"No evidence. As you know." The doctor gestured toward Jud. "No solid evidence of a break-in at our house. No evidence of the two calls being made by anyone but Jannie herself—because they were made from the very same area. And since you've tapped those two lines—nothing. Except a supposed call to the hospital—which no one else heard."

"Wait, back up. You think your wife made those phone calls *herself?*"

"Apparently so. She let it slip that she knows about cell phone tracing from watching true crime shows on TV. So she knew she couldn't just make up the calls—she actually had to receive them. I figure she bought a throwaway phone and dialed herself."

Janessa McNeil would *do* that? "But if she knows about call tracing, she'd know the calls would trace back to her own area."

"True. But that would just make it look even worse—like the man was stalking her. He was in close proximity."

Jud stared at a spot on the wall, trying to make sense of the doctor's suspicions. They did fit what little evidence he'd gathered. But Jud could not imagine them fitting Mrs. McNeil.

"You mentioned something about the man calling your wife's hospital room?"

McNeil shook his head. "That's what she claims. Now he's supposedly threatening Lauren. Talk about upping the ante. Believe me, I wouldn't let anything happen to my daughter, but I *know* that phone call never happened. Jannie tried to tell me a nurse overheard the conversation, but when I talked to the woman she didn't know anything about it."

Jud made a note. "What time did she say the call came in?"

McNeil shrugged. "I don't remember. Sometime yesterday."

"Yesterday? You never mentioned it."

McNeil looked away. "I . . . couldn't. I know our phone conversations have been brief. I'm sorry about that. But all these suspicions were rolling around in my head, and I had to sort them out. I didn't want to believe them. I really didn't." McNeil spread his hands. "But when you think about it, there's nothing, *not one thing* to substantiate her story. Nothing stacks up. And I'm just sick about this. Utterly sick."

What husband wouldn't be, if he believed such a thing about his wife? "But *why* would she do this?"

McNeil regarded him, as if assessing how much he knew. That chilling light in Jud's head grew a little brighter. After all, Sarah was pretty astute. Jud kept his face placid.

"I don't want my wife humiliated." The doctor spoke with his old force. "And I know you've already put manpower into this case. Plus falsely reporting a crime is a crime in itself. I don't want Jannie in trouble. This has gone far enough. I want you to drop the case."

Drop the case? "What if you're wrong? What if this stalker really exists?"

"He doesn't."

The man was certainly sure of himself.

Jud's gaze returned to the spot on the wall. He had to admit everything the doctor said could fit. But he still found the story hard to swallow.

Jud looked back to the doctor. One crucial piece remained missing. But apparently Jud was going to have to back McNeil into a corner before he'd admit it. "Tell me this. Could the man have placed infected ticks on your wife—but she didn't get Lyme?"

McNeil shrugged. "Yes, it's possible. Everyone reacts differently to the infection. Or maybe they never attached at all."

"So all the negative test results don't necessarily mean this man doesn't exist."

"I . . . true."

"And the phone calls coming from the area near your wife—maybe this bad guy really *was* that close."

The doctor leaned forward and looked Jud in the eye. "I'm telling you, she's lying. Close the case."

"I can't close a criminal investigation simply because a family member asks me to."

"*Do* it." McNeil's lips thinned. He straightened his back. "Do I need to tell your chief how you're wasting your time on a case with no evidence when a string of burglaries is yet to be solved?"

Jud tossed down his pen. The barb about the burglaries hit a little too close.

"Hear me, detective. I *don't want* any more embarrassment for Jannie."

Or maybe for himself?

Jud stabbed McNeil with a look. So the man wanted to play rough? Fine. "Dr. McNeil, there's one question you haven't yet answered. And I have no reason to continue listening unless you do. *Why* would your loyal, trustworthy wife do this?"

McNeil locked defiant eyes with Jud. Anger and resentment rattled the air. "Apparently she once again feels the need to survive."

"Survive what?"

"Or perhaps it's more like exact her revenge." And then, in a cold, self-rationalizing tone, McNeil told Jud why his wife had launched her outrageous scheme.

SUNDAY

Chapter 14

ON SUNDAY I WAS RELEASED FROM THE HOSPITAL AT NOON. I'd requested that Brock buy me a cane. He brought one to the hospital, a silver, ugly thing with rubberized handle. I badly needed it. I remained unsteady in my gait and weak-muscled. The burning on the bottoms of my feet had increased and only grew worse the longer I stood. Even with the cane I shuffled. And using the thing hurt my right hand and arm.

We drove home, the day bright and the silence in our car thick. I wore sunglasses, and still my eyes hurt. In the spotlight of Brock's suspicions, every one of my symptoms seemed to scream its existence. The cautious bending to get into his Mercedes. My painful hand outreached, trying to pull the door shut. Brock closed it for me. Did he resent that?

In my house I felt like a refugee come to beg. As if something had changed while I was gone, and I could no longer settle into its familiar comfort. Lauren was still at Katie's. Maria would bring her home around mid-afternoon. I caned my way across the kitchen to the freezer and opened it, staring at its contents. Meat needed to be taken out for dinner. What should I choose? And surely the laundry had piled up. Yesterday was Saturday, and the bed sheets hadn't been changed. My eyes took in the meat choices, hardened and frosted. Like my husband.

He closed the door leading to the garage. "Don't worry about dinner. I'll pick up something later."

"No, no, I'll cook." I had to. Just to prove there was still some normalcy about me. Although where I'd find the energy, I didn't know.

"Jannie, we need to talk."

Funny, how those words carried a kind of finality.

I edged back and closed the freezer door. Turned myself around. My feet bottoms sizzled, and the fatigue made me sway. I needed to sit down, but I wasn't about to suggest it.

Brock gestured with his head. "Let's go in the den."

The den. For a moment I couldn't remember what room that was.

Brock headed into the TV room. Through the pass-through window I watched him aim for his armchair. I made my slow way out of the kitchen to the couch and sat down, trying to keep my back straight, my face calm. What was I to do with the cane? I didn't want to rest my palms on its handle like some old dowager. I hesitated, then leaned it against a cushion so it wouldn't fall. I didn't want to have to bend over and retrieve it from the floor.

"What is it, Brock?" Maybe I could feign control of this conversation. "You want to discuss my f-faked illness?"

He sat, hands on his knees, his expression almost defensive. It took him a long while to respond.

"You know. Don't you, Jannie."

A statement, not a question.

I gave my head a tiny shake. *What?*

He pulled in air. Let it out. "About Alicia."

In drugged motion the name wafted through my brain. Alicia. One of his lab assistants.

"And me."

My head pulled back, my eyelids weighted. I think my heart stopped beating. I fixed on my husband's face, waiting for him to say more. To explain that it wasn't as it sounded. The second stretched out, my fingers rubbing against my jeans, my legs heavy as logs. How strange, hearing news that could upend my life, and I was just . . . sitting there.

"Actually," I heard myself say, "I didn't."

Was that a smirk that flashed? "Oh, I think you did."

My eyes slipped closed. What was the important topic here? Not the fact that my husband was apparently doing something horrible and immoral, but that I'd *known* about it? I took a deep breath. It ransacked my lungs. "Tell you what, B-Brock, why don't you humor me."

He leaned forward, elbows on his thighs, fingers laced. "I was prepared to have this talk three days ago."

Thursday—when Stalking Man first called. Well. Wasn't that quite the fated day.

"I'm leaving, Jannie. I'm moving in with her."

I floated to the ceiling and looked down, a detached spirit. At first my brain couldn't grasp what I'd heard. Then vague realization filtered in. Brock's plan to tell me three days ago. Then the weekend, Lauren staying at Katie's rather than at home. "You were with her. This weekend."

Brock shrugged.

"You'd planned that already?"

No answer.

What to ask next? Where to even go from here? "How old is this person?" Was I not young *enough* for him?

"That hardly matters."

I'd seen her at last year's Christmas function. She couldn't be even thirty yet. A real beauty. Dark-eyed and tanned, even in winter. An insane figure, accentuated in a perfectly fitted red dress. Brock had introduced us and given her a perfunctory peck on the cheek. At the time I'd thought *my husband works with* that *every day?*

My thoughts wandered further back. Our marital problems started well before Christmas. That party—he'd been with her even then.

A disgusted sound puffed from my throat. "I can't believe this." It was so . . . Hollywood. The successful older man taking up with the younger, beautiful woman at work. I knew men really did this—all too often. But only someone else's husband. Not mine. Never mine.

"What are you going to tell Lauren? You're going to leave your only . . . child for someone who's y-young enough to be your daughter?"

"Jan—"

"You'll break Lauren's heart. And for that I'll break you in two!" I picked up my cane and shook it at him, like some mad old lady. I'd have laughed if the whole thing wasn't so awful. Just look at me. Thirty-six years old and already ancient. Used up.

"Put that thing down."

The cane slipped from my hands, the pain in my knuckles too great to hold its weight. It hit the floor with a rattle that pierced my ears. I ogled the thing, shiny and slick, my mouth ajar and sweat trickling down my spine. Despair sucked me in until I nearly fell over. I grasped the sofa cushions, steadying myself. There. There went my heart, pulsing again. Draining so much energy.

How miserable that I was sick at this moment, my anger left with no way to vent, my muscles like puddles of water.

"I will talk to Lauren." Brock sounded so calm, so quiet. "We'll work it out. She'll come to visit me as often as possible. We can take joint custody. I'd never walk away from my daughter, you know that."

"You *are* walking away, Brock. You step through that door, and she stays here—that's w-walking away. Just try explaining to Lauren how *Alicia*"—I sing-songed the name—"is more important than she is."

He looked at his hands. *Hit a nerve, did I, Dr. McNeil?*

"And what am I supposed to do, Brock? I don't think I can even d-drive. You're just *leaving* us to fend for ourselves?"

"You'll get better."

"Will I, now."

"Yes." His voice sharpened. "Probably about as soon as I pack my things."

I glared at him. *"You're* the liar here, not me."

He pinned me with a look. "It takes two to make a marriage fall apart."

"Do tell. And what exactly is it that I've . . . done to you? Other than take care of you and our house and child. Other than love you"—my voice caught—"with my *entire life.*"

He looked away, his jaw set. "You've put me through a lot of worry in the past few days."

Well, excuse me.

"Brock. I didn't know you were leaving. Naïve as that makes me, I didn't know. This illness, the phone calls—they're not faked. I know you'd l-love to believe that. Makes it easier to walk out that door. 'Cause what kind of man leaves his w-wife when she can barely walk? Not to mention when some man's stalking her."

Brock stared at the floor. Shook his head.

I tore my eyes away from the sickening sight of him. Brought a hand to my forehead. *Should* I have known he had someone else? Had I been that stupid? All those late nights 'at work,' the months of his pulling away from me. Maybe I had known, but I hadn't allowed myself to *see.* How could I, after all Brock had done for me? That mistreated, ailment-faking child had grown up but was never quite whole until Brock stepped into her life with the missing pieces.

Now Brock was missing a few of his own. Like common sense. And morals and loyalty.

Out of nowhere, Stalking Man's voice played in my head. I looked back to Brock. "Tell me—would your p-professional reputation be ruined if you reversed your opinion on Lyme?"

His jaw tightened, and his narrowed gaze rose to mine. "Is that what this is all about? You want to bring me down. You want to ruin me."

Like you're ruining me?

All the same, I had to admit there was a certain logic to his accusation. He was leaving me for some young assistant at work. Someone who helped daily in the lab, on his research. Why shouldn't I strike back at him professionally?

Still, how quickly Brock had concluded that. Just three days ago who would have believed I was capable of such a thing? Who'd believe, that is, except someone just as low, who could recognize the wash of the very traits he was drowning in.

"How did you ever g-guess?" My tone ran as chilled and hard as a brick dam against snow melt. "Yes. I made it up. All the symptoms, the phone c-calls. My fear. I lied to you. Lied to the police. Launched a f-formal investigation into thin air. Which, I believe, is a . . . crime." Tears bit my eyes, but I blinked them back. I would not cry in front of this man. Not here, not now. Not *ever*. "If that's what you want to believe, Brock, go right ahead. Must make you feel better. Because only a louse would walk out on a s-sick wife just home from the hospital."

He jumped up. "I don't have to listen to this."

Sudden fear raked nails across my chest. This was really going to happen. Within an hour or two he'd be gone. "Brock, please. He threatened to infect Lauren, don't you hear? We can't let him get to Lauren!"

Brock whirled on me, then stomped over to shake a finger in my face. "*Don't* you bring my daughter into your little scheme, Jannie. Don't you dare! Because if you do, I'll take her away from you. That's a promise."

He jerked away and strode from the room. I sat like a stone, listening to the thump of his footsteps as he hurried upstairs to pack.

Chapter 15

BY THE TIME MARIA BROUGHT LAUREN HOME, LUGGING HER backpack and suitcase, Brock had thrown together two suitcases of clothes and put them in his car. Child returns, husband leaves. He was now in his office with the door closed. My insides had numbed. I hardly knew how to greet my own daughter.

"Sweetie." In the hall I leaned down, pasting a smile on my face. My feet were planted apart, one hand on the cane so I wouldn't fall over. Maria and Katie hung in the doorway, watching. I could feel their shock at my appearance.

"Mom!" Lauren hugged me gently, then pulled back, her eyes shiny. The freckles on her nose looked darker, or was that just my imagination? "I'm so glad you're home."

"Me too." I rubbed the top of her head, my heart turning inside out. What it would do to her to hear her father was leaving. "You and Katie take your things up to your room, okay?"

"Glad you're back." Katie touched my arm as she followed Lauren.

"Thanks, honey."

Maria shut the front door as we watched them disappear upstairs. She regarded me with a shake of her head. "Jannie, you look . . ."

"I know. Let's sit down."

I clumped into the den. To the couch where I'd heard the words that would change my life. Maria took the armchair. "Before I forget, Lauren has some homework to finish. She promised me she'd do it when she got home."

"Okay."

"So." Concern etched Maria's forehead. "They still don't know what's wrong with you?"

"Brock does. I'm faking. And he's leaving me."

Maria's chin tilted down. She looked at me through her white-blonde bangs, eyebrows raised. *"What?"*

In low tones I told her about Alicia. I said nothing about Stalking Man. That was too much for this conversation. And what if Maria didn't believe me either?

Her gaze coasted toward the stairs. She licked her lips. I watched her struggle to absorb this new reality. "He's going to tell Lauren before he leaves?"

"That's the plan."

Maria made a sound in her throat. "Oh. How *awful.* That's going to be . . ."

Yeah.

I shifted my position. My head felt so heavy, as if my neck didn't want to hold it up. "Look, I hate to ask you for anything m-more, but I'm going to need help getting Lauren to school until I can find someone around here to take her. Trouble is, none of her friends in this . . . neighborhood go to her school. Maybe I can hire somebody—"

"No, no, don't do that. Of course I'll help." Maria raked a hand through her hair. "I don't understand why Brock thinks you're faking. I mean, just 'cause you did that as a kid—"

Two sets of girl feet pounded down the stairs. Maria's mouth clamped shut.

"Mom, we want a snack!" Lauren and Katie made for the kitchen.

"Go ahead."

Dully, I watched the girls through the pass-through window. "We'll talk later," I whispered to Maria.

She nodded.

Ten minutes later, Maria and Katie prepared to leave. "I want you to call me tonight, tell me how you're doing." Maria firmed her lips in a non-smile.

Don't leave. Don't. Because when they did, Brock would have to talk to Lauren. And the secure world I'd spent nine years building for my daughter would crumble.

I pictured Stalking Man invading our home however long ago. Standing over my bed as I slept. At the thought of his coming back for Lauren, abject terror seized my throat. Somehow I would keep that fright to myself, not let it affect my daughter. But I couldn't shield her from her own father.

My body started to shake. I slumped over on the couch, then lifted my feet up to lie down. In the kitchen I could see the edge of Lauren's right shoulder as she sat at the table. A schoolbook thumped down before her.

Brock's footsteps sounded on the hardwood floor.

My eyes closed. I needed to get up, be a part of their conversation. Hold Lauren's hand. But my muscles wouldn't move.

Memories marched through my head. Brock after Lauren's birth, holding her for hours. Not even wanting to give her to me for feeding. His tea parties with five-year-old Lauren, both of them sitting cross-legged on the floor, surrounded by an array of stuffed animals and a tiny tea set. I'd taken a picture once, the two of them tipping dainty cups to their lips, Brock's pinky extended to match his daughter's.

Brock at the school play last year, insisting we sit on the front row so Lauren could see us during her performance.

How could he leave her? How could he leave *us?*

"Hey, Punkin." Brock's steps reached the kitchen.

"Hi, Daddy!" Lauren's chair scraped against the floor. Eyes still closed, I heard the rustle of clothes and pictured them hugging. The chair scraped again as she returned to her seat.

Fresh fear wound its way down my limbs. It curled and crept and stuck to my veins until I would burst with it. *How* was I going to do this? Where was I going to find the energy to take care of a crushed child?

"Whatcha working on?" Brock asked.

"Science."

I had to get up. I needed to go to her. My muscles gathered for the attempt to rise.

"Listen, Punkin."

I sat up, heart skidding. Swung my feet to the floor. Vertigo hit. I closed my eyes, fighting for equilibrium. Whoa. It hadn't been this hard to get up when Maria and the girls arrived.

"What?" Lauren's voice sounded so innocent, so unprepared.

Silence from the kitchen. I fumbled for my cane, thrust myself toward the edge of the couch. My feet needed to center under me so I could get up. My left hand pushed against the cushion until I managed to stand. I started to move toward the kitchen.

"What is it, Daddy?"

I reached the armchair. Where he'd sat when he told me. That armchair would never look the same again. I stepped around it. The sound of a long sigh reached my ears. *Brock.* It was a sigh of defeat.

"Just wanted to tell you I have to go on a trip for a week."

I made it to the threshold. Leaned against the doorjamb.

"No, I don't want you to go!" Lauren looked up at her dad, disappointment pulling at her profile.

Brock turned toward me, his eyes grazing mine before bouncing away. "Afraid I have to. In fact, I have to leave right now."

"Where are you going?"

"On a business trip. You know, boring stuff."

Coward. All the same, relief washed over me.

Lauren's shoulders slumped. "But it's Sunday night. And I just got *home.*"

"I don't want to go. But I'll call you every night, okay?"

Lauren glanced over her shoulder at me. "Who's going to take care of Mom?"

Brock stilled. "Guess you'll have to do that."

Lauren looked from him back to me, reticence scrunching her eyes. Even a nine-year-old knew how ridiculous that sounded.

How strong the pull of this Alicia must be. To make Brock do this.

Lauren got up. She and her dad hugged each other. Brock kissed her on the head. "Be a good girl, now."

"Where's your suitcase?"

"Already in the car. I'll talk to you soon. Be a good girl, okay?"

Lauren's head hung. "Yeah. Okay."

Brock turned toward the door leading to the garage, then veered toward me. He leaned in close enough to whisper without Lauren hearing.

"*You* tell her."

Then he was gone.

Chapter 16

THROUGH THE GLASS HE WATCHED THE ADULT FEMALE TICK crawl on a spindly branch. She was hungry.

In this spring season the tick was reaching the end of her life cycle. Hatched from an egg into larva in July nearly two years ago, she'd been no bigger than a period at the end of a sentence. She'd fed as a nymph and had a second feeding the following spring. That fall she molted into an adult. Denied a blood meal at that time, she'd gone dormant over the winter. Now she sought a meal once again.

He'd chosen this tick with purpose. She was big enough to be spotted with the naked eye. She'd grown significantly since her nymph stage, now measuring about one-eighth of an inch wide. The back of her body was black, seeping into bright red. She was noticeably bigger than her male counterpart, and much brighter. Males showed no red.

After her long-awaited feeding this female tick would lay eggs, then die.

If she fed at all.

He rocked back in his chair, arms folded, gaze drifting upward. A scene filled with Elyse rose in his mind, his wife's round cheeks flushed and large brown eyes bright. They were backpacking in Oregon, an hour from their home at the time and had just found the perfect campsite—a level area tucked in the woods and beside a stream. Elyse wore a blue T-shirt and jeans, her brown arms tanned and strong from weight-lifting. She flung her heavy backpack down with enthusiasm, turning in a complete circle, her ponytail bobbing as she nodded. "Yes, *yes*. This is *just* the kind of place I wanted!"

"What if there are bears?"

"Nuh-uh, I'll fight them for this spot!" She spread her arms wide and grinned.

That was Elyse, full of energy and light. Nothing got the best of her; nothing deterred her from exploring the world. At work, her third-grade students loved her, and at home Elyse exuded optimism in the midst of his melancholic spirit. She was his strength and supporter, his best friend and lover. She buoyed him up and urged him on when his personal demons threatened to overcome him. And she made sure he took his meds. Without them he tended to go a little crazy, conjure up things that weren't true. Elyse evened him out, gave him a reason to breathe.

She was his *life*.

He watched the tick venture upon a new twig, its eight legs moving in slow precision.

"We don't have Lyme in Oregon," the doctor had said when Elyse asked for the test. She'd gone to him with a mysterious weakness in her limbs and pain in her joints, a creeping depression that sucked away her sprightly demeanor and spat out listlessness. Some friend had suggested she might have Lyme. Elyse insisted on the test, which the grudging doctor ordered. Result: negative.

Five years crawled by before they discovered the truth, years during which the Lyme spirochetes deep inside her tissues reproduced and thrived and laid siege to her body. By the time of her diagnosis— at last an answer!—Elyse no longer walked.

One day he brought home a scientific journal containing the "Clinical Practice Guidelines for Lyme Disease," written by the fourteen-member committee under the auspices of the Infectious Diseases Society of America. By that time he and Elyse had moved to another state where she could be better treated. But their insurance was balking at continuing to cover the huge cost of antibiotics. His mouth twisted at the memory of lying beside his wife in bed as he read the guidelines that would render her more helpless than ever. "There is no convincing biologic evidence" for the existence of chronic Lyme, wrote the esteemed panel. Long-term antibiotic treatment was not warranted.

All those years of suffering—and these people were saying Elyse wasn't even sick. His fingers curled inward until his nails bit both palms. His body shook with an anger that would not be bound by muscle and sinew.

The IDSA committee had spoken. Insurance companies listened. After that their coverage for treatment dried up completely. Their debt mounted—until they could no longer pay for treatment at all. Without antibiotics, Elyse quickly grew worse. Her eyes couldn't stand light, and constant facial tics tugged at her mouth and cheeks. She lost memory, the ability to read. The will or energy to do anything. Her heart weakened.

He leaned forward and placed his finger against the glass, following the tick's crawl. The words from the TV interview all those years ago echoed in his head. One of the doctors on that committee, so sure of himself, so learned and wise: "Those claiming to have chronic Lyme disease do not, it's as simple as that. They may have some autoimmune issue caused by the presence of spirochetes long ago. Or they may need psychiatric counseling.

"People do not die from Lyme disease," the doctor declared a few moments later.

Two months after that, Elyse was gone. Cause of death on her certificate: Lyme disease.

"Promise me," she'd whispered as she lay in bed, unable to move. "Promise me you'll change this for other Lyme patients. You'll *do* something."

He could barely get the words out. "I promise."

Afterward he'd found an online list of patients who had died from Lyme—the memorialized kin Elyse had now joined. He was shocked to see the names of adults *and* children. The ages covered all generations. Seventy-seven, sixty-four, forty-seven. Elyse had been thirty-one. And the children. Age seventeen, eleven, five. Even babies could be born with Lyme from the mother, as the disease was able to cross the placental wall. Of course doctors like those on the committee would deny that possibility too.

Staring at that list on the monitor, he felt sudden heat track through his body. He shoved from his chair and paced, mounting anger pounding in his veins. All of it—Elyse's illness, her death—was so preventable. So *unbelievably stupid*. A few biased doctors could control the whole country like this? Could snap their fingers and launch their declarations from lofty laboratories and schools of medicine, far from the hue and cry of real patients and real pain? Then denigrate the doctors in the trenches who treated those patients no one else would treat. Their reported professional ties to patents and insurance companies, their arrogance in protecting their reputations at all costs—*all of it* was so disgustingly, ridiculously *wrong*.

What every doctor on that committee needed, he'd seethed to himself as he paced, was a whopping case of Lyme. They and their families, too. Let *them* watch their loved ones waste away. Let *them* watched their loved ones die.

He stomped across the room and back, arms swinging, fingers clawed. If he could get to every one of those men, he would. He *would*.

A hard swivel and he strode in the opposite direction, hands thrust in the air. When he reached the wall he jerked around again. Back and forth, back and forth he paced, cursing and crying, the minutes oozing into one thick, suffocating paste of grief and rage. Time plodded by without his awareness. His steps pounded and his fists punched the air until finally, spent and sweat-washed, he fell into the chair before his computer. There he'd slumped forward and listened to himself breathe.

Now, years later, he watched the tick with grim satisfaction, feeling the same sheen on his forehead.

I am not a monster.

Despite his fury over the years, the spittle of revenge, he had overcome. He'd built an entirely new life and career. In time memories of Elyse threatened to fade. Sometimes in his deadened brain he even thought, *Did she exist at all?* To keep her alive within his mind he'd reached deep inside what was left of himself. And he'd discovered a plagued but determined Don Quixote. He would change the system. Tilt at the windmills of that tight and righteous medical community. And he would win.

With a deep sigh, he stretched his tense muscles. These past few days had been utterly stressful. Things had not exactly gone as planned. And it wasn't easy living two lives.

His eyes fixed once again on the tick. Such a small, insignificant creature to be capable of carrying such a toxic load of misery.

He blinked his scratchy eyes and stood. Picked up the small, waiting vial—and opened the glass top to collect its precious cargo.

Chapter 17

LAUREN AND I ORDERED A PIZZA FOR DINNER. AT THE KITCHEN table, I stared at my plate, my stomach turning over.

"What's wrong?" Lauren held a half-eaten piece with pepperoni in her hand. My side of the pizza had the added mushrooms. A faint tomato stain edged one corner of her mouth.

I shook my head. "Just tired."

She took another bite and chewed. "It's not fair that Daddy had to leave as soon as you came home."

"I know."

Behind me I could feel the empty backyard. It was still light now, but what would we do after the sun set? I pictured myself dragging through the house, double-checking doors and windows. What good would that even do? They'd all been locked before.

After dinner, with Lauren's attention fixed on the TV, I made my way into Brock's office. I collapsed in the chair behind his desk and gazed about the room like a lost soul. All the wood was dark walnut. I'd have chosen cherry. It was brighter, warmer. It occurred to me I could sit here this week while I paid bills. I'd always used the kitchen table, my files squeezed into the end cabinet. Since the beginning of our marriage I'd written out checks for each bill. Yet never did I have my own place for the task. Why was that?

Jud Maxwell's card sat on the desk. Must have been the one he gave me, although I had no memory of putting it there. On impulse I picked up the phone and dialed his number. Did the man even work on Sunday?

"Jud Maxwell."

He'd answered so fast. My brain stalled. "Hi."

"This would be . . . ?"

Our phone line had blocked our caller ID. "Janessa McNeil."

"Oh. Mrs. McNeil."

Something about that *Oh*. Vague warning chimed in my head. "I'm home now. And Brock's . . . gone. Didn't have much time to talk before he left. I wanted to check about our phones. Are they still t-tapped in case that man calls again?"

And, by the way, how was I supposed to sleep in this house tonight?

"Glad to hear you're home." The detective's tone sounded cordial and . . . something else. Guarded? "Are you feeling better?"

I hesitated. "Afraid not."

A squeak filtered over the line, as if he'd leaned back in an old chair. "Sorry to hear that."

He said no more. Was he waiting for me? For no reason at all scenes from numerous cop shows ticked through my head. They were all the same—a tense-muscled suspect in an interrogation room, the casual-looking policeman waiting him out.

"So what about the phone t-tapping?"

"I heard that the man called your hospital room."

"Yes!" My throat tightened. "He threatened to . . . hurt Lauren. To infect her like he did me."

"With Lyme, you mean."

"Yes."

"But your Lyme test was negative."

I stared at the pen holder by Brock's monitor. The four pens in it were all alike—black and sleek. I pictured Brock holding one of them, bouncing it against the desk while he talked on the phone. About *me*. So he'd told Jud everything, had he? Including his suspicions of his wife?

"I need to be retested. The results may be wrong."

"I see."

"*Do* you? He threatened my *daughter*." My voice turned off-key. Shivers crawled around my body. "Listen, I'm here alone with Lauren, I'm s-sick, and *I want to know if you're listening to my phone calls!*"

"We have left the taps in place, Mrs. McNeil. But I have to be honest with you—we're not actively listening to the calls."

"Why?"

"I'm afraid we're lacking manpower at the moment. You may not have heard while you were in the hospital that three more burglaries occurred in Palo Alto over the weekend—and they all appear to be linked. Our chief has put every available man hour on that case."

"So . . . you're not doing anything to investigate that madman who's been calling me?"

Jud hesitated. "Mrs. McNeil, I wish I could be investigating your case. But at the moment we're swamped here, and my superior has not given me the go-ahead to spend the time unless something new comes up. The problem is, so far I have no real evidence to support your story. The hospital tests were all negative. And there was no evidence of a break-in at your house."

"You traced the two ph-phone calls. Brock told me. So you know I got those calls."

"Yes. We also know that both times the calls originated from the very same area where you were located."

"*Or you made them.*" So that wasn't just Brock's suspicion, but Jud Maxwell's as well? "I *didn't* make those calls."

"It's—"

"I didn't!"

Silence. I hunched over the phone, disbelieving. Not this too. I couldn't take it.

"Mrs. McNeil, I tend to believe you. But our investigations rely on evidence. We can't justify spending more time on this case if nothing pans out. But I'm *not* forgetting you. If something new comes up, something you can give me, please call. I'll look into it. Also in the meantime I have asked our patrols on the street to do drive-bys of your home."

I stared at the pens. So neat and precise. My mind plodded through the lack of evidence. But was there more? Had Brock told Jud Maxwell about my childhood faked sickness? And did he know Brock was having an affair with a lab assistant? Maybe Jud's wife, Sarah, had heard rumors. Maybe she'd even seen Brock and Alicia together. Maybe everybody on campus knew of my husband's affair. That Christmas party last year, when everyone greeted me, all smiles? I pictured Dane Melford, Brock's other assistant. We'd talked for some time at that party, and he told me over and over how wonderful Brock was. I thought of Dr. Sid Segal, another professor in the department, and one of Brock's biggest rivals. Harold Standish, a colleague and occasional golf partner of Brock's. Harold's son, Brad, also worked in the department. And countless other professors and researchers, their assistants and groupies. Did they all hiss innuendo behind my back? "*She doesn't know, does she? Look at her over there, watching Brock peck Alicia on the cheek.*"

Heat slid through me. I wanted to punch something.

"Did Brock talk to you? Did he t-tell you to stop your investigation?"

A beat passed. "I did ask him to report to me the hospital findings, remember? So yes, we've kept in touch."

He was hedging. I could hear it in his voice. "He told you things about me, didn't he."

"Such as?"

"Don't l-lie to me. I've had a husband lying to me for m-months."

Another awkward pause. Which told me I guessed right. Jud knew about the affair.

"*Did* Brock talk to you?"

I could feel his reticence. Finally he said, "Yes."

"What exactly did he say?"

"I'd rather not—"

"*What* did he say? You owe me that much."

That squeaky chair sounded again. "He told me about your marital issues, Mrs. McNeil."

Marital issues? "You mean his affair with Alicia Mays."

"Well—"

"Did he tell you he'd been p-planning to move out?"

"Yes."

The answer stung. This detective, this husband of Brock's administrative assistant, had known before *I* did. "What else did he say?"

"Mrs. McNeil, nothing your husband said would turn me aside from this case if I had anything to go on."

Dizziness swirled around me. From the pain in my body or the sickness in my gut, I didn't know. My breath rode shallow. "I don't have the . . ." What was the word? What was the *word*? "Energy to play twenty questions. *What else* did he tell you?"

I could practically hear the gears turning in the detective's head. I pictured him sitting at an old steel desk, uniformed police passing in the hallway. Should he refuse to say more of the confidential conversation? Or would his empathy with the sick, abandoned wife win out?

Jud Maxwell's tone dropped. "He did mention your abusive father. The sickness you faked as a child."

There it was. The puzzle pieces all fit. Brock's affair at work, his stellar standing at the school of medicine. Now his jilted wife was trying to ruin his career by upending his lifelong research in Lyme. What a clever woman that Janessa was, striking at the very thing that had brought Brock and his young, beautiful lab assistant together. What a way to seek revenge.

"And that's what I'm doing n-now, I suppose. Faking."

"Are you?"

My muscles ached, my lungs groaned, and I barely had the strength to hold my head up. It was taking every ounce of willpower I possessed to even have this conversation.

"Have you ever had Lyme disease, Mr. Maxwell?"

"No."

"You'd better hope you never do. Because I p-promise you, you'll *wish* you were faking."

"If the tests were negative, what makes you so sure you have Lyme?"

"Because my husband has been dead wrong about everything else!" I slammed down the receiver.

Long moments passed. I sat there, beyond numb, my thoughts everywhere and nowhere. Then, through the closed door I registered the sound of canned laughter from the television. Lauren giggling along with it.

My neck would no longer support my head. Every joint in my body throbbed. And those little spasms I was feeling were so strange. I lifted my right hand, twisting it to examine my forearm. An area about two inches wide tremored and twitched as if a bug writhed just beneath the skin. I watched with appalled fascination. What *was* that?

The skin crawl continued.

An hour later, as Lauren's bedtime approached, I couldn't wait to fall into bed myself. Slowly I caned around the house, checking locks on windows and doors. In the kitchen near the door to the garage sat our burglar alarm's control unit. I activated it to *Stay*. We could move around inside the house without tripping the laser beams, but opening any door or window on the ground floor would set the alarm off.

If only I'd been in the habit of setting the alarm every night. Stalking Man couldn't have gotten in. The stupidity. The alarm had been here since we moved into the house when Lauren was a baby, yet we never used it unless we left town. How could we have been so complacent?

I lingered in front of the control pad, resting my forehead against the wall. *If only, if only.* My life was suddenly filled with those pathetic two words. I had to change that. Had to *do* something about all of this.

But at that moment I had no strength for anything.

The phone rang. It was Maria. I'd forgotten to call her. "He didn't t-tell her," I whispered, afraid Lauren would hear. *"I'm* supposed to do it."

My friend made a sound in her throat. "Unbelievable."

Yeah. "I'll s-see you in the morning."

I managed to drag myself upstairs and into my room. There I gimped around the bed to Brock's nightstand on the other side. In the drawer of that nightstand lay his gun, a Smith & Wesson 637. Brock kept the bullets in the top drawer of his main dresser. I remembered that the gun held five rounds. And it was lightweight but had a pretty hefty recoil.

As Lauren took a shower I sat on the bed and loaded the gun. With my weak, painful fingers it took some time. I could only imagine those same hands trying to shoot. And how many years had it been since I used the thing? I'd never wanted to learn how to shoot in the first place. Guns scared me—especially with a child in the house.

But tonight, for the first time in my life, I would sleep with one loaded by my bed.

I placed the weapon and the box of bullets in the drawer of my nightstand.

When Lauren emerged from her shower I called her into my room. "You can sleep here tonight."

She bounced up and down. "I can sleep with *you?*" The multi-hued flowers on her pajamas reflected color in her cheeks. How different she would look if Brock had told her the truth.

"You bet."

She grinned. "Oh, yippee! I'll get Tito." She ran back into her room for the brown stuffed dog.

When she returned I locked the door. Lauren tilted her head. "Why're you so worried about the alarm and the door and everything?"

"No reason, except that your dad's not here. Just think it's safer, that's all."

She accepted my lame answer with a shrug of her shoulders and climbed into bed.

I couldn't sleep. The physical pain and the thoughts of Brock—with *her*—would not let me rest. Anger and sorrow and fear mashed together in my lungs until I could barely breathe. Questions whirled and tangled in my mind. How many nights had I lain here with Brock while his mind was on that woman? Why had he drawn away from me in the first place? What had I done? And Stalking Man—was he out there, watching the house? Did he know Brock had left? If I'd had the energy I'd have gotten up, paced the floor. Cleaned the house. *Something.* But the emotions' only outlet came in hot tears that slid down my temples and dripped into my ears.

If only I had a Bible beside the bed. I wanted to find that verse that had come to mind before: "*God is our refuge and our strength, a very present help in time of trouble.*" It had to be in the Psalms. My soul longed to read more verses, draw from them all the comfort that I could.

My exhausted eyes lifted to the radio clock on my bedside table. After eleven. Surely this had been the longest day of my life.

Except for tomorrow.

MONDAY

Chapter 18

WHEN I AWOKE AROUND SIX O'CLOCK I FELT AS THOUGH I'D been up all night. No refreshment from sleep in the slightest. Could I even get out of bed?

I rolled over and reached for my cane on the floor. Eased back the covers. In slow, cautious motion I managed to sit up and move my legs over the side of the bed. My brain told me I couldn't do this. I should listen. Did I want to fall on the floor as I had in the kitchen those few days—that lifetime—ago? This time I may not get up.

How many days of this until Brock realized he was wrong—that I really was sick? How many days until he returned home to take care of me?

My cane positioned just right, leaning forward, I gathered all the strength I could find and pushed to my shaky feet. For a moment I hung there, testing my body. Everything hurt. The worst flu could not bring this kind of pain in my muscles. And my joints—this must be what rheumatoid arthritis felt like.

Somehow I crossed the treacherous and rolling path to the bathroom. By the time I came out a few minutes later I could think of nothing but returning to bed.

Propping my pillows behind me, I half sat up, watching the clock until I needed to wake Lauren. She lay on her side facing me, a hand curled around Tito. One thought rang clear in my muddled head. I could not live like this and take care of my daughter. I had to get a diagnosis. Treatment. I had to get well—for Lauren.

At seven o'clock I woke her by a light rubbing of her head. She breathed in deeply, rising cognizance twitching across her face. Her eyes opened in sleepiness, then blinked. One side of her mouth curved. "Mmm."

"Wake up, sleepyhead."

She swallowed. "Not yet."

"Yes. Yet."

I touched a finger to her face. "Look at you, even lovelier than yesterday. The Pretty Fairy came and k-kissed you again last night."

Lauren smiled. "How'd she know I was in your room?"

"The Pretty Fairy always knows."

Lauren yawned, then sat up and surveyed me. "You feeling any better?"

I pulled my lower lip between my teeth. What was the point of faking it? She'd see right through me. "Afraid not. Can you get d-dressed and just have some . . . cereal for breakfast? Maria will be by to pick you up for school."

Lauren nodded, her eyebrows knit. "I'm sorry, Mom." She slid from bed and walked around the end of it, carrying Tito.

"Oh, wait, Lauren. You'll need to turn off the alarm." She could use the second control pad near the master bedroom door. "Otherwise it'll go off when you g-go outside."

"How?"

I told her the sequence of buttons to push. She followed my directions, and the control pad's red light switched to green.

One night in the house—safe. How many more nights would I lie awake and wonder until Stalking Man was caught?

And just who was going to catch him?

I needed to get downstairs, check around the house. Even if the alarm had been on all night, what if . . . something? I couldn't let Lauren just wander around down there by herself.

Once more I hauled myself out of bed. As Lauren dressed I pulled on a robe and made my way to the stairs. At the top I stood looking down, dank dread in my chest. I may as well have been stranded on top of a mountain.

The gun. I'd left the thing loaded in my nightstand. What if Lauren went back into my room for something and happened to open that drawer?

Slowly I returned to my room. With the door closed I pulled the weapon out of the drawer. I clumped into my walk-in closet and laid it high on a shelf out of Lauren's reach. Tonight I'd return it to my nightstand.

Back at the stairs I descended one at a time, gripping my cane in one hand and holding on to the banister with the other. Going down was much harder than coming up. It required more leg strength to lower myself down. If I fell now and broke something—then what?

Would Brock claim I'd staged that, too?

After an eternity I reached the bottom and stumbled across the hall into the kitchen. I opened the sliding door and peered into the backyard. No footprints on the deck, across the grass. I gazed to my right at the ground near the sturdy-limbed tree growing close to the house. Numerous times we'd had to trim the tree's branches because they nearly touched the upstairs window in our dressing room. That trunk would make a great hiding place for someone sneaking through the yard. But I saw no footprints there either.

Spent, I relocked the door and collapsed into a chair at the table to wait for Lauren. She soon appeared, hair combed and looking cute in a pink cotton top and jeans with stitched rosebuds on the sides. Lauren loved flowers on her clothes. She poured herself a bowl of cereal and milk and settled next to me at the table.

"Don't talk to any . . . strangers around school. Okay? Especially men."

Lauren's mouth stopped mid-crunch as she fixed me with a questioning look. She finished her bite and swallowed. "Why're you saying that? Why is everybody saying that to me?"

"What do you mean, everybody?"

"Daddy said it two days ago."

Ah. So there had been a time when Brock believed me.

"And now you're locking the doors and turning on the alarm and everything."

"The doors are always l-locked at night."

She gave me a look. I raised my eyebrows and said no more. Lauren's gaze fell to her cereal bowl. After a moment she shook her head and sighed. "Well, you don't need to make me scared."

"Am I making you scared?"

"*Yes.*"

My heart panged. "Sorry. Didn't mean to."

She frowned. "Something's weird, is all. I mean just . . . everything."

A kid's antennae. I thought back to my own childhood, to walking in the door every day after school. The moment I crossed the threshold I'd stop, sensing the air for my father's mood.

I would have to be more careful. But how to protect Lauren without frightening her?

At 7:45 Maria arrived. By then I lay on the couch. Lauren had just unlocked the front door, then trotted upstairs to brush her teeth. Katie pounded up to find her.

Maria stood over me, worry sketched into her forehead. "How are you?"

The tone of her question said she needn't ask. Surely I looked terrible.

"Lauren doesn't look upset. Did you tell her?"

"I couldn't."

She gave an empathetic nod. "What was Brock's excuse for leaving?"

"A . . ." The word eluded me. "That thing when you . . . A business trip. For a week."

Maria planted a hand on her hip and looked away, digesting the news. By the look on her face it soured her stomach. "So." She focused on me again. "You going to tell her tonight?"

"No. I mean, this can't l-last." My voice caught. "Brock has to see I'm really s-sick and come back."

Maria gazed at me, doubt pulling at her mouth. "Sure."

We regarded each other.

"What else can I do for you today, Jannie?"

Maria worked part-time in the public high school library. She wasn't free to help me during the day. "I'll be f-fine." I aimed a grim smile at her. "Think I'll just camp out right here. You're doing enough getting Lauren to school and back."

The girls trotted down the stairs, ready and bristling for the day. So much energy. Lauren leaned over to kiss me on the cheek. "Bye, Mom!"

"Bye, honey." I almost said *stay safe,* but bit back the words.

After they'd left, the house rang with unnatural silence.

I closed my eyes.

The next thing I knew the clock read after 10:00. My brain felt fuzzy. Stalking Man's words filtered by in slow motion: *"After they're done testing you for all the things they won't find, go to a doctor who knows how to treat Lyme."*

I needed to do that. But everything within me fought it. What a horrendous, ridiculous situation. My own husband wouldn't listen, and now my only recourse was to follow the advice of my tormentor? The sick man who'd done this to me and now threatened my daughter?

My lips twisted. I *wouldn't* do what he said. Whatever he wanted, I should do just the opposite. He didn't deserve satisfaction from his evil. He deserved punishment and ruin.

A half hour seethed by as I envisioned confronting the man. Proving to Brock and the police he was real. I would prevail here. Some way.

The anger tired me. Its clods began to break up, crumble apart. In its place formed defeat. I couldn't catch this man in such a state of sickness. Neither would I woo my husband back. Truth was, Brock saw what he wanted to see. He'd already planned on leaving me. I'd just given him the perfect excuse.

Stalking Man was my enemy. Yet he was the only one who seemed to know how to help.

A long sigh escaped me. My hand rubbed across my forehead as if to buff away the knowledge that prickled there.

I needed medical help. And I wasn't going to find it among Brock's colleagues. My only recourse was to cross the Rubicon, defect to the other side. Go to the people Brock had built a career on disdaining.

I had to find a Lyme doctor.

Chapter 19

THERE WAS A CERTAIN IRONIC JUSTICE IN USING MY HUSBAND'S computer to learn about chronic Lyme disease.

In pajamas, robe, and slippers I propped myself up in Brock's chair, staring at the monitor. My brain was running slower than the Internet. For a moment I couldn't even think what words I should type into Google's search. I needed to find a doctor, but something made me key in *Brock McNeil Lyme*. Thousands of hits popped up.

I dug in. My reading was slow and plodding, but I kept at it. On web page after web page I read of Brock's insistence that Lyme is "hard to catch and easy to cure." That it is "overdiagnosed and overtreated." His name also appeared on articles run in the most prestigious of medical journals. In 2001 his committee's findings on Lyme disease were published in *The New England Journal of Medicine*. Ten years ago. I remembered when that happened. I'd been pregnant with Lauren. At the time I was thrilled at my brilliant husband's success. In that article Brock and the committee stressed that a short round of antibiotics was all that was needed to cure Lyme.

I also read web pages written by Lyme patients or their loved ones in which my husband's name seemed almost a curse. Because of doctors like him, they claimed, diagnosis and treatment for chronic Lyme were difficult to find.

Both of these sides couldn't be right. But how could Brock and his esteemed colleagues be wrong? The whole nation believed them. And *The New England Journal of Medicine* was no slouch of a publication.

My head began to pound. As my fatigue grew I slumped lower in the chair. I longed to lie down, take a nap. But I wanted answers.

As I read statements from doctors on the other side of the argument, I saw a pattern begin to emerge. Researchers like Brock often defined Lyme disease in very narrow terms, ignoring the huge list of potential symptoms patients were facing. Patients fitting these researchers' limited definition of Lyme were used in their studies, while others were disqualified. Meanwhile, doctors treating chronic Lyme spoke of how differently it could affect each patient, especially in the presence of coinfections that often accompanied the disease. Patients with Lyme plus coinfections were typically much sicker. And treating each illness required different medication.

Coinfections. Stalking Man had mentioned those. *Did* I have a combination of diseases, as he claimed? Is that why I'd gotten so sick?

Lyme was far bigger, the experts said, and much more complex than the Brock McNeils of the world would admit. Studies of the spiral-shaped bacteria or "spirochete" that caused the illness showed how cunning and adaptable it was. In different environments it could change its outer coat of protein, making it invisible to the body's immune system. It could hide in the body's cells. Other times it could wall up like an enemy in a fort by forming a hard outer shell or *cyst* that most antibiotics could not penetrate.

All the various medications needed for long-term treatment were expensive. Insurance companies didn't want to pay.

"Hasn't your dear husband testified on behalf of insurance companies at numerous trials?" Stalking Man's cynical words tracked through my mind. *"I believe he's been paid for his hard work on the stand."*

Uneasiness gnawed at my gut.

My processing abilities were slowing, but I pressed on. I had to read many paragraphs three and four times before I could retain the information. I read about Lyme symptoms—of which I had plenty. I gazed at pictures of the deer tick that carried *Borellia burgdorferi,* the Lyme spirochete. How small the ticks could be. But the ones in California had an easy-to-spot marking—black turning to red on its back.

I typed in a new search: *Lyme tests.*

Many more hits surfaced. I delved into the background of the tests' development—apparently another major issue at the heart of the Lyme wars. Tests measured the presence of certain antibodies in the blood, which the body produced in response to different proteins in the spirochete. Years ago when the criteria for reading the Western blot test were developed, the "bands" of antibodies chosen for inclusion in test results were so controversial they'd caused a huge ruckus in the medical community. For some inexplicable reason numerous bands exclusive to Lyme had been excluded from the criteria. Still the Centers for Disease Control had adopted these criteria, and doctors across the country used them to this day.

Also at issue was the series in which CDC testing was done. The CDC process was to give a test called the ELISA first. Then, if the ELISA showed positive—and only if that was the case—run its Western blot. The Lyme community insisted the ELISA test was unreliable, which resulted in many patients slipping through the cracks thanks to a false negative result.

Stalking Man's words about my Lyme test results mocked me: *"Of course it's wrong."*

The saddest part was how much damage a false negative result could inflict. Lyme *could* be easily fixed if treated soon after a tick bite. But delays gave the spirochetes time to reproduce and burrow deep into body tissue. Worse, patients were often misdiagnosed with ailments such as Chronic Fatigue Syndrome, MS, fibromyalgia, arthritis, depression, and other illnesses. The misdiagnosed patients may then be given steroids to calm their swollen joints. The steroids suppressed the immune system, allowing Lyme spirochetes to reproduce all the more. The patient inevitably worsened. All because of a wrong test result.

In more recent years a few labs had sprung up that ran their own tests for Lyme, whose criteria for reading Western blot tests included bands of antibodies that better covered the spectrum of the disease. And they administered both the ELISA and Western blot tests at once. To floundering patients who'd fought symptoms like mine for years, these more reliable and complete tests finally gave them a diagnosis: Lyme. But researchers like Brock stood by the CDC criteria. All else to them was mere quackery, leading to so-called overdiagnosis.

I sat back in my chair, considering that. If Brock was wrong, what a double whammy for Lyme patients. First they were denied a diagnosis because of ineffective testing. Then, when they got worse as a result, they were denied the treatment they needed to halt the disease.

Rubbing my neck, I checked the clock. Twelve thirty. I had to eat something. I shuffled into the kitchen and chose a can of soup from the pantry. Leaning against the counter for support, I tried to pull back the tab on its lid. It wouldn't come. I pulled harder, pain shooting through my knuckles.

My hands were too weak to open a can of soup?

I set my teeth on edge and tried again. The lid began to roll back. By the time I had the whole thing off, tears filled my eyes. My hands and fingers throbbed. That would be the last one. No more opening cans for me.

What would I eat?

I poured the soup into a bowl and heated it in the microwave.

Shuffled it over to the table. The bright sunlight streaming through the sliding glass door pierced my eyes all the way to the back of my head. I rummaged in our junk drawer for a pair of old sunglasses and shoved them on. The pain had intensified everywhere in my body. I made my way to a cabinet to swallow three extra-strength aspirin.

Finally I sat down at the table to eat.

Oh. I brought a hand to my cheek. I still hadn't looked for a doctor. What was wrong with me? That's what I'd planned to do in the first place.

I concentrated on eating. Slowly the soup disappeared. When I was done I stood up and gazed with longing at the couch in the den. With much effort I turned away and headed back to the office. I collapsed into the desk chair and hooked my cane over one of its arms. The light was less bright in here. I slid my sunglasses on my head. Surveyed the computer.

Where . . . ? What was I . . . ?

I clicked the search button. Up rose all the hits for *Lyme tests.* My eye fell on one site—evidently the story of a young patient. I followed it.

My heart wrenching, I read the testimony of Karen Forshner, mother of Jamie, who'd contracted Lyme from her while still in the womb—another possibility Brock contested. Soon after birth Jamie became very ill. Lyme tests, even the CDC ones, returned a positive diagnosis. He was treated and got better. The antibiotics were stopped. And he relapsed. With more treatment he improved again—until doctors said the treatment had to stop. This cycle happened again and again. Electron microscope pictures of Jamie's tissue showed the presence of spirochete-like structures after treatment. But skeptics said they weren't *burgdorferi.* Treatment ceased for good while the Forshners awaited new tests. Over a year went by. Jamie relapsed, fell into seizures and died.

He was five years old.

Karen quoted Brock as one of the leading voices insisting Jamie did not have Lyme. Brock declared that the spirochetes would not survive a short-term bout of antibiotics.

Jamie's autopsy results proved Lyme spirochetes were still in his brain.

"If public policy was prevention oriented instead of anti-antibiotic hysteria oriented," Karen had said, "my son would be alive today. I am not alone. Other mothers have also lost their children."

I sat back, gulping air. Brock's writings about Lyme helped cause the death of a *child*? I stared at the desk, trying to wrap my mind around the thought. How did Brock sleep at night? How did he *live* with himself?

Only one way. By clinging to his opinion. If he changed now, if he refuted his own findings over the years, he'd have to face the fact that he'd helped cause pain and suffering, even death, to innocent patients.

No wonder he refused to believe me.

A second horrendous thought hit. *This* was the disease Stalking Man had threatened to infect my daughter with. I hadn't known Lyme could kill. I clearly remembered Brock insisting no one ever died from Lyme.

My weary eyes focused again on the screen. Jamie's story had taken place in the late '80s to early '90s. Brock would have been in his thirties. Young enough in his career to make a mistake. Yet he hadn't changed his tune since.

Chest tight, I read more stories. They were easier to process since they weren't full of scientific information. But the reading was so much harder. This wasn't cold data on tests and spirochetes and what constituted the disease. These were stories about real, suffering people. Those who went undiagnosed for years—until a Lyme-literate doctor finally sent them for proper testing. Children who lost years of school, adults who went from athletic to bed-ridden. Bad enough they fought such horrible illness, but at the same time they had to fight the medical community. Doctors didn't want to treat them. Insurance companies didn't want to cover their meds or disability. Many of these patients went into severe debt. Some of the doctors who did finally treat them—with positive results—were hauled before medical boards and saw their licenses revoked. *Then* they were sued by the insurance companies, who wanted compensation for the medications they'd covered for the "false diagnoses."

Dr. Brock McNeil had testified in some of those trials.

These Lyme doctors lost everything. Still their patients flocked to support them, staging rallies and raising their voices. "When will we finally be heard?" they cried. "When will science finally open its eyes to our plight?"

Nausea roiled in my stomach. How had I not known this? How had I not realized what was going on out there?

My head dropped, chin nearly touching my chest. How had I not known? Because I'd only heard Brock's side, his research. Seen his success in the eyes of the medical community. But all along there had been thousands of patients—with symptoms like mine—who longed to be well.

I leaned back in my chair, spent and sick to the core. I thought of Brock in his research every day, teaching his classes. So far removed from these patients' outcry. If he were forced to face these debilitated people every day as the Lyme doctors did, would he remain as insensitive? As certain of his beliefs?

Instead he was hidden away in his shiny lab. With his shiny little mistress.

"I want you to change your husband's mind."

No way would I ever be able to do that. No way.

I pressed the back of my hand to my forehead. Took deep breaths. My mind slid away. For a long time I sat there in suspended consciousness . . .

Doctor.

The memory arose from nowhere, and my brain snapped back. I still needed to find a doctor.

My fingers groped their way to the keyboard. I typed in *Lyme literate doctors* and hit *Search*. Over 12,000 sites came up. My exhausted eyes started to run down the list when a name snagged. *Carol Johannis.* I turned it over in my mind. Dr. Johannis. Yes. I'd heard Brock speak that name in derogatory terms. Some vague memory whispered she was local.

I jumped to a new search: *Carol Johannis Lyme.* When the hits appeared I followed the top three. Dr. Johannis practiced in Palo Alto. According to a patient who'd talked about her in a chat forum, she specialized in Lyme. I even read an account of her publicly confronting Dr. Brock McNeil for his misleading statements about the disease.

No wonder he sneered at her name.

I picked up the phone.

Chapter 20

BY THE TIME I FELL ON THE COUCH, WEARING MY SUNGLASSES, I had a mere half hour to rest until Maria brought Lauren home. Too late, I knew this wasn't going to work. I couldn't stay up all day and have any energy left for Lauren. Just the thought of seeing her, of having to talk, loomed overwhelming. *Breathing* was hard.

At least I'd possessed enough presence of mind to unlock the front door first. Once I was down I wouldn't be moving again for a while. And I was too empty to care that I'd left myself vulnerable. If Stalking Man wanted to walk into my house—let him. He couldn't hurt me worse than he already had.

Within minutes I fell asleep. It seemed in no time Lauren burst through the door, startling me awake. "Hi, Mom!" She ran into the den and hovered over me, shedding her backpack on the floor with a dull thud. "How come you're wearing sunglasses?"

Maria's and Katy's footsteps sounded in the hall. I heard the door shut. Soon all three gazed down at me. I tried to smile but couldn't.

"It's just too . . ." I searched for the word. It rolled here and there, hiding in the crannies of my brain. "The light . . ."

"Too bright for you?" Maria's eyes rose to the window.

Bright. That was it. "Y-yes."

"I'll close the shades for you." Maria moved to the window and lowered them.

Why hadn't I thought of that?

Lauren's face scrunched up. "You're talking funny again, Mom. Worse than this morning."

Exhaustion, that was the problem. I could feel it blanketing my body, my head. I'd pushed myself too much. Now I was paying.

"I'm okay. I just . . . talk slow."

Lauren nodded, doubt pulling at her brow. "Can Katy and I get something to eat?"

"Yeah."

The girls headed for the kitchen.

"Hear from Brock today?" Maria perched on the edge of the couch near my legs. She kept her voice down.

"No."

She stared at the floor, our thoughts thick between us.

"I found a doctor who treats Lyme. Got in tomorrow. Amazing. They had a c-cancellation. Said that . . . hardly ever happens."

"Well, that's good you got in so fast." She frowned. "But I thought you were tested for Lyme already."

"I was. But I need a better test."

"Oh." She shrugged—a gesture that went right through me. How few people knew about these Lyme wars. "What time is the appointment? How will you get there?"

"Eight thirty. I'll call a c-cab."

"No, Jannie—"

"You go to work right after taking the g-girls to school. I'll be okay. Really."

Maria saw I needed to rest and soon gathered Katy to leave. When

they'd gone I pushed myself to sit up. "Lauren, please come get your
. . . stuff in here. I can't carry it."

She walked into the den, eating the last of a cereal bar, and picked
up the backpack. I slogged my way into the kitchen and sat down at
the table with her. Hooked my cane onto the edge of Brock's chair.
"School okay?"

"Uh-huh." She pushed bangs out of her eyes and unzipped her
pack. "Can we call Dad?"

"Maybe after dinner." I shifted in my chair. It was hard to get
comfortable. "So . . . see any strange people around school today?"

Lauren plumped out her lips. "I see strange people every day. I'm
in fourth grade."

I smiled.

She pushed back her chair. "I gotta go to the bathroom." Out of
the kitchen she trotted.

I reached for her backpack to pull out books, but it was too heavy
to drag close enough to me. My hand fell on the front of the pack, to
the small zippered area where Lauren carried lunch money and pencils.
I could at least take out a pencil for her. Wow. What a big help.

Why was I even sitting here? Lauren never liked me looking over
her shoulder while she did homework. Guilt had pushed me into that
chair, plain and simple. Her dad wasn't coming back, and somehow
that was my fault. If I'd only been a better . . . something.

Indignation trekked up my spine. It was *not* my fault.

From a distance I heard the bathroom door close.

Heaving a sigh, I tugged the small compartment's zipper open.
Reached inside and felt for a pencil. My fingers closed on a small
bottle.

What was that?

I pulled it out. Held it in front of my face. It was clear plastic.
Empty. Except for a bug crawling along the bottom.

Deer tick.

The realization socked me in the gut.

A cry erupted from me. I dropped the bottle. It hit the table with a *click* and bounced. My hand scrambled for it—and knocked it over the edge. The thing plunked onto the hardwood floor and bounced again. Heart tripping, I jerked my chair backward and leaned over, searching. My leg banged into my cane, and it fell with a *whap!*

Where was the vial?

I fumbled off my sunglasses and dropped them onto the table. Light stabbed my eyes. I squeezed them shut and leaned over farther, blinking hard. Maybe it was right under my chair.

What if that thing got loose in my house?

From far away I heard the toilet flush.

No. I lunged downward, groping for my cane. Had to get up. Had to look. My fingertips grazed the sleek gray metal and I snatched it up. Banged it into position to support me. Pain shot through my knuckles. With my left hand I shoved from my chair into space, struggling for balance. I found it . . . lost it . . . then listed upright. Took a step backward. My frantic gaze swept the floor. No bottle. One palm on the table, I leaned down and peered underneath.

There. Way over on the other side. Its bottom pointed toward me. I didn't see the tick.

The bathroom door opened. Lauren's footsteps sounded in the hall.

As fast as I could I edged around the table. Adrenaline raced through my weak body, making me sway and shake. Somehow I had to reach that area, get all the way down to pick up the bottle.

"Mom, what're you doing?"

I tottered forward, my head turning toward Lauren—and felt myself tip. My legs gave out. I pitched like a fallen tree and landed hard on my side. "Ungh." Breath whooshed out of me. My cane went flying.

"Mom!"

My neck muscles melted. My head sank to the floor.

For a moment I lay there, disoriented. Lauren ran to me and flung herself down. "Mom, Mom!" She grasped my shoulder and shook. It felt like a freight train tossing me.

I winced. "I'm . . . okay." The words puffed out, barely audible.

"No, you're not!" She jumped up. "I'm calling Daddy."

"No, *don't.*"

She thudded over to the phone, picked it up.

"Lauren, don't!"

"But you need—"

"No!" I pressed a hand to my forehead. "He's . . . busy. Nothing he can do. Just . . . come help me up."

The receiver rattled. Lauren scurried over to me.

Where was the bottle? The tick? I *did not* want Lauren to see it.

"What do I do?" Lauren crouched beside me, her nose running and face tear-stained.

"Help me sit up."

I held out my hand. She gripped it hard. I gritted my teeth against the pain. "Pull. Easy."

She stood up, planted her feet and pulled. My joints from fingers to shoulder screamed. After agonizing seconds I slumped into a sitting position, gasping. The hurting didn't subside.

Lauren let go, her hands to her mouth. "You okay?"

For a moment my tongue wouldn't work. "Yeah. Just . . . let me rest." I aimed a look to my far left, my peripheral vision grazing the bottle. I moved my head around, stretching my aching neck. How was I going to stand the pain of getting to my feet? Already it made me nauseous. But the thought of that tick in the bottle, lying on the same floor . . .

"Okay. Think you can get me all the way up?"

Fresh tears flooded Lauren's eyes. "I don't know."

"Let's try. If not I'll scoot to the s-sink and pull myself up." I forced the corners of my mouth upward. "Silly, huh."

No smile from Lauren. Her expression pinched with fear for her helpless mother. I just wanted to hold her to my chest and tell her everything would be all right. That's what mothers did for their children. "It's okay, Lauren." I placed both my hands in hers. Eased myself around until my feet were in place. "Okay, let's try."

Lauren leaned back, tugging at me with all her might. I couldn't help her. Not at all. Pure dead weight, and the *pain*.

"Stop!"

She let go. I leaned over, chin to my chest, and panted.

Lauren crumpled down beside me.

I patted her arm, trying to say *"It's okay, I'm fine"* but no words would come.

The tick, the tick.

"Let me just . . . slide myself over to—"

"What's that?"

My pounding head turned toward Lauren. She was staring over my shoulder.

"There's a little bottle on the floor."

"It's nothing."

"Did you drop it?"

"No." Lie after lie. I was becoming a natural at lying to my daughter.

"I'll get it."

"Lauren, *stop*."

She crawled around me toward the table. Wedged herself between it and the wall.

"Lauren, no!"

She reached for it. Picked it up. "What's wrong, Mom? It's just a bottle." She wiggled out and turned around. Held the thing up. It was empty. No top.

Lauren stuck her forefinger inside and turned it upside down to rest on her fingertip. "See?"

Chapter 21

SEATED BEFORE PILES OF PAPER ON HIS DESK, JUD SIGHED AS he tried to concentrate on his notes about the burglaries. So far they had plenty of nothing. Jud had to wonder how effective he was being on the case. His mind kept drifting to Janessa McNeil. He'd told her the truth when he said he tended to believe her—despite her husband's insistence she'd faked the whole scenario. Jud couldn't really point to anything to support his opinion other than his gut feeling. But his gut didn't let him down often.

Plus, something didn't sit right with Brock McNeil. Even with all the circumstantial evidence pointing to the fact that Janessa may be lying, why would her husband be so adamant the case be closed? Why not give his wife any benefit of the doubt—particularly since her safety was involved?

Last night when Jud should have been sleeping, he'd found himself again perched at his home computer, researching the world of Lyme.

"Hey, Jud." Stan Mulligan, one of Jud's fellow detectives, knocked on his open office door. Stan was a bear of a man at 6'4", 250 pounds. His buzzed hair and hard-set jaw made him look like someone you wouldn't want to meet in a dark alley. "We got a possible foreign print off Fletcher." Fletcher was the street where the most recent burglary had occurred.

"Any match?"

Stan shrugged. "We're running it." His eyes fell to Jud's notes. "You find anything we missed in that pile of yours?"

"No."

They exchanged a weary look.

"Hear anything new on that Lyme case?" Stan arched his back. Jud heard a series of cracks.

"Nothing I can use. This Lyme war thing is all new to me. In my spare time at home I keep trying to figure out the players."

Stan tilted his beefy head, thinking. "Know who you should talk to? Walt Rosenbaum—left here three years ago to work on the San Jose force? He's got Lyme pretty bad, last I heard from him."

Jud remembered Walt. Muscular young guy, always working out. Talkative. And never afraid to say exactly what was on his mind. Jud couldn't imagine him brought down by illness. "You have his number?"

"Think so." Stan pulled his cell phone from his pocket and hit some buttons. Jud wondered how the man's large fingers could even work the keys. "Yeah, here's his home." Stan rattled off the digits.

Jud jotted them down. "Thanks."

Stan lumbered off and Jud turned again to his burglary notes. But Walt Rosenbaum's number called to him. On impulse he picked up his phone and dialed.

Surprisingly Walt answered.

"Hi, this is Jud Maxwell from Palo Alto PD. Long time no see. How ya been?"

"Jud, what a surprise. Yeah, I could be better, but maybe you heard. I was diagnosed with Lyme disease six months ago. It's gotten so bad I can't even work. I'm home on disability."

Jud listened as Walt gave a rundown of his symptoms. He didn't stutter like Janessa McNeil, but other things were an eerie echo of Janessa's claims: terrible fatigue, lost strength in his legs. If Walt left the house he went in a wheelchair. His heart fluttered, every joint hurt, and half the time he couldn't think.

Sounded a *lot* like Mrs. McNeil.

"But enough of my problems. What's up with you, Jud?"

"Actually, I need to talk to you about a case I'm working that involves Lyme." Briefly he told Walt the details, leaving out the names.

"Wow, that is crazy. This doctor—you wouldn't be talking about Brock McNeil, by any chance?"

"How'd you guess?"

"Really? McNeil?" Walt snorted. "Man. You got any leads?"

"That's why I called. Thought maybe you could give me some general direction. McNeil said the perp had to be someone in the Lyme community—and certainly that's what the phone calls seem to indicate."

"He oughtta know. Fact is, everybody in the Lyme community hates Brock McNeil. Of all the know-it-all docs who insist there's no such thing as chronic Lyme, he's at the top. It's doctors like McNeil who've put me on this couch instead of working. First it took me two years to get diagnosed because the tests work so badly."

Janessa McNeil's words rose in Jud's mind: *"I need to be retested. The results might be wrong."*

"Then when I finally was diagnosed, I was already chronic. But McNeil and his cronies say three to four weeks of antibiotics will fix it. Which it won't. Still, my insurance listens to *them*, so then it dried up. Then I lost my job." Bitterness tinged Walt's voice. "My wife's working, but it's pretty hard on just her salary and the disability. Plus we got a first-grader."

Jud's heart went out to the man. "I'm really sorry to hear all this, Walt. Can't be easy."

"No. But I'll make it."

Jud gazed at his burglary notes. The case he should be working on right now. "So, Walt, you're saying it's not just a few Lyme patients—those more involved in advocacy, for example—who would know McNeil's name?"

"No, no. Anybody who has Lyme knows that name. 'Cause once you have this disease you quickly find out you have to fight for yourself. So you hop online to learn who else out there has Lyme and can tell you the ropes. Things like where to find a doctor and what treatments work, diet, basically the new way you have to live. Doesn't take long before you're knee deep in the Lyme wars yourself. You quickly see who's who."

Jud leaned back in his chair, and it squeaked. Stupid thing. He needed to oil it. "Have you heard anyone make any kind of threats against McNeil?"

"Not out loud. But I'll bet you there's not a Lyme patient out there who hasn't thought what Brock McNeil needs is a taste of his own disease."

The words seemed to echo over the line. "Really."

"No kidding. 'Course, actually *doing* something like this is pretty insane. And going after his wife—that's cold."

"If you were investigating this case, where would you start?"

Walt made a *tsk*ing sound. "With no solid leads, hard to say. Could be anybody in the country who's got a beef against McNeil."

"Not necessarily someone in this area?"

"Lyme patients are everywhere. Lots of 'em are back east. But thing is, if your perp is an active Lyme sufferer, the guy's not likely to be pulling off something like this. He'd have to have a real mild case, so you'd wonder why he's so mad. So maybe it's someone who watched a family member . . ."

Walt fell silent. Jud waited him out.

"You know what?" Walt took a breath and let it out. "Now that

I think about going after the woman instead of the doc himself—maybe it's like an eye for an eye, you know? In this case a wife for a wife."

"Someone whose wife has Lyme."

"Yeah. Doesn't that make sense? If you're a criminal mind."

Yes. Jud supposed it did. "Any thoughts on who?"

"Not a one. Lotta women with Lyme out there. Lotta ticked-off husbands—pardon the pun. And it's just a theory to begin with. Maybe I'm wrong. But I'll keep my ears open in the online forums and such."

Online forums. Jud should look into those himself. If he found the time. Lack of sleep was beginning to catch up with him.

From down the hall he heard a familiar voice. The chief was headed his direction. Jud leaned toward his desk. "Thanks a lot, Walt. I have to go, but keep in touch if you run across anything."

"No problem, man. It'll give me something to do."

Jud hung up the phone just as the chief stuck his head in the door.

"Maxwell. Anything new on the burglaries?"

Chapter 22

I FROZE, GAPING AT THE EMPTY VIAL TURNED UPSIDE DOWN on Lauren's finger. My throat convulsed in a swallow. "Get off the floor."

"Huh?"

"Get off the floor right now!"

Lauren stood up. "What's *wrong* with you?"

"Where's the top?" I threw frenetic glances around the floor.

"There is no top."

"Here. Somewhere." I shifted one hundred eighty degrees. Peered around chair legs, toward the cabinets, the stove.

"Where'd this thing come from, anyway?" Lauren slid the bottle off her finger and onto the table. It sat there mocking me. So *empty*.

I couldn't see the top. It must have popped off when the vial fell to the floor. How far had it bounced? The tick had a hard back. If it had bounced too, maybe it landed close to the top.

No need to panic. We'd find it.

"Lauren." I worked to keep my voice even. "I was looking at that b-bottle before I fell. It had a . . . bug in it."

"A bug?"

"I dropped it. Now the bug's gone, and we . . . need to find it. I don't want it l-loose in the kitchen. Can you p-please look?"

She made a face. "Is it a spider?"

"No."

"I *hate* bugs."

"I know." I licked my lips. "It has some red on its back."

"Where'd it come from? Why'd you have a bug?"

My voice rose. "Just look, okay?" I took a breath, calming myself. "Please."

Lauren gave me an apprehensive glance, then bent over, scanning the floor. She peered around the table and chairs, then worked her way up to the stove area. "Here's the top." She picked it up. "See?"

"Okay, good. Maybe the bug's nearby."

Lauren continued her search. I watched from the floor, besieged by visions of Stalking Man. How close he'd gotten to Lauren to place that bottle in her backpack! He was sending me a message: *I can get to your daughter. You can't protect her.* I wanted to jump up, grab Lauren, and whisk her away. To somewhere, anywhere.

But I couldn't even rise from the floor.

What if it was on her already? She'd been crawling around. What if it was on me?

I held out my arms, checked them all over. Looked at my feet. I pulled my pajama bottoms up each leg as far as possible, ran my hands over my skin. I felt in my hair, my neck, down my chest and around toward my back. No tick.

Lauren had reached the refrigerator. Next she headed for the stove, head down and hair swinging. Looking. Finally she straightened with a frightened sigh. Put a hand on her hip. "I can't find it."

"It has to be here somewhere."

"I looked everywhere, Mom."

"Look again!"

"It's *not* here."

"Lauren! Look again."

"But—" She tipped back her head and gazed at the ceiling. Her mouth began to tremble, and a tear slipped from her eye. "I don't know what's going on."

I stared at her. So many frustrations and questions in her words. She didn't understand my illness. Why her dad had left on a sudden "trip." He usually gave her plenty of warning before he left town. Why her mother was so paranoid and on edge with her. Most of all, why I, who didn't like bugs any more than she did, had brought one into the house.

My hips hurt from sitting on the floor for so long. And the back of my neck creaked and swayed, as if it couldn't support my head much longer. "I'm sorry. I don't mean . . . to yell."

Where was the tick? Was it on my daughter?

I searched the length of floor between me and the sink. The overbright light hurt my eyes, but I couldn't put on sunglasses now. No sign of the creature. With much effort I scooted over until I could reach up and wrap my fingers around the sink's lip. Could I lift myself up as I had days ago? Last time I'd possessed more strength in my arms. I breathed a prayer, positioned my legs under me—and pulled.

Pain grabbed my fingers, hands, and arms. I nearly let go. Gritting my teeth, I willed myself to pull until I stood, shaking, hanging over the sink. For a moment all I could do was gasp. "Please bring me my . . ." The word wouldn't come. I gestured toward the thing I needed.

Lauren brought it. *Cane.*

"Thanks."

I had to search the floor, her body. The tick was here, somewhere.

Turning to Lauren, I did my best to smile. I ran my fingers over her face, wiping away the wetness. "It'll be okay."

She nodded, but another tear slipped down her cheek.

"Come on." I nudged her to my chest and hugged her with one

hand. She melted into me, sniffing. I leaned against the counter for support. When Lauren drew back, her expression was resolute. I wiped her face again. "Let's go around and look together, okay?"

We made a slow trek around the kitchen, gazes glued to the floor. With each step—and no sight of the tick—my body tingled more. That horrible thing was loose in my house. I wouldn't have been more frightened if it was a poisonous snake. At least snakes were bigger, easier to spot. This insidious, disease-carrying tick—surely Stalking Man had made sure it was infected—could hide in so many places. Then crawl on Lauren without her feeling a thing.

"L-look under the bottoms of the cabinets." All around the kitchen a section of wood came down, the cabinets set back from it a number of inches. The tick could crawl up on the other side of that facing.

"I did that."

"No, you didn't."

"But—"

"Lauren. *Do* it."

Reluctantly she squatted, her palms on the floor. I cringed. Lowering her face close to the hardwood, she bent her head to check under the edges of the wood. A foot at a time, she moved forward, checking the long row.

She stood up, arching her back. "I can't see under there all that well."

Was it under the facing? Or somewhere else? The cabinets on the other side of the kitchen were too far away. Still . . . I gazed at them, feeling nausea. "Go do the same thing over there." I pointed to the far cabinets.

"But I can't see."

"Try."

Slump-shouldered, Lauren sighed her way to the area and crouched down once more. Muscles tense, I watched the floor in front of her, making sure it was clear as she inched forward.

At the end of the cabinets, she stood. "Okay, that's it."

My body listed to one side. *God, please help me.* "Come sit down." I clumped to the table and collapsed in my chair. Lauren fell into hers and regarded me, her mouth bent.

I laid my cane on the table and turned to her. From the recesses of my mind rose Brock's threat: *"Don't you bring my daughter into your little scheme, Jannie. If you do, I'll take her away from you."*

I placed a hand under Lauren's chin. "Let's make sure the bug's not on you."

Her face scrunched up. She jerked back. "You think it is?" Her breath came out in little puffs. "Get it *off* me!"

"Stand up first and let me look you over."

"Oh!" She pumped her hands in the air. "Where *is* it, will it bite?"

"Lauren, stand up."

"But will it *bite?"*

"I don't know."

Lauren stood up, her head low, running frantic hands down the front of her body. "What kind of bug is it?"

"Not sure. Put your arms out straight."

She shot them out, trembling. I scanned her clothes from the top down to her feet. "Turn around."

She whirled and stopped, little noises escaping from her lips. "Do you see it?"

"No."

"Ohhh."

My heart banged around in my ribs. I would spot it easily if it was there, right? Surely I would. It was big enough. "Lauren, it's okay. It may not . . . be on you at all. I'm just making sure."

"But what if it *bites* me?"

My hand reached out and lifted up her shirt. I placed my palm on her back. "Come closer." She jumped backward. I slid my hand all the way up to her neck, feeling the bony shoulder blades, the bump of her spine. "Turn around again." Leaning forward, I used both hands, feeling her sides, up to her chest, her neck.

What if I did find it? Could it have dug into her skin already? I'd have to twist it out of her. Lauren would freak.

But I could not find it on her upper body anywhere.

Lauren's eyes glistened. "What if it's there and you just didn't see it?"

"Sit down. Let's look at your legs."

She threw herself into her chair and yanked up a pant leg.

"Feel upward as far as you can, sweetie."

She groped around her calf, a sick look on her face, then checked the other leg. Fresh tears spilled. "Maybe it's up higher."

Lauren jerked to her feet and yanked down the zipper of her jeans. She tore the pants down, then kicked them off. "Do you see it?" She faced me, then spun around, showing me the back of her legs. I saw nothing but her little-girl skin, the blue flowers on her white panties.

"No." Another possibility hit. A long shot, but I had to check. "Let me check your hair."

She shuddered. "Not in my haaair!" Her hands flew to her head, fingers scrambling across her scalp. "I don't want it in my hair!"

"Lauren, stop. Let me."

She bent her head far over, close to my chest. I swept my hands through her thick strands of hair, then onto her head. Felt the front, the back, behind her ears, down to her neck. Her dark tresses could so easily hide the tick. But it wasn't there. Still, what if . . . ? I drew her closer and picked through her hair as if searching for lice.

Lauren's hands gripped my knees. She leaned against me, the weight making me hiss in pain.

She let out a wail. "Did you find it?"

"N-no."

A sob escaped her. "Mom, I'm scared!"

"I know, just . . ."

My fingers picked and searched, picked and searched.

"I want to call Daddy!"

"No! We can't."

"Why?"

"He's . . . in meetings. We can't bother him now."

"He'll get out of the meeting for me."

"No, Lauren."

No tick. It wasn't on her. Anywhere. I was ninety-eight percent sure.

But that other two percent . . .

"Stand up," I told her. "It's not on you."

She straightened, her eyes dark and eyebrows furrowed. "Then where is it?"

"I don't know."

"You sure you saw one at all?"

My heart twinged. Was my daughter starting to doubt me now? "I'm sure."

"*Where* did it come from?"

I gazed into her clouded face, my chest heavy and thick. What in the world was I supposed to tell her? A man was stalking us, and my own husband didn't believe me. And the police were too busy to care.

"Mom!" Lauren shivered.

"It was in your backpack."

"*My* backpack?"

I nodded. "I found it in your front zipper compartment. Someone must have put it there as a trick."

"But who would do that?" Her cheeks reddened. She looked away, her lips pressing and one hand finding her hip. Then she swung back to me. "I bet it's that stupid Paul Paxley. He teases me all the time, and I can't stand him anyway!" Her eyes glistened with righteous indignation, and her lips pulled. "I'm gonna tell the teacher on him tomorrow."

"Lauren, no. You don't know who did it. And we . . . found the bottle, and so that's the end of it."

"It's not the end. We don't know where the bug is!"

My chin dropped. The last spate of energy in my body melted right out of me. If I didn't make it to the couch—now—I'd fall right out of the chair.

Suddenly I couldn't pull in enough air. My body tipped, my head swam. "Oh." My mouth dropped, and I sucked in huge, grating breaths as if I'd just shot to the surface of water after nearly drowning.

"Mom?"

Still not enough oxygen. Black shapes swirled through my eyesight. Any second, I'd go down. I grabbed the edge of the table and leaned over the wood. Turned my head to one side and laid it down. My legs shook, and my arms, my fingers. Yawning dread swept through me. I couldn't breathe. I *could not* breathe.

"Mom!" Lauren shook my shoulder. "Mommeeee!"

I tried to answer, to calm her, but couldn't. *More air, more.* I dragged it in, my lungs wheezing like rusted bellows, the rasp gritty in my throat. My chest rose and fell, pushing my torso up from the table. My sight faded more . . .

The blackening stopped.

I felt a change in my body, as if a blocked airway had expanded. The sense of suffocation subsided, my breaths not quite as frenzied. The screams in my brain died down. Still I lay bent over the table, pulling in air until my lungs could hold no more, pushing it out, pulling it in again.

"Mom?" Fear coated Lauren's voice.

My breathing steadied. My vision cleared.

"I'm . . . okay. Just . . . felt dizzy."

I gave myself another moment, then cautiously raised my torso from the table. My fingers slipped off the edge of the wood. I hung there, assessing my heartbeat, my balance. It had passed. That horrible death-grip feeling of being buried alive was gone.

My throat convulsed. "I need to lie down."

In a blur I felt for my cane, pushed to my unsteady feet. I shuffled into the den and fell upon the couch, spent and wracked with pain. "L-Lauren," I croaked. "You have to get . . ."

My throat closed up. I tried to push out the words, but they wouldn't come. Fatigue rolled its boulder-like body onto my chest, crushing my lungs, my mouth. My mind shrieked for me to *do something, save your daughter!* but I couldn't even keep my eyes open. They blinked and fluttered . . . and then glued shut.

My last waking thought was of the tiny time bomb crawling loose in the kitchen.

Chapter 23

FEELING HIT ME FIRST. THE THROB OF MY BODY, THE WEIGHT of my chest with every breath. Then sound—or lack of it. I floated up, up, in a dark, dank cave . . .

My eyes opened. I lay on my back, staring through a haze at the den ceiling, a block of dread in my chest. The light was so bright. Didn't I have sunglasses? "L-Lauren?"

"What?" The response, heavy with accusation, came from the kitchen.

"You okay?"

"Fine." Still sullen.

"Your homework done?"

"Almost."

My gaze wandered to the clock on the wall. Just after 5:00. I'd been asleep . . . what? An hour?

The tick. The memory washed over me in a frigid shiver.

"Lauren, get out of the kitchen!"

"What?"

"G-get out. Now!"

Her chair scraped. She appeared in the doorway, frowning. "If you're still worried about the bug, it's not there. Believe me, I looked everywhere. Like *three* times." She folded her arms, brimming with indignation. I'd scared her for no reason. Scared her with one of the things I knew she hated most.

"I'm s-sorry. I just . . ." I turned my gaze away from her, floundering and sick at heart. The tick was there. It was *still there.*

She sniffed, then walked to the armchair and plopped into it. Her voice softened. "You feeling any better?"

Jud Maxwell's words whispered from the recesses of my mind: *"If something new comes up, something you can give me, please call."* He should know. About the tick. About how close Stalking Man had gotten to my daughter.

The phone sat in its cradle on the table behind my head. In slow twist I turned on my side and fumbled for the receiver. My body felt like it was pushing through water.

Wait. What was Jud's number?

I rolled to my back. Lauren watched me, lingering anger blending into sympathy. My eyes blinked at the phone, as if it would tell me what to do. I laid it in my lap. "Lauren, I need you to g-get something for me."

"What?"

"A business card. On Daddy's desk. Name on it is Jud Maxwell."

She heaved a sigh and rose. I listened to her footsteps as she went through the hall, to the office and back. She stood behind the couch and thrust the card toward me. "Here."

"Thanks." I took the card and touched her hand. "You still scared?"

She shrugged. "The whole time I did my homework, I kept my feet off the floor."

I nodded, sick at heart.

Lauren rubbed her arms. "Is Jud Maxwell that detective who was here?"

The card felt hot in my fingers. "Yes."

"Why do you want to call him?"

When I was a small child I'd hated my mother's lack of explanations. Actions and words that made no sense would flow around me, and I could never glean the answer to *why*. Why was my daddy in bed? Why did he look sick? Why wasn't he home? Why was my mom's face bruised? I felt locked out from the truth, never sure what to expect. But sure that when it came I would never know why. In time I learned. My father started hitting *me*. And the effects of his drinking spilled from the bedroom through the entire house. The secrets then rested upon my shoulders as well as my mother's. I had to hide our shame from the rest of the world.

I'd vowed nothing like that would ever happen in my own home, with my own children. No hiding, no lies. No dodging questions when Lauren *knew* something was amiss. Nothing was more important than my daughter's ability to trust me.

I licked my lips. "To tell him about the bug in your backpack."

Lauren's nose scrunched. "You're going to tell him *that*? Whoever did it at school's really gonna get into trouble."

"I just don't want . . . anyone hurting you."

She regarded me, her lips pressed. Doubt flicked across her face—and it pierced to my soul.

"I don't like you sick. It makes you . . ." Lauren shook her head.

I worked to give her a reassuring smile. "I'm going to the doctor tomorrow."

"You've just *been* at the hospital for three days."

"I know but . . . this is a different doctor."

"Will he make you better?"

"She." I swallowed. "Yes. I think so."

Lauren bit the inside of her cheek.

"Why don't you watch TV up in my . . . upstairs? Since I need to make the call from here."

Her eyebrows rose. "You're gonna let me watch TV in *your* bedroom?" For some reason lying on her parents' king-sized bed to watch TV had always been the ultimate in decadence for Lauren.

"Yeah. Just for now. Before you go . . . do I have sunglasses?"

She gave me a look. "They're in the kitchen."

"Oh. Right. Could you get them for me?"

She headed to the kitchen, stopping at the threshold to check the floor. In seconds she returned. I put the sunglasses on. Ah. So much easier on my eyes.

"Can I go upstairs now?"

"Yeah. Close the door, okay?"

"Okay." Lauren swiveled and trotted off before I could change my mind.

I adjusted my aching neck against the pillow and looked dully at the card. For a moment I couldn't think how to hold it to see the number and dial at the same time. Wouldn't I need a third hand for that? Such a problem. I closed my eyes, fighting to logic my way through. If I couldn't even do this, how was I going to convince Jud to listen?

Up and down my legs I felt those strange little muscle twitches, like bugs wriggling under my skin. I read the first two numbers off the card and hit the buttons on the receiver. Repeated with two more at a time. Finally a phone rang on the other end of the line.

"Jud Maxwell."

For a split second, fear nearly made me hang up. "Hi. It's J-Jannie. McNeil."

"Yes, Mrs. McNeil."

"I . . . There was a tick in Lauren's backpack. In a little . . . bottle. He had to put it there."

"A tick?"

"A deer tick. They carry L-Lyme. I saw online what they look like."

Jud made a sound in his throat. "You and Lauren okay?"

Just great. "Uh-huh."

"Do you have this bottle with the tick inside?"

"Yes. No."

"Which is it?"

"The bottle, yes. But I dropped it. The t-tick fell out. Can't find it. Looked all over." A chill knocked down my spine.

"You can't find it?"

"Had L-Lauren look. Everywhere in the kitchen." My voice crimped. "We have to f-find it. It could bite her!"

Silence. I could imagine his thoughts. How convenient for me to have lost the main piece of evidence. If Brock heard of this he'd be furious. I could only imagine his ravings. I couldn't deal with that. Not on top of everything else.

"P-please. You have to believe me."

Jud's chair squeaked. "So you have the bottle, correct?"

"Yes."

"Okay. I'll come over and get it, and we can talk more about this. All right?"

My eyes burned. "Yes. Thank you."

"Give me, say, twenty minutes."

"Okay." My finger hit the *off* button. The phone fell against my stomach.

Thank You, God. Thank You, thank You.

Surely Jud would find the tick. Then he'd believe me completely. Brock would have to believe me. He'd come home . . .

I lay staring at the ceiling, entertaining desperate dreams of all my problems fading away. Then I dropped back into hard reality.

How would I get up to answer the door when the detective arrived?

Chapter 24

HE DROVE DOWN THE STREET AS A SUIT-CLAD MAN STEPPED onto the house's porch and reached for the doorbell. The man was too far away for him to tell who it was.

His foot jerked off the accelerator for a split second, then he regained his equilibrium. No need for concern, no matter who it was. He was just a man driving by in an unknown car. Besides, the dark toupee and mustache concealed his features.

The door of the house opened, and the man disappeared inside.

It was a heady thing, being a savior. Few were called, fewer still up to the task. In every Lyme patient's story he read on the Internet, in every Lyme patient's face he saw at rallies on TV, he saw Elyse. Heard her voice.

"Promise me you'll change it for others."

This world was full of injustice, yet so many sat on the sidelines and did nothing. This disease, these Lyme wars were costing people their quality of life, some their very lives themselves. It required focus, *genius* to accomplish what he had done. What were a few sick lives to save the masses?

As he drove past the house, he dared no more than a glance at it.

Had she found the tick yet?

His lips curled. What a sight that would be when she did.

Try to catch me now. Try to keep me from your precious Lauren.

Chapter 25

I'D MANAGED TO SIT UP ON THE COUCH. I SQUINTED THROUGH the window to watch for Jud Maxwell's car. I'd opened the shades, which didn't help my eyes any. But I wanted to reach the front door before Jud rang the bell and alerted Lauren. Thoughts trudged through my muddied brain—plans on what I could say, what I could do to make the detective do something. That tick had to carry Lyme. And what else was it—three coinfections? Which meant it would be proof of what Stalking Man had done to me. Even Brock would have to believe my story.

My body so wanted to lie down. The mere idea of walking to the door exhausted me.

Finally I saw a car pull to the curb. The detective got out, carrying something. A kit? And his tape recorder. Somehow I managed to push to my feet. Against the floor my cane made a hollow, indignant sound. The sound of my heart. My life.

When I pulled back the door Jud Maxwell was reaching for the bell.

Despite the sunglasses, the sun hit my eyes like a wall of fire.

I squeezed them shut. "Come in." I stepped back, washed in *déjà vu* of this same scene mere days ago. The detective stepped inside. "Please follow," I gasped. "In here. Need to sit down."

"Are you feeling any better?"

His voice came from behind as I made for the beckoning couch. "Worse. I see a doctor tomorrow."

"You've seen a lot of doctors lately."

"None that could help."

I dared not look back to check his expression. If he still thought I was faking all of this, I'd never convince him of anything.

"Please. Sit." I half-gestured toward the armchair and slumped onto the couch. Laid my cane across the cushions.

He remained standing. Set his kit and recorder on the coffee table. "Where's the bottle?"

My mind blanked. I stared at him, all too aware of long seconds clicking by. Heat pulsed in my cheeks. The mental fog made me feel so utterly stupid. It would be impossible to explain to someone the lack I felt in my brain. Synapses as useless as unplugged electrical cords.

Then, suddenly—they connected. "In the kitchen. Some . . . where. You can see."

Jud's eyes lingered on me for a moment, a hand on his hip. The knot of his dark blue tie lay askew. The tie didn't match his suit all that well. Did Sarah not dress him? The way I always dressed Brock, matching his ties to suits. He was never any good at that sort of thing.

The way I *used* to dress Brock.

A sob rolled up my throat. I thrust it back down.

Jud opened his kit and pulled out two white gloves—the kind used to gather evidence. The sight of them turned my stomach. This was my *house*. Now it had become a crime scene.

He disappeared into the kitchen. His footsteps stopped. Moved again.

Silence.

Had Alicia matched Brock's tie this morning? How had he even known which ones to pack? How *could* he manage without me?

Jud returned wearing the gloves. In one hand was the vial, cover and all. Had I put that top on? Maybe Lauren had done it. "This it?" He held it up.

I nodded, my thoughts lingering on Brock. "Still empty."

Oh good, how smart that sounded. What did I expect—the tick to morph back inside through the plastic? My eyes shut. This was a mistake. I never should have called the detective. He'd walk out of here thinking worse of me than before.

Jud opened the kit and pulled out a small paper bag. He dropped the vial inside, folded over the top and pulled a pen from his pocket to label it. He set the bag on the table. "I saw your daughter's backpack. You said the bottle was in there?"

"In the . . . small zipper part in front."

"Did you look through the rest of her pack?"

I blinked. Why hadn't I? "Once I saw the tick I—"

"Understood. Let me bring it in here, and we'll go through it, okay?"

"Okay."

Jud went to the kitchen and returned, carrying the backpack with both hands. Moving the paper bag and recorder to the floor, he set the pack on the table. Squatted down. One by one he pulled out the items that symbolized my Lauren. Textbooks, notebooks. Pens. A tiny stuffed animal. An old invitation to a birthday party she'd already attended. A hair clip, notes from her friends. Half a candy bar in its wrapping. An old test, graded *B*. My heart clutched at each item. Every one spelled trust and innocence, my daughter's life now strewn in pieces on the floor.

Brock, how could you leave her?

The backpack lay empty. Jud ran his hand inside each zippered section. He stood, arching his back, and spread his hands. "Nothing else out of the ordinary."

"No."

Jud thought for a moment. "You say you dropped the tick. In what area?"

"The kitchen. By the table. W-would you look?"

"Yeah."

Once again he disappeared. After a time I saw him through the pass-through window, bent low. I sagged on the couch like a half-stuffed ragdoll, my thoughts bending from the tick to Brock and back again. Sudden anger steamed up inside me, rattled around my ribs, then petered away. No energy to sustain it.

I don't know how long I waited. My eyes found the clock twice, but they looked through it, the time not registering. What did it matter anyway?

Jud appeared. "I've looked all over and can't find it."

Of course he wouldn't. Why should anything go right for me today? "It's really small."

"Yeah. Easy to miss."

I raised my eyes to his. Did he believe me?

"You'll keep looking for it?"

I nodded. You bet I would.

"If you find it I want you to put it in something and call me right away."

"I will."

Jud took off the gloves and put them in his kit. "Where's your daughter?"

"Upstairs. Watching TV in my room." I rubbed my chin with the back of my hand. My knuckles twinged, making me wince.

He sat down in the armchair. "I need you to tell me everything about the tick. When you first saw the bottle. How you dropped it. Everything. I'll record your story. All right?"

My *story*. Not *the facts*. A Freudian slip? I nodded. Waited in silence while he readied the recorder and spoke our names and the date into it.

"Okay, tell me what happened."

I told him. With halting words and a mind that twisted and stuttered, I related finding the bottle, then dropping it. My falling down. Lauren's and my desperate search for the tick. "But I didn't tell her what it was. Just called it a b-bug." I swallowed. I couldn't talk much more. It was so *tiring*. "Sh-she wanted to know if it would . . ." My eyes fell to the recorder. I could feel my lungs struggling to suck in air. "When they . . ." I floundered, then tapped my teeth. "Bugs that . . ."

Jud frowned. "Bite?"

"Yes. Bite. I said it could. So we had to find it."

He nodded. "All right. Anything else?"

My gaze drifted to the fireplace. How long since we'd had a fire? Last winter. Brock had made it.

Brock. Come back to me. I have to get you back.

I shook my head.

"Okay." Jud leaned over and turned off the recorder. "Thanks. Now I need to talk to Lauren."

My muscles tensed. "Why?"

"I need to hear her side of the story about the bottle. And I need to ask her if she saw anyone she didn't know around her backpack today."

"But she's already scared enough. I don't want her . . ."

He looked at me, an unreadable expression on his face. Compassion? A blend of pity and judgment? "I understand. But you've called me with this news, and now I have to follow it through."

"Don't tell Brock." The plea just blurted out. "Please."

Jud's eyes held mine. He tilted his head in a half nod. "I'd like to take her in the office where I met with you and your husband, if I may."

"Not here? With me?"

"I need to talk to her alone."

I focused on my lap. *Alone.* Of course. To see if her answers corroborated her crazy mother's story. "Would you call her down? I can't . . ."

He walked behind me into the hallway, to the bottom of the stairs and called Lauren's name. After two tries I heard the door to my bedroom open, sounds from the TV waft out.

"What?" Her response was clipped, wary.

"It's Detective Maxwell, remember me? I was here the other day to talk to your parents. I'd like to talk to you now, all right?"

A long pause. I could feel Lauren's hesitation. Here was one more thing in an already strange day. A strange week. "Okay." A moment later her feet hit the hall floor.

"Let's go in your dad's office, okay?"

Another pause. "Mom?"

The discomfort in her voice pierced me. I should get up, demand to be with her. "It's okay, honey. You go talk to him."

Their footsteps faded behind me. I heard a door shut. Once again I waited, my body listing over, my mind at half-stun. I longed to return all of Lauren's things into her pack. She would not be happy to see them gone through like this, so scattered. But I couldn't get down to the floor. And my last bit of energy was waning.

I moved my cane to the floor. Lay down and closed my eyes. How was I going to take care of Lauren by myself, day after day?

About twenty minutes later Lauren and the detective emerged from the office to stand over the back of the couch, gazing down at me. I tried to sit up, embarrassed to be lying down in Jud's presence. But my body wouldn't budge.

"It's okay." He waved a hand at me. "Stay where you are."

I looked at Lauren. "You all right?" She was eyeing her possessions on the floor without an ounce of surprise. "We had to—"

"It's okay, he told me." She shrugged. "I'll put them away later."

I turned a questioning gaze on Jud. He lifted a hand as if to say *I have a way with kids.*

"Mom, can I go back upstairs and watch TV?"

My eyes searched her face. Was this stoicism, or had Jud truly put her fears at ease? "Sure."

Lauren trotted off. Jud came around the couch. "Please." I gestured toward the armchair. He took it. With great effort I pulled myself to sit up. "Well?"

He leaned forward, legs apart, hands clasped between his knees. "She told me what happened. She told me everything you did. Except, of course, she came on the scene after you'd dropped the bottle. So she never actually saw you pull the bottle from her backpack."

Point taken. Once again my story could be suspect. "Did she see anyone at school?"

"No. But when I pressed her she did remember that she'd left her backpack lying on the grass near the parents' pick-up area. She happened to find a cell phone lying on the grass and ran to turn it into the office."

That was Lauren. Ever honest. Caring about someone else's loss. I shook my head. "If she hadn't done that, he maybe couldn't have—"

"True. Or maybe he'd have tried some other way."

I fixed Jud with a look. "You believe me? About all this?"

"There's no doubt in my mind you're very sick. And I haven't been happy about not being able to spend more time on your case. I've done some research online about this disease and the so-called Lyme wars. Just so I could understand the context. I've also checked into Lyme symptoms. Yours seem right on the money."

He'd taken the time to research? My eyes welled, I couldn't help it. "Thank you." The words came out a raspy whisper.

Jud hesitated, as if searching for delicate words. "However, I still don't have much to go on in this case. And meanwhile we're getting all this pressure on the local burglaries. I'd love to have a bit of hard evidence so I could show my superior this case deserves more of my attention."

I could only nod. At least . . . this.

He pointed toward the bag. "I'm going to take that vial to be tested for fingerprints. I'll let you know what we find. Which reminds me, I need to get yours and Lauren's prints so we can rule them out. I brought what I need to take them in this kit."

My relief fizzled. "Lauren's prints? What do I tell her? What did *you* tell her?"

He tapped his thumbs together. "We all want to shield our kids. I understand that. I got two of my own. But in this case, Lauren already knows funny things are going on. I think it's better to tell her the truth than allow her imagination to run wild. Kids know when you're lying."

I thought of my childhood. Yes, they did.

"I'll be going to Lauren's school tomorrow. I want to alert her principal about the possibility of someone harassing her. I don't need to tell them the whole story. But if this guy's really out to harm Lauren, we need to have precautions in place."

"Yes. Good. Thank you."

Jud rose. "Let me call Lauren back down for the prints. I should have done that a minute ago." He scratched his jaw. "Is Dr. McNeil coming home early tonight? You look like you could really use some help getting around."

His offhand remark slapped me in the face. I looked away, shame curling through me. Brock wasn't heartless, yet he'd left me in this state. I must have caused him to want to leave. Somehow. Some way.

But wait a minute—Jud already knew about this.

"He's moved out. Just like he told you he was planning to do."

Incredulity swept over Jud's face. "When did this happen?"

"Last night. Why are you acting like you didn't know?"

Jud made a sound in his throat. "Your husband told me he'd been planning on leaving. But the way he talked, I figured after you got sick he put it off."

Wasn't his judgment of Brock just a little late? I turned my head to look up at him. "You knew about the affair for m-months, didn't you? Your wife knew. Nobody told me. Now he's gone."

Jud's head drew back. "Actually we didn't, not for sure. Not until your husband came to see me on Saturday." His hand found his tie and smoothed it. "But Sarah suspected."

My lips pressed. "And at the Christmas party neither of you said a thing."

I knew I was being unfair. I didn't know Sarah and certainly not Jud well enough for either of them to voice a mere suspicion. But I didn't care. Right now I needed the detective to stand by me. "Just don't . . . abandon me now."

Jud gazed at me for a moment, then gave a curt nod.

He turned away to call Lauren.

When she came down Jud took her fingerprints first. Lauren was fascinated but full of questions. "You're not doing this just because you think somebody at school gave me that bottle, are you?"

Jud glanced at me. "No."

"Then who do you think did it?"

"Lauren." I shook my head at Jud. "We'll talk about it after the detective's gone."

"But—"

"Later."

Lauren gave me a long, hurt look. "Well, fine. I need to put my stuff away." As Jud and I watched she busied herself replacing all the items in her backpack. Had I been able to supervise, I'd have nudged her to throw out the old notes, the half-eaten candy bar. But to a nine-year-old, every item was precious.

When done she lugged the pack into the kitchen. I heard it land on the table. Wordlessly, she retreated upstairs.

When Jud reached for my hand to take my prints, I flinched. My fingers were so tender.

"That hurt?" He let go of my hand.

"Yeah. The joints."

He touched me again gently. Still the procedure hurt. He had to press on my fingers and move them side to side to make sure the prints were complete. I said nothing, but my jaw clenched, and a single tear rolled down my cheek. The pain in my body, the pain in my heart— together they were too much. I just wanted to hide. To sleep and not feel anything.

Jud saw the tear but pretended he didn't. I wiped it away with the back of my hand, too tired to feel ashamed for crying.

He packed up his things and prepared to leave. "I'll let you know if we find anything on the bottle."

"Thanks."

He shifted on his feet. "Mrs. McNeil, I'm really sorry all this has happened to you."

I nodded. "Thanks for coming."

He gave me a tight smile, then headed for the door. I listened to it open and close. A moment later a car started up outside. Drove away.

Now what?

I would have to talk to Lauren. Tell her we suspected an unknown man had left that bug in her backpack. She would want to know why. And I would say . . . ?

Not now. Too much for me to face. I lay back down.

"Mom!" Lauren's feet pounded down the stairs. She appeared at the back of the couch, holding out the phone receiver from my bedroom. "Dad wants to talk to you." She screwed up her face and whispered, "He sounds mad."

Something deep within me clunked, like a metal door slamming shut. "You called him?"

She pushed up her bottom lip. "I told him about the detective and the fingerprints, thinking maybe he'd explain. Since *you* wouldn't tell me what's going on."

Oh, Lauren, no.

She thrust the phone toward me.

"Janessa!" Brock's voice spat from the receiver. He hadn't called me my full name in years. "Come to the phone right now!"

Lauren's lips pulled wide in a *yikes* expression. Her eyes rounded.

All thoughts I'd entertained of Brock listening to me, of him coming back, dropped through my stomach like a stone.

"*Janessa!*"

He wouldn't forgive me for this. For refusing to heed his threat. For scaring Lauren. No way. Whatever had happened to this point would pale beside the fury Brock would now unleash on me.

With trembling fingers I took the phone and held it to my ear. "I'm here."

Chapter 26

WHEN I WAS TEN MY FATHER ACCUSED ME OF STEALING TWO dollars from his wallet. Never mind that I hadn't touched it, much less stolen the money. In his drunken mind two dollars were missing and I had to be the culprit. He threw my door open as I lay on my bed, reading. The smell of alcohol and sweat blew in with him. I jumped so hard my book slid onto the floor.

"Where's my money?"

His face was red and his hair stuck up. He planted his feet apart, leaning toward me. Now I could smell the whisky straight from his breath.

"What money?"

"You took it!"

"No, I didn't."

"Yes, you did!"

A claw-like hand grabbed for me. I scooted out of his reach toward the headboard and cringed. "I didn't take anything, Daddy, I really didn't."

Desperate prayers welled within me. *Please God, please, please.*

"Two dollars!" Spittle flecked my father's lips. His voice turned hard and bitter. "I clothe you and feed you. Work hard to keep a roof over your head—and you steal from me."

No denials would stop him. He had his own belief and it was right simply because he thought it so. He jumped onto my bed and sank his fingers into my arm. Yanked me to the floor. The breath knocked clean out of me.

I don't know which hurt worse, the blows or accusations. One ripped my body; the other burned my soul. When my father finally staggered off, cussing, I crawled back onto my bed and curled into a ball, sobbing. "No, I didn't." My fist bounced against the covers again and again. "I didn't, I *didn't*."

For an hour I lay there crying until I finally fell asleep. When I awoke, head pounding and muscles aching, the injustice and helplessness of it all descended upon me in a smothering cloud. I started to shake. At any time in the future my father could once again determine his own reality. At any time he could come back, accuse me of something I hadn't done, perhaps something far worse. And what would I do?

How would I defend myself to a person whose ears wouldn't *listen?*

Neither did Brock listen now as I stuttered my story of the bottle, and the tick, and the man who'd gotten so close to Lauren. I sank into the couch, arm barely able to hold the telephone, battered by his vehemence. This hurt far worse than my father. There may have been no physical blows, but Brock had been the man who'd picked me up and helped me heal from my abusive childhood. For him to turn into a version of my father, to berate me in such a way, to *not believe* me—

I could not take it.

Lauren hung back, wide-eyed, hearing her dad's tone if not his words. "Go," I mouthed at her, but she refused to leave. And I didn't have the energy to make her.

"I told you not to bring Lauren into this!" Brock raged for the third time. "Checking her all over for a tick? Are you *crazy?* You scared her to death!"

"I was s-scared too. That it was on her."

"And you called Jud Maxwell to come over!"

What—Brock had exclusive rights to phone the police?

"Janessa!"

"Yes. I did."

He blew frustration over the line. "When are you going to stop this charade?"

"When are going to stop being so c-cruel?"

Lauren edged around the sofa, arms crossed and shoulders bent. She sat on the edge of the armchair, pale-faced, watching me. Never before had she heard me and Brock fight.

Brock huffed again. "I know revenge when I see it. And don't think it doesn't sadden me. I thought such things were beneath you. Particularly dragging Lauren into your scheme."

"Why can't you b-believe I'm sick?"

"Maybe you are! But it's not Lyme, tests have proved that. You're only pursuing that to get back at me."

It hit me again, hard. The picture of me at ten, cowering and crying on my bed after my father had beaten me. And something within me cracked, a fissure small but deep. Out of it poured the bubbling lava of indignation. I did *not* deserve this. "Get back at you for what, Brock?" Despite the anger my voice caught. Or maybe because of it. "Since you're . . . such a *great* guy."

Fat tears spilled from Lauren's eyes. "I'm sorry I called him."

Something sounded on Brock's end. A door closing? A book dropped? "I'm coming to get her."

A moment passed before his words registered. "What?"

"I'm coming to get Lauren. Pack up some clothes for her."

I nearly laughed. Sure, I had the strength to do that. "And take her where?"

A beat passed. "To where I'm staying."

"And where would that be, Brock?"

"You know."

"Say it." I caught Lauren's eyes, but there was no stopping me now. This ugly truth could no longer be hidden, not if Brock showed up at our door. "Say where . . . you are."

"I'll be there in an hour. Have her ready."

"You're not t-taking Lauren from me."

"I warned you."

The thought of Lauren wrenched from me, taken to *her* house. What did Alicia know of mothering? What did she know of my daughter?

"You're n-not. You c-can't just take a child from her . . ." The word lost itself in my head. I chased it, but it fell down my throat and into my chest. Rolled around and wailed. This could not be happening— Brock taking Lauren away. My mind would burst apart. *"Please."*

"Then stop me."

How could I stop him? I could barely move from the couch.

"You can't take care of her, right, Janessa? Being so sick as you are. Lauren said you fell down. Can barely walk. You can hardly talk to me. How are you going to get her to school? Make her dinner? *How* do you plan to take care of her?"

"I—"

"And if she's in so much danger, some crazed man stalking her with infected ticks"—he snorted—"just how do *you* plan to protect her?"

The question stabbed me. How *could* I? But I was her mother. My child could not be taken from her *mother.*

"If you don't want me to take her, Jannie, get better. Now. Stop the dramatizing. Show me you're able to get up and get around."

Tears slid down my temples. My *charade* traded in for keeping Lauren, was that it? "I *can* take care of her. I'll m-manage."

Lauren gripped the edge of the armchair. Her face was pinched, her eyes searching mine for answers, for stability. "Where does he want me to go?"

I pulled the receiver away from my ear. "He wants to take you to stay somewhere else."

"Where?" Her expression held the memory of our separation while I was in the hospital. "I don't want to go anywhere."

"Did you tell her, Janessa?" This from Brock on the phone. "Did you tell her why I left, like I asked you to?"

Asked me to? He'd walked away like a coward and thrown the demand in my face. "That's your job. Since you created the . . . situation." I couldn't believe we were having this conversation, with Lauren hearing half of it. How had Brock and I come to this? How could he pull the very foundation out from under the child he so loved?

He made a sound of disgust. "Forget an hour, I'm coming now."

The line cut off.

In a daze, I positioned the receiver in front of my face, one weak finger searching for the *off* button. Pieces of me floated up and away, my brain chanting a mantra—*this isn't real, this isn't real.* As far as Brock had fallen, I had to believe he'd fill Lauren's ears with lies about me. I couldn't stand that. Couldn't bear to lose anything more. Not my daughter. Anything but Lauren.

Imagine if we'd had a second child. Brock would be taking that one, too. I'd so wanted another baby, but Brock wouldn't hear of it. One was enough. He was getting too old to start over.

I *could* take care of Lauren. Somehow. I'd already gotten her rides to and from school. She and I could heat soup together, if nothing else. She could open the cans. And I *had* to watch over her. At least I knew to check for ticks when she came home from school. That may scare her, yes, but taking a chance was far more frightening. Brock wouldn't do that. He'd tell her it was all nonsense.

"Mom." Lauren gripped her fingers and pushed them against her chin. "What's going *on?*"

I looked at her, and my heart broke. Just fell into shattered pieces. Two choices here, both miserable. I could tell Lauren myself, now. Or let the truth come out when Brock arrived and we fought some more.

"Your dad . . ." I pictured the two of them in their tea parties. And the time Brock took her to the daddy/daughter dance at school. He'd worn a pink tie to match her dress—a color he hated. He'd ordered her a pink rosebud corsage. "He doesn't w-want to live with me anymore." Me, just *me.* I couldn't let Lauren think it was her fault.

Her face scrunched up. "What?"

"He has . . . he l-likes someone else now. Some other person. He's not on a business trip. He's staying with her. And he m-misses you. He wants to take you there."

"*No!* I don't want to go!" Her eyebrows slanted upward. "What do you mean he likes someone else?"

I swallowed. "He doesn't want to l-live here, Lauren."

Her mouth dropped open, and her cheeks blanched. "Are you getting a *divorce?*"

Divorce. What a horrible word. A word for other families, for couples who didn't know how to love each other. Not us. My throat nearly closed. "I don't know, honey."

She jumped to her feet. "You can't! I won't let you!"

"I don't want to, Lauren. Believe me."

"But Dad does?"

"I don't know."

Lauren's face crumpled. She leaned forward like a tree uprooted in the wind, then stumbled to the couch. She collapsed on her knees, arms crossed over her forehead, and fell on my chest, sobbing. Pain from the physical hit ripped through me. I gasped, shaking. Bit back my cry. Her weight upon me felt like an avalanche, but for the world

I wouldn't move her. I brought both my hands to her head, stroked her hair.

"I'm not *going* with him." Her voice muffled into my shirt. "I'm staying here with you!"

At that moment I didn't know who I hated worse—the man who'd made me so sick, or my husband. At least Stalking Man didn't know me. Had never loved me.

Lauren cried and cried. Heat from her face and arms radiated into my chest, every tremor throbbing me with pain. Finally she raised up, hair sticking to her cheeks and skin red. Defiance burned in her eyes. "Who is she?"

I blinked at her, startled. The question sounded so grown up, something the wife would demand to know. Was it in the female genes, this righteous indignation against betrayal?

"Someone he works with."

"What's her name?"

"Alicia."

Lauren's features twisted as if she'd bitten into the sourest candy. "I *hate* that name."

I heard the faint sound of the garage door opening.

Brock.

Chapter 27

JUD STOOD IN CHIEF KRAMINSKY'S OFFICE, BITING HIS TONGUE as he listened to the man's harangue. Kraminsky sat in the chair behind his desk, his typically ruddy face even redder than usual. The day—and lack of leads on the burglaries—had not gone well for him.

"So you have this vial—surely covered in Janessa McNeil's own fingerprints, as well as her daughter's—so who knows what else you'll be able to pull off of it." The chief shook his head. "But no tick. Once again no evidence of any kind. Just her story."

"Just her story. And the fact that she's mighty sick."

"Which also has yet to be proven."

Jud sighed. "You been talking to Brock McNeil?" As soon as the words blurted from his mouth, he wished they hadn't.

Kraminsky rose to his full 5'10" height. He leaned toward Jud, planting both palms on his desk. "I've got a string of unsolved burglaries here with *plenty* of evidence they really happened! *And* I got the media all over my back. I don't need some civilian doctor telling me not to pursue this crazy case of yours. With what little you've got,

I can figure that out on my own. Bring me something on your case, Maxwell! Then we'll talk."

Jud wasn't about to back down now. "You can't be telling me to not even test the vial for prints."

The chief waved a hand. "Sure, sure, test it. And if you find something, great. But what if you don't?" Kraminsky raised his bushy eyebrows.

What if he didn't?

The guy could have worn gloves.

Or Janessa McNeil could be lying. If she *was* lying, she deserved an Oscar. The woman looked so sick.

"If I don't . . ." Jud left the words hanging in the air. He spread his hands in a gesture of futility and turned to leave the chief's office.

Back behind his own desk, Jud stared at his stacks of files, still stewing. He tapped a fingernail against his teeth. Not since yesterday had he talked to Brock McNeil—just before the doctor took his wife home from the hospital. Apparently, as far as McNeil was concerned, the case *was* closed. Just because he wanted it to be. What kind of arrogance was that?

Jud glared at the phone, an impulsive thought kicking around in his head. Maybe he ought to check in with McNeil. Not quite sure what information the doctor could give him that would help. But it was better than just sitting here all riled up. Besides a call would likely rattle McNeil's cage, and right now Jud figured the man deserved it. Jud couldn't forget the look on Janessa McNeil's face when she told him her husband had moved out.

On the other hand Sarah may not take too well to Jud irking one of her bosses. She was finding herself in a rather awkward position between him and McNeil.

Jud weighed his options, then leaned forward to snatch up the receiver. Rather than searching for McNeil's direct number, Jud punched in the digits he knew so well.

"Department of Medicine, this is Sarah."

"Hello, gorgeous." He pictured his wife at her desk, brown eyes dancing. She got those little crinkles around her eyes when she smiled.

"Oh, you say that to all your wives."

He laughed. "Can you put me through to McNeil?"

"If you insist." Her voice lowered. "Don't be a pill, you hear? I'd like to keep my job."

"You know he left his wife last night?"

Sarah drew in a breath. "He actually did that? *Now?*"

"Yup. Moved in with Alicia."

Shocked silence. "Oh. That's just . . . awful."

Jud could imagine his wife's concern running from Janessa McNeil to her coworkers. With McNeil and Alicia living together, their relationship couldn't remain secret for long. Everyone in the department would learn of their affair. There would be upheaval. Sarah hated upheaval.

"Okay, forget everything I said." Sarah sounded disgusted. "Bug him all you want. I have another call coming in. Talk to you tonight."

She clicked off, and a phone rang in Jud's ear. No answer. Eventually Sarah picked up again. "No good, huh?"

"Nope."

She sighed. "I was gone from my desk for about fifteen minutes, so for all I know he left." She still sounded upset. Jud wished he hadn't told her until tonight. "But let me try the lab."

More rings—two, three. The fourth one cut off.

"Lab. Dane Melford."

Jud's chin sank. "Oh, hi, Mr. Melford. Detective Maxwell here. I was trying to reach Dr. McNeil."

"He had to leave. Sorry. Is there something I can do for you?"

"No, thanks. I'll try reaching him on his cell phone."

"I don't . . . Uh, do you think it could wait awhile?"

"Wait?"

"Perhaps now is not the best time. He left in a hurry. Said he had something at home to take care of."

Really. *"Home* meaning . . . ?"

Dane hesitated, as if the question confused him. "Where his family lives. His house."

Ah. Apparently Dane didn't know his boss had moved in with Alicia either. McNeil sure knew how to keep his secrets. "Everything all right at his house?"

"I didn't want to ask. I just supposed Mrs. McNeil needed his help doing something."

McNeil helping his wife? Now there was a switch.

Jud shifted in his chair. "I see. All right, I'll give it some time before I call him, then. While I have you, Dane—you have any other thoughts for me concerning the case?"

"Not really. Well, maybe one thing I thought of this morning, for what it's worth. You might try going online and seeing if there are any chat rooms where people talk about Lyme. Maybe you'd find someone who's vocal and upset. I know that's a long shot . . ."

"Not a bad idea. I actually heard the same thing from someone else. But he called them forums, not chat rooms."

"Forums, okay. Tell you what, when I go home tonight I'll get on my computer and help you look. If I find anything I'll let you know."

So McNeil was hiding more than one secret from his lab assistant. If Dane Melford knew his boss wanted this case closed, he wouldn't be offering his help. "Appreciate that."

Jud hung up the phone and sat back, thinking. This case continued to get more strange by the minute. But his impulse to call the doctor had ebbed. Last thing he wanted to do was get between Mr. and Mrs. McNeil. That poor woman needed all the help she could wring from her jerk of a husband.

He dropped the receiver back in its cradle.

Chapter 28

AT THE SOUND OF BROCK'S ARRIVAL, EVERYTHING WITHIN me clamped down. If there was an ounce of adrenalin left in my body, I needed it now.

"Lauren, I need to get up."

She stood and retreated a few steps, giving me room to edge my legs around till my feet touched the floor. Her back remained stiff, her jaw set. She'd heard the garage door too, but she was not about to turn around to face her father as he stepped into the room.

The kitchen door opened and closed. I leaned over, fumbling for my cane. Lauren picked it up and handed it to me.

Brock appeared at the threshold of the den.

Sensing his presence, Lauren tensed and folded her arms. Her stubborn head would not turn.

I fought to stand. To be the epitome of that old saying "I'm not going to take this lying down." Never before had I known so deeply what that meant. Lying down meant weakness, acceptance. Nothing within me accepted what my husband was trying to do. Feeling Brock's eyes on me, the disgusted curl of his lips, I positioned my feet, my cane.

Scooted myself toward the edge of the couch. With valiant effort—and a thudding, sickening hurt in my joints—I tried to rise. The first time I fell back. And the second. Lauren stepped forward to help. I waved her away. Fact is, I hurt too much for her to pull me up this time.

Third time's charm. I ended up on my unbalanced feet.

Brock glared at me. Did any compassion exist somewhere in his anger? I thought I saw a flicker, something in his eyes.

He walked forward, annoyed gaze sweeping the room. "Lauren, where's your suitcase?"

Just like that—"*Lauren, where's your suitcase?*" No explanation to his daughter, no apology for ripping her from her home. My heart folded in on itself. A week ago Brock would never have imagined treating his beloved child this way. He wasn't really like this. He wasn't.

She whirled on him. "I'm *not* going with you! I want to stay with Mom!"

His face softened. "You can't stay here, Peanut. Your mom's not well enough to take care of you."

"So who's gonna take care of *her?*"

Brock spread his hands. "Come on, Lauren. We can talk about this later. Right now we just need to get you packed. I don't want you to be without something you'd miss. Bring your stuffed animals, your blankets, whatever you want."

"I don't like Alicia!"

Brock recoiled. He shot a dark, accusing look at me. "Go upstairs and pack." His voice hardened. "Now. If you don't, I'll do it for you, and you might not like the clothes I pick."

The bottoms of my feet burned, and my ankles trembled. With both hands I gripped my cane for support, but their finite strength was already waning. And holding myself up hurt every joint. I began to sway. "B-Brock . . ."

I wasn't going to manage this. It was either sit down or tumble over. I backed up to the couch, bent my knees, and let myself fall. My body smacked the back of the couch, lifting my legs off the floor. My feet landed with a thud, stunning my legs with pain. Air gushed from my mouth.

"Lauren." My throat closed, tears biting my eyes. I didn't want her to see what was to come between me and Brock. "Get some . . . things together, okay? Then we'll talk."

She shook her head, her mouth flattened and pulling wide. "I don't *want* to."

"I know. But please. For me."

I gave her what I hoped was a reassuring smile. She looked from me to her dad. He nodded. Lauren's gaze dropped to the floor. With a giant sigh she turned to walk around the couch. She went around my end, keeping a distance from her father.

We waited until her footsteps faded up the stairs.

Something in the air shifted. Brock regarded me as if suddenly unsure of himself. He walked to his armchair and dropped into it. "Are you really sick?"

I nodded. My eyes wouldn't rise to his.

He drew in a long breath. "If you are, we need to get you some help. Maybe you should go back to the hospital."

"For what? More negative tests?"

His mouth opened, then shut. "Maybe you could get your mother out here to stay with you."

"My *mother?* Sure. That would be an immense relief."

"Maybe some friends then. They could take turns."

While you ignore my needs. "I'm going to a d-doctor tomorrow. One who treats Lyme."

He tipped his head back and regarded the ceiling. All remnants of sympathy for me melted from his face. "So we're back to that."

"We n-never left."

"Who's the doctor?"

"Carol Johannis."

"Carol Johannis." Brock sneered. "Of course. Who else?" He narrowed his eyes at me. "You know she's publicly testified against my findings." He shook his head. "Of course you do. That's why you chose her."

I looked at my lap. Why even fight his accusations?

"How do you even know her, Janessa?"

"I don't. I found her online."

"Ah. Sure. Great way to find a doctor."

My insides were trembling like a gelatin unmolded. I sagged deeper into the couch cushions. "Brock. That m-man. He put the tick in her . . ." I waved a hand in the air. "Her thing. You have to believe me."

"And now that tick is here. Somewhere loose in the kitchen."

I said nothing. I knew how crazy it sounded.

"Janessa. If your story is true, and there *is* an infected tick loose in this house, *why in the world* would you want to keep Lauren here?"

His question shot to the core of me. I felt the blood drain from my face. No answer would come, because Brock was right. He was *right*. I could only stare at him as the horrible realization spread over me. I could not fight his logic. He'd trapped me.

Lauren was really leaving. I was really going to lose her.

I'd get her back, of course. This was just temporary. Until this nightmare ended.

When my mouth finally moved my jaw creaked, as if it didn't want to form the words. "You'll have to w-watch her, Brock."

Even then I couldn't stand the thought of it. Maybe I could still stop him from taking Lauren. If I went to an attorney, fought him in court. But how to answer the accusation that she was in more danger here than with her father? *If* my story was real. And if it wasn't . . . why should the court allow her to stay with such a vengeful mother?

Grief bored into my heart. I fixed my eyes upon the coffee table, seeing nothing, unable to move. Any moment now I would just dry up and blow away. I could. Not. *Do* this.

"All the more reason for me to take her," Brock said. "Since you claim your 'man' got into this house at night. Like I said before, at least now he won't know where to find her."

He let the sarcastic words fly like arrows. Amazingly, they bounced off. I simply couldn't hurt any more deeply than I already did.

"Jud's going to t-talk to her principal at school." I still stared at the table. "The teachers will . . . know."

Brock drummed his fingers on the edge of the armchair. "Great. So he's intent on pursuing this. Sounds like you've covered all the bases. All you need now is that Lyme diagnosis. Which no doubt Carol Johannis will be all too happy to give you." He snorted. "Just wait till she tells her colleagues you're her patient. The Lyme advocates will be all over you."

I raised my gaze to him. Bitterness accentuated the planes of his face. Did he think so little of Dr. Johannis to believe she'd breach doctor/patient confidentiality? And even if he did—what about *my* bitterness, my anger? He'd walked away from me into some other woman's arms. He was taking my child. What did I have left?

"Brock, please. Just check Lauren when she . . . gets home from school. For ticks."

"Jannie, I am *not* scaring her any more with this nonsense. She'll be fine."

"What if she's not?"

"She *will* be!"

"But—"

"Janessa, stop it! Stop it right now!" Brock leapt to his feet. "I'm not hearing any more of your lies." He strode out of the room into the hallway. "Lauren!" He shouted up the stairs. "What's taking you so long?"

Her voice floated down. "I have all this stuff to bring."

"Just pack a few things. We can come back later. Get down here."

"I have to—"

"Get down here now!"

I huddled on the couch, hands in my lap. Thinking if I tried real hard to wake up from this nightmare, maybe I would.

Brock returned to pace the room.

"Who's going to take her to s-school?" I glared up at him.

"I will."

"What about picking her up?"

"Don't worry, I'll handle it."

"You're at w-work. You're never available in the m-middle of the afternoon."

"I'll figure it out."

I glared at him. "Don't you dare send that Alicia to get Lauren at school. Lauren will hate you for it."

"Jannie. *Stop it.*"

"Who's she going to stay with until you're done with work? Huh, Brock? Your little mistress?"

He stomped to the couch and towered over me, his face crimson. "Jannie, *shut up.*" He glared at me, fire in his eyes.

I drew in my shoulders. Was he going to hit me? My heart hammered, but I couldn't stop. This was my *child* at stake. "Y-you have no idea what it m-means to take care of Lauren by yourself."

"I said I'll handle it, all right?"

"No, you—"

He slapped both hands against my shoulders and shook me. Hard. My head flopped and rattled. Pain coursed from my neck to my toes. "Unhh." A strangled cry erupted from my throat.

"Stop talking, you hear?" His teeth gritted, a vein pulsing in his neck. He was a Brock I didn't know, a man I'd never seen. *"Don't* you say *another* word!"

He pushed me back against the couch and stalked out of the room. His footfalls smacked against the hardwood floor. "Lauren! Get down here right now!"

The years fell away, and I flew back to the house of my childhood. Back to cringing on the bed after my father had beaten me. How had I gotten here? How had my life spun so out of control?

I started to shake. I was going to lose it, right here, right now. *Jannie, pull yourself together.* But I had not an ounce of strength left. The voice within me spoke louder. *Yes, you can. For Lauren's sake.*

My limbs pulsed. I pushed down a sob. Brock hadn't meant to shake me. He'd just . . . snapped. He'd never touched me like that before. Never.

I brought trembling hands to my cheeks. Wiped away the tears. The voice inside me was right. I couldn't let Lauren watch me fall apart.

Minutes later she came downstairs, toting her stuffed animal and favorite blanket. Brock carried her suitcase. With a force beyond myself I managed to give her a weak smile, tell her she'd be all right. Lauren put down her things and bent to give me a hug. She buried her face against my neck, and I smelled the lingering strawberry of her last shampoo.

"I love you, Mom."

"I love you too, sweetie."

"Get well."

"I will. I'll be fine." She pulled back, and I tried to smile again. "Call me after s-school tomorrow."

This wasn't happening. It *wasn't.*

She nodded, eyes welling.

Brock moved to the kitchen threshold. "Come on, Lauren, let's go."

Mouth trembling, she picked up her stuffed animal and blanket. Followed her dad, shoulders slumping.

"L-Lauren." She turned. "Be careful of strangers."

"Oh, for—" Brock shot me a look of scorn.

Lauren's widened eyes slid from him to me. Her chin raised in a semblance of a nod.

Next thing I knew—they were gone.

Chapter 29

IN THE SUDDEN STILLNESS THE HOUSE FELT LIKE A VACUUM, snatching the air right out of my lungs. At first I thought it was my emotional state. Now with Lauren gone, I *could* lose it.

But no. It was happening again, like before in the kitchen. I couldn't breathe.

I leaned back to give my chest room, gasping. No good. Why couldn't I feel any oxygen? My brain started screaming for it, the demented room devoid of even an ounce. I choked and pulled inward . . . choked again.

This was worse than before. Maybe a heart attack . . .

The walls spun. Dirt clods crowded into my vision.

Down, get down!

I wriggled my aching body until I lay prone, lungs sucking and blowing. Suffocation covered my face.

This is it. I'm going to die.

I dragged in another breath—and an ounce of oxygen radiated through my body. I grasped for more and felt it spread through my limbs, a living, preserving stream. It trickled, then flowed harder. I wanted more of it. A river. I wanted to drown in it.

Over a few minutes my breathing steadied. Still deep and hungry but evening out. I lay there and sucked in air, thinking of nothing but the rise and fall of my chest.

The sense of dying sank, then was swept away. I lay still, chest fluttering.

All the pain of Lauren's absence flooded back.

I cried then, sobs rattling in my throat and tears washing down my temples. I cried for my weakness, and my unrelenting pain, for Brock's hardness, and that tick in my kitchen. I cried for the detective who couldn't help me, for the fear of living in my own house, Stalking Man's utter lack of mercy. I cried until my head pounded, and my body shook, and the tears dried up.

Shaking, I lay there. Wasted.

Scenes from my childhood soon plowed into my head. My father hitting me, my mother doing *nothing* to stop him. Then Brock and his accusations, the cold stone of his face.

Anger set in.

I could not stay on the couch any longer. I needed . . . something. Comfort from somewhere, or my very soul would burst.

My body pulled itself to sit up. My hand reached for my cane. I struggled to stand, swaying. My feet shuffled me around the couch, through the hall, past the bottom of the stairs where Brock had just stood. Where Lauren had come down with her suitcase. I stumbled into Brock's office only to know I couldn't stand to be there either. Around I turned and toward the kitchen. How long it took to get there. Then—over to the cabinet where I kept my files for bills.

And my Bible.

My left hand grabbed the book, but it was too heavy to lift with one hand. I rested my cane against the counter, then leaned my body against it, freeing both hands to pull out the book. Heart thumping,

I managed to push the Bible in the crook of my left arm and hold it against my body. I plucked up my cane and headed for the table. Dropped the Bible upon it. I pulled out a chair and fell into the seat. Laid my cane across on the table.

God, I need . . . You have to do something!

My fingers opened the Bible. I flipped pages until I landed in the Psalms. Yes, that's what I needed! Prayers like King David prayed when he fled from Saul for his life in the wilderness. When he cried out to God to *help*. I wanted words of anger, prayers hurled at God. I wanted bitter complaints and demands. I wanted God to know what He had done to me.

My blurry eyes fell on Psalm 69. I took off my sunglasses to see the words better.

"Save me, O God, for the waters have threatened my life. I have sunk in deep mire, and there is no foothold; I have come into deep waters, and a flood overflows me."

Yes, God, that's me!

"I am weary with my crying; my throat is parched. My eyes fail while I wait for my God. Those who hate me without a cause are more than the hairs of my head; Those who would destroy me are powerful."

A groan escaped me. My hand turned pages again, seeking. I landed on Psalm 77.

"My voice rises to God, and He will hear me. In the day of my trouble I sought the Lord; In the night my hand was stretched out without weariness."

More pages turned, almost as if my hands moved by themselves. My eyes skimmed words here, there, until they took in a verse in the middle of Psalm 94: *"If I should say, "My foot has slipped," Your lovingkindness, O LORD, will hold me up."*

Really? So where was His love now? I leaned back and raised my eyes to the ceiling. "God, are You there? I sure don't feel You. I feel all alone. Please help me. Do . . . *something*."

My right hand drifted from the Bible onto my lap. As suddenly as it had come, the fury-filled energy melted away. I leaned forward and lowered my head. Any minute I could fall out of the chair. I didn't hear God speak. I saw no lightning, and my body hurt just as badly. But a line of one psalm chanted in my head: *"My voice rises to God, and He will hear me. My voice rises to God, and He will hear me. My voice rises . . ."*

This was a choice. I could believe that verse—or not.

Well, why should I? Everything in my life had gone wrong. My future, everything I *was* lay in ruins.

"My voice rises to God, and He will hear me . . ."

My head came up. I pulled in a deep breath. Wiped a hand over my face.

"I choose to believe." I said it aloud. My face tipped toward the heavens. "Hear that?" Defiance tinged the words. "I *choose* to believe."

What else did I have?

Still no lightning. No warm healing through my body. Just a quiet thought that this was right. That God would help. Regardless of my nightmare, He was worthy to be trusted.

Okay, God. Okay. But you still better do something.

A moment passed. I pushed back from the table—and remembered the tick.

My feet jerked off the floor. I leaned over to inspect my slippered feet but saw nothing. Pulled up my pajama bottoms. Checked carefully. Everywhere. Pulled off my slippers and examined my feet.

No tick.

Brock's words pecked at me: *"If there's an infected tick loose in this house, why in the world would you want to keep Lauren here?"*

I put my slippers back on. Lowered both feet to the floor. Why should I care now where the tick was? So what if it bit me? I couldn't feel any worse.

Exhaustion rose, swirled me around like tide water on a beach. I staggered to my feet, picked up my cane, and clumped back to the sofa. The new center of my world. I fell upon it, sick, lonely, with no fight left in my body.

My voice rises to God, and He will hear me.

Maria sludged into my thoughts. I needed to tell her not to come in the morning to pick up Lauren. I reached for the phone and called her. Told her the news in a deadened tone that frightened her and me both.

"I can't believe this, Jannie. Are you okay? Should I come over and stay with you?"

"Maria, you have your own family."

"But who's going to help you?"

"I'll b-be okay."

"Poor Lauren. She's going to be so confused."

"I know. It's . . ." My words ran out. Sleep beckoned, a deep, dark well. "Maria, I need to . . . go now. I'm k-kind of . . . tired."

She sighed into my ear. "Okay, Jannie. I'm so sorry. I'll be praying for you. And I'll check on you tomorrow."

"Thanks."

I clicked off the line and fumbled the receiver into its holder. Then I closed my eyes, leaned out over the blackness, and tumbled into it headlong.

Chapter 30

I AWOKE TO DARKNESS.

Seconds passed as I fought to comprehend where I was. I lay on my back on the den sofa, blinking toward the kitchen. Pale light from a streetlamp filtered in through the front window, tainting the room in a sickly glow. The armchair—Brock's chair—hulked before me, empty and mocking. My cane lay across the coffee table, a reminder of who I'd become. I could make out the shape of the wall clock but couldn't read it.

The memories flooded back. My fight with Brock. The way he'd shaken me. His taking Lauren. That tick somewhere in the kitchen. Or was it in this room by now?

The stillness of the house stretched into a dark canvas that spread over me, stifling and filling me with dread. I needed to get up, go to the bathroom. But my joints pulsed with pain, and lead weights held me down.

I *felt* him then. Stalking Man.

Panic spritzed through me from head to toe. The hairs on my arms bristled. In my mind I leapt up and ran to flick the nearest light switch.

The vision jarred me, a cruel reminder of the health I'd lost and what I'd become. An invalid and sitting duck for the man who, of all people in the world, had chosen me as his target.

Had he come back now to kill me?

Had I activated the alarm?

I fought to sit up. Leaning to my left, I reached for the lamp sitting on the side table and turned it on. Illumination popped into the room, startling my sensitive eyes. I turned away and looked into the kitchen through the pass-through window. I saw no one.

The clock read 11:35.

Chill, Jannie. There's no one here.

Maybe. Maybe not. Nothing in my world made sense anymore. Nothing was predictable.

Stalking Man had broken into my home to put ticks on me. The deed was done and the result just what he wanted: I was beyond sick. Why should he return now?

I needed to check the house.

Through will more than strength I struggled to my feet, the cane handle slick against my palm. My knees screamed as I gimped across the room to the wall switch to flick on the overhead light. I stepped into the kitchen and lit it up as well. An empty room. Barren. My Bible lay on the kitchen table. Beside it, my sunglasses. I couldn't remember putting the glasses there.

Was it just a couple weeks ago in here we'd begun Mother's Day with a breakfast Brock made for me? Lauren had given me a card, its envelope decorated in hand-drawn flowers.

Even then the Lyme spirochetes had been within me. Embedding into tissues throughout my body.

My hunched form now reflected in the sliding glass door. Beyond it the backyard loomed black and huge, a thousand unseen eyes watching me. I hit a switch by the door, and floodlight filled the yard. I pressed close to the glass, peering out. I could not see every foot of the area. There were trees and bushes, a gazebo and hot tub—all places Stalking Man could hide behind. I angled to survey the tree near the far side of the house. He could be behind it, for all I knew. And of course there was all that open space beyond our yard. Was he back there somewhere?

I stood for some time, blinking in the light. The floods were so very bright, they may as well have been the sun.

Nothing moved.

An ice pick pain hit me behind my eyes. I flicked the floods off.

I turned away and noticed the alarm pad light shining green. Not activated. I clumped over to turn it on. The light blinked into red.

Now what? Suppose I'd just trapped Stalking Man *inside* the house.

I checked the lock on the sliding glass door. Should have done that when I was standing there. It was secure.

Slowly I made my way around the bottom floor, peering at windows, the front door. All seemed tight.

He could be on the upper level.

My eyes rose to the staircase. I licked my lips, knowing I should check. Just to show myself he wasn't here, that I was being foolish. But I hadn't the energy to tackle those steps.

"Are you up there?"

My muscles jerked at the sound of my own trembling voice. Blood whooshed a *thud-thud* in my ears. For a moment I froze, expecting to hear something. A footfall. The whisper of clothing. Air swirled about me, cold and full of portent. My legs started to shake.

How stupid was this? Stalking Man wasn't here. No one was in this house but me. Not my husband. Not even my daughter. Just me and my runaway imagination. And my suddenly hopeless life.

The gun's up there!

The sudden memory hit me in the gut. I'd forgotten all about that gun. It had been up there all day in my closet—and I'd sent Lauren into my room—alone—to watch TV. The weapon was high on a shelf but still. My daughter and a loaded gun in the *same room.*

Air puffed from my lips. What had I been thinking? I never would have done such a thing before.

I had to get that gun. I needed it down here. With me.

Grunting, I forced my shaky legs to take one stair at a time. Halfway up I stopped to rest, leaning on the banister and my cane. When I finally reached the top I was sure my legs would no longer hold me. Somehow I made it to my bedroom closet and picked up the gun. Now to carry it back downstairs. What if I fell and dropped it? What if it went off?

I sank onto the bed and took out the bullets. Put them and the weapon in the pocket of my robe. Panting hard, I made my way back to the steps—and down. At the bottom I nearly collapsed.

I needed rest. But I also needed food.

In the kitchen, alone, at midnight, I pulled cheese and lunch meat from the refrigerator and sat down to eat. At the table I reloaded the gun.

The gaping back hole of my backyard pulled at my eyes once more. Why had I parked myself in front of the glass door? My nerves crawled with the thought that *he* was out there. Hadn't I turned the flood lights on a little while ago? Why had I turned them off? I was too tired to get up and turn them on again.

Through my chugging brain filtered the memory that I had an appointment in the morning at 8:30 with Dr. Carol Johannis. I'd have to call a cab. It would be oh, so tiring to get to her office and back, but I could hardly wait. I needed a listening ear.

Positive tests.

Vindication.

I ate the meat and cheese, my mind on half numb. Took a drink from my water glass, my fingers shaky and weak. It was difficult to even hold that much weight in my hand. Twice I nearly dropped the glass. As I set it down my gaze wandered past my reflection in the sliding door, the first few inches of the back deck barely visible.

That's when I saw the box.

Chapter 31

THE MIND CAN PLAY A CREATIVE LIST OF TRICKS EVEN WHEN it's well. Had it done that now, invaded as it was by sickness? I gaped at the box, trying to convince myself that my brain was conjuring it. But that thing had not been there when I stood peering out into the floodlit yard just twenty minutes ago.

Had it?

I struggled to my feet and leaned against the table, heart thumping. My arm hairs raised again as I felt my vulnerability, lit up in the room for Stalking Man to see. He *was* out there, wasn't he. Gloating at my startled reaction. Maybe he'd been following my movements through the house, through one back window to the next.

My bleary eyes focused on the box.

Jud Whatshisname. The detective. I should call him.

Right, Jannie, and wake the man up. And what would he find when he got over here—*if* he came at all? An empty box on the deck?

My feet took me to the door. The lock felt cold against my fingers, as if warning me not to open it. What if Stalking Man was right around the corner, waiting to jump me?

I flicked on the floodlights. The backyard shot into bright. I winced. Outside I saw the deck, its steps onto green grass, the bushes along the fence. The trees and gazebo and hot tub. All as before.

I unlocked the door and slid it back. Cool night air hit my face. With my cane I rocked the box. Something moved inside, sliding from one side to the other. Whatever it was it couldn't weigh more than a pound. More ticks?

It would have to be a very big bottle.

I leaned my cane against the wall and held onto the door jamb, slowly leaning down to reach the box. No way was I stepping outside to retrieve it. My hand brushed a top flap, not taped down. I grabbed it and pulled the box over the threshold.

Panting, I relocked the door. This time I left the floodlights on. Only then did I think to lower the beige fabric blinds compressed in a tight long rectangle along the top of the door. I couldn't remember the last time I'd used that shade.

I picked up the box and set it on the table. Held my breath and pushed back the flaps.

Inside lay a cheap-looking cell phone. I stared at it.

The thing rang.

"Ah!" I jerked back. A second ring. It went off a third time while I gaped at it. Should I pick it up?

Next thing I knew, I held the phone in my hand. My finger found the *talk* button.

"How are you feeling, Janessa?"

The voice—*his* voice—ran low and deep. *This isn't what he sounds like in normal life, is it?* If he had a normal life.

Emotions whirled within me. Anger, despair, indignation. The final one—abject fear—sank me into the nearest chair. "Are you in my backyard?"

"It's been too long since I visited your home."

Visited? "Why do you keep c-coming back? What do you want?"

"Your husband has left, I see. Gone to another woman." He made a sound low in his throat. "Of all things I hadn't foreseen that."

That made two of us.

I licked my lips. "You're following us." What was the man—invisible?

He chuckled, an evil sound. "I've seen the patrol cars drive by your place. And I can guess they've tapped your phone. After our talk you can throw out your new toy, by the way. And no point in tracing this call. It'll only lead to nobody."

I ran a hand across my forehead, no words forming. This man was beyond me. Too clever. Too vicious.

Silence strung out. Odd, my jumbled thoughts. I hated this man but didn't want to sever the tenuous line between us. He was my enemy, yet the only one who understood what was happening to my body. Not that he cared. But then, neither did my husband.

"You find my little gift in your daughter's backpack?"

The tick. My eyes roved the kitchen floor, as if it might appear at its mere mention.

"You s-stay away from my daughter!" I slumped forward, panic stealing through my lungs. "You don't need Lauren. You have *me.*"

"And what good are you doing me, Mrs. McNeil?" He spat the words. "Can you tell me one thing your husband is doing that shows he's willing to take a second look at his research findings? All I see is him moving *away* from you."

The names and faces of all the Lyme patients I'd read about online scrolled through my mind. Their struggles. How they fought to convince the medical world of their plight. This man didn't deserve to be counted among them. "You don't care about Lyme patients! You're just a terrorist."

The phone line seemed to chill. *"Don't* you tell me who I care about. Don't you *dare* tell me."

"Then why did you do this? Why would you wish it on anybody?"

"Not anybody. Just Doc Brock's wife."

"Why not *him?*" After all, wasn't Brock the real target? "Why me?"

I heard the slow hiss of expelled air. "I know what it's like to see a wife suffer."

My mouth opened, then closed. Something told me he hadn't planned on letting that clue about himself slip. A bit of humanity. A *reason.* "What happened?"

"What do *you* care?"

"I know what she's feeling."

"Felt."

"What?"

"She's dead." The words were thin and flat.

"From Lyme?"

No response, as if the stupid question wasn't worth an answer. My insides iced over. I thought of the listed names of victims on that web site, from small child to the elderly. I remembered the tirades against my husband, how again and again his research had blocked long term treatment. How would I feel about Dr. Brock McNeil if I'd lost a loved one to Lyme?

Empathy swelled in me, only to quickly scab over. This man fancied himself some White Knight for the Lyme awareness community? A self-righteous advocate who'd suffered so much he could do anything he pleased? Guess again. He didn't deserve to be any part of those people. He'd purposely made me sick. Now he was threatening Lauren. No one but a monster would wish the very disease that killed his wife on someone else, especially a child.

I dropped my head in the palm of one hand. How could I fight this man? His hatred went too deep, too cold. "I'm sorry."

"I don't want your sympathy. I want your action. You have forty-eight hours to talk some sense into your husband, got that, Janessa? Within forty-eight hours I want to see him issue a statement that he's rethinking his stance on chronic Lyme disease. That watching you suffer from it has opened his eyes."

Right. I didn't even have a positive diagnosis yet. "And if he doesn't?"

"I'll get to Lauren. Don't think I won't. And then I'll go down the list of the committee members. They all have wives and children of their own."

No. My body started to vibrate. Now I had not just Lauren to protect, but all the other families as well? I could barely walk. Half the time I couldn't think clearly. How was I supposed to save all these innocent people?

I swallowed hard. "L-listen to me. Brock won't . . . He's not . . ."

"What choice do you have, Mrs. McNeil?"

"But—"

"What choice?"

"None! But Brock isn't listening."

"You want your daughter to feel like you do right now?"

"No!"

"You want to be responsible for the other families?"

"I—"

"Then I suggest you *make* your husband listen."

"Call *him*. Please. He doesn't b-believe you even exist."

"Where does he think that tick in your daughter's backpack came from? You?"

"I . . . I lost it."

"What?"

"The tick."

A beat of silence. "You *lost* it?"

"It's somewhere in my kitchen."

"Somewhere in your—" He snorted. "So find it."

"I can't." My tone hardened. "If you'll remember you made me so sick I can hardly move."

Air seeped over the line. "How. *Stupid.* Are you?"

My fingers curled. If only I had his neck to wrap them around. "Pretty stupid. But then—you did that to me too."

"Do you know how many illnesses that tick is carrying?"

Let me guess—Lyme and three coinfections. This man was utterly mad. "So send me another one. The m-mail will do just fine. Better yet, send it straight to the L-Lyme lab. I'm sure they'll concede it carries the diseases."

"Janessa—"

"You don't need me at all!" Tears scratched my eyes. "Why bother with stupid me?"

A moment passed. I could feel his seething.

"Are you quite through?"

No. Yes. My veins ran so steaming I could barely speak. "Why?" The whisper hissed out of me. "Why are doing this? Who *are* you?"

He laughed, a grating sound. "Perhaps it hasn't occurred to you, Mrs. McNeil, that I enjoy seeing you suffer."

As his wife had suffered? And merely because I was married to Brock McNeil? "So you're nothing but a sadist. And here I thought you wanted to help p-people suffering from Lyme."

"I *am* helping them!" Anger seemed to erase his calm. Now every word shook, as if I'd plucked at the core of him. "It's what my wife wanted. One day they'll thank me. Every one of them."

"She wanted you to help—or hurt?"

Something smacked on his end of the line, like a fist against wood. "I *am* helping! I *am*! I'm keeping my promise to her!"

"Was she a g-good woman?"

"The best." His voice caught. The sound chilled me. He seemed like a bomb ready to blow, but my own anger ran too deep to stop now.

"Then why should she be p-proud of you? Harming another wife. Threatening a child. She'd never approve."

"Shut up!"

"If she were still alive, she'd *divorce* you."

"Shut—"

"She hates you from the grave."

"Shut *up!*" I heard a crash. Hard breaths spat over the line. "Don't you *ever* say anything like that again. Ever!"

What was I thinking, goading this unstable man into a rage?

We sat there, I in my sane world and he in his insanity, his panting like slaps in my ears.

I swallowed, my throat beyond dry. "I know you're helping." I forced my tone to remain comforting, even as my heart galloped. "And I want to do what you say. I want to c-convince Brock to change his mind. But no matter what I do, he won't listen."

"Even when his daughter's health is on the line?"

"He doesn't *believe* me."

"You keep getting strange calls."

My teeth gritted. "He doesn't b-believe that either."

"And you're obviously sick. In front of his very eyes."

"He doesn't *care!*" The words burst from me, then throbbed in the air of my empty, abandoned house. So much for keeping calm. There it was—the mean, ugly truth I hadn't wanted to admit even to myself.

Brock didn't care.

Not today. Not tomorrow. He didn't love me anymore. He wasn't coming back. He *didn't care.*

I heard the slow intake of breath, as if Stalking Man had looked into the very face of evil. "Then he truly is a beast, isn't he?"

A sob snagged in my throat. "Please. Just don't—"

"Forty-eight hours."

"But how do I—"

"I won't contact you again."

"No, wait. Don't hang up!"

The line deadened.

"Hello? Hello!"

Nothing.

"Hello!"

I lowered the phone to the table and started to cry. Tears fell into my plate until I pushed it away, the very smell of lunch meat now disgusting. I hunched there, small, sick and beaten, and crossed my arms over my chest, hugging myself when no one else would.

Forty-eight hours.

I could phone Brock right now and tell him about this new call. But I knew he would just declare me an even bigger liar. He'd rant at me for continuing in my madness. And Jud Maxwell was off duty by now. Besides, what proof would I have to offer the detective that I hadn't bought the cell myself and called it from yet another throw-away phone? If he could trace the call, it would surely show that it had originated from this area. Just like before.

"God, please . . ." I could whisper no more. Not the smallest of prayers. Could only hope those two words were all God needed to hear. My mind scrambled for the psalms I'd read, but I only remembered one phrase.

My foot has slipped.

I sat at the table, rocking, rocking. Hopelessness welled in my lungs until I thought I would drown. This man was beyond crazy. To spend so much time—and resources—planning such crimes.

What was I supposed to do?

A long time passed, until the tears finally dried up. By that time I barely clung to the chair. I stared at the wall, my chest fiery with pain. Minutes ticked by as I made no move. Little by little the anguish seeped away. In its place trickled a new awareness, something too big, too out there to even consider in my demolished state—yet there it was.

No one was going to help me protect Lauren or anyone else. No one. I had no physical strength and a fraction of my mental power. But somehow, some way, no matter what it cost me—I would have to stop this madman.

TUESDAY

Chapter 32

IN THE MORNING I AWOKE ON THE COUCH WITH NO MEMORY of having gotten there. The clock read 6:00. My body felt no better for having slept. In fact it fought me to merely sit up, as if my limbs were weighted with lead, my chest with steel. My hand trembled so much as I reached for my cane that I wasn't sure I'd be able to hold it.

A phone lay on the coffee table. I frowned at it. The den receiver sat in its stand on the side table. So this second one was from . . . ? Maybe upstairs?

Yes. Lauren had brought it down last night.

I stuck the phone in my robe pocket and made my way to the bathroom. After that I stood at the bottom of the stairs, looking up. I had to shower. Had to make myself at least half presentable for my doctor's appointment. But I may as well have been looking at Mount Olympus.

In my head I heard Stalking Man's voice.

"Don't you ever say that again. Ever!"

What about that cell phone I found last night? Was it still on the kitchen table?

I needed to call Jud. Tell him I'd heard from Stalking Man again. Although—what good would that do? Another call that lead nowhere. Another phone yielding no prints.

I placed my right foot on the first stair. Held on to the banister as tightly as my painful fingers could—and pulled myself up. I stood there panting, feeling dizzy. If I fell my legs would not get me up. Breathing a prayer, I attacked the next step. And the next. Good thing I'd woken up as early as I did. It must have taken me fifteen minutes to reach the top. By then sweat ran down my face, and groans rode on my every breath.

But I'd done it.

I clumped my way into the master bathroom, grateful as never before that we had a separate walk-in shower. Stepping over the edge of a tub would have been a nightmare.

No, Jannie, not we *have a separate shower.* You. *Brock doesn't live here anymore.*

At the bed I stopped to pull the receiver from my pocket and place it in its stand. Then I noticed the red light on the burglar alarm pad. It took a minute to remember the code to turn the alarm off. The light switched to green.

By the time I came out of the shower, got dressed, and dried my hair, I felt as if I'd run a marathon—through chest-deep mud. It was 7:00. I had to get downstairs, eat something. Call a cab.

Once again, going down the stairs was harder than coming up. How much a normal body works, without a person giving it a thought. The tensile elasticity of ankles and feet to keep you stable, to turn corners. The strength of your legs to lower you down a step. As I struggled to reach the lower floor, at least my mind had something immediate to consume it. When I finally hit the hall, all my fears flooded back. Stalking Man. Lauren. Forty-eight hours.

No. I'd been given forty-eight hours at midnight. Last night. That was seven hours ago. Now I had . . . how many left?

Panic seized me. Lauren would be at school within the hour. Had Jud called the principal yet? Would they watch her with extra care? For all I knew Stalking Man would renege on his two-day warning and go after her now.

I reached the kitchen and pulled sliced ham and cheese from the refrigerator. Poured myself a glass of milk—which I typically never drank. Protein. On the table sat the cell phone. I'd placed it back in the box. Also on the table were my sunglasses. And Brock's gun. I frowned at the weapon. When had I put it there? The long shade was still lowered, covering the sliding glass door. Just as well. Less light to stab my eyes.

But through the fabric the backyard looked so bright.

I shuffled to the sliding door and edged back the shade. The floodlights were on. Must have been on all night. I turned and flicked them off.

My feet burned and prickled as if I'd stuck them in fire. I collapsed into a kitchen chair to eat. Five minutes later I was done and needed to get up again. I had to . . . do something.

What?

My eyes half closed as I focused on the table. I felt the gears in my brain go around and around, finding no connection. The Internet on dial-up—stuck. The world seemed to fall away, leaving me suspended . . .

Something clicked inside my head. I brought up my chin. *Telephone.* I had to call for a cab. And talk to Jud Maxwell.

His business card was . . . where?

I pushed to my feet, grimacing at the pain on my soles. In a half daze I found the phone book, only to forget why I'd pulled it out. When I finally remembered, I couldn't think what letter *cab* started with. Or should I look under that other word. Which was . . .

Something. *T?*

Taxi.

By the time I managed to call a cab it was 7:45. I told the company to send the driver up to my door. That I might need help getting out to the car.

My mind went blank again. Was there something else I'd meant to do?

Put the gun away.

I picked it off the table and stuck it in a cabinet on top of the plates.

That done, I shuffled to the front bathroom to brush my teeth. As soon as I finished, the telephone sounded. Five rings shrilled the air before I reached the receiver near the den sofa. It was Maria.

"Jannie, how are you?"

"Okay."

"Any better?"

"No. I'm g-going to the doctor now."

"You still taking a cab?"

"Yeah."

"Oh, Jannie, I should be taking you."

"You can't."

"I know, but still."

The doorbell rang. I swayed on my feet. "Taxi's here. Have to go."

"Okay. I want to hear what happens."

Yeah. Me too.

I replaced the phone, anxiety spritzing through me. Where was my purse? I hadn't seen it in days.

It seemed like an hour passed before I reached the door. I opened it—and sunlight skewered my eyes. I gasped and stumbled back.

"Whoa!" A rotund cabbie jumped over the threshold and caught me. "You okay, ma'am?" He smelled of cigarettes, his face lined and brown.

My head nodded. "I . . ." My hand circled in the air. "I need . . ."

"You need to be staying home, is what you need." He held me firmly by the elbow. The pain from his fingers pooled air in my throat.

"No. I'm going to . . . doctor."

"I'm taking you to the doctor?"

"Yes."

Empathy creased his features. "You got no family to take you?"

I only looked at him. Any moment I was going to fall over. Why had I thought I could do this? A shaky breath heaved from my lungs.

His face softened more. "Hey, it's okay. We'll get you there. Maybe you should go to the emergency room instead."

"No. Doctor."

He shrugged. "Okay, if you say so." The cabbie looked me over. "You got everything you need?"

I shook my head. "P . . . P . . ."

"Purse?"

"Yes."

"Where is it?"

I stared at him. My face must have looked like a blank slate. He shook his head—*oh, boy*—then glanced around. "Can you give me a clue?"

My body swayed. "I have to sit down."

He sighed. This was hardly the way for him to make money.

"I'll p—pay you. For your time."

"No worries. Come on." He led me into the den, where I fell into the armchair. "Now, where's your purse?"

When had I last seen it? Did I have it in the hospital? Did Brock bring it out of his car? Maybe he'd put it in my Lexus. That's where I usually kept it.

I pointed back toward the kitchen. "Garage. Car."

"You think it's in your car? Okay." He hurried out of the room. I heard the door to the garage open and close behind me. My eyes drooped shut. How crazy this was. A complete stranger—a man—in my home. Searching for my purse. And me, helpless. This is what

I had been brought to. This is what Stalking Man—and Brock—had done to me.

The cabbie returned, carrying my purse. "Found it." He smiled for the first time. "Ready now?"

"On the kitchen table. Sunglasses."

"Okay." He strode out again and returned seconds later, sunglasses in hand. He held them out to me, and I gratefully put them on.

"Ready to rock and roll?" He held his hand out to help me up.

I waved it away. "Need to do it myself. Hurts when you touch me."

He scratched his forehead and stood back to watch my struggles. "What is this you got, anyway?"

"Lyme."

"*This* is Lyme?" He gave a low whistle. "Man."

Chapter 33

BY THE TIME WE GOT TO THE TAXI I WAS SHAKING. I TOLD THE cab driver the address of Dr. Johannis's office, amazed that I remembered it. My fingers fumbled inside my purse, seeking my wallet. What if I had no cash? When I saw I had over $100 in bills, I nearly cried. I paid him a large tip. "Can you come back? Take me home?"

"When?"

"Don't know. I'll call."

He handed me a card for his company. "Ask for Tony B. If I'm available, I'll come."

"Thank you. Very much."

"You need help getting in the building?"

I regarded the short distance. He'd pulled up in the parking lot right near a side door. "I'll be okay." Gathering what energy remained in my body, I hoisted myself from the car.

Fortunately Dr. Johannis's office was on the first floor and near that side door. I checked in with her receptionist, who told me the doctor was running about fifteen minutes late. Wonderful. She handed me a clipboard with papers to fill out. I collapsed into a waiting room

chair and leaned my head against the wall. I had no energy to fill out
the papers but knew I must. First items on the papers: name, address,
nearest of kin. *Oh, no.* I stared at the last one, castigating myself. I
should have thought of this. No way could I put Brock's name on that
line.

I left it blank.

Next—symptoms. An unending list of them, with boxes for
me to check. Sore throat and fevers. No. Sore/burning soles. Yes!
How did they know that? Joint pain—fingers, toes, ankles, wrists,
knees, elbows, hips, shoulders. Yes, yes, yes to all. Joint swelling.
I held out a hand, peered at my knuckles. They *were* bigger. Stiffness,
muscle pain, muscle weakness. Confusion, difficulty thinking. Yes!
Forgetting words, poor attention span. Had they spied on me to
write this list? Disorientation, anxiety, tremors, light sensitivity. Odd
muscle twitching. Yes—that strange wriggling beneath my skin. I'd
been feeling that again this morning. Vertigo, lightheadedness, air
hunger.

Air hunger. Those awful spells I'd had! What a perfect way to
describe them.

Chest wall pain, extreme fatigue, sleeping with no refreshment.
Yes, yes, yes.

The symptoms continued. Some I didn't have. But to have checked
so many. Just the sight of all the marked boxes left me woozy. When
did these symptoms start? the form asked. I stared at the brown
carpet, trying to count back the days. My mind wouldn't work. Every
time I began counting backwards the days would fall out of my head.
Finally I gave up. I'd need to look at a calendar.

Were you bitten by a tick? Yes. When? I left it blank.

When I finished I lay the clipboard in my lap, too tired to rise and
give it to the receptionist.

Time blurred. I think I fell asleep. The next thing I knew a nurse
was touching my shoulder. "Mrs. McNeil? The doctor's ready to see

you now. Here, I'll take that." She held out her hand for the clipboard. "You need help getting up?"

"No. Thanks."

In slow procession she led me down a hallway and into an examining room. I eyed the paper-sheeted gurney and knew I wouldn't be able to balance upon it. "Sit here." The nurse motioned to a chair with arms.

I sat like a rag doll as she went through the typical nurse routine of blood pressure and temperature readings. "Okay, sit tight and the doctor will be right with you." The nurse left, closing the door behind her.

Sit tight. What else could I do? Now that the moment had come to see a bona fide Lyme-literate doctor, part of me wanted to flee the building. What if *she* said I didn't have Lyme? Any diagnosis would be better than not knowing. But I'd gone through so many tests for everything else. What was left?

A knock sounded on the door, jilting my nerves. It opened, and in walked a woman in her fifties, trim, with bobbed brown hair and large eyes. She couldn't have stood over five feet five, but an air of assurance and strength entered the room with her. No white coat. Just slacks and a blouse. She carried the clipboard with my telltale papers. "Hello." She gave me a sunny smile. "I'm Dr. Johannis."

I managed a weak smile in return. "Hi."

She surveyed me. "Boy, my nurse is right. You look really sick. I'm glad we were able to get you in so quickly."

A lump welled in my throat. Just to have a doctor admit I *looked* unhealthy. "Yeah."

"I understand you think you have Lyme." She sat in a chair opposite mine and plucked a pen from a pocket in her blouse. "I've looked through your symptom list here. You've certainly checked a lot of them."

I nodded.

"When did they start?"

"I don't . . . I need a calendar."

"Here you go." She pointed to a large one on the wall. I hadn't even noticed it. "You're not the first patient who's needed it. You need to look back a few months?"

"No, just . . ." My gaze faltered around on the calendar until I found today's date—Tuesday. That day I'd started to feel much worse—when I'd fallen in the kitchen—had to be weeks ago. It seemed like another lifetime. But I'd only been home a couple days from the hospital. And only been there a few days. I counted backwards, and my mouth fell open. It couldn't be. That had been just last Thursday. *Five days ago.*

Just six days ago I'd thought I had the flu? I'd had my hope to get better soon, a husband, a daughter. I couldn't grasp that. Surely I'd been through a time warp.

"Thursday I got worse. Last Thursday. I'd been s-sick for about three weeks before that. I just thought it was the . . . flu. Until Thursday."

"Okay." She jotted a note. "Your form says you were bitten by a tick. How long ago was that?"

"I don't know."

"You have any idea? One month? Two, three?"

I held her eyes, feeling the thump of my heart. Maybe I shouldn't have come. How could I go through this exam without telling her everything? I didn't know when I'd been bitten. Stalking Man said the ticks carried Lyme and three coinfections. Shouldn't I tell her that? But how could I?

My head shook.

Dr. Johannis made another note. "All right. Tell me what happened last Thursday."

In halting words I told her. My weakness and fatigue that day. Falling in the kitchen. My stay at the hospital. The slew of tests—all negative. Including the one for Lyme.

When I was done, Dr. Johannis shook her head. "You poor thing. Amazing they were able to run all those tests so quickly."

Not if you're Brock McNeil's wife. I shrugged.

She set down the clipboard. "Okay, let's take a look at you."

The doctor allowed me to stay in the chair as she gently examined my hands, wrists, and ankles. She poked around in my chest, stopping when I gasped. "That really hurts, huh?"

Oh, yeah.

She handed me my cane. "Can you stand up for me? I want to check your balance."

I fought to my feet, leaning on the cane. She motioned to it. "Can you stand without it?"

"I'm afraid I'll tip over."

She had me close my eyes—which caused me to sway, even with the cane. She watched me walk a few steps, then stopped the examination. Dr. Johannis shook her head. "I often do much more to check for balance and ability to move." Her voice lightened. "But obviously you're rather lacking in that department." She smiled again. "Come on next door into my office, and we'll talk." She pointed left. "There's a much more comfortable chair in there for you. You need help getting there, or is it too painful?"

Gratitude seeped through me. She understood that it hurt to be touched. She *knew.* "I'll do it, thanks."

Her lips pushed together. "Follow me in, then. Take your time." She strode out.

Heart fluttering, I pushed to my unsteady feet.

Chapter 34

I HOBBLED THROUGH THE DOOR OF DR. JOHANNIS'S EXAMINING
room and around the corner into a surprisingly pretty office. Tex-
tured blue walls, a shiny oak desk. A large, healthy fern in one corner.
Dr. Johannis took the chair behind her desk and motioned to one on
my side. "Please."

With little grace I lowered myself into the seat. Hooked my cane
over its arm.

Dr. Johannis pushed my papers aside and leaned forward, hands
clasped. "Well, I certainly suspect you have Lyme. You present many
common symptoms."

Lyme. The dreaded disease I'd read online. All those patients—
sick for years. But just to hear a doctor say it. Not deny it.

"We'll test you for it, of course. After we're done here you can see
my lab technician. He'll take your blood and send it out for testing."

"To that Lyme lab? Not the CDC . . . thing." All I needed was
another negative result.

"Yes, to the Lyme lab. I don't find the CDC test nearly as reliable.
They too often result in a false negative—perhaps what happened to

you. Still, the Lyme lab tests aren't perfect either. *Borrelia*—the bacteria that cause Lyme—are very formidable creatures. They can change their outer coat to make themselves invisible to the body's immune system— and therefore to the tests. So a negative result on any test doesn't mean you don't have Lyme. In the end Lyme is a clinical diagnosis."

"Those doctors didn't think so. When the Lyme test said n-negative, they pushed it aside." As did Brock. Never had I heard him say Lyme is a clinical diagnosis—that symptoms outweighed test results.

"Yeah, well. That's the way it goes."

Clearly Dr. Johannis didn't want to talk against her colleagues.

I took a deep breath. My body felt *so* tired. But at the moment my brain was half working, and if I was prepared to go head-to-head against Stalking Man, I had much to learn. "The CDC Western blot tests sometimes are false negative because of the bands of antibodies they don't include, right? I read about it."

She nodded. "You'll see two results on your tests from the Lyme lab. One will be their results, the other will be what the CDC would say. Often with a positive from the lab, the CDC result reads negative. You'll be able to see the individual bands that are positive. One of the biggest problems is that numerous bands specific only to Lyme aren't included in CDC Western blot results. For example: band number thirty-one—which refers to an antibody for a protein on *Borrelia's* outer surface called OspA. This protein is so Lyme-specific it was used to make the Lyme vaccine back in the nineties. Yet the CDC doesn't include its antibody in determining test results."

Vaguely I remembered reading that detail. "Why?"

Dr. Johannis lifted a hand. "There are lots of unanswered *whys* in the Lyme world, I'm afraid."

I was beginning to see that.

"At any rate, I'll also order tests for coinfections. Many times Lyme isn't the only disease the tick was carrying. You may also have

Erlichiosis, Babesiosis, and other coinfections. The problem is, each one needs to be treated differently. For example, Babesiosis isn't a bacteria, it's a parasite in the malaria family. Therefore it won't be killed off by antibiotic treatments for Lyme. Overall, if you treat for Lyme alone and ignore coinfections, you won't get better. So we have to look at the total package."

Relief washed through me. She'd test for everything. I wouldn't have to push her to do that.

Dr. Johannis leaned back in her chair. "Anything else you want to ask before we draw your blood?"

"Treatment is around four w-weeks of antibiotics if you catch L-Lyme early enough, right? Are we catching it early enough for me?"

"Well, you look pretty sick. Your tests will show results in two different categories. Results labeled IgM show a positive or negative for Lyme introduced into the body in the last six months. The IgG category refers to six months or more. You could have a positive IgM and a negative IgG, meaning you've contracted in approximately the last six months. If so, you're not yet into the full chronic stage of Lyme. That stage is much harder to treat and takes far longer.

"However there are other factors that can make one patient's case harder to treat than another's. One, as I mentioned is coinfection. A second is the germ load in your body. Just how heavily infected are you? Another is simply each person's unique response to Lyme— where the spirochetes go in that particular body, the strength of the immune system, and other factors. You look to me like you could have had Lyme for over six months. On the other hand, not necessarily. You may just be a person it happens to hit very hard. Clearly once you started having symptoms they progressed quickly."

My eyes blinked a few times, my brain trying to process all she'd said. "Those patients that aren't diagnosed for years? They get r-really sick."

Dr. Johannis nodded. "Unfortunately, yes. They can get far more sick than you are. Those cases take a long time to treat. And some of those patients will get better, then relapse." She lifted a hand. "It's not easy science, treating Lyme. It's experience over the years, seeing what works, what doesn't. There's still so much we don't know about the disease."

Except for Brock. He seemed to know everything. Sitting there in Dr. Johannis's office, I could grasp more than ever the difference between her and my husband. He in his laboratory and classroom, she facing very ill patients who begged her to help them get well.

I wasn't being fair, keeping things from her like this. I was trusting her to tell me the truth. She was trusting me as her patient to do the same.

"Mrs. McNeil?" Dr. Johannis gave me a little smile. "Looked like you went off there for a minute. Something else on your mind?"

My veins heated. Why had she asked that?

Mentally I scrambled for some question to cover myself. A blurry memory surfaced—something Stalking Man had said about Brock's research. "I heard something about Lyme needing a . . . narrow definition in order for v-vaccines to sell. What does that mean?"

Dr. Johannis pulled in her mouth. "That could be another long discussion. I'll try for a short answer. We were just talking about how Lyme affects people differently—when it hits, how it hits. And also that it's a disease requiring a clinical diagnosis, since the tests don't always work. That makes Lyme a very nebulous sort of illness. Before you can create a vaccine you must do many things. One is to determine what part of the bacteria is infectious. I won't go into all of that right now. Another, as you say is to define the illness it's supposed to protect against. A more narrow definition, say one that calls for a specific set of symptoms, makes things easier." The doctor tilted her head. "That's a layman's answer and barely scratches the surface. But does that make sense?"

I focused on the desk, trying to process her words. "So . . . if someone is working on a v-vaccine, it would be better for that person to narrowly define Lyme."

"Well, the challenges in creating a vaccine are very convoluted. But looking back, some have wondered if the increasingly restrictive definition of Lyme was partly brought about by the development of the vaccine that was eventually taken off the market in 2002."

Restrictive definition . . .

Was Brock's research basically motivated by money, as Stalking Man suggested? The thought sickened me. For years I'd thought of Brock as caring for others. Had I been wrong all along about *that*, too? My eyes closed. What *else* about Brock didn't I know?

"Jannie, what is it? You look troubled."

"No, it's . . . I just . . ." I looked Dr. Johannis straight on. And then, just like that, the words leapt from my tongue. "I'm not who you think I am." My eyes widened. *Why* had I said that?

Confusion flicked across Dr. Johannis's face. "Your name's not Janessa McNeil?"

My body weighted to the chair. How to get out of this? "No. I mean, yes. I am. But . . ."

I should leave right now. Find another doctor. What I could not do was tell this woman my story—and watch her disbelieve me. I could take no more accusations. No more sneers.

The doctor's pen lowered. She placed it on her desk and leaned forward. "Mrs. McNeil?"

My throat heaved in a swallow. "I'm Brock McNeil's wife."

The news rippled across her features. She sat up straighter, her mouth pulling in. The doctor stared at her desk, as if wondering which question to ask first. She spread her hands. "Is this a set-up?"

"No. I'm really sick. Wish I wasn't."

She nodded slowly. "I can see that. Does your husband know you're here?"

I pictured Brock's scoffing at the mere mention of her name. "Yes."

"But he doesn't approve."

"No. He thinks I'm faking."

"Why would you be faking?"

My eyes burned. I wiped a weak hand across my forehead. "You have to believe me. I just w-want someone to *believe* me."

"I do believe you. I'm listening."

Maybe it was the compassion on her face, maybe it was just that I felt so exhausted and alone. Maybe at that point I simply didn't know how to back out. For whatever reason—I told her. Everything. Once I got started, I couldn't stop. The phone calls, all I remembered that Stalking Man had told me. Brock's affair, and his leaving. The vial with the tick inside. The detective's request—almost a pleading—for evidence he could use. I tripped over words, sometimes forgot them altogether. Dr. Johannis didn't rush me. She just let me talk until my brain shuttered and my tongue lay thick in my mouth.

Finally I sat back, a worn and begging supplicant.

Dr. Johannis's gaze drifted across the office. Her eyebrows rose, and I saw a slight shake of her head, as if she couldn't fathom my tale. Moments passed. For the first time I heard the ticking of a clock on her wall.

She drew a breath and looked at me, empathy softening her mouth. "First of all, I believe you."

My eyes welled. I felt stupid for crying. Seemed I'd cried more in the last few days than the past decade. But I was too tired to fight the tears. "Thank you."

Dr. Johannis laced her hands together. "I hardly know where to begin." She tapped a finger against her desk. "I find myself trying to think like this man who's been calling you. Just to try to understand him. I suppose, in his perverted logic, he *is* helping the Lyme community. And I can see where he'd get the idea." She rubbed her temple. "You hear about the legislation regarding Lyme that passed in Connecticut in 2009?"

I shook my head.

"It was a bill—passed unanimously—that allows doctors in that state to treat Lyme long term without repercussions from the medical board. California also has a law that allows doctors to treat Lyme as they see fit. But Connecticut"— she shook her head—"that's the ground zero state for Lyme. Amazing how long it took for *that* state to come around. Anyway, it happened because two state representatives came face-to-face with Lyme through illnesses of their family members. One representative's mom got it, and the other's husband fought a life-threatening case. Seeing loved ones go through such a difficult disease—that tends to diffuse the notion that it's 'hard to get and easy to cure.'" She raised her hands. "So I can see where this guy would expect your husband to come around in the same way."

A shiver ran down my back. Stalking Man was insane but smart. Bad combination.

"And the fact that he contacted you this month. Did you know May is Lyme Awareness Month?"

"No."

"It is. Every year the Lyme community gets more media in May. You'll hear public service announcements about the disease, that sort of thing. There are rallies, people speaking out."

I raised my chin in a nod. What little energy I had was trickling away.

Dr. Johannis seemed to pick up on that fact. "Okay, so let's get down to what to do next. I didn't hear you say you called the detective after that last phone call."

Had I? My gaze roved back to the fern. I'd meant to. But I couldn't remember . . .

"No. Don't think I did."

"Well, that's critical. You should do it. Matter of fact, I should call the detective for you right now."

"But—"

"Let me back up a minute. The Lyme lab can take a week or even longer to get blood test results back to me. And they don't hurry for anybody. But your case is different—you've got police involved and an alleged crime. If we have a detective hand-carry your blood to the lab and ask for a rush, they'll listen."

"But I don't want them to know who I am. I mean—that I'm Brock's wife."

Dr. Johannis shook her head. "McNeil's a fairly common name. That in itself isn't going to give you away. And I'm certainly not going to tell them. Now, how did you get here? Surely you didn't drive."

The doctor was storming ahead, her alert brain thinking of details far faster than mine could. "A cab."

"Ah, so no one's waiting to take you back. I'll call the detective. See if he can take your blood to the lab and then take you home. Do you have his number with you?"

My mind blanked. How had I ever called it in the first place? The answer surfaced. His card. I had left it . . . somewhere in the house. "No. But his name's Jud Maxwell. With the Palo Alto department."

She reached for her phone. "I'll find it." She called information and picked up her pen to write down the number, then dialed it. "Jud Maxwell, please." In a moment I could hear his voice filter from the receiver. "This is Doctor Carol Johannis in Palo Alto. I'm here with Janessa McNeil, a new patient. She's told me what's going on. First I want to tell you that her symptoms strongly indicate that she has Lyme. We're about to do blood tests on her to be sure."

I sat back in my chair, her voice fading. As if I watched her on screen with the sound turned low, I heard her talk to the detective, telling him about Stalking Man's latest phone call.

His wife died from Lyme. Suddenly it hit me how important that fact was. It was our first real clue.

Dr. Johannis listened as the detective replied. I couldn't tell what he was saying. Suddenly my body felt even more limp. I slumped over, craving the ability to lie down. The doctor pulled the receiver from her ear. "You all right?"

"Yeah. I . . . just so . . ."

She firmed her mouth and nodded. "I'll get him over here." She raised the phone. "Detective, Mrs. McNeil's about had it. How about if you . . ."

Her words faded amid a ringing in my ears. My eyelids would not stay up. Somebody had opened trap doors in both my feet, draining out all my energy.

Dr. Johannis hung up the phone and stood, crackling with purpose. I fixed her with a dull stare. Had I ever been that energetic? That able to *think*?

"All right, Mrs. McNeil, let's get you to the tech to draw your blood."

"J . . ." I wanted to tell her to use my first name. What was it? "Jannie."

"Okay. Jannie." She came around and stood by my chair. "I'm going to have to help you up, or you won't make it."

"Uh-huh."

The world glazed over as people came and went and fussed about me. A lab tech drew multiple vials of blood. Jud Maxwell arrived. I rallied enough to pester him with questions. Had he talked to the school? Did the principal and teachers know to watch Lauren closely? Yes, he told me. He'd been there. Gave the school just enough information to let them know Lauren may be in danger. They were watching. They promised to be diligent.

"You sure? You really went there?" I wanted to go myself, make sure Lauren was all right. Grief welled up in me. This was too much, losing Brock and now my only child. I needed them. I needed to take care of them.

"Yes, Mrs. McNeil. They are being extra careful with her."

"Okay. Thanks so much." But I couldn't rest. Stalking Man was out there. He'd already broken into my home, eluded the police department's drive-bys enough to return and leave a box on my porch.

When I was all done and the doctor paid—straight out of my pocket, since she didn't take insurance—Jud prepared to help me out to his car.

"Insist to the lab you need the results today," Dr. Johannis said. "That way hopefully you'll get them by the end of the afternoon."

"All right. Can you help me find patients across the country who've died from Lyme?"

"I'll try. Jannie mentioned she found a list online, but that doesn't mean it's complete."

Could Stalking Man's wife be in that list? Maybe I'd even read her story.

Jud considered the doctor. "What are your thoughts on who this could be?"

She shook her head. "You've got a wide range of suspects, I'm afraid. Anyone who's been sick with Lyme or had a loved one sick knows about the Lyme controversy in the medical community—and would know Dr. McNeil's stand on the subject. The Lyme community is highly networked and astute about the disease. They *have* to be, because they must be actively involved in their own treatment. Of course the big narrowing factor is that his wife died from the disease. *If* he's telling the truth. But bottom line, your suspect could have come from anywhere."

Jud nodded. "Yeah, looks that way. Makes my job all the harder."

During the ride to the lab I leaned back in my seat, too overwhelmed to talk. At the lab I waited in the car while the detective carried my blood inside. Dr. Johannis had said she would call ahead to alert the techs he was coming. Jud returned after about fifteen minutes.

"Sorry that took so long."

"What happened?"

"They're going to get on the tests right away. Your doctor should get a call at the end of the day."

Today. Maybe, finally, I would have a diagnosis. Never before had I understood how powerful that word is for those who are sick.

Jud started the car—and took me home.

The detective helped me inside the house and got me to the couch. I fell upon it and melted into the cushions. I didn't bother to take off my sunglasses. Jud brought me a drink of water, then returned to his car for some items. I knew he would bag the cell phone as evidence. He returned with, among other things, a flashlight. I frowned at it.

"I'm going to find that tick."

"Oh." Thank God. "Wait. Gun. In a cabinet. It's loaded." Amazing that I'd remembered that.

Jud gave me a little smile. "I'll be looking closer to the floor."

He went to work in the kitchen . . . and my body was snatched up and swept away, clutched in the talons of sleep.

Chapter 35

"MRS. MCNEIL? MRS. MCNEIL."

My name drifted to me from some distant source. I swam in a dark river, going in circles. The water rose and tossed me out on a bank.

"Janessa."

My eyes opened. I lay on the couch. The blurry figure of Jud Maxwell stood over me. "Hmm?"

"Sorry to wake you."

I blinked, becoming aware that I still wore my sunglasses. "S'okay. What time is it?"

"Just before noon."

Noon. What time was that? My mind chugged. I should know what the word meant, but I just couldn't . . .

Clear thought lit up my brain. Noon. Twelve in the daytime. Stalking Man had given me forty-eight hours last night at midnight.

I had . . . thirty-six hours left. To do . . . something.

"I've got the cell phone bagged," Jud said. "I'll take it back for prints. And we'll try to run a search on that phone call you received."

I shifted, then pulled myself to sit up. Nudged my legs to the floor. Only then did memory of why he was here surge in my head. "Did you find the tick?"

He pulled his top lip between his teeth. "No."

"*No?*"

He sighed. "I looked everywhere. Used the flashlight. Got down on the floor and checked under the cabinet overhangs, under the table."

No. This couldn't be. "Maybe it crawled in here."

"I checked here too—up to a point. It would take a team of people to do a thorough search of your house. A tick's pretty small."

"Why would you need to search the whole house?"

"Maybe we wouldn't. Obviously we'd start from the kitchen and fan out. It couldn't have crawled too far, I don't think. But it may have hitched a ride on clothing and fallen off somewhere else. Maybe even upstairs."

His unspoken words rang loud and clear. No way would he be allowed to get a team out here to search. "So. We back to square one? No evidence."

He backed up to the armchair and sat down. Leaned forward to clasp his hands between his knees. "As I've told you, it's not that I haven't believed you. But I just need some tangible evidence that leads me somewhere."

And self-righteous Stalking Man had wanted to provide it. He'd expected me to find that tick. "You heard a doctor say I'm sick."

"I never doubted that."

"Looks like it's Lyme."

"And we'll have the test results soon. If they're positive, that'll be a tangible piece of evidence."

We stared at each other.

"So what do we do now?" Fear curled up my spine. "I have thirty-six hours. Then he g-goes after Lauren."

"We won't let that happen."

"How do you plan on stopping it?"

"For one, I'll talk to your husband. Make sure he understands what's at stake. Two, I'll fight with all I've got to put an officer at the address where Brock is staying."

"He won't listen. You don't understand Brock; he's too deep in . . . denial now. Brock never admits he's w-wrong. Besides, this man is too clever." My voice was rising. "He'll see your posted m-man. He won't go into that . . . wherever they're staying. He'll wait till Lauren's at school. And I can't be with her there. I can't p-protect her!"

"We will, Mrs. McNeil. I promise you, we won't let anything happen to your daughter."

I fixed him with a glare. "What if you get no more evidence than before? What if n-nothing on that cell phone is traceable? As for my illness—I could have purposely infected myself, all to try to keep my husband. So you tell me. What are your . . . superiors really going to say about putting m-manpower on watching the place where Lauren is staying? Or her school?

He spread his hands. "I—"

"You can't promise me, can you."

"I will not let anything happen to your daughter. Even if I have to watch her myself, off duty."

"You're *on* duty while she's at school!"

"Mrs. McNeil, I'm going to talk to your husband. I *will* convince him that Lauren is in danger. Even if he doesn't want to admit he's been wrong about you, surely he'll take precautions for his daughter."

Maybe. Maybe not. Maybe he'd dig his heels in, all the more outraged that I'd taken things this far. Who could predict what he would do? I didn't know the man anymore.

Jud cleared his throat. "Also, we can't rule out this cell phone yet." He pointed to the bagged evidence. "We'll see where it leads."

"Nowhere. You know that. It's why he took the chance of coming here to bring me a n-new one. He knows this home phone and my . . . regular cell were tapped. He's been ahead of you all along." My words may have been halting, but there was no mistaking the barb in my tone.

Jud Maxwell stood. "I hope to change that."

"Hope's not enough." My insides writhed. *When* was this going to come to an end?

The detective put his hands on his hips. "I'm sorry you're so upset, Mrs. McNeil. I can understand why. Believe me, I'm as frustrated as you are. This case is on my mind a lot."

Was it? I pondered that, the whirlwind inside me losing a little momentum. I hadn't the energy to sustain anger for any length of time.

Maybe Jud was more of an ally than I'd thought.

But what good was having an ally that wasn't able to help me? He couldn't even find a tick in my kitchen.

"Well." I know my response sounded stilted. "Thank you."

He gave a little nod. "I'll be in touch. The lab will fax the results to your doctor. She's agreed to contact me immediately. And call you as well."

What would Brock say when he heard? Would he even accept positive results from the Lyme lab? Not likely. Maybe he'd storm over here and berate me some more. Or worse. I shuddered.

"What is it?" Jud's keen detective's eye didn't miss a thing.

Heat flicked through my veins.

"Mrs. McNeil?"

"Nothing. I was just . . . thinking about Brock."

He surveyed me. I could feel his suspicion rising, as if he'd sensed my fear. "Has your husband threatened you in some way?"

In an instant I was twelve years old, looking at myself in the bathroom mirror. How to explain the bruises on my face this time? The truth was too shameful. We never told the truth about that.

I fixed my gaze on the floor, glad for the sunglasses to hide my eyes. I could not bring myself to admit this. Jud's wife worked with Brock.

"No."

The detective eyed me for another long moment, then looked away with a sigh. "I'm here if you need me."

I nodded.

Jud let himself out. I stayed on the couch, staring at the fireplace. I needed to get up but couldn't find the energy. Brock's face filled my head—so full of rage, the vein pulsing in his neck. Despair clouded over me, descending until my body choked in it. Even so, my mind screamed for me to *do something*. How could I just sit there and let the minutes slide by? Knowing, no matter Jud Maxwell's good intentions, that he likely wouldn't find Stalking Man before the thirty-six hours ran out.

"Don't you ever say anything like that again. Ever!"

How foolish I'd been. Why had I bated Stalking Man like that? If I hadn't made him so mad, maybe he'd never have flung out that deadline. And now he'd said he wouldn't contact me anymore. As much as his calls terrified me, the silence was worse. I had no hint as to what he was doing.

This whole thing was insane. I sat trapped in my own body while my daughter and other wives, other children were threatened. I would go mad with this. And how could I even trust Stalking Man would *wait* forty-eight hours?

"God, why won't You help me?" I tipped my head to the ceiling. *"Why?"*

No response. Nothing.

My insides started to churn. This wasn't fair. Why was everything falling apart at once? My feeble fist beat against the sofa cushion. It was no more than a tap, but in my mind I punched through a wall. I wanted to run through the house, screaming.

Breath snagged in my throat. My lungs flashed the need for more oxygen. In seconds the air hunger hit full force. I slumped over to lie down on the couch, heaving for breath. The world dotted and rolled, then blacked altogether. My limbs froze. My fingers clawed. I raked in fragments of air in grating, desperate strangles.

After an eternity a small passageway in my throat opened. I gulped and choked—and found more oxygen. I sucked it in for all I was worth, feeling my lungs loosen, death's grip fall away.

For long minutes I lay there, only breathing, breathing until my respiration returned to normal. As if it had never happened. As if I'd imagined the whole thing.

I sat up, still light-headed. If skeptics had witnessed that scene, they'd surely have said I was faking. It had to *look* fake. Coming out of nowhere. Then gone, just like that.

"God, how do they do this?" All those patients who'd had Lyme for years with no diagnosis, who'd lost their families and friends. How did they survive?

My throat had dried out. I struggled to my feet and caned into the kitchen to slug down a glass of water. My gaze landed on my Bible lying on the table. It called to me—or maybe my soul called to it. I sat down and thumbed through the Psalms, seeking more verses of comfort. Something, anything to get me through the rest of this day. The pages landed on Psalm 103: *"Bless the LORD, O my soul; And all that is within me, bless His Holy name. Bless the LORD, O my soul, and forget none of His benefits. Who pardons all your iniquities; Who heals all your diseases—"*

Oh, yeah? He hadn't healed mine.

My hand moved to slap the Bible shut, then stopped. Like magnets my eyes were pulled again to verses one and two: *"Bless the LORD, O my soul; And all that is within me, bless His Holy name. Bless the LORD, O my soul, and forget none of His benefits."*

I stared at the words, my spine stiffening. Why should I praise God? *Now?* In the middle of this nightmare?

"Who pardons all your iniquities."

Well, yes He had. But still—

"Bless the LORD, O my soul."

I pushed the Bible away and sat back in the chair, my jaw hardening. Was God laughing at me? Rubbing it in? He knew how sick I was. He knew the last thing I wanted to do was thank Him for that.

I scowled at the table. Until a thought began to nag me.

Maybe it didn't matter what I wanted. Maybe praising God was a matter of will. Wasn't He still God, whether I was sick or not?

My finger ran along the page of the Bible, feeling its smoothness. Tightness swelled in my throat. For a long time I couldn't form a single word. Then my mouth opened. "My soul, praise the Lord. I praise You, God. I do."

Something inside me loosened a little. I lowered my head and fixed my gaze on the table . . . until the wood blurred and I stared through it. My thoughts muddied.

Time passed. I could feel myself hanging there, yet no clear thought would form.

Lyme Awareness Month.

The words suddenly emerged from a marshy bank in my memory. My brain chugged into gear once more. May—Lyme Awareness Month. The month when the media pays more attention to the disease . . .

An idea surfaced. I raised my head. The thought flashed feebly, a beacon in thick fog. I followed the light, knowing I still wasn't processing all that clearly. Was this leading me down a dangerous path?

The idea grew brighter.

Lauren. The other wives and children Stalking Man had threatened. Not to mention all those Lyme patients out there who needed the world to know about their plight. If I did this I could help them all at the same time.

One problem. I didn't have my test results yet—proof that I had Lyme. They would be critical in backing up my story.

My story. That's all I had. But it was powerful.

I could barely move or think. I couldn't begin to know who Stalking Man might be. He could have come from any state in the country. Neither could I trust that Jud Maxwell would find the man before he got to Lauren, then moved on to his next victim. But in our last call I'd found his Achilles' heel. I couldn't go chase him down. But maybe I could shake him up.

I wiped my sweaty forehead. Jud Maxwell wouldn't want this. He'd claim it would get in the way of his investigation. And Brock would be livid. My heart stumbled at that thought. If there existed even a tiny chance I could ever get him back—this plan would ruin it. Yes, he'd treated me terribly. He didn't deserve me. But was I really ready to burn the bridge between us after twelve years of marriage?

And what about Lauren? What would she think? She was the most important of all.

If this plan worked, I'd get my daughter back. Nothing mattered more than that.

Flash, flash went the beacon.

Still, my pulse trembled. There would be no turning back.

I sat there for some time, weighing the risks, realizing that with my dimmed ability to process I couldn't think through them all.

Something within me gave way, and I pushed to my feet. Before I could change my mind, I clomped over to pick up the phone.

Chapter 36

THE VIAL CONTAINED AN INFECTED TICK IN ITS NYMPH STAGE, like the ones he'd placed on Janessa. So small and black it wouldn't likely be seen amid the roots of dark hair. Lauren had hair like her mother's.

He stuck a hand in his pocket, feeling the vial's smoothness, reassuring himself it was still there.

The library computer sat empty. He took a chair at the small cubicle and logged in. Brought up the Internet.

"She hates you from the grave."

His heels dug into the floor.

He typed in the URL for MapQuest.

The last twenty-four hours he'd had trouble sleeping. Maybe because he hadn't taken his bipolar meds in four days. He should. His moods would then even out. But he needed this manic stage to fuel him. Even now he could feel the fire in his veins, the zing of energy. Made him powerful. Invincible.

MapQuest came up. He placed the cursor in the start box and typed in the library's address. Then leaned back to pull a piece of paper with a Los Angeles area address from his left pocket. He typed that in the end box. Hit *get directions.*

There they came. How convenient, the Internet. It was the web that had allowed him to find all the home addresses in the first place.

With a few more clicks he printed the document.

The trip would take six hours. He'd leave Friday at dinner time. Drive into the night.

This committee member's wife would be a fast hit. He'd follow her to the grocery store, something like that. Brush up against her. Another tiny tick. Who would think to even look for it?

He closed out of the Internet. Rose to retrieve the directions from the printer.

On the way out of the library he checked his watch. Just past noon.

In three hours Lauren would get out of school.

Chapter 37

🦎 FOR HALF AN HOUR I TALKED TO TV REPORTER RHONDA
Laverly, one of the mainstays on the local ABC channel's six o'clock
news. Rhonda was blonde and blue-eyed, a tiny thing but exuding
energy and passion for her stories. My stuttered speech was so frus-
trating, especially against her clipped sentences. Reporters are always
pushed for time. Before I was long into my story, Rhonda interrupted
to ask if she could tape the conversation.

"On one condition. I want you to. Film me. I want to show the
world what L-Lyme is like." Not to mention I had a few choice words
to throw out there for Stalking Man.

"Let's hear all you've got to say first." Rhonda turned on her
recorder. "Go."

She'd made no promises, but I forged ahead anyway. What did
I have to lose?

Rhonda heard me out, clearly fascinated. When I finished, she
told me she'd do some checking on my story. "If it all checks out I'll
see what I can do about getting a camera crew out to your house this
afternoon."

She ended the call with a terse promise to phone me back as soon as she could.

By the time I hung up I shook with exhaustion. I ate a sandwich and collapsed on the couch.

Before long the phone rang. It was Jud.

"I just got a phone call from a reporter. She said you contacted her about the case."

Here it came. "What did you tell her?"

"That I can't talk about an ongoing investigation."

As I suspected. But the answer would be all Rhonda needed.

"Mrs. McNeil, I'm not convinced you're doing the right thing. We try to be strategic about going to the media—and think through how much information we give them."

"I don't have time to *think.*" Too late I realized how bad that sounded. "I have to do this interview to protect my daughter. And all those other families out there this guy has threatened."

"What interview?"

"I'm hoping they'll tape it this afternoon. The reporter's going to try to make the six o'clock n-news."

Jud sighed.

"There's a bigger . . . reason I'm doing this," I said. "This man—he's been so calm up to now, but I heard him g-get mad on that last phone call. I'm going to make him mad again. He'll make a wrong m-move, like call my home phone. You still got the line tapped?"

"Yes."

"Then you'll finally be able to hear him. You can trace to his location."

"You can't predict that's what he'll do."

No I couldn't. Not exactly. But he'd do something, I could feel it. Jud hadn't heard the calls. He didn't know Stalking Man like I did.

Jud tried to talk me out of going forward. I told him it was too late for that. Besides, what else did we have? Stalking Man had eluded us at every turn. I was a mother. My daughter had been threatened. I *had* to do something.

A click sounded in my ear—notice of another caller. I held out the receiver and peered at the ID.

"Jud? The reporter's phoning now. Hang on a m-minute." My finger hovered over the phone button. For a moment I couldn't remember which one to push. *Flash.* I hit it to move to the other call. "Hi, Rhonda?"

"We're a go. We'll be at your house in about forty-five minutes. You'll be ready?"

"Yes. Give me t-time to get to the door. I'm slow."

"We need every second we can get. Can you unlock it now? We'll knock and come on in."

"Okay."

"See you soon." She hung up.

I flashed back to Jud. "They're coming over right now for the interview."

He paused. "All right." His tone sounded resigned. "Look, do one thing for me. Don't mention the part about the suspect's wife dying from Lyme. He may not have realized he slipped up about that, and it's a big lead I can follow. If we don't catch him soon, maybe in time we'll decide to put that information out to the public. But not yet."

"Okay."

We hung up. Half-dazed, I replaced the receiver. This was really going to happen.

For a moment I considered going upstairs, trying to fix myself up. I must look terrible. But I had no energy to waste struggling with steps. Problem was, the more tired I became, the more my speech stumbled and my mind fogged. Plus the interview was about my being sick. Why try to hide it?

I heaved to my feet and clomped to the front door. Unlocked it. Then headed to the sofa to wait. Within minutes the phone rang again. The ID read Brock's cell phone. I stared at the numbers, dread encircling my heart. I couldn't handle this confrontation right now.

I set the receiver back in its base. It rang a second time, jangling my nerves. A third and fourth. The answering machine kicked on in the kitchen. The beep had barely sounded when Brock's irate voice barreled to my ears.

"I know you're there. Pick up *right now*." Pause. "Pick up, Janessa!"

Muscles shriveling, I turned my head away from the phone. Thank heaven Brock wasn't in this room with me. No telling what he would do.

"Janessa!"

My anxious gaze landed on the clock. *Lauren.*

My arm reached to pick up the phone before I could stop it. "Brock. Who's going to pick up Lauren?" Despite my demand, my voice angled sideways with fear. For the first time I realized I'd almost rather face Stalking Man than my own husband.

"What are you doing? A reporter called my office. A *reporter!"*

"Brock, *who* is picking up Lauren?"

"You'd better recant whatever story you told her right now. Do you realize how idiotic you're going to look? The police don't have one shred of evidence your story's even true." He blew air over the line, hot enough to singe my ear. "Jud Maxwell told me about the supposed latest phone call. Even if you didn't make this whole thing up and Lauren really was in danger, we could protect her."

If.

"I get what you're trying to do now, Janessa. You want to bring me down. In front of everyone. Make no mistake, *you're* the one who'll be brought down. You want your dirty laundry aired in public—you'll get all of it. I'll tell them about your childhood faked illnesses. I'll tell them you're jealous and can't let go. That you're an unfit mother who's losing her mind, who scared her own daughter to death, frantically searching for ticks all over her body. You will lose your daughter, Janessa. Permanently. I will sue for custody, and I *will win*."

No. Anything but losing Lauren for good.

But Brock would do it. And he would win. Brock always won. He was the one with the resources, the reputation. The charisma. What was I but a sick mother who could barely take care of herself, much less her child.

My body shook. I could call the reporter back right now and tell her not to come. Work this out somehow with Brock. When I got my test results, he'd believe me then. Maybe when he talked to my doctor . . .

Who was I kidding? Dr. McNeil put little stock in the Lyme lab's diagnosis. And he had no respect for Carol Johannis. I swallowed hard, fighting for strength to stand up to this man. "Brock. *Who* is picking up Lauren?"

He cursed under his breath. "I am!"

"Just please . . . g-go early. Be there when she comes out."

"Who are *you* to tell me how to take care of my daughter? I'm not the one making her crawl on the floor looking for a deadly tick." His tone was pure acid.

No. He was the one who'd left her. Who'd put some mistress above her. My eyes closed, my chin falling to my chest. I could feel my mind shutting down. "Where will she . . . be? While you're t-teaching."

"Janessa. Call that reporter back and recant your story. Now."

My insides were melting. The last bit of strength had drained out of me, and Rhonda would soon be at my door. I wouldn't be able to do the interview.

"B . . ." What was my husband's name? "W-watch Lauren. Please. Check her for . . ." That bug. That . . . thing. "T-ticks."

He exploded in a stream of curses.

I pulled the phone from my ear and gaped at it. How did I turn the thing off? My glazed eyes searched the buttons but nothing made sense. Brock's voice still spat into the room.

My hand reached for the phone base and dropped the receiver into it. I heard a click, and Brock's voice cut off.

I slumped to the right until my head hit the sofa cushions. My body twisted, my feet still on the floor. The position made my hips ache, but I couldn't think how to fix it.

Wait. I needed to call the reporter. Tell her I was too sick . . .

Where was the phone?

The world fell away. The next thing I knew my doorbell was ringing.

Chapter 38

AS SOON AS JUD TURNED OFF HIS CAR IN THE POLICE STATION parking lot, he looked up Brock McNeil's cell number and dialed it. His adrenaline pumped with each ring of the phone in his ear. No more excuses that this case was all a farce. Not after a doctor all but confirmed Janessa McNeil had Lyme. And the lead about the suspect's wife having died from the disease—that was huge.

Once in awhile the stars aligned. The new information on this case happened to coincide with a hit on the foreign fingerprint from the Fletcher burglary. When the print had been run through the system it came up with a match—a known drug dealer in the area. Stan Mulligan and another detective were following up. With the reported threat to Lauren McNeil, and a doctor's opinion that her mother did have Lyme, the chief had given Jud the immediate go-ahead to turn his attention to this case.

If only Janessa McNeil hadn't jumped the gun with the reporter. Jud had a nagging feeling about that interview.

As Jud got out of the car, Doctor Johannis's voice echoed in his head. *"You've got a wide range of suspects, I'm afraid. Anyone who's been sick with Lyme . . .*" The same suspicions Walt Rosenbaum had spoken of. Also similar to Dane Melford's thoughts.

Although Jud hadn't heard back from either man.

No answer on McNeil's cell. His canned message clicked on. "This is Doctor McNeil. Sorry I'm unavailable. Please leave a message." *Beep.*

Jud pushed down his frustration. "Dr. McNeil, this is Detective Maxwell. I need to talk to you as soon as possible. The man who has been calling your wife—and yes, I believe he exists—is now threatening to infect your daughter with Lyme. I've met with the principal at Lauren's school. He has been alerted to the situation and has briefed his staff to be particularly vigilant regarding your daughter. Please give me a call." Jud rattled off his cell number and disconnected.

He leaned against his car and punched in the number to the department of medicine. Sarah answered.

"Hi, babe. Dr. McNeil around?"

"He's in class. When he gets out he said he's going to pick his daughter up at school."

"Okay. I've left a message on his cell phone. But when you see him, tell him I called."

"Something up?"

"Plenty. But I gotta run now. Talk to you tonight."

Jud strode across the parking lot, headed to his office. He had a date with his computer—searching online for women who'd died from Lyme disease.

Chapter 39

THE FRONT DOOR OPENED, AND A FEMALE VOICE CALLED, "Jannie, it's Rhonda."

Footsteps sounded in the hallway. The clack of high heels. A second, heavier tread. "Jannie?"

"Here." My voice barely rose from the couch. I struggled to sit up.

Rhonda strode around the couch to stand before me, clad in a blue suit to match her eyes, her hair perfectly coifed. Energy crackled around her. A cameraman in tow lugged his equipment. "Jannie?" She bent down to peer at me, clearly shocked at what she saw. "You all right?"

"Just tired." I couldn't do this—even if I found the strength. I couldn't lose Lauren. A sob kicked up my throat.

"Hey, it's okay." Rhonda touched my cheek. "I'll get you some water." She disappeared into the kitchen. Cabinets opened. The faucet ran. She hurried back in, a woman pressed for every second, trying to show compassion but with no time to spare.

She handed me the glass. I downed the water.

"That's good." Rhonda took it from me and walked over to the pass-through window to set it on the counter. She trotted back to the center of the den and surveyed the room, the front window with shades drawn. I couldn't remember pulling down those shades. "We'll have to leave her there," Rhonda said to the cameraman. "Maybe shoot her straight on? There's still too much backlight from the window. Second camera on me can go near the window. I'll sit here." She pointed to a spot near the coffee table.

The cameraman gauged the distance from me to the opposite wall. "Not much room. Can we shove back the couch?"

Her eyes narrowed. "Yeah. We can move it all the way back to the wall."

My mouth opened to protest, tell Rhonda I couldn't go through with it. But no words came.

"Jannie, this is Bill." Rhonda pointed to the cameraman.

"Hi, Jannie." He nodded at me, then moved to the coffee table, pushing it far to my right, toward the kitchen. Rhonda shoved the small side table further left until it rested against the wall near the windows.

"Okay. Jannie, just stay where you are. We're going to move the couch back." She took my end, Bill on the other, and they scooted the couch across the hardwood floor to the back wall. Rhonda stood, panting, and adjusted her suit coat. "That work?"

Bill eyed the scene. "Yeah, it'll do." He began setting up his equipment.

Still I could say nothing. My body felt half there and half on some distant plane.

Rhonda sat beside me, her voice gentling. "I'll pull up a kitchen chair not too far from you, and we'll just talk, okay? You going to make it?"

I stared at my lap, voices and threats jumbling in my head. Stalking Man's. Brock's. One would hurt my daughter if I didn't catch him in time. The other would take her from me if I tried. Both scenarios were unbearable. If I'd possessed the strength, I'd have groaned and wailed. Shook my hands at the heavens.

"Jannie?"

I raised my weary eyes to Rhonda's. She watched me, her expression fraught with tension. When she saw my head come up, she smoothed the lines from her face. But her eyes gave away her concerns. I ogled her, my stomach turning over as a realization dawned. This seasoned reporter saw herself teetering on the brink of not just a big story, but a huge one. The details were bizarre. And that kind of story often went national. Rhonda would be the one to break it. No wonder she and her station were pushing the time so much, trying to fit this in at the last minute. Willing to go ahead with the story even before I had test results.

National. Why hadn't I thought of this? Once I took the cork out of the genie bottle, how to control the genie?

No way could I handle having the story told across the country. My mother would see it. She'd hound me. What if reporters from everywhere ended up on my front lawn? Or filming Lauren as she went to school? They'd snoop into our lives, find out everything about us. Brock would insist to an entire nation I was just trying to ruin him.

No. I couldn't do this. Absolutely not.

"I'll help you through the questions, all right?" Rhonda pressed. "It'll be okay. This story will help find the man who's been harassing you."

I stared at her, my body glued to the couch. Finally my mouth opened to say no. Instead I heard, "I'll need to k-keep my sunglasses on."

She shot me a relieved smile. "That's okay." She leapt to her feet. "Just rest while we finish setting up."

I closed my eyes and slumped back against the sofa. What had I done? What *thing* inside me drove me to go through with this? How

I would even manage to speak when the camera came on—I didn't know.

God is our refuge and strength, a very present help in trouble.

My mind still reeled, but my soul clung to the verse. It was all I had.

Through closed lids I sensed the room brightening. I opened my eyes to see lights turned on, aimed at me. Harsh lights. I winced and turned away.

"Are those too bright?" Rhonda asked.

I knew they needed the illumination. All the better to display my ravaged body to viewers. "I'll keep my eyes closed." Viewers wouldn't be able to see behind my sunglasses anyway.

My neck struggled to hold my head up. Rhonda arranged a throw pillow behind me for support. And before I knew it the cameras started rolling.

Rhonda was good. Pressed for time and knowing I had little strength, she didn't probe me to retell the entire story I'd given her over the phone. No doubt she'd fill in the background parts herself for the segment. I could visualize her now, setting up the scene. Explaining to viewers who my husband was, why I'd become the target of a madman. She now asked me pointed questions about my symptoms, about Stalking Man's threats. In strained speech, using strength I didn't know I possessed, I told her of falling in the kitchen. Stalking Man's chilling words in that first phone call: *"Welcome to the Lyme wars, Janessa."*

"Briefly tell me about the Lyme wars," Rhonda said. "What does that mean?"

Briefly? The situation was so convoluted. My brain scrambled to process a reply. "Some doctors like my husband believe that two to four weeks of . . . antibiotics cures Lyme. Even if you've had it for y-years. But many Lyme patients are still sick after that. They want longer treatment so they can. Get better. Because of doctors like my husband they have a hard time . . . getting it. Treatment. Other doctors who do treat them longer can g-get in trouble for it."

"And what do *you* believe, Mrs. McNeil?"

My lips parted. Never since the day I met Brock had I dreamed of speaking against him publicly. He'd awakened me to self-confidence; I supported him in return. But now . . . All those suffering Lyme patients who weren't believed, as Brock refused to believe me. How could I turn my back on them? I'd *become* one of them.

"Look up stories of Lyme patients online. They're *horrible*. You'll s-see how sick they are—for years. And doctors don't listen. Bad enough to be this s-sick"—I gestured toward myself—"but to go undiagnosed. Hear some doctors even say it's all in y-your head . . ."

"So your husband is wrong."

"The m-medical world needs to take a new look at Lyme. Many doctors are given w-wrong information about the disease. They're told Lyme isn't in their state. Or they're t-told to rely on . . . tests that have never been reliable. Doctors need to throw off their b-biases. Look at research with fresh eyes."

Rhonda nodded. "Sounds like this man who infected you has made his point. This is the kind of publicity he wanted. Does it bother you to play right into his hands by giving this interview?"

My head pulled back. I hadn't thought of it like that. But her question gave me the chance I was looking for. "I want to h-help Lyme patients. They are sufferers. But this man." My voice turned bitter. "He thinks he's some s-savior for all Lyme patients. He doesn't deserve to be a part of the L-Lyme advocate community. He's not a helper. He's a . . . terrorist. His cause may be right, but the w-way he's doing it is so *wrong*. What good person would purposely g-give someone this disease? And now he's threatening to infect my daughter!"

Tears scratched my eyes, and one fell to catch on the inner edge of my sunglasses. I thrust a finger under their frame to wipe the tear away.

"Why do you think the police can't catch this man?"

"They will. Maybe with the . . . public's help. Maybe someone out there knows s-something."

Rhonda made an empathetic sound in her throat. "And what keeps you going, Mrs. McNeil? This is obviously very traumatic for you."

"Determination to protect others, including my daughter. Most of all, God."

"Your faith?"

"Yes. The Psalms help. They t-teach me to trust. And to praise God. Even now."

"It must be hard to be thankful when things are going so badly."

I tried to smile but failed. "I don't f-feel like it. But . . . I've praised him lots of t-times when I knew other people were suffering. Is God any less God just b-because *I'm* the one who's now in trouble?"

My words ran out—and all energy with them. Just like that. My shoulders slumped. I shook my head. "I can't . . . I'm done."

"One more question?"

"N-no. Can't."

"Okay." Rhonda nodded at Bill. The cameras stopped rolling. He turned off the lights.

I lay prone on the couch while the two of them hurriedly packed up their equipment. Rhonda bent over me before they rushed out the door. "You'll be okay here?"

A rhetorical question. Not like she would stay and help. I nodded.

Rhonda turned to go. I brushed her hand. She swiveled back.

"Y-you want more exclusive . . . stuff from me?"

"Absolutely."

"Of everything I said, *don't* cut what I said about the man being a terrorist. Run all of that part. If you don't, I w-won't talk to you again."

She surveyed me, the gears of her reporter mind spinning. "And if I do?"

"C-call me anytime."

She dipped her head, checked her watch—and was gone.

The clock read 2:30. Lauren would soon be out of school. I twisted around to pick up the phone and dialed Maria's cell.

"Jannie! How *are* you?"

"Can you g-go five minutes early to school? Be there before the kids come out."

"Sure. Why—?"

"Watch Lauren as she comes out of the building. Every s-second. Brock's picking her up. Make sure no other man gets c-close to her."

"Jannie, what's this about?"

My chest would barely rise to breathe. "I'm . . . tired. Can't talk now. Watch ABC news at 6:00."

Silence. *"What?* You're scaring me."

"I have to go now." Somehow I managed to click off the line.

There. I'd done all I could do. My body would take no more.

The phone dropped to the hardwood floor with a clatter. I fell off a cliff into sleep.

Chapter 40

 THREE THIRTY.

Lauren sat outside his office at an empty desk. She'd been picked up from school and would now stay here, doing her homework, until the work day was done. She wasn't happy about it. Her face carried a scowl, her lips drawn in a hard line. "Dad, I want to go to *home!*" she'd declared more than once. "I want to see Mom!"

This was no place for a nine-year-old to spend the afternoon. Home is where she should be. If it hadn't fallen apart. Where would she go tomorrow after school? And the day after that?

Fine, so this was a temporary solution. For today at least it suited his needs.

He stopped by Lauren's desk and leaned down to see what she was working on. Math. One of his favorite subjects. "Need any help?"

She twisted up to glower at him. Dark half circles discolored the skin below her eyes. She clearly hadn't slept much last night. Too much trauma. "No."

"Want a drink?"

"No."

"You sure?"

She pursed her mouth. "Like what?"

"I can get you a Coke."

She tapped her pencil against the textbook. "Okay."

The things it took to placate a kid.

The nearest vending machine was on the first floor. He strode through the central area past Sarah's desk and down a flight of steps, thinking of Elyse. So many years it had been since they were married. Since he'd lost her. They'd wanted kids. She never had time.

His nerves popped and jarred, his whole body on edge. It wasn't merely the lack of his secret meds. Pretending to be someone you're not comes with a price.

He reached the vending machine and drew quarters out of his pocket—the same one that contained the vial. *Ch-ch-chink* went the money as he dropped it through the slot. He pressed the button for Coke—and down rolled a can. How predictable and right.

On the empty staircase he stopped to set down the can of soda. From his pocket he pulled the vial. Held it up to watch the tiny creature crawl along the bottom. For the last few hours he'd hidden the small bottle in a drawer, its top off, to allow the tick some air. Oxygen—and now food.

He dumped the tiny nymph onto his palm. Closed his fingers around it. The vial went back into his pocket.

Two at a time he took the remaining stairs. He passed Sarah's desk, shooting her a quick smile. Approached Lauren from behind and set the Coke down beside her. "Here you go."

She looked up and gave him a tight smile. "Thanks."

He held his hand just above her head and uncurled his fingers. Patted her dark, thick hair. "See there. I'm not all bad."

Chapter 41

A RINGING PHONE SOUNDED ON A DISTANT PLANE. THEN CLOSER.

I started awake, my half-open eyes bleary and my limbs sucked into the couch. I still wore my sunglasses. The ring came again, from somewhere on the floor. With great effort I leaned over the edge of the cushions and searched the hardwood. My aching hand picked up the receiver.

"Hello." My voice was little more than a grunt.

"Jannie? It's Dr. Johannis."

"Oh." *Test results!* "Hi."

"You don't sound good. You doing all right?"

"I was s-sleeping."

"Ah, sorry to disturb you. I have the test results from the lab."

Here it came. What if she said it wasn't Lyme? "Okay." My heart fluttered.

"Well, you certainly are positive for Lyme. Highly positive, in fact. Your IgM—that's current infection—shows multiple plus signs in numerous bands. Even so, as we discussed, according to CDC standard bands, you would indeed show negative."

My brain scrambled to keep up with her words. Positive. I did have Lyme. I had a diagnosis! But only because of these special Lyme tests. The recognized standard testing would have let me fall through the cracks. Again. As sick as I was.

"Your IgG, that is infection over six months, is negative," Dr. Johannis continued. "That means you were infected within the last six months."

I rubbed my forehead. "Uh-huh." How I wanted to say more. I wanted to get up and dance. Just knowing my enemy for certain sent hope surging through my veins.

"You also have three coinfections." Dr. Johannis's tone remained even, but I knew what she was thinking. *Three of them.* Just as Stalking Man had said.

This was evidence, right? For Jud.

"The coinfections are Erlichiosis, Babesiosis, and Bartonella. The combination of these with Lyme could be a factor in your getting so sick so fast. In particular Bartonella tends to add to the encephalitis— your inability to process thought and overall mental confusion. It can also help cause that pain on the bottom of your feet."

My throat convulsed in a swallow. This *was* good news, right? Proof of my claims about Stalking Man. But the longer Dr. Johannis talked, the more I realized my troubles had only just begun. Because now I knew for sure I had to battle the awful disease of Lyme. *And* three other illnesses.

"Does this happen to most people? The coinfections?"

"Often, yes. Maybe not all three. That's a whopping load, mixed with Lyme. But the presence of any coinfection worsens the symptoms."

So I wasn't alone. Right now that didn't seem to help. "How long till I get well?"

Dr. Johannis drew in a breath. "It's hard to say. We'll have to see how you react to the medications. And I can't give them to you all at once. I'll design a treatment plan for you, and you'll need to follow it carefully. But all in all, we're probably talking six months. Quite possibly longer."

Six months. My heart curled in on itself. That long—without Lauren?

"But that's all together, r-right? I mean, I'll get . . . better during that time." Well enough to take care of my daughter. If Brock followed through on his threat and sued for custody, I would have to prove I was well enough to care for her.

"Jannie." The doctor's voice softened. "I know you want to get well quickly. I'll do all I can to help. But you have to understand this will take time."

I didn't *have* time. Panic clutched at my chest.

If Stalking Man could only be caught soon. Then I wouldn't have to worry about Lauren's safety. And Brock would look terrible to a judge for not believing me about the danger to me and Lauren. For walking out on me when I was so sick. As for my health, I could hire someone to come in and cook until I felt better. That person could drive Lauren to school. That would work. Judges don't take children away from their mothers just because they're sick.

"Jannie, you there?"

"Huh?"

"I was saying you have to be prepared to get worse before you get better. In your research about Lyme, you read about Herxheimer reactions?"

Maybe. Yes. No. "I think so."

"These herxes, as they're called, occur when the Lyme spirochetes are killed. As they die off they release toxins in the body—faster than the liver and kidneys can deal with them. These toxins cause symptoms to worsen. Herxes typically start two to three days after you begin an antibiotic. You're sick enough already that I imagine your herxes could put you to bed until they play out."

Bedridden? And living alone? "How l-long do they last?"

"Depends on the drugs and your reaction. Three to five days is usually the worst of it."

I closed my eyes. "So, you mean *every* time I start a different drug, that will happen?"

"That's the pattern. We've also seen a general pattern of herxing every four weeks. This appears to coincide with the life cycle of *Borrelia*. So all in all, I want you to understand you're entering a real fight here. I do think you can come out on the other side and be healthy again. Fortunately you're being diagnosed within six months of infection. Otherwise it would take a lot longer to treat you."

A distracted thought floated into my brain. How ironic. If Stalking Man hadn't been so driven to harass me, to try to change Brock's medical opinion *now*, I'd have gotten far worse. If it hadn't been for my attacker, I wouldn't even have a diagnosis.

But then, what good would I have been to his "savior" cause? With Brock's committee set to release their findings in the fall, Stalking Man needed me as his poster child now.

Well, he'd gotten his wish.

"This is . . . scary." My limbs trembled.

"I know. But I'll help you through it."

I pulled in a breath that shuddered down my lungs. "So now what?"

"Call my office in the morning and make an appointment. I'll tell my assistants to work you in as soon as possible. Then we'll discuss your treatment and get you started on the antibiotics."

After which I'd get worse. *Oh, God help.* How could I feel any worse than I did now?

"In the meantime watch your diet. This is very important. Stick with protein and avoid carbohydrates. Stay away from caffeine, alcohol, and sugar—both refined and natural, as from fruits. *Borrelia* thrive in an environment high in sugar."

"Okay."

"I will call Detective Maxwell next and tell him these findings. Also, Jannie, a reporter has called my office, asking about your case. I want you to know I did not leak any information to the press."

"I know. I did."

"You did?"

"I want to flush him out. This m-man. Before he hurts . . . someone else. It's supposed to be on the six o'clock news tonight."

News. What time was it? My blurry eyes rose to the clock. Five forty.

Five forty! Lauren got out of school long ago.

"I see," Dr. Johannis said.

See what? What had we been talking about?

"I informed the reporter I can't talk about any of my patients. I'm sure she knew that already."

"Yes."

Dr. Johannis sighed. "Well. Guess I'd better get home and turn on the news. What channel?"

"ABC."

"Okay. Hope you catch the guy, Jannie."

Me too. "Thanks."

We disconnected.

With sluggish limbs I heaved myself off the couch to head for the bathroom. From there I went to the kitchen. At the refrigerator I pulled out more slices of cheese and lunch meat. Protein. As I retrieved a side plate from the cabinet I saw Brock's gun lying on top of the big plates. I left it there.

By the time I fell back upon the couch, exhausted and feet burning, it was nearly six. Where was Lauren? Was she all right? I reached for the receiver to call Brock's cell phone—and it rang. I jumped. The ID read a local number I didn't recognize.

My lungs chilled. Stalking Man?

Holding my breath, I picked up the phone. "Hello?"

"Mom!"

Air seeped from my lungs. "Lauren. Where are you? How are you?"

"I'm finally back from Dad's work." Her voice held the peeved tone she reserved for relating a fight with some friend. "I had to sit there for hours and do my homework. He just brought me here, then he turned around and went back."

How thoughtless of Brock to make Lauren sit at his work, when he could have brought her here.

"I don't want to do that again tomorrow, Mom. I just want to come home."

"I'll bet. I want you here, too."

"Yeah, tell that to Dad."

"How's . . ." I could barely form the name. "Alicia?"

"She's pretty. And I don't like her."

"Does she t-treat you okay?"

"I guess."

"And your dad?"

"He's just . . . he's all tied up in knots or something. It's like he doesn't know what to do with me."

He most likely didn't. Bringing the child from a twelve-year marriage into a mistress's house couldn't feel comfortable. Even for someone as confident as Brock.

Lauren's voice lowered to a near whisper. "He's still really mad at you."

"How do you know?"

"He won't even talk about you. I say I want to come home and he just like growls at me." Her words choked. "Mom, I want to come *hooome.*"

My heart turned over. "You will. Soon as I can g-get you back."

She sniffed. "Are you any better?"

I hesitated. "No."

Air seeped over the line. "I'm sorry."

"I'll be okay."

The news. Where was the TV remote?

A horrible thought struck me. What if Lauren heard about the segment from a friend? Surely somebody would call her. Maybe even Katie. Or if not a phone call tonight—someone at school tomorrow would talk. And children could be so cruel. They'd tease Lauren. Make fun of me to her face—the way I look, my stuttering speech. Some boy was apparently teasing her already. He'd have a heyday now. As if she wasn't already going through enough.

Why hadn't I thought of this? It was so obvious.

My eyes closed. At that dreadful moment I could almost grasp that Brock had been right to take Lauren. I wasn't thinking straight these days. How could I care for her properly?

The thought deflated air from my lungs.

"L-Lauren." I swallowed. "I might be on the n-news tonight. On TV."

"Dad told me." She sounded almost accusing. "Alicia's supposed to tape it for him."

Oh, no. "What did he say?"

"That you're all mad about Alicia, so you're trying to hurt him at work. Or something like that."

My stomach roiled. How *could* he?

"And it all has to do with that detective who came to our house. Stories you're telling him."

My mouth opened to protest, then snapped shut. Is this what Brock and I had come to? Hurling accusations at each other through our daughter? I couldn't do that to Lauren.

"Honey, I'm not m-making up stories."

"Then why doesn't Dad believe you?"

Why was he making *any* of his recent choices? "I don't know. I just . . . I wouldn't lie to you. I only w-want to keep you safe. I love you so much."

"I know. I love you too." She sniffed again. "I want to come home."

I stared at the coffee table, trying to see down the dark tunnel of the next six months. Multiple antibiotics. Symptoms worsening. If my brain slowed down any more, would I be able to think at all?

"I want you home, Lauren. I really do. We'll . . . work on it. Okay?"

She heaved a sigh. "Okay."

"Was your dad waiting for you when you got out of school?"

"Yeah. I went right to his car."

Surprising. I'd have expected Brock to be late, kept away by work. Maybe part of him did believe me.

"Then where did you go?"

"To his office building. I told you that."

"Oh. Right."

My eyes blinked at the clock. Six.

I heard Lauren's name called from the background. A female voice.

"I have to go now, Mom. Alicia says it's time for dinner."

Alicia. The very name sent bitter waves through me. And she was cooking for *my* daughter.

At least Lauren would eat a meal. I couldn't cook for her at all.

My throat heated. "Okay, honey," I whispered. "Hope it's good."

We hung up. I found the TV remote on the side table, near the phone. Hadn't noticed it there before. For a long moment I stared at it, fishing in the thick waters of my mind. How did you work the thing?

The answer surfaced.

I switched on the TV to Channel Seven—and waited for the news story that would help me catch Stalking Man.

Chapter 42

MY STORY WAS THE LEAD TEASER FOR THE NEWS—A "BIZARRE medical crime." I knew what being the main teaser meant. They would run the story last, luring viewers to watch the entire show before satisfying their curiosity.

By the time the segment started to air my heart thrashed and my throat ran dry. If they didn't include my tirade against Stalking Man this would all be for nothing. *No*, I tried to tell myself, *that wasn't true.* Maybe someone out there would know who this man was. Maybe just taking the story public would be the answer.

But leads from the public could take weeks. I needed help *now*.

The screen flashed to a scene of Rhonda on the sidewalk in front of my house. I cringed. They'd filmed her lead-in here? I didn't want my house shown.

". . . in Palo Alto." Rhonda stood in her blue suit, looking perfect as always. "Janessa McNeil's husband, Dr. Brock McNeil, is a professor and researcher at the Stanford School of Medicine—and the chair of an important national committee whose published findings on Lyme disease drive standardized treatment across the country . . ."

Was Brock watching this? Was Lauren?

The scene changed to a close-up of me. I gasped. How *awful* I looked, even in sunglasses. Pale and exhausted, the mental confusion casting a blank pallor to my expression. Horrified, I watched myself on TV as I answered questions, tripping over words, my facial muscles contorting as I fought to process. *That's* how I looked when I spoke?

The story segued from me to Rhonda numerous times as she filled in more details between my responses. I heard myself give answers I had no memory of speaking.

Come on, come on. Run my words against Stalking Man.

They did. Everything I'd insisted to Rhonda that she keep in the story. At least, all I could remember.

God, let it be enough. Please.

Near the end of the interview Rhonda asked me where I found the strength to deal with all this. I sat amazed at my answer about God and reading the Psalms. About learning how to praise Him even now. It was all true, of course, but I had never spoken so openly about my faith. Now I'd done it on TV.

As soon as the interview ended, the phone rang. My nerves surged white hot. I peered at the ID, already starting to tremble. But it was only Maria's number.

Breath returned as I picked up the phone. "Hi."

"Jannie, I had no idea! Why didn't you *tell* me?"

"I don't know. It was . . . Brock and everything."

"And he left you—in the middle of *this*. As if the sickness wasn't enough."

"He didn't believe me." Would he now?

"How could he not? Since when did you turn into some huge liar?"

"Since my husband w-wants to leave his wife, and she schemes to g-get him back." Or was it to get back at him?

"Are you *kidding* me? That's absolutely crazy!"

Maria was right. It *was* crazy. Brock's actions suddenly loomed so absurd that I wondered anew at how far he had fallen. How he could possibly justify himself.

We talked until my energy ran low and I had to lie down. I told Maria about my test results, the coinfections appearing just as Stalking Man said they would. By the time I hung up, my throat was dry and I had to get up for water. I clumped to the kitchen, feeling the silence of the house. Vaguely I wondered if the tick was still in the room somewhere. No matter, I didn't need the thing as evidence now. Testing it would likely show the same results as my own blood. But still, to know it was in the house. When Lauren came back I'd have to check her every day. Make sure she always wore shoes in here.

As I filled a glass of water, a vibrating dread settled over me. The house was so still. As if it was waiting for . . . something.

I looked at the phone, willing it to ring. Even so, my nerves sizzled at the thought.

Had Stalking Man watched the news?

When he did call, I'd have to keep my wits about me. I should get him to talk about his wife—tell me her name. Maybe she was included in that online list.

Water guzzled down, I set the glass in the sink. That dread wavered and rumbled around me. Even in my stomach I felt it. The hairs on my arms rose. I peered through the window above the sink out to the backyard. It was barely past seven o'clock. Still a couple hours of daylight left. But already the coming night loomed ominous.

I shuffled over to the sliding glass door and pulled back the long shade to check the lock. Secure.

With effort I turned, my gaze finding the alarm's key pad on the wall by the garage door. I shuffled to it and turned it on. The light changed from green to red.

For a moment I stood, feeling the burn on the bottoms of my feet, the thump of my heart. Listening to the house.

The phone rang.

The sound shot right through me. I reared back—and dropped my cane. It fell with a soul-shaking crash.

My body wobbled. I groped wildly for the table's edge, seeking support. My trembling hand found it and hung on for all it was worth.

A second ring.

I stared at my cane. No way to lean down and retrieve it. As a third ring shattered the kitchen I shuffled toward the receiver, leaning on the table . . . the back of a chair. Between the last chair and the counter spanned about four feet. I let go, my arms thrashing as I flung myself toward the granite like a wobbling toddler. My right hand whacked against the counter's edge, spinning pain up to my shoulder. At the last minute I grabbed on and held. Rested my weight against the solid structure as I fumbled for the phone—no time to check the ID.

"Hello?"

"Mrs. McNeil, it's Jud Maxwell."

"Oh." My legs weakened. I leaned over the counter, puffing as my last ounce of strength trickled down a black hole.

"Are you okay?"

"I . . . yes." I managed a glance over my shoulder, seeing the cane on the floor. "Just . . . wasn't near the . . . phone."

Dizziness hit. I had to sit down. "Jud, can I . . . c-call you b-back?"

"Sure."

"Wait. What's your n-number?"

He started to tell me, but I had nothing to write with, and no way would I remember it. "Wait. I'm not . . . I can't . . ."

"How about your phone ID? It probably caught it."

Oh. Right. "Okay. Call you back."

I lay the receiver down, still clutching the counter. Found the button to end the call—and pushed it.

My eyes clouded. I didn't have much time. Somehow I managed to turn and lunge back to the chair. I collapsed into its seat and rested my head on the table. Deep breaths. In. Out. In. Out. Slowly the darkness split apart, hazed away.

With caution, I sat up. My cane lay about three feet from me. I curled my fingers under the seat and pushed off with my feet to scoot the chair. It moved an inch. I scooted again and again—until finally it rested near my cane. I reached out a foot and dragged the bottom of the cane closer. Now to lean down and get it without falling out of the chair.

One hand grasping the seat, I curled forward until my fingers brushed the cane. An inch farther, and they closed around the gray metal. A small cry of victory fell from my lips as I lifted the stupid thing.

For a moment I sat, eyes closed. Breathing.

Jud.

I gauged my distance from the phone. I now sat about a third of the way toward the door to the den. Better to head for the couch, where I could lie down.

With my final bit of effort I heaved to my feet and stumbled to the sofa. I fell on its cushions, gasping. Wondering if my arms would lift to pick up the phone from the table behind my head. I felt so much worse—even from just a few hours ago.

Ten minutes passed before I could twist my body enough to drag the receiver to my ear.

Jud's number sat in the call log. How did I dial it? I ogled the various buttons, my brain chugging through mud. At some point the thickness cleared. I pressed a button—and the number dialed itself. Jud answered on the first ring.

"It's me. Jannie."

"You all right?"

"Uh-huh. Lying down now."

"Good. I won't keep you. Just wanted you to know I caught the interview here at the station. I appreciate your doing what I asked."

Which was . . . ? I couldn't remember. "You r-ready to trace his number when he calls?"

"I've got a man listening to your home line. Turn off your cell phone so the man will have to contact your home. I've also got a car surveilling your street."

Something in Jud's voice told me he didn't expect Stalking Man to call. That, if anything, I may have driven him away.

Jud was wrong. He had to be.

"Good." The phone started to slip from my ear. I couldn't talk much longer.

"Meanwhile I've been on the computer, looking into women who've died from Lyme," Jud continued. "I've compiled a list from a number of different sites. Now I'm going to go through and see what I can find about each one."

"Okay."

"I haven't been able to get hold of Dr. McNeil. I have left him four messages since this afternoon, three on his cell and one at work."

"He won't pick up when he sees your ID. He's furious at me about the interview. He'll view you as an enemy, since you're listening to me."

Jud sighed. "Sorry that's the case."

"Yeah." My head spun. "Have . . . to go now."

"All right. Keep in touch."

His words barely registered. I clicked off the line and dropped the phone onto my stomach.

My eyes closed. I stumbled into edgy sleep—and dreams of a bug-eyed man.

Chapter 43

WHEN I WOKE UP THE ROOM WAS NEARLY DARK. WEAK LIGHT filtered from a streetlamp through the front window shades.

He never called.

My heart sank. *No, no, no.* I'd set a trap for Stalking Man—and he didn't fall for it. That TV interview—all for nothing. I should have known I couldn't predict his actions. With my slow brain, how could I strategize anything?

It was no use. Stalking Man would never be found, my sickness was going to drag out, and who knew when I'd ever get Lauren back? I might as well die right now.

For a long time I lay there, depression wrapping me in cold arms. Until a tiny voice whispered that I had to keep fighting. For Lauren's sake.

The telephone lay on my stomach. How had it gotten there? I twisted around to put it back on its base. With a deep sigh I sat up and turned on the three-way lamp by the sofa to low. I took off my sunglasses and tossed them on the coffee table. Gathered my cane to stand up. I shuffled to the bathroom, then found myself heading to Brock's office and computer. I had to find something worthwhile to do.

Wait. It was *my* office now.

At the desk I heaved myself into the chair and switched on the computer. While it booted up my mind faded out. When I blinked myself into awareness some minutes later, the screen was ready.

Where had I read that list of Lyme victims?

I checked the computer's history, surprised that I remembered how to do that. My brain was seeming to wake up a little. Soon I found the page I was looking for and clicked to it. Up came the list of those who'd died from Lyme. I needed to print it out. Then it would be easier to retrieve if Stalking Man ever did decide to call. Maybe he just hadn't watched the six o'clock news. Maybe he'd see the segment if it ran again later tonight. Or tomorrow.

When I clicked the command to print, the machine only whirred. An error box popped up. The printer was out of paper.

Where did Brock keep it?

I opened the top drawer on the right, then the middle one and the bottom. No paper. Started with the drawers on the left. The second drawer contained a light-colored manila folder with Brock's handwriting on the tab. My eyes grazed over the label as I began closing the drawer.

The words on the folder tab registered. *Lyme research.* I slid the drawer open again and stared at the folder. Picked it up.

Inside was a document in two columns. On the left was a research paper copyrighted in 2008 by the American Society for Microbiology. Five researchers from the University of California, Davis had written the paper, titled "Persistence of *Borrelia burgdorferi* Following Antibiotic Treatment in Mice." On the right were notes in Brock's handwriting.

My eyes went first to the abstract of the paper summarizing the research. I had to read it four times before I could begin to process it. Mice infected with Lyme spirochetes had been treated with antibiotics for one month, some during the early stage of infection at three weeks, and some after four months of infection. Tissues from the mice were then examined for the presence of spirochetes. In some mice—particularly those not treated until the four-month stage—spirochetes could still be found. When ticks were allowed to feed on these mice, they picked up the spirochetes and later transmitted them to previously uninfected mice.

Whoa.

This research proved that four weeks of antibiotics weren't enough to kill all Lyme infection, as Brock and his committee contended.

2008. Three years ago. The only reason Brock would keep a copy of research findings such as these would be to refute them.

My gaze wandered to his handwritten notes. Opposite the explanation of the set-up for the research article, he'd written: *Replicated 2009.* To the right of the statement that some mice still retained *Borrelia*, he noted: *Similar findings, esp. in mice treated at four months.* Beside the text about ticks picking up the infection and transmitting it to other mice, he wrote: *Concur.*

I blinked at the notes. *Replicated 2009.* Brock had done similar research two years ago? And it had resulted in the same findings?

This couldn't be. I must be reading it wrong.

I read the abstract again, then Brock's notes. *Concur.* There was no other way to interpret that word. Brock's research agreed with the previous trials. He'd tried to refute it—and failed.

The file dropped from my hands onto the desk. I sank back against the chair, trying to take this in. Brock had proved himself wrong. Yet he was holding fast to his mantra of many years—one month of antibiotics was the maximum needed to eradicate Lyme.

Were his findings for the committee this year going to reflect the results in these notes? They would have to. But then—why was Brock still so insistent about his previous theory? Why would he fight Stalking Man's demand with such righteous indignation?

I stared at the papers until the words blurred. My brain chugged and whirred, but I couldn't make sense of it. My body chilled and goose bumps popped out on my arms, as if my heart sensed something my mind refused to see.

Brock, why have you been lying about this?

Shivering, I picked up the document and flipped through it. Brock's notes gave details as to his replication of the research's process. Underneath that document lay a second one—cryptic notes of further research done by Brock, dated July 2010.

Ah, here it came. Refuting results.

But no. This was a different study. *Does presence of coinfection reduce results of antibiotic treatment of Borrelia?*

Coinfection? My nerves began to tingle.

Three mice groups, first infected with Borrelia burgdorferi plus Erlichiosis; second with added Bartonella; third with added Babesia. Results: mice treated with antibiotics for Lyme one month . . .

Understanding punched me in the chest. Brock's third group of mice would have been infected by a tick carrying the exact diseases I had: Lyme and the same three coinfections.

What a coincidence.

I stared across the office, fighting to process. Just *how* much of a coincidence was this? Apparently many people had one or more coinfections along with Lyme. But how many had these exact three?

If I could only think better. If I could only make these bizarre puzzle pieces fit in a way that made sense. Clearly I was overlooking something. Because the suspicion that wanted to emerge couldn't be right.

The tingling in my nerves grew stronger. In time my entire body vibrated with it.

My breath shallowed, and I felt dizzy. I yearned to lie down, but no way. I had to stay in the chair and think this through. This was too important. Too . . . earth-shattering.

I rubbed a hand over my face.

Okay. Point one: Brock had known for the past few years that his theory was wrong. What would he have done when he discovered that?

The right thing would be to publish his findings. He'd set out to prove a trial was flawed in some way, only to replicate its results. That was big news, especially for the chairperson of such a powerful committee. But Brock had said nothing. He'd hidden his findings in a drawer—at home, away from his lab.

Had no one at his lab known of this research? Maybe he'd done it on his own.

Unless Alicia knew. If she'd seen those results, she'd never tell anyone. Her loyalty to Dr. Brock McNeil would have only drawn the two of them closer.

Had that been the start of their relationship?

My heart tumbled and dipped. I swallowed hard.

Point two: Brock was a man who would never admit he was wrong. And as a doctor he'd built his reputation on his opinion about Lyme. Brock had been so outspoken and highly regarded in the field that he'd been chosen as chairperson of his committee.

So what would *this* man do when confronted with such a startling new reality about Lyme? My eyes burned. I closed them . . . and tried to concentrate.

Maybe he would find a way to fade from the limelight for awhile. A way to step down from the committee without questions.

But how to do that?

The idea hit me like a tidal wave.

What if he was forced by a madman from the Lyme advocate community to change his opinion for the safety of his wife and child? Then, what if the dedicated Dr. McNeil, even in the face of such horrific threats, refused to go against his conscience? Instead, he would step down as chairperson, allowing the committee to continue in its work without hindrance from his personal problems.

No. Impossible.

And yet . . .

Speaking of personal problems, what if, at the same time, Brock wanted to leave his wife for his lab assistant—the one person who knew the truth? And, of course, he wanted custody of his daughter . . .

A groan rose up my throat.

I shook my head. No. Still impossible. Brock would never do such a thing. He'd never purposely make me sick.

But he had ticks in his lab with the exact same diseases.

Still, I couldn't believe it. Even with all Brock had done—his growing so distant, then leaving me, his anger and refusal to believe my story, the way he'd shaken me—I just couldn't. Wasn't my brain plugged up? I wasn't thinking clearly. Surely I'd overlooked something.

Yes! Like Stalking Man's voice. That wasn't Brock.

But that voice had been altered. I knew that. It was always low and gruff.

Could Brock disguise his voice that much?

What about the wife who'd died from Lyme? Stalking Man had sounded so sincere, so angry when he talked about that. Had it just been a cover-up excuse? An act? Brock certainly had never been married before.

Or had he?

The thought turned my blood to water.

Had he?

Was there a past to Brock I'd never known?

I thought of when we'd met, how much older Brock was than I. He made no mention of a previous marriage. At the time I'd thought *Wow, such a handsome man—a bachelor for this long?*

Was Brock really that duplicitous? Could he be two people—the man I knew and the man he really was?

I shook my head. That was *crazy*. The stuff of crime movies. It wasn't Brock. Couldn't be. Besides, Stalking Man had talked about going after the families of other committee members. If it was Brock, why would he go that far?

To cover his tracks.

No. *No.*

The phone rang. My whole body jumped. I stared at the receiver, my soggy mind about to burst. Not now. I couldn't talk to anyone.

It hit me then. Brock had never been with me when Stalking Man called. And he'd been supposedly "out of town" the night the man broke in and placed that tick on me. Then Brock had played along, even calling Jud Maxwell. But he soon tried to stop the investigation.

A second ring. A third.

I could barely breathe. On automatic I picked up the receiver and stared dull-eyed at the ID.

Brock's cell phone.

Don't answer it. Don't!

Flailing hope within me had to hear his voice. Had to hear something to remind me none of this could be true.

I pushed the button to connect. "Hello." My voice croaked.

"Well, what an evening I've had." Brock's words spat. "First your favorite detective has been calling me all day. Then I watched your interview that Alicia taped for me. That was quite a performance, Jannie."

I floundered for a response. "I didn't ask to get sick."

"And I didn't ask *you* to go tearing down my name on TV!"

"I didn't t-tear down your name."

"You most certainly did. You made it very clear where you stand on the subject of treating Lyme."

Which you know to be right. Our breaths collided over the line.

I swallowed. "Where's Lauren, is she okay?"

"She's here with me. Where she's going to stay."

My mind whirled. So many things I wanted to ask.

"You and that doctor of yours sure have Jud Maxwell fooled."

"So I somehow staged my new test results?"

"I honestly can't figure out what you've done. But you know good and well I've never put any stock in that lab's tests."

Stalking Man's forty-eight hour deadline rose in my mind. Had that been just a ruse? Brock would never hurt Lauren.

But then, I never would have believed he'd hurt me.

Had he done this? Could Brock really be my true stalker?

And now he had my daughter . . .

Heat surged through my bones. "I want you to bring Lauren home right now!"

"I thought you were sick. From the looks of you on TV, you can't even take care of yourself."

"I can take care of my daughter. I want her back here and safe. *Now.*"

"She's safe here while you *convalesce.*" Brock sneered the word. "You can't have it both ways, Janessa. You've trapped yourself in your own game."

My game?

"Tell me the truth, Brock. You know I'll need more than four weeks of . . . treatment for the Lyme, don't you?"

"You don't have Lyme."

"You know I do."

"Oh yeah, and some crazy man broke in during the night and infected you."

Yes, Brock. Some night when you were "gone." Or so you say. Was it really you? Why did you go to the trouble to break in? Did you want me to have nightmares?

"You want to destroy me professionally, don't you, Janessa. And maybe a part of you still wants to make me feel sorry for you."

I stared at his research notes on the desk.

"Well guess what—you won't destroy me. And I'm *not* coming back to you."

"Brock." Was that my own tongue speaking? "I found your research notes. They show the sp-spirochetes are still alive after f-four weeks of treatment."

Silence.

Tears burned my eyes. "You know that four weeks of . . . antibiotics aren't enough, don't you? You've known for s-some time. What were you going to do, ignore those findings? Just go on with your c-committee?"

"Janessa, you have no idea what you're talking about. My research is ongoing. Those findings were in *mice*, not people." Sarcasm bent his tone. "Besides, your mind is too jumbled to think straight. Remember?"

My spine stiffened. If I couldn't think, it's because he'd made me this way. My husband. The man who'd helped me overcome my past. The father of my child.

He'd done this, hadn't he. Really done it. "What do you want from me, Brock?" My voice shook. "What do you w-want that you haven't already taken?"

"Stop this ridiculous charade. And recant that TV interview—publicly."

"You should be happy about that interview. All the more reason for you to step down from being chairman of your committee."

"What are you *talking* about?"

"That's why you did this, right? You needed a reason to be *forced* to leave."

His silence throbbed.

Stunned are you, Brock, that I'd figure it out? "I'll get Lauren back when they hear what you've done to me."

"Get over it, Janessa, lots of husbands leave their wives."

"Don't p-play dumb with me, Brock. I'm talking about the threatening phone calls. *You* made them. *You* put the . . . ticks on me and made me sick—"

"What?"

My throat closed up.

"Janessa, you have flat out gone over the edge." Brock's voice rose. "Don't you dare go claiming I've done any of this to you! I will not have some vendetta of yours ruining my entire career. You hear me? This is it! It stops *right now.*"

What little strength I had was waning. What did it matter? I'd lost everything. But I'd go down fighting. "You did this. I know it. I'm calling Jud."

Brock snorted. "You tell this to Jud and you *will* be sorry."

"I'm not l-listening to your threats anymore. I'm c-calling him."

"Janessa, don't you do it!"

"I will."

"Think what you're doing."

"I'm calling him."

"You—" He cursed. "What is it going to take to *shut you up?*"

Suddenly I realized my vulnerability—so alone and weak. "He's got an officer watching the house, you know."

"Good! Maybe you'll catch your bad guy." Brock's derisive laugh was like acid. "Oh, right, that's *me.*"

My mind spun. Lauren was with Brock. She'd been with him since after school.

"Jud will arrest you. It's over, Brock."

"Janessa, I'm warning you one last time—"

"I'm calling him *right now.* I'm telling him everything."

"You are insane!" Brock's voice hissed. "I'm coming over there, and I *will* make you listen."

Fear ricocheted down my spine. "No! I don't want you here."

"It's *my* house."

"You left it!"

The phone slammed in my ear.

Chapter 44

THE RECEIVER DROPPED TO THE DESK WITH A CLATTER. I fumbled to pick it up, my heart churning. I'd done it now. Why had I opened my mouth? I should have called Jud Maxwell first, told him everything. He'd have gone to Brock. I'd be safe.

Had to call Jud. Immediately.

My desperate eyes peered at the phone. I smashed it to my ear. No dial tone.

Why?

Frantically I searched the buttons on the receiver. But my brain just . . . hovered.

Maybe I needed to turn the phone off, then back on. I hit the *off* button. Then *talk*.

The most beautiful dial tone I'd ever heard sounded.

I poised a finger to call Jud, then froze. What was his number? My gaze darted around the desk. His card must be here somewhere.

Couldn't see it.

I picked up the file with Brock's notes, looked underneath. Nothing. My trembling hands threw the file back down.

Where was the card?

Hadn't I talked to Jud hours ago? I fought to remember which room I'd been in—and flashed an image of myself on the couch. The side table. Jud's number must be there.

I pushed back from the desk and swept up my cane. An odd mix of adrenaline and exhaustion whirled through my limbs, making them shake all the more. I tried to get up three times before I succeeded. Then for a suspended second I couldn't remember what I needed.

Card. Den.

I wobbled out of the office, through the living room and hall. Time seemed to slow, my feet shuffling yet barely moving me. With my every step fear sank its claws deeper into my lungs. By the time I reached the den I was sweating. I clumped over to the side table, expecting to see a white rectangle. It wasn't there. *No.* I moved around to the front of the couch, looked on the coffee table. My sunglasses were there. No card.

How had I dialed Jud's number?

Wait, hadn't he called *me*? So when did I last have the card?

Maybe I'd taken it into another room.

I stumbled through the den and into the kitchen. Flipped on the overhead light. Leaning weakly against the threshold I scanned the table, the counters. No card.

Tears scratched my eyes. This was so *stupid*. Why couldn't I remember this one thing? Slumped against the doorjamb, I tried to fight through the brain fog. The harder I tried the thicker it became. A tear slipped down my cheek.

The gun.

My chin came up. At least I could get that. And I knew where it was. Upstairs in the closet. On the shelf, where I'd put it out of Lauren's reach.

All the way upstairs. Would my legs make the climb?

I turned around to cane through the den, the hallway. To the stairs. I was moving even slower. At the bottom of the steps I almost gave up. What did it matter? Let Brock come. What more could he do to me?

My foot has slipped. From somewhere in the depths of me the words surfaced. "God," I moaned, "help."

I lifted my foot on the first stair and pulled myself up, grunting. Took the second, and the third. Every few steps I had to rest, panting, even while a voice in my head shouted *hurry, hurry, hurry!* An eternity passed before I reached the top. Dizziness washed over me as I made the turn to clump down the hall. The master suite was so far away. I just wanted to reach the bed, fall down on it and not get up. Let whatever happened, happen.

Lauren's face flashed in my mind.

I had to keep fighting. For my daughter.

My breath came in gasps as I crossed into the room. The bed called to me but I didn't dare give it a glance. I made it to the closet, peered up toward the higher shelves. My head didn't want to lift.

No sign of the gun.

I moved closer to the painted shelves, seeking that black and silver against white. It wasn't there. Not on any shelf. Not *anywhere*.

Sweat trickled down my spine. My eyes closed. No card, no gun. Had I made them both up? Was I dreaming all of this?

Black on white. A picture swelled in my mind. The gun was in the cabinet downstairs. On top of the plates.

"*No.*" I sank against the wall. The kitchen was a thousand miles away. I'd never make it back down there. My muscles were no firmer than sand.

With baby steps I turned myself around, headed out of the closet. Pain ricocheted from my hand holding the cane. And the back of my neck ached something fierce. Soon I wouldn't be able to hold my head up.

My eyes grazed the clock. Nearly 11:00. How long had it been since Brock called? How long would it take him to get here?

I didn't even know where Alicia lived.

One thing I did know. If I collapsed on the bed, I wouldn't get up for a long time.

Memories of my childhood swept over me. Of lying on my bed, trapped and helpless before the fate of my father's hands.

From father to husband.

My feet turned and pointed me out the door.

At the top of the stairs I swayed like a woman hanging over a precipice. How to get down all those steps? My legs couldn't hold me.

My hands turned clammy. I had to do something. I *needed* that gun.

With a force outside myself I set a shaking foot on the first stair. Holding on to the banister with my weak hand, I lowered my other foot. One more. Just one more. I managed another stair. Then I allowed my knees to collapse and fell back—hard—to sit at the top of the steps, my feet two stairs below. The jolt shot pain up my back, into my head. My eyes clouded.

I placed my cane lengthwise on the steps, bit my lip, and pushed the silver metal off. It rattled to the bottom.

Here goes. Using both hands to push, I slipped down the top step on my rear. Adjusted my legs one step farther down. Then repeated the process. Every muscle and joint begged me to stop, but I kept on, doggedly, my eyes fixed on the bottom as if it were a golden prize. Down. Down. Down. After a year I reached the landing. I scooted across it and turned. Almost there. I lowered myself down one step. Then with my feet on the hall floor, I gathered my cane, not knowing if I'd ever stand up.

Please, God. Please.

Cane on one side, holding the banister on the other, I fought to rise. On the fourth try I made it.

No blood remained in my veins. My chest heaved as I struggled toward the kitchen, my mouth open and gasping. Air throttled down my throat like the sound of someone dying, the *clunk, clunk* of my cane an echo through the quavering house.

When I reached the threshold of the kitchen, out of nowhere rose a vivid thought: Jud's number was trapped in my phone's ID. I didn't need his card.

My nerves bristled. First the card, then the gun. My brain was nothing but a hole-riddled pan trying to hold water.

By the time I reached the cabinet my lungs burned. I opened the door. There sat the gun. I reached for it, brought it down. It was still loaded, I remembered that much. I set it on the counter and reached for the phone to call Jud Maxwell. Pushed *talk*—and stared at the receiver. How did I find Jud's stored number?

From somewhere upstairs I heard the crack of glass.

Chapter 45

JUD STRAIGHTENED HIS BACK AND ARCHED HIS NECK SIDE TO side. He was still at the computer in his office. Hadn't stopped to go home or even eat. An hour ago he'd phoned Sarah to tell her not to wait up for him.

He'd heard nothing from the officer manning Janessa McNeil's home line. And nothing from Mrs. McNeil since just after the TV interview. His suspect was keeping silent—as Jud had guessed he would. He could only hope they hadn't driven the man underground.

With a sigh he focused again on his monitor. He'd gone through about half his list of adult female victims of Lyme, Googling each name to see what he could find about the husband. Did any of those men have criminal records? Did any of their names come up attached to threatening comments in some Lyme forum?

The husbands weren't always easy to find. In numerous cases they didn't share the wife's last name.

So far—nothing.

Jud buffed his face and checked the clock. He'd run down one more name. Then he really needed to put something in his stomach.

He typed the name plus *Lyme* into Google search and hit enter. Up popped a number of hits. One was the list from which he'd culled the name. The tenth link down looked like an obituary. Good. They always named next of kin. He followed it.

With tired eyes he scanned the text. The husband's name at the bottom snapped his chin up.

Jud stilled.

He shook his head and read the name again. *What?* This was impossible. Maybe just some other man by this same name.

But what a coincidence. Jud was a detective. He rarely believed in coincidence.

Still, none of this fit. The marriage. The state.

Jud stared at the monitor, calculating the years since this obituary. Maybe . . .

He backed up to the search results and surveyed the other links. Followed one after another, but many didn't mention the husband. Those that did failed to confirm Jud's burning suspicions. Frustration mounting, he typed in a new search, using the husband's and wife's names together, plus *Lyme* and the state. A few hits came up. One looked like some article on Lyme. Jud clicked on it.

At the top of the article sat a paragraph of text about the author. And the man's picture.

Jud gaped at the photo. It was him. Younger to be sure. But definitely him.

Brock McNeil.

Jud snatched up his cell phone.

Chapter 46

I FROZE, MY MIND SLOGGING TO PROCESS THE NOISE.

Glass . . . a window?

Brock.

Another crack sounded, followed by the tinkle of glass.

The backyard tree with branches reaching to our window. He must have climbed that tree.

I dropped the phone. My hand swept up the gun. I turned, heart skipping, thinking nothing but *run! Hide!* I dropped the gun in my robe pocket and moved out of the kitchen as fast as my shaky limbs would take me. Heat flooded my veins. I'd never get there fast enough.

I hit the hallway, knowing I'd have to pass the stairs. How soon before he broke out the window enough to crawl through? Would he hear the thump of my cane? I tried to place it without sound, but that slowed me down. Nausea roiled in my stomach. I fought to move faster.

My feet shuffled me past the bottom of the stairs. I pulled myself forward, forward, toward the living room and office. No energy remained in my body. Panic alone fueled me.

Brock. He knew the upstairs window wouldn't trip the alarm system. And he knew police were on the street. Had he parked a block away, run through the open space into our backyard?

That was crazy. The Brock I knew would never *do* that.

A sob clogged my throat. My own husband was here to kill me. To silence me for good. Then he'd flee back to his mistress, who'd tell the police he'd never left her side. Lauren was long asleep and would never know. And the mysterious Stalking Man would now be wanted for murder—and never found.

No. Not true. My mind wasn't thinking straight . . .

I passed through the living room, ears straining for any sound from upstairs. Did I hear a tread on the carpet?

My nerves sizzled, my hand weakening on the cane. Almost there. Almost . . .

I reached the office. Turned off the overhead light. Dim illumination filtered from the hallway.

My feet tottered to the desk. I pulled the rolling chair away and stared at the hollow space underneath the piece of furniture. Once I got down there I wouldn't be getting up.

Leaning against the desk, I pushed my cane to lie beneath it on the floor. Then, holding onto the edge with both hands, I lowered myself to sit on the floor. I fell the last half a foot. The pain took my breath away.

My eyes blurred. Brock would be coming any minute. I reached behind me for the chair and rolled it close. Scooted my body underneath the desk and pulled the chair up to the opening. I shoved myself back, leaning against the front panel wall of the desk. Breath gurgled up my windpipe, my chest swelling for air like a pumped balloon. I swallowed hard, fighting to quiet my gasps.

Too late I remembered the phone sitting on the desk. *No.* My heart lurched. I'd meant to grab it, call Jud while I was hiding.

A footstep sounded on the hall's hardwood floor.

My quivering hand dug in my pocket for the gun. I slid it out and wrapped both palms around its handle, my finger finding the trigger. I held it chest high, pointed toward the opening—and waited. My arms trembled, the weapon barrel wavering. How would I hold it steady enough to shoot?

If I shot at all.

Yes, I *would*. I wasn't a helpless child anymore, cowering in her room from her father's rages. I was a mother, with a daughter who needed me. I'd promised her we'd be together again.

The footsteps moved away from me, toward the den. I cocked my head, eyes closed, listening with my entire body.

Their sound faded. Maybe he was in the kitchen.

My insides started to shake. They quaked and heaved until vertigo muzzled my head, my eyes. Twice I nearly dropped the gun. I gripped it tighter, my knuckles throbbing.

Something sounded. I held my breath.

A step. A second. Coming back through the hall. So firm and steady. No need to call my name or hurry. Time was on his side.

Desperate hope writhed. Brock would search the house and think I'd gone. He wouldn't find me underneath here. As soon as he left I'd struggle up. Somehow. Get to the phone. I just had to keep quiet. Muffle my breathing.

The footfalls hit the office floor.

My jaw dropped open, oxygen pulled into my mouth in silent globs. The gun jittered so hard in my hands I knew I would drop it.

Please, God, let him pass by.

Only a minute, no longer. There weren't many places in here for me to hide. He'd be gone soon. Just one more minute . . .

The footsteps crossed the room behind me. He was checking beyond the armchairs. They halted, then returned. Started around the desk.

This is it, Jannie, hold on, hold on. My finger tightened around the trigger. I would shoot Brock. I would.

The words of that psalm flooded my mind: *"My voice rises to God, and He will hear me."* With every fiber I prayed for God's strength, for His help. My father had abused me. Now my husband wanted me dead. But my Heavenly Father was here. He *was.*

The footfalls crossed in front of the desk. In the dimness through the chair legs I could just make out Brock's dark pants as he passed by. All breath stopped.

I grasped the gun and counted the never-ending seconds. He would turn around now. Leave the room.

Dots skipped before my eyes. Flames shot down my limbs. *Come on, come on . . .*

The footfalls turned. Just beyond the chair the pant legs reappeared. They stopped before the desk.

The gun dipped and shook, my heart grinding, yet no blood flowed. The dots in my vision stuck together, blocking half my sight. I blinked my eyes, turning my gaze downward—and caught the horrific sight of my cane's hooked top sticking out just past the edge of the desk. Would he see it in the dark?

"My voice rises to God, and He will hear me . . ."

Brock took one step forward, then halted again. His clothes rustled.

"Ah." He said it low in his throat, followed by a satisfied chuckle. Almost as if he were proud of my resourcefulness. He moved to one side of the chair. It began to roll.

Don't do it, Brock, I'll shoot you. I will.

I clutched the gun, my hands smacking up and down. But even as the chair rolled back, back, out of the way, I knew I couldn't do it. I could not shoot my husband. The man I'd once loved. *Still* loved. The father my child so adored. How could I kill him and ever face Lauren again?

My head buzzed. I was going to faint.

The chair stopped rolling. Brock moved toward the desk. Clothes rustled once more as his legs began to bend.

A sob spilled from my lips.

Brock stilled at the sound. Then stooped down. I made out his arms. His shoulders.

No, Brock, please!

My trigger finger would not move.

His face peered under the desk. Did I see a smile?

"Found you, Janessa."

No, no.

He reached for me.

My finger jerked.

A gunshot shattered my ears.

Chapter 47

EVERYTHING BLURRED INTO CHAOS. THE GUN KICKED HARD in my tender hands. My body spasmed, and my head smacked against the back of the desk. I cried out and dropped the weapon. It fell on my lap. I swept it off.

Brock reeled backward from his squat and slumped over on the floor. He didn't move.

I screamed. Screamed again—then couldn't stop. Panic ricocheted through me until I thought I would explode. I could only see Brock's body up to his shoulders. Had I shot him in the head? What had I done, what had I *done?* I had to get out from under the desk, help him. Maybe he was alive. But I could barely move, and he lay right in front of the opening. I'd never be able to crawl over him. Never be able to get to the phone and call for help. How long would I be trapped in this little area with my own shrieks sizzling my ears, and my limbs too weak to move, and this acrid smell, and my husband, the father of my child, *dying?*

My throat turned ragged, and still I screamed.

A sudden earsplitting sound jangled my nerves. My shrieks cut off, my hands flying to my ears. Too loud, so loud, what *was* it?

The alarm.

I choked a breath. The police. They'd heard the gunshot.

"Here! Help!" But the constant ringing drowned out my cries. I struggled to scoot forward, my limbs barely working. "In here!"

The alarm stopped. The sudden silence buzzed my head.

I broke into sobs. Tried to drag myself from under the desk, but there lay Brock. My husband, and I'd killed him.

"Jannie?"

From some other plane I heard my name called. "H-here! In the . . ." What room was I in?

Running footsteps sounded in the hall.

"Jannie, where are you?"

"Here." I slumped over, chin to my chest. My head reeled.

The room lit up. Footsteps ran toward the desk. "What the—"

I raised my heavy head to see legs appear near Brock. The policeman bent down to look at my husband. Reached to touch his neck. *"What—?"*

The officer dropped to his knees and peered under the desk. In a terrifying hallucination, I saw Brock's face.

"No! Get away!"

"It's okay, it's okay." The man jumped up and dragged the body aside. Squatted down and held his hand out to me. "Come on now. It's me. Let's get you out of there."

"No!" I cowered back.

"Jannie, come on. I won't hurt you."

His face swam before me. My husband's face. Talking. Alive. "B-Brock?"

"Yeah. It's me. It's okay now."

"Brock?"

"Jannie." He reached out and clasped my wrist. "Come on now. I've got you."

The world went black.

Chapter 48

MY EYES BLINKED OPEN TO OVER-BRIGHT LIGHT. I WINCED. For a moment I knew nothing. Saw only the ceiling of our den, felt the sofa cushions beneath my legs. Then memory flooded my brain. A moan escaped my throat.

Brock's pinched face appeared above me. He stooped down and took my hand. His touch was gentle. "Welcome back. You've been out for awhile."

I stared at him. My Lyme brain whirred but kicked up only grit.

He gave me a tight smile. "Everything's okay. The officer who was patrolling outside is here."

Vaguely I registered a man's voice from the other side of the house, the squawk of an answering radio. "But I sh-shot—"

"I know." Brock's face contorted. "I'm so sorry you had to face that alone."

"But . . ."

"Dane worked for me for two years. I had no idea. I still can't . . . I just don't understand how this happened."

Who?

"But it's over, Jannie. He's dead."

"I sh-shot *you*."

"Me? No."

"But you . . ."

"It was Dane Melford. Remember him?" Brock spoke as if addressing a confused child. "My lab assistant."

My tongue wouldn't work.

"He apparently got in through the window upstairs."

Breaking glass. I remembered that. I licked my lips. "It wasn't you."

"I came in to help you, remember? I was trying to get you out from under the desk."

I could only stare at him.

"Jannie, it's okay now. You're just still in shock."

"I thought . . . You didn't make those phone calls? Infect me with Lyme?"

"Of course not. Don't tell me you really believed that."

Why shouldn't I have?

"Jannie, I'd never do anything like that to you. How could you even think such a thing?"

Because . . . because it made sense at the time.

Hadn't it?

I felt so numb. I couldn't even rejoice that my daughter's father wasn't dead. That I hadn't killed him. "I never thought you'd leave me either."

Guilt flicked across Brock's forehead. A moment passed before he spoke. "I'm so sorry I didn't believe you. I just had no idea. I thought you were making the whole thing up to get back at me. But I should have known. Should have listened."

My throat tightened. For a moment I couldn't speak. "You stopped listening to me a long time ago."

Brock looked away. "I should have believed you were sick." He shifted to his knees. "But the story about the man and the phone calls just sounded so crazy. And I still can't understand how Dane . . ."

Dane Melford. The name was just sinking in. Brock's loyal assistant. Had always been so nice to me.

Sympathy for Brock twinged. Betrayal never felt good. "Why'd he do it?"

Brock rubbed his cheek hard. For the first time I realized how shell-shocked he looked. "I talked to Jud Maxwell on the phone. He's on his way over here. He'd just found a picture of Dane online. Dane had a sick wife who died."

"But he'd never been married."

"I guess he lied about that. Apparently he lied about a lot of things."

I couldn't respond. Too much to take in.

Brock shook his head. "He claimed his wife died from Lyme."

"*Claimed.*" Same old Brock. My sympathy waned.

I pulled my hand from his. So much this man—my own husband—had done to me. "I thought it was you. I thought I'd shot *you.*"

Brock eyed me, his mouth opening.

"Do you get that, Brock? *Do* you? You say Dane lied. Well, you lied to *me.* Abandoned me for someone else. Refused to believe my . . . pain and fear. Took my d-daughter away from me. When I heard the window b-break, I thought it was you. I got the gun and hid from *you.*"

Horror crept across his face. He rocked back on his heels. "You wanted to kill *me?*"

How thick *was* this man? Could he not see what he'd done to me? What he'd driven me to? "Wanted? No. Never. In fact I couldn't, even when you—he—leaned down by that desk and grabbed for me. Even when I knew I was going to die. But then my finger jerked, and—" Tears bit my eyes. I turned my head away.

No reply from Brock. For once he'd been shocked to silence.

I lay there and cried. Still Brock said nothing.

A horrible thought hit. My head shifted back to Brock, my voice sharp. "Where's Lauren?"

"With Alicia." Defensiveness edged his tone. "Sound asleep."

"You took her to your office after school. Was D-Dane there?"

Brock's eyes widened. "We saw him when we came in. And she sat outside his cubicle doing homework."

"He threatened to give her Lyme, Brock." Panic clutched my throat. "He could have put a tick on her!"

Brock's face paled.

"You have to go check her all over. Right now!"

He pushed to his feet. "I'll call Alicia."

"She won't—"

"Alicia knows what ticks look like, Jannie." His voice had hardened. He thrust a hand in his hair. Stared at the floor. "She'll be okay. Even if he did put a tick on her, it hasn't had time to start transmitting the spirochetes."

"You sure?"

"Yes." He gave me a look. "There's no controversy about *that*."

We stared at each other, thinking too many thoughts to speak.

I heard the front door open. "Dr. McNeil?"

I knew that terse voice. Jud Maxwell.

"In here." Brock strode around the couch. I looked over the back of the sofa to see Jud appear at the den's threshold. He looked out of breath, shaken.

"Got here fast as I could." Jud gazed past Brock toward me. He hurried into the den, around the furniture. Brock followed. "Mrs. McNeil. You all right?"

No. My head nodded. "I k-killed him."

Only then did it begin to sink in. I'd killed a man. Someone I'd known and trusted. Fresh tears welled in my eyes.

Jud shook his head. "It's okay, you're safe. That's what matters."

"Will I be . . . arrested?"

He gave me a wan smile. "Don't you worry about that. We'll clear this up."

"I want to say again that I'm sorry I didn't call you back today." Brock faced the detective, remorse in his expression. "I shouldn't have ignored you."

Jud waved the apology away. "That last call to your cell just a little while ago—when I found Melford's picture on the computer, I thought of you immediately. I had to let you know. When I couldn't reach you, I dialed here. But the phone was busy."

Brock nodded. "It was off the hook."

It was?

Vaguely I remembered trying to call Jud. Dropping the receiver when I heard the glass break.

The detective looked back to me. "I'm sorry, Mrs. McNeil. So sorry. I should have discovered this sooner."

"Don't . . . You did what you could."

Our eyes held for a moment.

Jud gestured toward the office with his chin. "I've got to go in there." He swiped his forehead. "We'll have other officers responding. I'm afraid your house is about to be turned into a crime scene. But you stay where you are. For the moment you're fine in here."

"Okay." Brock stepped aside to let the detective pass.

"Be back in to talk to you soon as I can." Jud hurried from the room.

Brock turned away, reaching into his pocket. He pulled out his cell phone and hit a button. I heard a number automatically dial.

Alicia.

How many months had that auto dial been on my husband's phone?

He wandered into the kitchen as he began speaking. I heard the words *wake up Lauren* and *tick*, then could hear no more.

My eyes closed. From deep inside my body started to shake. I needed water. And I felt so weak. Like I would never, ever get off the couch again.

I don't know how many minutes passed before Brock returned, slipping the cell phone back into his pocket. He ventured no closer than his armchair.

My armchair.

His gaze met mine. So many unspoken words thrummed between us.

He spread his hands. "What you did tonight, Jannie—it's amazing. Really. You stopped a madman."

By the grace of God. Still, my husband's help would have been appreciated.

"At least you can rest now." Brock gave me tight smile. "It's over."

His words struck to the core of me. I looked away, feeling more weary than ever. And so very alone.

"Over, Brock? Far from it. I still have Lyme."

THREE MONTHS LATER

Epilogue

LAUREN AND I WERE AT THE KITCHEN TABLE ON A FRIDAY morning when she saw it. I noticed her glance at the floor, then do a double take. She frowned, her mouth stopping in mid-crunch of her cereal. Then her eyes widened. She dropped the spoon into her bowl, got up and crept toward the counter.

I turned to follow her focus. "What is it?"

A speck of red on the hardwood caught my eye.

Lauren squatted down a safe distance away and pointed. "Look."

The tick.

"Oh." My breath stopped. The nightmare of last May came hurling back.

As if it owned the world, the tick started crawling toward Lauren. She jumped to the safety of her chair and lifted her feet. "Where'd it come from?"

I watched it, too stunned to reply. We'd managed to convince ourselves the tick had found its way outside at some point while the back door was open. But all these months it had been here. *Here.* My skin tingled.

"Get it, Mom!" Lauren's face scrunched up.

I rallied myself. "I will." I tried to keep my voice light, even as my heart skidded. We'd had three months to heal emotionally, yet even now the fear rested just below the surface. Lauren still slept with me every night. And every night we turned on the alarm.

I pushed to my feet, reaching for my cane. "You're going to have to help me. You know I can't lean over."

"I don't wanna touch that thing!"

"You won't have to touch it. Just get a glass for me."

"But I'll have to walk past it."

"Never mind, I'll get the glass." Skirting the tick, I edged over to open the cabinet. After three months of antibiotics I moved better these days. But I was far from well. And some days—when the herxes hit—I could barely make it around the house.

I pulled down a tall glass and held it out to Lauren. The tick was now a few feet from her chair. "Set this down in front of it so I can push it inside."

She made a face but did as she was told. I held on to the table and used my cane to nudge the tick over the edge of the glass. "There. Now turn it up."

"What if it jumps back out?"

"Ticks don't jump."

She eyed me.

"Come on, Lauren, before he crawls out of there."

She righted the glass. The tick slid to the bottom.

Lauren set it on the counter near the stove and backed away. She shuddered. "Where *was* it?"

I watched its legs move, feeling for bearings. "Must have been up under that lip of wood by the cabinets."

"All that time it didn't eat?"

A shiver ran through me. "Guess not."

Lauren's eyes met mine. "Does it have Lyme?"

Probably.

"It's the one Dane put in my backpack, isn't it?"

Lauren remembered Dane. All too well. How nice he'd been to her that afternoon when she'd done her homework outside his office. He bought her a Coke. And he patted her head. No doubt that's when he released the tiny tick in its nymph stage. Alicia found the tick on Lauren's scalp that same night. Brock pulled it out with tweezers. Lab tests confirmed it carried *Borrelia*. But, thank God, the tick had not been attached to Lauren long enough to transmit the spirochetes.

"Yup. Imagine so."

The old anxiety rattled inside me. Mentally I recited a psalm. *When I am afraid, I will trust in You. In God, whose word I praise . . .*

We watched the tick move across the bottom of the glass.

"What're you going to do with it, Mom?"

I wanted to kill it. Smash it flat. "I think I'll put it in a little plastic bag and take it to Detective Maxwell."

Lauren pulled her head back. "What's *he* want with it?"

I shrugged. "Maybe nothing. But maybe just as a last bit of evidence, he'll have it tested to see what it carries."

Or maybe he'd do that out of mere curiosity. The case was officially closed. Even though Dane was dead, Jud had dug into his background, uncovering the what and who, trying to piece together the why. The police had to be sure he'd acted alone. Apparently Dane had married young, to a woman named Elyse. She'd been infected with Lyme and, like so many patients, wasn't diagnosed for years. She had a particularly hard case and, despite months of antibiotics, could not get well. Then her insurance ran out, her treatment stopped— and she died. Upon autopsy spirochetes were found in the tissue surrounding her heart.

Dane had years to swim in his bitterness—until he vowed to do something about it. Jud surmised that he'd planned his attack for years, purposely hiring on as a lab assistant to Brock. The two years he worked with his nemesis he apparently learned Brock's out-of-town schedule, and most likely cased our house to see the layout of windows and doors.

The thought of the man's painstaking cunning still brought me chills.

Lauren moved her lips around. Her eyes wouldn't leave the tick. "I want to tell Daddy we found it. Think he's at work yet?"

I glanced at the clock. After 8:00. "Yes."

Since Lauren had come back to live with me two months ago, she called her dad at least once a day. And every other weekend she stayed with Brock and Alicia. Brock and I only spoke when we had to, mostly regarding our daughter. Too much hurt hung between us.

Lauren hurried to pick up the phone.

A few hours later I drove Lauren to Katie's to spend the night. Katie's family had been gone on vacation, and the girls wanted as many sleepovers as they could have before school started. I'd only begun driving again in the past three weeks, so I took it slow. But I could do it. And I could think better. And talk without stuttering—well, most of the time.

The tick rode along with us in a plastic bag, tightly sealed.

The minute Katie opened her front door Lauren launched into her story about finding the tick. Now that the thing was safely ensconced in plastic, she made herself sound oh, so brave.

"I can't believe it showed up, just like that." Maria shook her head.

I gave her a look. *Chalk it up to one of the many crazy things that have happened to me.*

The girls soon pounded down the hall to Katie's room. I settled at Maria's kitchen table as she made me a latte—decaf coffee, no sugar. My Lyme diet reigned supreme.

"So how are you?" Maria poured milk into a metal cup.

"Okay. I have my good days and bad days, as you know. But I'm fighting it."

"How much longer will you need treatment?"

I sighed. "Don't know. Months yet. Still, I'm one of the fortunate ones. At least I have a diagnosis and a doctor who knows how to treat me. And so far my insurance continues to cover the medication. That's far more than a lot of Lyme sufferers have."

She nodded.

We fell silent as Maria foamed the milk at the espresso machine.

She poured the coffee and milk together. "Did the divorce papers come?"

My gaze fell to the table. "Yeah."

She made a sound in her throat. "When?"

"Last week."

Maria set the drink before me. Handed me a napkin. "I'm so sorry, Jannie."

I managed a smile. "Well, not like I didn't know he was going to file."

Brock had promised not to fight me over details—perhaps due to his guilt over not believing me. Lauren and I would stay in the house. He'd provide me with child support, of course, and alimony until I was well enough to work.

As for Brock's work—and views on Lyme—nothing had changed. He remained in his position at Stanford School of Medicine. His research continued. And the committee he chaired had published its latest findings on Lyme. Findings that further narrowed the parameters of the disease, which meant diagnosis and treatment would be even harder for many patients to obtain. I knew firsthand that was indeed happening from talking to Lyme sufferers across the country. After Dane's death my news story had gone national.

I found myself speaking out on behalf of the Lyme community often these days.

I sipped the foam on my drink while Maria made a latte for herself. "So Lauren's staying until Sunday, right? And we'll get her back to you at church."

"That's the plan. Unless I take a sudden downturn and can't go."

It had happened before a number of times, but now I managed to make the service most Sundays. For all I'd survived, God surely deserved my praise. And the people at Maria's church—now *my* church—had been so kind to me. That first horrible month of treatment, when Lauren still lived with her dad, many had brought me dinners and driven me to the doctor—even before they knew me.

Maria shrugged. "Well, if that happens, no worries. We'll just drive Lauren back to you." She settled at the table with her latte. "Lauren looks good. I don't see that lost little girl look in her eyes so much."

"She's hanging in there. Getting used to her new life."

Used to her parents not living together, and shuttling back and forth between homes. She was also getting used to Alicia. For Lauren's sake, I was glad to see that. Still, my heart panged whenever she spoke of their shopping or going places together. Things I longed to do with my daughter—and couldn't.

One day. My health *would* return to me.

Maria and I talked for an hour, until I felt myself tiring. I needed to get home and rest. But I still had to stop by Jud Maxwell's office. He was expecting me.

I hugged Maria, kissed Lauren good-bye, and caned out to my car.

Twenty minutes later as I made my slow way into the police station to see Jud, the bagged tick sat in my purse. I could feel my body weakening. Any time I pushed myself to do too much, my symptoms flared.

In Jud's small office I held the plastic bag out to him with a small flourish. "Here it is."

"Look at that." Jud shot me a nonplused grin.

"Will you test it at the . . . L-Lyme lab?" Uh-oh, I was starting to stutter. A sign of my weariness.

He lifted a shoulder. "Maybe. We'll at least keep it with the case files. It's nice to know it's out of your house."

No kidding.

Jud motioned to the chair before his desk. "Please. Sit down. You look worn out."

It was kind of him to notice. But then, he would. Jud had become a friend to me and Lauren. He'd stopped by the house on a couple occasions to see how we were getting along. And his wife, Sarah, called occasionally to check up on me, even if that did put her in a bit of an awkward position. Neither she nor Jud approved of Brock's relationship with Alicia. But Sarah did still work for Brock.

"Thanks." I settled into the chair.

Jud held up a finger. "I have something for you." He opened a drawer in his desk and pulled out a manila file. "These are extra copies for you to keep. All the stuff I uncovered about Dane Melford."

I eyed the folder, not sure how much I wanted to know. "Anything n-new?"

Jud rested his elbows on the desk and steepled his fingers. "A few pieces that might help clarify why he did what he did. For one thing, he was bipolar and on meds. He'd been diagnosed as a teenager. If he went off his meds, that could have added to his instability. I also managed to track down some of his old friends from school. They told me Dane had a self-righteous, obsessive streak even then. Seemed to just be in his make-up."

Hardly an excuse for what he'd done to me. "He sure m-managed to seem normal when he worked with Brock."

Jud gave me a grim smile. "He sure did."

Fatigue weighed my chest. I really needed to get home. "Jud, thank you. I need to g-go now." With effort I pushed to my feet.

He nodded. "I'll walk you to your car." Jud picked up the file and ushered me out.

When I reached home it was nearly one o'clock. The house felt so still and empty. Brock gone, Lauren gone. But I was not alone.

Too tired to eat, I headed straight for the couch and collapsed upon it. After a few hours' rest I'd be ready to get up again. And with God's help I'd tackle the rest of the day.

As my eyes closed, my two favorite verses from Psalm 94 rose in my mind: "*If I should say, 'My foot has slipped,' Your lovingkindness, O LORD, will hold me up. When my anxious thoughts multiply within me, your consolations delight my soul.*"

Such comforting words. Again and again they had proved true.

I mouthed them silently until I fell asleep.

A Note from Brandilyn Collins

🐝 I HAVEN'T JUST STUDIED LYME. I'VE LIVED IT.

Remember Jannie McNeil's fall in her kitchen, and her inability to get up? That's straight out of my own life. When Lyme hit me, it came fast and hard. Until that day I had been a healthy, fit, five-miles-a-day runner. Fortunately I had a friend who recognized the symptoms and insisted I go for testing. From there I linked up with a Lyme-literate doctor. Most fortunate of all, God chose to miraculously heal me from the disease months later. But not before I'd lived the nightmare of Lyme. Six years later in 2009 I was reinfected with the disease and managed to conquer it after six months of antibiotic treatment.

I remember slumping in the waiting room of my doctor in 2003, so sick I could not remain sitting in the chair. (They had to move me to the doctor's personal padded armchair with footrest in a private office.) Hanging on the waiting-room wall was a framed newspaper article summarizing the 2001 findings written in *The New England Journal of Medicine*. (While Brock McNeil's part in writing those findings is fictional, they are very real.) The newspaper article explained how researchers had once again proved that Lyme was never chronic and was, in fact, very easy to treat with a short-term round of antibiotics. People claiming months or years of crippling symptoms from the disease were just *wrong*.

What those know-it-alls need, I thought with an admittedly un-Christian attitude, *is a real good case of Lyme*.

And so the idea for this novel was born. It would take another seven years before I was ready to write it.

In *Over the Edge* the background information about Lyme disease and the Lyme wars is straight out of my research. To this day many Lyme patients have to fight for diagnosis and treatment. But beyond that, this book is a work of fiction. The characters are in no way real. Brock McNeil does not represent any one doctor. Rather, he arose from my own imagination as a combination of researchers who still deny the existence of chronic Lyme as an active infection. In placing him at the Stanford School of Medicine I'm casting no aspersions on that respected institution. It simply provided a setting for my story. One other fictional point to note: In *Over the Edge* Jannie's test results from the Lyme lab were available within about six hours. I wrote it that way to keep my story moving. In reality, results could not be ready that quickly.

Now, fiction aside, let's talk about the realities of Lyme.

The Lyme wars go back a number of decades. It's a complex war with complex arguments, but simplified it comes down to these two sides: Lyme-literate doctors—working in the trenches with very sick patients—who believe long-term antibiotic treatment is effective, vs. doctors aligned with such powerful entities as the Centers for Disease Control (CDC) and the Infectious Diseases Society of America (IDSA), who deny the existence of chronic Lyme as an active infection. This latter group of doctors instead insist that long-term patients suffer from a post-Lyme treatment syndrome—some form of autoimmune disease as yet unknown and undefined. This "syndrome" should only be treated symptomatically, they say, and not with antibiotics.

As *Over the Edge* depicts, the Lyme wars arise from these four factors, which form a vicious circle:

First, *Ineffective testing.* The CDC criteria for administering and interpreting tests have been controversial since they were approved in 1994. First the CDC insists on a two-tier form of testing, starting with the ELISA test, then proceeding to the Western blot *only when the ELISA is positive.* Unfortunately all too often a negative ELISA is a false negative because of the test's poor sensitivity. (Although the CDC insists the test *is* sensitive.) So many patients are lost right there.

Those who do test positive move on to the Western blot, which looks for antibodies to *Borrelia burgdorferi* in the blood that reveal themselves in the form of stripes or "bands." Each band refers to a certain type of antibody and is indicated on the test results by a given number. Even when the test for Lyme was first developed many doctors protested the inclusion and exclusion of certain bands. One of the biggest arguments was over band 31—an antibody to a protein on *Borrelia's* outer surface called OspA that is exclusive to Lyme. Yet this band was not included as a positive indicator on the test, while other bands that were less important were included. In order to test positive for Lyme, a patient must see a certain number of the included bands indicate positive. Many patients fall short of that required number of positive bands, often due to the fact that Lyme-specific bands that should have been included as significant were not. Overall, as a result of these controversial criteria, patients can see "negative" false results as much as thirty to forty percent of the time.

To counteract the CDC's ineffective criteria for testing, labs such as IGeneX in Palo Alto, California, have designed their own criteria that include the Lyme-specific bands that the CDC's criteria do not. IGeneX tests also search for more than one strain of *Borrelia*, while the most common test kit in other labs looks for only one strain— B31, the original strain found on Long Island. Lyme-literate doctors often send blood to labs such as IGeneX. Meanwhile the CDC and medical community at large do not recognize results from such labs as legitimate. Like Jannie McNeil, in 2009 my results from IGeneX were positive for Lyme according to IGeneX criteria, but negative according to CDC criteria. As sick as I was with Lyme, if I'd relied on standard diagnostic criteria, I would have remained undiagnosed and untreated. That unfortunate scenario happens again and again for Lyme sufferers.

Second, *Lack of education among doctors.* Lyme-literate docs are few and far between. The rest simply don't know enough about the disease, relying on outdated information as to where Lyme is found and what its symptoms are. For example, to this day many doctors still believe the old axiom that a patient must present the erythema migrans or "bull's-eye" rash in order to have Lyme. While the E.M. rash is a strong indication of Lyme when it occurs, many patients never have it. I didn't. The CDC itself looked at 119,965 Lyme patients between the years of 1992 and 2004, finding that only 68 percent of them had the rash. Other research indicates the rash, when present, resembles the infamous "bull's-eye" only 9 percent of the time. In addition you'll still hear docs in many states swear that Lyme is never found there— even when they'll admit it occurs in nearby states. Amazing. I wonder how those ticks know to stop at the state borders.

I know a twenty-year-old who was once healthy and outgoing. Now she lies bedridden, unable to walk or even hold a phone to her ear. She knows of receiving four tick bites, three of which caused the definitive bull's-eye rash. Even so her doctor insisted there was no reason to test for Lyme. "We don't have Lyme in this state," she was told. If she had been treated early on, she probably would be well today. But instead she went years without a diagnosis or treatment. All the while the spirochetes within her body reproduced and spread throughout all her systems.

I'm also left to wonder about the upcoming ranks of doctors and nurses. A couple years ago a nursing student in Washington state was telling me about her class on diseases. When they came to Lyme, the instructor said, "No need to bother with learning about that one. It's pretty rare, and we don't have it in this state." Wrong and wrong. I know people in Washington who are fighting Lyme. It's frightening to think that the health-care providers of tomorrow are being taught the old, incorrect axioms.

As one Lyme-literate doctor explained to me, at the heart of many doctors' inability to recognize Lyme is the incorrect application of the CDC surveillance criteria for Lyme. The role of the CDC is surveillance of disease in the U.S. Therefore the criteria the CDC establishes to determine if someone has a particular disease is very stringent. In surveilling cases of Lyme nationwide the organization wants to make very sure every person it counts as a Lyme patient indeed has Lyme. But these stringent criteria—which include presentation of only a few certain symptoms and a positive test result according to CDC criteria, among other things—are being misused as *diagnostic criteria* in doctors' examining rooms. The CDC web site itself says its "surveillance case definition was developed for national reporting of Lyme disease; it is not intended to be used in clinical diagnosis." Yet from doctor's office to doctor's office, the criteria *are* being used to diagnose, no matter how strongly a patient might present other known symptoms of Lyme.

Third, *Doctors' fear of treating chronic Lyme.* Many of the doctors who treat Lyme with long-term antibiotics are taking a great risk. Some Lyme-literate docs have had their licenses pulled. They've been sued by insurance companies, who didn't want to cover the expensive drugs. Even a reputable doctor who recognizes a case of Lyme may refuse to admit it because he simply does not want to get caught in the Lyme war crossfire.

I remember talking on the phone with one desperate man in Oregon who was very sick. "I've had three tests for Lyme," he told me. "All three were positive. Plus I have many obvious Lyme symptoms.

But after every test my doctor insists it's a false positive and still refuses to treat me."

Fourth, *Misdiagnosis*. Since the patients are really sick and Lyme is ruled out through misuse of the CDC criteria and poor testing—well, they must have something. That "something" often is misdiagnosed as Chronic Fatigue Syndrome, Fibromyalgia, Multiple Sclerosis, Parkinson's, Rheumatoid Arthritis, and other diseases. Either that or the symptoms are just "all in their head." (Which some doctors have been known to claim.) The problem with misdiagnosis isn't just the lack of right treatment, but the introduction of *wrong* treatment. For example, CFS patients are often given steroids to combat their swollen, painful joints. The problem is, steroids suppress the immune system and therefore are never given when a doctor knows a patient has an active infection of any kind. Bacteria are left to thrive in an immune-suppressed body. The Lyme patient gets worse.

Such is the unfortunate story of the twenty-year-old mentioned above. Since she "couldn't have Lyme" in the state in which she lived, she was diagnosed with CFS and put on steroids for months. She became much worse. Her Lyme was allowed to run rampant for years until someone finally pointed her to a Lyme-literate doctor for testing. But by then she was bedridden.

In the last few years Lyme proponents have seen some breakthroughs regarding the medical community's resistance to treating chronic Lyme. On July 1, 2009 a bill in Connecticut took effect that allows licensed physicians to administer long-term treatment to diagnosed Lyme patients and prohibits the Department of Public Health and the Connecticut Medical Examining Board from taking disciplinary action against doctors for such treatment. (Dr. Carol Johannis spoke of this legislation with Jannie.) A victory for Lyme patients, to be sure— albeit too late for some Lyme-treating doctors. Still, how amazing that it took until 2009 for this to happen in *Connecticut*—considered the ground zero state for Lyme and home to the town for which the disease is named.

In 2006, five years after that 2001 article I read in my doctor's waiting room, IDSA published its updated *Clinical Practice Guidelines* for Lyme. These guidelines further narrowed the parameters of the disease, thereby further limiting ability to treat. The IDSA guidelines are no small thing. Insurance companies cite them as reason not to pay for treatment, and medical boards quote them as proof chronic Lyme doesn't exist—that is, the bacteria causing Lyme are completely eradicated from the body after the recommended two to four weeks of antibiotics. As a result of the IDSA guidelines doctors would remain wrongly educated about the disease and refuse treatment.

Incensed they'd been had once again, Lyme patients rallied—literally. In time the attorney general of Connecticut launched an antitrust investigation into IDSA and the guidelines. From the looks of it, too many of the doctors on the IDSA panel had reputations and money at stake, apparently causing them to ignore dissenting views and research findings about Lyme. In May 2008 the Connecticut attorney general announced that his investigation had indeed uncovered serious flaws in the IDSA guideline-writing process, including conflicts of money interests, quashing of research that pointed to the existence of chronic Lyme, a biased chairman who handpicked doctors who believed as he did, and more. As a result a new review panel, consisting of doctors with reportedly no conflicting interests, would be created—again under the auspices of IDSA—to relook at the guidelines.

In 2009 a national hearing was held, during which physicians and scientists on both sides of the debate presented their research data regarding Lyme to the review panel. Some of the presentations arguing against the IDSA guidelines included:

1. Dr. Benjamin Luft, from SUNY Stony Brook, who presented evidence that Lyme bacteria can indeed persist in the body beyond the IDSA-recommended two to four weeks of antibiotic treatment.

2. A dissection of the four peer-reviewed IDSA studies, which showed that two of them were based on serious flaws, while the other two showed that patients did improve after six weeks of IV antibiotics. Since the four studies were based on only 207 patients in total and administering only one antibiotic, presenters argued that much more study was needed.

3. Dr. Ray Stricker and others, who presented studies that showed the two-tier standardized Lyme test lacks the sensitivity required to be accurate, missing eighty-eight out of every two hundred Lyme patients. The CDC spokesperson, Barbara Johnson, stood by the tests, although it was shown her endorsement was based on a ten-year-old study of a mere twenty-six patients.

After the hearing everyone waited for the pronouncement of the review panel. The panel said it would have findings by December of 2009, but 2010 rolled around with no announcement. The Lyme community remained skeptical. After all, the chair of the panel was a past president of IDSA. In April of 2010 the review panel finally announced its findings: bottom line, the current IDSA guidelines would stand. Specifically, the panel declared:

1. "There is no convincing biologic evidence for the existence of symptomatic chronic B. Burgdorferi infections among patients after receipt of recommended treatment regimens for Lyme disease."

2. "Antibiotic therapy has not proved to be useful and is not recommended for patients with chronic (>6 months) subjective symptoms after recommended treatment regimens." Controlled clinic trials for extended antibiotic treatment demonstrated "considerable risk of harm," and "little benefit." Therefore the risk/benefit ratio "strongly discourages" prolonged antibiotics.

3. The case reports of "perceived clinical improvement" during

prolonged antibiotic treatment, including those presented at the 2009 hearings, were "intrinsically incapable of hypothesis-testing." These reports were pronounced tainted for various reasons, one being that many participating patients' diagnoses of Lyme was questionable because they weren't tested under current CDC standards.

That's right—the very testing criteria that are inaccurate to begin with. Such a declaration from the review panel is one example of the cyclical reasoning that has arisen ever since the narrowly-defined Lyme symptoms and testing criteria were established in 1994. Often the cyclical reasoning goes something like this: only the CDC criteria are correct . . . therefore studies should include only patients meeting the CDC criteria . . . therefore results of said studies prove the CDC criteria are correct.

In short, all findings from the hearing that proved *Borrelia burgdorferi* exist after the IDSA-recommended two to four weeks of antibiotics were completely discounted.

In *Over the Edge*, Jannie reads an abstract of research that proves *Borrelia* continue to exist in mice after the recommended four weeks of treatment. This was taken from the article "Persistence of *Borrelia burgdorferi* following Antibiotic Treatment in Mice" by Emir Hodzic, Sunlian Feng, Kevin Holden, Kimberly J. Freet, and Stephen W. Barthold from the University of California at Davis. The full paper can be found online at: http://aac.asm.org/cgi/content/abstract/52/5/1728.

In 2009 the film crew of the award-winning Lyme documentary *Under Our Skin* interviewed Dr. Willy Burgdorfer, the scientist who discovered the spirochete that causes Lyme—which was named after the doctor. Dr. Burgdorfer had been retired since 1986.

When asked what he thought about the current Lyme wars, he responded, "The controversy in Lyme disease research is a shameful affair . . . The whole thing is politically tainted. Money goes to people who have, for the past thirty years, produced the same thing—nothing.

Serology has to be started from scratch with people who don't know beforehand the results of their research. There are lots of physicians around who wouldn't touch a Lyme disease patient. So [this] shame includes [them.]" His biggest regret in the aftermath of his discovery of *Borrelia burdoferi* is "that the technology used to diagnose and treat Lyme Disease wasn't worked all the way through. It [was based on] only a few results, then published. And later on, people [wanted] to take them back."

But even years later, at least as of the writing of this novel, they haven't been taken back. And so, for chronic Lyme sufferers, the fight goes on.

I wrote *Over the Edge* to tell a good suspense story. But beyond mere entertainment, I wanted to help shed light on the difficult struggles of thousands of Lyme patients in this country. I hope the novel helps individuals out there. Perhaps you. Perhaps someone you love.

If you are experiencing muscle weakness, joint pain, confused thinking, or other symptoms mentioned in this story, you owe it to yourself to be properly tested for Lyme. Don't allow doctors in your area to dissuade you from tests by claiming it doesn't exist in your state. And to ensure results are as accurate as possible, have your blood sent to a lab dedicated to testing for Lyme. There are numerous organizations and online sites that can help with information. I list a few of them here.

1. Lyme Disease Association. "Readiness through prevention, education, research, and patient support." This is an all-volunteer national nonprofit organization. (http://www.lymediseaseassociation.org)

2. International Lyme and Associated Diseases Society. A nonprofit organization. (www.ilads.org)

3. Lyme Disease Network. "*A nonprofit foundation dedicated to public education of the prevention and treatment of Lyme disease and other tick-borne illnesses.*" The Lyme Disease Network offers local support groups,

online forums for questions and answers, a newsletter, and much more. (http://lyme.net)

4. The Lyme Disease Foundation, *"the premier nonprofit dedicated to finding solutions for tick-borne disorders."* LDF was cofounded by Karen Vanderhoof-Forschner and Thomas E. Forschner, whose young son, Jamie, died in 1991 during a relapse of Lyme disease. (http://www. lyme.org/front.htm)

5. Canadian Lyme Disease Foundation. *"A federally registered charitable organization dedicated to promoting research, education, diagnosis, and treatment of Lyme and associated diseases since 2003."* (www.canlyme.com)

6. California Lyme Disease Association. *"The California Lyme Disease Association (CALDA) is a non-profit corporation acting as the central voice for all tick-borne disease issues in California and a supporting voice for national issues."* CALDA publishes the Lyme Times; was instrumental in establishing the Lyme Disease Advisory Committee (LDAC), which advises the California Department of Public Health on matters concerning Lyme disease; and is active in legislation regarding Lyme. (http://www.lymedisease.org)

7. Lyme Disease Research Database. Covering *"Lyme disease symptoms, treatment, diagnosis, prevention, and research."* Members receive access to the large database of LDRD resources. (http://www.lyme-disease-research-database.com)

8. *Lyme-Aware.* This organization was formed to *"create a unity among all of the [Lyme] organizations, websites, blogs, authors, etc."* (www. lyme-aware.org)

9. *Advanced Topics in Lyme Disease* by Dr. Joseph J. Burrascano. This is an in depth medical abstract about the symptoms and treatment of the disease. The symptom checklist is particularly helpful if you are experiencing symptoms that might be caused by Lyme. (http://www. lymenet.org/BurrGuide200810.pdf)

10. *Under Our Skin*, an award-winning documentary that follows the stories of numerous Lyme patients and includes interviews with

doctors on both sides of the Lyme wars. *Under Our Skin* is well worth watching. It is both heartbreaking and hopeful. You can see firsthand what the symptoms of Lyme look like. And you'll be amazed at certain doctors' attitudes against recognizing the chronic form of the disease. You can order a DVD of the documentary from its web site at http://underourskin.com.

11. *Cure Unknown*, by scientific journalist Pamela Weintraub. This book is a highly researched and fascinating look into the Lyme wars, from their beginning history to present day. Weintraub and her entire family were infected with Lyme disease after moving to an idyllic setting in Connecticut. Her ensuing years of discovery about the disease and its controversy within the medical community make for a richly detailed and often horrifying picture of the patients and doctors embroiled in the battle.

12. My own web sites contain answers to questions about Lyme disease and links to helpful organizations. See www.brandilyncollins.com and www.seatbeltsuspense.com. The story of my miraculous healing from my first bout with Lyme is on www.brandilyncollins.com. On my Lyme-*Over the Edge* blog are many incredible stories of Lyme patients and their struggles. Read these stories, and you'll understand how they suffer, and why they continue to cry out for proper testing and treatment. (www.lyme-overtheedge.blospot.com)

Finally, dear readers, I always love to hear from you. You can contact me from my web site. I am also on Facebook: www.facebook.com/brandilyncollinsseatbeltsuspense and Twitter: www.twitter.com/brandilyn.

God's blessings and health to all of you.

Acknowledgments

MUCH OF MY RESEARCH FOR THIS STORY WAS GAINED THROUGH living with the disease myself and talking to numerous doctors over the years. Also very helpful were writings by the organizations listed in my author's note, as well as the book and documentary film I mentioned—*Cure Unknown* and *Under our Skin*. I also studied countless papers of clinical trials regarding Lyme, and read transcripts of hearings about the disease.

For help with specific issues in the book, I turned to a few wonderful people.

First, my particular thanks to these experts in the field of Lyme, who reviewed *Over the Edge* regarding facts about Lyme disease, its testing and treatment, and the controversy of the Lyme wars:

Dr. Christine Green, a highly knowledgeable Lyme-literate doctor who has treated the disease for years.

Jim Wilson, president and founder of the Canadian Lyme Disease Foundation.

Dr. Nick S. Harris, President/CEO of IGeneX, Inc.

Thanks to Mark Mynheir, whose career in law enforcement spans well over two decades. With all his experience in working as a narcotics agent, on a S.W.A.T. team, and as a homicide detective, Mark proved very helpful in telling me about the latest information on tracing phone calls. Mark Young, a retired police officer with over thirty years' experience, was also helpful with the phone tracing issues and with explaining how a detective might handle Jannie McNeil's strange case. You can blame me, not these two professionals, for any police work in the story that doesn't completely align with their guidance.

Dr. Richard Mabry, now retired, guided me through Jannie's stay in the hospital and the tests that she would face.

My thanks again to all of these experts. Any factual errors remaining in the story are mine.

Discussion Questions

1. How did Jannie's childhood experiences as the daughter of an alcoholic help define her marriage?

2. If you experienced the sudden symptoms Jannie experienced at the beginning of the book, what would you think was wrong?

3. If you know someone with Lyme disease, how are their symptoms similar to or different from Jannie's?

4. Describe a time in your life when you willed yourself to praise God through difficulty.

5. To what extent did Jannie's desire to have the perfect home and marriage allow her to close her eyes to hints that her husband was having an affair?

6. Did you ever feel any sympathy for Stalking Man? Why or why not?

7. Did you ever feel any sympathy for Brock? Why or why not?

8. How did Jannie exhibit strength in the midst of her body and mind being so weak?

9. Psalms 94:17–18 says, "If the LORD had not been my help, I would soon rest in the silence of death. If I say, 'My foot is slipping,' Your faithful love will support me, LORD" (HCSB). To what time in your life does this verse most apply?

10. What Bible verse has been particularly helpful to you when you were going through a difficult time?

11. What was the most tense part of the story for you?

12. What part of the story most surprised you?

13. At the end of the book, how is Jannie a better person for having gone through her trials?

14. Describe a difficult experience in your own life that has made you a better, stronger person.

15. Did you want Jannie and Brock to get back together at the end? Why or why not?

16. At the beginning of the book Stalking Man spills ticks "over the edge" of their bottle onto Jannie. At the end Jannie nudges the tick in her kitchen "over the edge" of a glass to capture it. What symbolism is there in the use of the book's title in these two scenes?

17. What have you learned about Lyme disease and its treatment from reading *Over the Edge*?

BRANDILYN
COLLINS
SEATBELT SUSPENSE®

SeatbeltSuspense.com

B&H
FICTION

Sometimes

the truth hides where **no one** expects to find it.

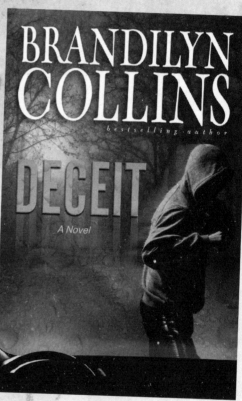

BRANDILYN COLLINS

bestselling author

DECEIT

A Novel

Joanne Weeks knows Baxter Jackson killed Linda—his second wife and Joanne's best friend—six years ago. But Baxter, a church elder and beloved member of the town, walks the streets a free man. The police tell Joanne to leave well enough alone, but she is determined to bring him down. Using her skills as a professional skip tracer, she sets out to locate the only person who may be able to put Baxter behind bars. Melissa Harkoff was a traumatized sixteen-year-old foster child in the Jackson household when Linda disappeared. At the time Melissa claimed to know nothing of Linda's whereabouts—but was she lying?

In relentless style, Deceit careens between Joanne's pursuit of the truth—which puts her own life in danger—and the events of six years' past, when Melissa came to live with the Jacksons. What really happened in that household? Beneath the veneer of perfection lies a story of shakeable faith, choices, and the lure of deceit.

Read the first chapter at: http://brandilyncollins.com/books/excerpts/deceit.html

When your worst fear comes true.

EXPOSURE

Someone is watching Kaycee Raye. But who will believe her? Everyone knows she's a little crazy. Kaycee's popular syndicated newspaper column pokes fun at her own paranoia and multiple fears. The police in her small town are well aware she makes money writing of her experiences. Worse yet, she has no proof of the threats. Pictures of a dead man mysteriously appear in her home—then vanish before police arrive. Multisensory images flood Kaycee's mind. Where is all this coming from?

Maybe she is going over the edge.

High action and psychological suspense collide in this story of terror, twists, and desperate faith. The startling questions surrounding Kaycee pile high. Her descent to answers may prove more than she can survive.

Read the first chapter at: http://brandilyncollins.com/books/excerpts/exposure.html

BRANDILYN
COLLINS
bestselling author

dark
pursuit

The Top Christian Fiction Suspense Novel of 2007
~*Library Journal* for *Crimson Eve*

Novelist Darell Brooke lived for his title as King of Suspense—until an auto accident left him unable to concentrate. Two years later, recluse and bitter, he wants one thing: to plot a new novel and regain his reputation.

Kaitlan Sering, his twenty-two-year-old granddaughter, once lived for drugs. After she stole from Darell, he cut her off. Now she's rebuilding her life.

But in Kaitlan's town two women have been murdered, and she's about to discover a third. She's even more shocked to realize the culprit—her boyfriend, Craig, the police chief's son.

Desperate, Kaitlan flees to her estranged grandfather. For over forty years, Darell Brooke has lived suspense. Surely he'll devise a plan to trap the cunning Craig.

But can Darell's muddled mind do it? And—if he tries—with what motivation? For Kaitlan's plight may be the stunning answer to the elusive plot he seeks...

Read an excerpt at: http://brandilyncollins.com/books/excerpts/dp.html

Kanner Lake series

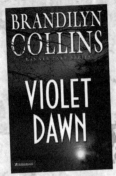

Paige Williams slips into her hot tub in the blackness of night—and finds herself face to face with death. Alone, terrified, fleeing a dark past, Paige must make an unthinkable choice.

In *Violet Dawn*, hurtling events and richly drawn characters collide in a breathless story of murder, revenge and the need to belong. One woman's secrets unleash an entire town's pursuit, and the truth proves as elusive as the killer in their midst.

Leslie Brymes hurries out to her car on a typical work day morning—and discovers a dead body inside.

Why was the corpse left for her to find? And what is the meaning of the message pinned to its chest?

In *Coral Moon*, the senseless murder of a beloved Kanner Lake citizen spirals the small Idaho town into a terrifying glimpse of spiritual forces beyond our world. What appears true seems impossible.

Or is it?

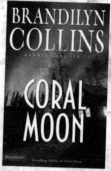

Realtor Carla Radling shows an "English gentleman" a lakeside estate—and finds herself facing a gun. Who has hired this assassin to kill her, and why?

Forced on the run, Carla must uncover the scathing secrets of her past. Secrets that could destroy some very powerful people. Perhaps even change the face of a nation...

On a beautiful Saturday morning the nationally read "Scenes and Beans" bloggers gather at Java Joint for a special celebration. Chaos erupts when three gunmen burst in and take them all hostage. One person is shot and dumped outside.

Police Chief Vince Edwards must negotiate with the desperate trio. The gunmen insist on communicating through the "comments" section of the blog—so all the world can hear their story. What they demand, Vince can't possibly provide. But if he doesn't, over a dozen beloved Kanner Lake citizens will die...

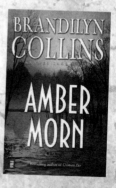

Read the first chapters at: http://brandilyncollins.com/books

Hidden Faces series

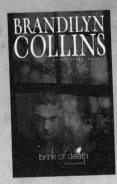

When a neighbor is killed, desperate detectives ask courtroom artist Annie Kingston to question the victim's traumatized daughter, Erin, and draw a composite of the suspect. But what if Annie's lack of experience leads Erin astray? The detectives could end up searching for a face that doesn't exist. Leaving the real killer free to stalk the neighborhood...

For twenty years, a killer has eluded capture for a brutal double murder. Now, forensic artist Annie Kingston has agreed to draw the updated face of Bill Bland for the popular television show *American Fugitive*.

To do so, Annie must intimately learn Bland's traits and personality. But as she descends into his criminal mind and world, someone is determined to stop her.

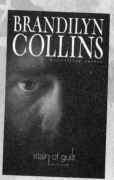

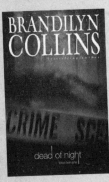

A string of murders terrorizes citizens in the Redding, California area. Forensic artist Annie Kingston must draw the unknown victims for identification. Dread mounts. Who will be taken next? Under a crushing oppression, Annie and other Christians are driven to pray for God's intervention as they've never prayed before.

After witnessing a shooting at a convenience store, forensic artist Annie Kingston must draw a composite of the suspect. She and friend Chelsea Adams soon find themselves snared in a terrifying battle against time, greed, and a deadly opponent. If they tell the police, will their story be believed?

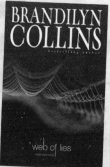

Read the first chapters at: http://brandilyncollins.com/books